Rondo Allegro

Also by Sherwood Smith:

DANSE DE LA FOLIE

Rondo Allegro

Sherwood Smith

First published 2014 by Book View Café Publishing Cooperative
P.O. Box 1624
Cedar Crest, NM 87008-1624
www.bookviewcafe.com

Print edition 2017
ISBN 978-1-61138-660-8

Cover design by Pati Nagle
Cover art *María Cristina de Borbón-Dos Sicilias, reina de España*
by Vicente López y Portaña
Interior design by Marissa Doyle

Rondo Allegro

One

AS THE EIGHTEENTH CENTURY drew to a close, it seemed that all the European world was at war.

A newly widowed woman peered out the rain-streaked windows in hopes that the post had brought a letter from her younger son, which never came; a boy shivered on the deck of a sloop-of-war, sobbing silently in fear and loss as voices shouted in an incomprehensible language around him; a girl walked out of the cook shop where she had been bound, and made up a new name by the time she reached the crossroads.

All three will be met with, one by one, but my story really begins on a simmering June day in Palermo, Sicily, 1799, as two men stood in an archway under carvings of laughing demons. They gazed out at a young lady, each man with very different thoughts.

The young lady sat on the rim of the fountain, staring upward. She appeared to be singing softly, though no sound carried across the sun-drenched courtyard.

Young lady? The younger man, a naval master and commander with his single epaulette, was dismayed. She looked little more than a girl.

The elder, a discreetly dressed intelligence officer, watched the commander covertly until the naval gentleman spoke: "You say her father is connected to a ducal family?"

"Yes. We had the father investigated, of course, before we approached him," the intelligence officer replied in a low tone. "As you would be justified in thinking, what noble gentleman, even a foreigner, performs as a musician in someone else's court? But the fact is indisputable: her father's cousin is the Duke of Ponte San Bernardo. Signor Ludovisi is considered a part of Naples's royal household, but unlike the rest of the titled rabble from various courts hanging on around either the royal family or our legation, he is a master violinist."

"Where is Ponte San Bernardo? Or should I say, what?"

"It lies north, in one of the valleys, Captain Duncannon." The intelligence officer knew exactly where it lay, but he believed that naval gentlemen—though capital on the waters—were ignorant as children when on land. He waved his hand airily northward. "The title goes back to Frederick III in 1453, which sounds more impressive than it is, as he reputedly handed coronets out like coins on his way to his coronation. This one was in honor of a bridge built by the Ludovisi, a cadet branch of the Ludovisi of Bologna. The duchy itself is the size of an inkblot, where they seem to mainly grow grapes, goats, and children. The girl will inherit nothing. There are numerous cousins in the direct line of inheritance. But it sounds well, does it not? A connection with a duke always sounds well."

The intelligence officer paused to take in the effect of these words on the captain. "You perceive I give you the truth, sir."

The captain made a gesture that could have meant anything, but would have conveyed to anyone who knew him his opinion of any 'truth' offered by intelligence officers. "So he is not a paid musician, yet he takes money from agents from Whitehall?" His expression was habitually severe, heightened by his hawk nose and strong chin; now his mouth thinned. "He's a spy?"

"Not at all, not at all, Captain Duncannon! He is a master musician, and in the world of music, gifts are understood," the intelligence officer soothed, hiding his disgust. Really, these naval officers were so simple! "He receives monetary gifts from King Ferdinand from time to time, usually to acknowledge royal favor after an exceptional performance. Our contributions are regarded in the same light, gifts from His Majesty's government, to an observer who has English interests at heart, due to his wife being English."

"Another word for observer is spy," thought the captain, who did not, in fact, like or trust the low-voiced, soft-stepping intelligence officers. Reason insisted that such men were loyal to king and country, but Captain Duncannon's private belief was that there would be far fewer wars if the spies would all go home and employ themselves more honestly.

That was neither here nor there. So this impoverished cousin to a duke spied for England, but who was to say he wasn't also being given pecuniary "gifts" by the French, the Spaniards, the Russians, the Ottomans, or any other Mediterranean interest?

The captain studied with growing doubt the young woman — girl — sitting there so patiently in the middle of that infernal courtyard.

The intelligence officer cleared his throat, and made another attempt. "As you can see, she appears well-bred. Not even swarthy, as so many Italians are."

She was a thin slip of a girl, wearing a plain round gown, her plank-colored brown hair pulled untidily back into two braids.

The intelligence officer, who had introduced himself only as Mr. Jones, was an expert observer of his fellow man, and perceived his companion's misgivings. Time was pressing, and Nelson's trusted Captain Troubridge had insisted that young Duncannon — at three-and-twenty, he was known privately by the younger officers of the fleet as The Perennial Bachelor — would best serve their purposes.

Mr. Jones lowered his voice to scarcely above a whisper. "I needn't repeat that Nelson personally takes an interest. I know it's irregular, and what's more important, he knows. I was given to understand that anyone who obliges him in this way is sure to make post sooner than later."

'Captain' was a courtesy; Duncannon was only a very new commander, his hope, like all his peers, that the rumors of fresh trouble from the French would last long enough for him to gain his step. Once you made it to post, you were on the list for life. Peace could break out, but you would be safely on the ladder to admiral. A shipless master and commander was no better than a lieutenant.

"All you need do is marry her," Mr. Jones repeated. "In front of the old man. After which he promises to disclose certain information that Nelson believes is crucial to the retaking of Naples. Signor Ludovisi won't last out the week, the physician insists. After that, you may do what you wish with the girl."

Duncannon turned Mr. Jones's way. "Is she a papist? If so it won't do. But you said her mother was English."

"Lady Hamilton assures me that the girl's mother always brought her to church with the English legation."

"Who are the mother's people?"

Mr. Jones shrugged. "The maternal grandfather, it is rumored, was well-born but a scapegrace, who married against his family's wishes and took his wife and daughter to Europe. His wife died, leaving him with a daughter named Eugenia. He ran out of money, or was cut off, and using his wife's name, took up teaching the sword to noble-born boys in Florence. We know nothing for certain of his wife's people; 'Johnson' encompasses, shall we say, many possibilities?"

As does Jones, the captain thought, disliking the man's insinuations.

"Miss Eugenia Johnson was a governess until she married Ludovisi, produced our young lady, and died. There you have it all. If you consider this background unsatisfactory, you are possessed of a near relation who is a bishop, Troubridge tells me. With his aid, you can easily extricate yourself from the legalities."

Mr. Jones, perceiving the lengthening of Duncannon's hang-gallows face, understood that he had made a false step and changed his tack. "Troubridge took care to assure me that though Naples's court is known far and wide as a hotbed of scandal, there is no evidence of her name among the whispers. I myself investigated, and it's true. Until the mother died last year, whilst teaching French to some of the royal children, this young lady was apparently counted among the miscellany in the royal wing. As they are, she is a pupil under Maestro Paisiello."

The man's insinuation about his great-uncle the bishop was no more than Duncannon had been thinking himself. But hearing the thought spoken out loud irked his sense of what was just. Troubridge himself had sent Duncannon toiling through the summer sun to this benighted palazzo, on A mission of some delicacy, eh? Nelson would entrust it to few, I need hardly tell you.

Jones, again hazarding a guess at the trend of the captain's thoughts, said persuasively, "Lady Hamilton is clamoring to put together the wedding. She cannot do enough for the English in this way. Fremantle testifies to that."

The use of Captain Fremantle's name had the effect that Jones had hoped. Duncannon said slowly, "Considering the circumstances, I see little reason to make a spectacle."

"Then it becomes the simpler," Jones said, bowing. "We'll have it at Ludovisi's bedside, as he requested. Shall I carry your assent to Nelson, then?"

"I condition only for assurance that the lady understands what is going forward, and freely consents."

"I will put a discreet inquiry in motion at once."

Signorina Anna Maria Ludovisi sat in the strange courtyard of Palazzo Palagonia, which had been the only palace large enough that could house King Ferdinand, Queen Maria Carolina, the English legate Sir William Hamilton and his lady, and their court. They had taken up the principal suites, leaving the musicians and servants to find what quarters they could.

It was this scramble for a place to stay, under the hot Sicilian sun, that had struck Anna's father down.

Though he had been considered old when he married, Anna had never thought her smiling father aged until quite suddenly, the year before, when her mother had died soon after her little brother's birth. Since then Papa had been ailing, and soon after they reached this horrible palace, he had collapsed.

She looked around, trying to fight the ever-present tears. The riot of statuary had seemed so pretty from a distance, but once she'd stepped close enough to see it, she'd found the statues of human-faced monsters unsettling. The entire palace was like that, a strange, even unpleasant place, making her feel as if she had somehow stepped from her own life with Mama and Papa into one of the darker operas.

She shut her eyes, relieved when she heard the whisper of

men's voices stop, and their footsteps fade away. Numb with exhaustion, and aware of the ache of grief pressing at the edges of her consciousness, she comforted herself with a mental review of one of Guglielmi's more cheerful melodies, one taught to the royal children as part of their musical education. She could not bear to think about her father, slipping inexorably beyond even her and her maid's most devoted nursing.

Presently she spied the approach of one of Lady Hamilton's Neapolitan servants.

Anna liked and admired Lady Hamilton, who was beloved by everybody who knew her. She made no pretense of hiding her humble beginnings as Miss Emma Hart before her marriage to the legate. Anna had admired Lady Hamilton as a child, seeing her weekly at the English church services at the legation, before she was old enough to be invited to sing when Lady Hamilton performed her Attitudes.

So her heavy heart lifted when the maid crossed the courtyard to say, "Her ladyship wishes to speak to you, Signorina Anna."

Anna followed the maid through the fantastical hallways to a room full of marble inset. At least there were no monsters or satyrs here.

Lady Hamilton was alone, was gowned in the filmy draperies that she preferred, a style that had changed decades of fashion. No one in court now wore broad panniers or tight-waisted satin or brocade gowns.

She had carefully rehearsed what she was going to say to the violinist's girl. She felt sorry for the child, but uppermost in her mind was her desire to please dear Nelson.

"There you are, my child," Lady Hamilton said, greeting Anna with a warm embrace against her soft, generous flesh. As always, she smelled delicious, her diaphanous draperies rustling as she drew Anna to sit on the couch beside her. "Now, dry your tears, have a comfit, and listen to me." Lady Hamilton's round cheeks dimpled, and her glorious smile invited Anna to intimacy.

Anna glanced at the silver trays full of delicacies, but her stomach had closed. Lady Hamilton took no notice; her mind was taken up with her purpose.

Lady Hamilton waited until Anna had pocketed her soggy

handkerchief, then said, "I am so very sorry, dear Anna, but the medical men are all agreed that your good papa is not likely to rise from his sickbed. And, like a good father, his last thoughts are of you, his beloved daughter. Our honored Admiral Lord Nelson has taken a personal interest in the case himself. He wishes to see you comfortably placed in marriage to Captain Duncannon, one of his most respected young officers."

Anna sank her teeth into her lower lip. 'Comfortably placed' would be a pension so that she might continue her singing. Not marriage to a total stranger.

Lady Hamilton, studying her tear-blotched face, said shrewdly, "It is no different than any other young lady of birth could expect. Why, our own dear Queen Maria Carolina was sent to Naples from Austria, after her sister died of the smallpox, not knowing the language, and scarcely sixteen years of age."

She was also sent to marry a king, Anna was thinking — but having no wish to marry a king (least of all a king like King Ferdinand IV) she managed the words, "If my father asks it of me, then I shall obey."

Lady Hamilton leaned forward to kiss Anna's cheek. "I shall set everything in train. You need do nothing but present yourself like the good girl I know you to be. You have always served as the model of a dutiful daughter, and your dear mama I know would applaud, for time and again she said how often she prayed you would marry an English gentleman."

"She did indeed."

It was all true. Anna's mother was used to discuss every English ship that came in, gleaning news of any eligible gentlemen, even when Anna was small; when they were alone together, Anna's mother had longingly described the cool, verdant English summers in spectacular gardens, and how much better life was in England, in an effort to transfer her love for England to her daughter.

It was also true that Anna was dutiful. 'Deference' was inculcated into all the palace children who dealt with the many princes and princesses.

Anna's mother had said once, after coming back to their rooms tired and worn from teaching willful royal children, "You must learn how to defer and deflect, the way my father taught his pupils with their swords. Then deference is a defense. But only if you learn to deflect and stand your ground; giving way until they overwhelm you will leave you with no retreat, and helpless. Never," she said seriously, as the palace buzzed with the news that one of the spoilt young princesses had caused her father to cast an old servant into prison, "never let them get you helpless."

I am helpless now, Anna thought, wiping her eyes. But she said out loud, "Thank you, my lady," and curtseyed.

Lady Hamilton smiled, embraced her, then briskly sent her away. Anna understood then that she was a problem that Lady Hamilton now regarded as solved.

Her father lay in a small room in the far wing. Lady Hamilton had seen to it that he had a window, even if the chamber was scarcely wide enough for the bed, small table, and chair. Stable smells wafted in, and the great noise and clatter as King Ferdinand and his entourage prepared to go out hunting, as they did every day, in all weathers.

Anna's maid, Parrette Duflot, stood on guard outside the door, as fierce as she was small. "He's awake, Mademoiselle. With him by." Parrette tossed her head on the 'him', which Anna understood to mean Beppe, who was as loyal to the Signor as Parrette was to her mistress.

Anna thanked Parrette and noiselessly let herself into the chamber. She found her father just as she'd left him, his head looking incongruously small on the great pillow the Hamiltons had sent especially. Beppe sat in attendance, a rough-looking article indeed as he gave Anna a short nod of respect. Most people did not get that much.

"Has he woken at all?" Anna whispered.

"He opened his eyes long enough for me to get some watered wine into him," Beppe replied, his weather-beaten, scarred face sober. "So. You will do as he asks, Signorina Anna Maria?"

As always, he pronounced her second name the Italian way, the 'i' pronounced with a hard E, instead of the 'eye' that Anna's mother had insisted on. The English pronunciation. But Anna never corrected him, which annoyed Parrette.

"Lady Hamilton says that she sees it as my duty..."

"But?" Beppe prompted. "I hear it, 'but'?" He lifted his shoulder. "You will be an English lady, as la Signora wished."

Her father's voice startled her, husky and low. "You will do as I asked, my treasure?" He spoke English with difficulty, but there was less chance of being understood if they were overheard from below the open window. "You will marry a well-born Englishman. You shall have a fine house, and a gentlewoman's rank. This, your beloved mother also wished for you."

"Why cannot we go to your home, Papa? You might recover, if you need not work, and I take up no space at all."

"No, and no." Papa struggled up on his pillow, sweat breaking out on his forehead from the effort. "My cousin is a buffoon, in spite of his grand title, and his wife a viper. She despised my beloved Eugenia for being English, and would use you as a drudge. I vowed I would only return to be buried. You will never go near them. Promise me!"

"If this is what you wish, Papa," Anna said, slightly giddy, as if the ground heaved under her feet.

Papa lay back, his breath shuddering. Beppe moved swiftly to help him. "Your medicine?"

"I do not need it," Papa said, pushing away Beppe's hand. "Now that I know my little Anna will be provided for. Mr. Jones promises this English captain is from a good family. That was important to my dear Eugenia. Brave—he won his promotion at the Battle of the Nile. That is important to me. I can face mia Eugenia dolce in Heaven, knowing that you will be well established."

"Papa—"

Her father's brow contracted and he made a weary move with his hand. "Beppe, fetch the priest. And the English divine. We'll have it right. There is little time. I feel death sitting on my chest, heavier than stone."

Parrette was waiting for Anna when she left her father's room, her thin brows a line and her vivid black eyes assessing. "So." The maid gave a short nod. "There is to be a wedding." She sighed, and spoke more to herself, "I believe it falls to me to instruct you in what that means."

Two

ALL PARTIES WERE SATISFIED, except for the two principals.

Captain Duncannon had been forced to listen to Jones promise the old man that his daughter would gain a house and a position in society, full knowing that he owned little more than his uniform, sword, and sea trunk. And as for society, he had turned his back on it when he took up his naval career.

Anna was too grief-stricken to think past her Papa's weakened breathing.

Parrette was resigned, too experienced with the vagaries of the world to voice any objection. She lost an entire night in her efforts to think out what she must say to Anna about what to expect once the ring was on her finger, but those efforts — the carefully chosen words — were largely wasted, she discovered the next morning. If Anna heard one word in twenty, that was the extent of her comprehension. Her thoughts were entirely taken up with her father.

Grief had become a boulder behind Anna's ribs by her wedding day. The westering sun cast an ochre glow around the crowd gathered tightly against the prince's bed to witness the transformation of Signorina Ludovisi to Mrs. Duncannon.

The marriage ceremony was conducted first by a priest, after which her father was promised extreme unction. While that was done, the company moved to a pretty courtyard where commenced a second ceremony, mercifully quick, overseen by an

English minister connected to the fleet: this man, Anna noted with inward relief, pronounced 'Maria' the English way. She hoped that augured well, or as well as this strange situation could ever be.

Her first contact with her husband was when he slid a ring upon her finger. It did not fit, of course; that seemed emblematic of her life, she thought as tears dripped down her face. She looked away quickly, closing her hand around the ring and surreptitiously thumbing away the tears with the other, aware that she was observed by her husband of five minutes as they walked back to her father's room to sign the marriage papers.

Anna's father had insisted on having his violin at his bedside. He had intended to play a wedding piece, but his hands faltered, and he fell back, defeated by his own struggle for breath.

Mr. Jones gestured toward the newlyweds. "May I suggest that the bride and groom step into the adjoining chamber, where I understand her ladyship has ordered refreshments to be laid out?"

"Go," Signor Ludovisi said to his daughter, his voice slurring. "I will keep my end of the bargain. Talk to your young man. Get acquainted."

The door closed behind them and the English chaplain sent by Captain Troubridge, who gracefully offered his congratulations to the bride.

The chaplain was an older man, face red under his wig. His imperturbable demeanor steadied Anna enough to enable her to glance at Captain Duncannon again, this time taking in more than the blue coat and single epaulette of a commander.

Like many of Nelson's captains, he wore his dark hair short. It curled slightly over his heavy collar in back, and brushed over his high forehead. His eyes were well spaced, with little lines at the corners from squinting in wind and weather, a characteristic shared by all the naval men she had encountered. He was very tall, his nose rather beak-like, reminding her of an eagle, and his chin long and firm, all of which seemed to render him even taller. His mouth seemed well shaped, but was too tight for her to descry expression. He looked very old to her; when his gaze encountered hers, she dropped her eyes, reluctant to be caught staring.

A servant began to circulate, bearing a heavy tray of chased silver piled high with luscious fruits. Another servant carried goblets of a chilled champagne punch. Anna was a married woman now, and so she could taste such things. Strange, how a few words changed everything. Would she be expected to dress as a married woman? If so, how was she to pay for new fabric?

From the far room she could hear men's voices, though not what they said. She knew that her father had had some dealings with the English, though no one had thought to share with her the particulars. Apparently this business could not wait. She hoped some of it would prove to settle her affairs comfortably, though how remained a mystery.

"May I fetch you a glass of champagne?" Captain Duncannon asked politely—her husband's first words to her.

Anna perceived that she had let a silence build, and blushed. She knew that it was for the wife, the hostess, to speak, to make everyone comfortable, but that was beyond her. All she could say was, "Thank you."

The captain obligingly turned away, affording her a moment to pull her handkerchief from her pocket and hastily scrub her eyes dry. Then she straightened, the little linen square crushed in her fist. She must exert herself, and learn what was expected of her.

The captain brought the champagne to her, and she raised the glass to her lips. The unexpected scent from the popping bubbles nearly made her sneeze, and her first cautious sip was even more disagreeable. Had the stuff turned?

Yet no one complained as the divine and the captain drank to one another, uttering polite compliments of the day. Anna ventured another sip, and then a third larger one. This one made her shudder, but it was followed by a sense of warmth from with-in that she found both strange and mildly pleasant. It gave her enough courage to stand under her husband's scrutiny, for when she looked up, she discovered his gaze upon her.

He stared, his heart sinking. His bride was a thin little maid in a plain, neat muslin gown, her thick brown hair bound up unsteadily on her head, her unremarkable face blotchy with tears. The uncertain angle of her chin, her very straight posture, called his sisters to mind. Addressing her as he would one of them, he said, "Have you lived here all your life?"

She replied seriously, "Not here, precisely, but in Naples, yes."

She spoke clear English, though with a strong French accent. "Soon after my parents arrived here from Florence—in fact, it is said that the monstrous earthquake in Calabria was at fault for bringing me into the world thus precipitously, for they were passing through when the first one struck." She closed her mouth, blushing. The champagne seemed to have loosened her tongue.

Duncannon made a polite noise, but inwardly he was appalled. That made her what, not quite sixteen? His sisters were seventeen and twelve; in memory they were mere children. He knew girls married young more often than not, but her youth placed her firmly in a category with Mary and Harriet.

At least so young a girl could scarcely harbor any expectations of him. He had not seen his sisters for ages, but he recollected that they liked talking about their harps and singing and dancing. "I was told you study music under the Maestro. Do you play the violin, then?"

"Badly, sir." She was barely audible.

"The fortepiano? The harp?" He named the proper instruments of a well-brought-up young lady.

"A little of the one, but not of the other, sir."

"Your English is excellent, and I am given to understand you speak French as well. I take it you also speak Italian?"

"Oh, yes, sir. And Neapolitan."

"Accomplished indeed!"

Observed narrowly by Parrette from the doorway, the two continued their awkward conversation. He asked her which of the Maestro's pieces she had heard of late. As the captain was partial to music—indeed, he spent his occasional liberty attending concerts when he could get them—they talked about the latest opera by the great Paisiello.

Anna became a trifle more animated as she praised the opera, Duncannon found, to his relief. (It being easier to think of her as 'the young lady' than as his wife, though signing his name had brought home the truth of his experience.)

But when they had exchanged all the possible polite superlatives, she agreeing with everything he said, conversation faltered, and he had no idea what to do next.

Jones rescued him with his reappearance, Troubridge behind

him. They signaled with twitches of chins and furtive gestures with the hands not carrying their hats. The captain excused himself, leaving the young lady in company with the divine, who continued to talk about Mozart, his particular favorite.

"We've heard all we're going to," Troubridge said when Duncannon drew near. "If you will report directly to Nelson, Duncannon, pray carry my compliments, and add that we are going to corroborate some of the details before we rejoin you. If you leave now, you should be able to make the tide," he added.

Duncannon resolutely hid his relief at the prospect of soon being out of the situation. Except that he wasn't out of it. He had spoken the words. He had signed his name. He had woken a single man that day, and he would sleep alone again that night in his cabin, though with the knowledge that he possessed a wife.

"The young lady?" he asked.

Jones said smoothly, "Lady Hamilton insisted that nothing material will change."

"And after the father succumbs? I heard you promise him the girl would gain a house and position in society, and in the necessity of the situation, I did not deny it. Need I remind you that I cannot offer either of these things? Therefore, I believe it ought to fall to you to initiate a dissolution. At the same time, my own sense of honor requires me to insist you guarantee that the young lady, however briefly she bears my name, will not suffer thereby."

Troubridge heard in the lengthening of Captain Duncannon's vowels a hint of the dashing captain who had sailed under the guns of the enemy at the Nile, and turned to Jones. "I believe you assured us that Whitehall would cooperate in this matter."

The intelligence officer knew very well that 'Whitehall' could mean an entirely different set of men if the government changed, and that old promises were very often discarded by the newcomers. But his orders had been clear. "May I remind you gentlemen that the young lady is housed in a royal palace, with every evidence of continuing there, under the patronage of Lady Hamilton? Therefore her position may be regarded as secure, until I obtain instructions from London on how to proceed."

Troubridge eyed Jones, then turned to Duncannon. "Once we have settled affairs in Naples, Nelson shall speak to Lord Keith on your behalf. You will not be the loser for your cooperative spirit. Nelson stipulated for that in specific."

Mr. Jones bowed.

"Very well," Duncannon said.

He returned to the young lady and took his leave in form, deciding that the least said, the less chance of awkwardness.

She responded so faintly he could scarcely hear her, and he wondered how much she truly comprehended of the situation. But that is the government's problem, he thought as he walked away. Even so, he was aware of a sense of guilt, as if he were beating a cowardly retreat.

Parrette watched him go, then shifted her attention to Anna, who gazed nowhere as she absently turned the ring around and around on her finger. She looked so pale, so sad, that Parrette's heart ached for her.

Anna was unaware of anyone else's sensibilities. Her entire attention was focused on that ring. It itched, or perhaps she only thought it did, for gold did not raise rashes. Parrette had told her that it was one of Lady Hamilton's trinkets, brought all the way from England, and provided at the last moment.

Anna was aware of a sense of relief. She had had no firm expectations, knowing that naval wives did not always follow their husbands aboard their ships: some lived ashore as housing could be got, and others remained in England, as for example did Lady Nelson. It seemed she was to be one of the second group. Just as well, she thought, for she could not bear to leave her Papa when he was so ill.

The captain's departure served as a general signal. Very soon Anna had given her last curtsey and received her last congratulation. Her mouth ached from the effort of smiling.

As the servants carried off the dishes, Anna rejoined Parrette in the hallway. "Your Papa is asleep, Mademoiselle, parbleu! Madame, I should say." Parrette rolled her eyes expressively. "The English kept him talking, oh, forever, but he seemed easier when they were gone and was able to see the priest."

"Perhaps, now that he has discharged whatever it is he felt his duty," Anna said with faint hope, "he might rest well, and recover."

Parrette clasped her hands in fervent agreement.

Anna retired early, too exhausted to think beyond the morrow.

She woke to the news that her father had sunk into a coma, and two nights later, as Anna woke abruptly from an exhausted doze while sitting on a hassock at her father's bedside, she discovered that the hand in hers had gone loose and lifeless. A glance revealed the truth, that his spirit had fled.

Three

THOUGH ADMIRAL NELSON HAD become as important to the Neapolitan court as the English legates, this marriage between one of his commanders and the daughter of one of the court musicians did not cause a ripple. Lady Hamilton would have made case for a splendid celebration of the sort she loved, but she had been adjured to keep it select, even private, the excuse being the father's sinking.

Devoted to Nelson as she was, she acquiesced without demur, and the marriage was known only to those few who had attended. After it, the girl was left in peace to grieve, and the captain was immediately ordered to support the fleet in its impending rescue of Naples.

As for Anna, there was so much for her to do that she scarcely had time for grief, and no time at all to comprehend her sudden change in state. Though she knew she was a married woman, she felt that she was an orphan.

With Captain Duncannon gone so soon after the wedding, the only evidence of her marriage was the ill-fitting ring on her finger. It did not seen like a wedding ring at all; it was more like another of the trinkets that Lady Hamilton had given her from time to time as a reward for her singing. Some of them even had worth: Emma had received a pair of diamond earrings for providing the 'voice of an angel' from behind the curtain at the Attitudes when the English navy first arrived.

As Anna set herself to the task of disposing of her father's few belongings, Parrette made it her business to glean what information she could about Captain Duncannon.

When Anna came at last to the packing of her father's music, most written out in his own dear hand, Parrette came in to report. "Captain Duncannon was sent directly from here to Naples."

Anna wiped her brow. "I thought as much."

"I also learned that he has been promoted from a ten gun brig to a recently captured French vessel called Danae."

"Mother of Perseus," Anna said approvingly.

Parrette, whose awareness of the classics was roughly coequal to her interest, which is to say scant, went right on to what did interest her. "He was used to be called Wild Harry, which brought him to the notice of Captain Nelson. Catalina, whose brother's wife's uncle knows the purser aboard the Danae, says that among the officers of the fleet, he is called the Perennial Bachelor."

Anna fanned herself with an extra copy of a Mozart motet as she considered these words, then said, "At all events, he is not one now."

Parrette pursed her lips. "Il y a anguille sous la roche," she muttered, but under her breath. When it came to men, and their often-incomprehensible doings, she always smelled a rat.

Then, feeling guilty for her forebodings, she busied herself with scrubbing the already-clean chamber, as Anna turned back to her sad task.

Reality set in under a heavy thunderstorm when Parrette and Anna stood alongside the coach under dripping umbrellas, half the King's musicians ranged at a respectful distance, as Papa's casket departed on the coach to his final resting place in Ponte San Bernardo.

Beppe paid no heed to the rain dripping from his hat onto his face as he said to Anna, "You'll be safe with the English." He remembered the autocratic duchess; even if the French had not been making war up and down the Italian peninsula, there would have been no good life for La Signorina Anna in Ponte San Bernardo.

Anna whispered, "I believe I will. Here," and she pushed a

purse into his hands. "Here is the half the money from the sale of Papa's things. He would have wanted you to be comfortable while accompanying him…" She swallowed the word home, remembering how many times her father had insisted that 'home' was his wife and daughter. Her throat tightened painfully. "To his last rest."

Beppe took the purse, which was regrettably light, and pressed a kiss on the back of her black glove. Then he was gone.

"He'll drink it up at the first tavern," Parrette declared.

"He's a good man," Anna said, by habit.

"Scélérat! Les lazarones are no good," Parrette muttered, though now that he was leaving, she could acknowledge that at least he had been loyal to the signor.

Each morning following Beppe's departure—the time Anna had been used to sit with her parents, talking about music in three languages—she sat alone, looking out the windows at the heat-shimmering stones of the courtyard below.

Each day brought increasingly horrific reports from Naples, and in the meantime, Anna remained in her rooms, uncertain what to do. Lady Hamilton departed with Admiral Lord Nelson aboard the Foudroyant, and Parrette brought back the exciting news that the legate's wife was interceding with the queen on behalf of Neapolitans, from poor to rich, as Nelson's force hunted down all Jacobins to be put to death.

Rumors ran both wild and bloody, the one consistent report that the English had succeeded in driving the French away.

Days sped by, one much like another, then it was time for everyone to be on the move again, and in the midst of the chaos, Anna was summoned to Lady Hamilton, whom she found in a cabin aboard the English ship, people bustling about dodging the mariners who tended the complication of ropes and sails.

"My dearest child," Lady Hamilton exclaimed when she saw Anna, raising her voice to be heard over the bawling of a boatswain a few feet directly overhead. To a maid importuning her from behind, "No, no, the silk, please. Carry it to Mrs. Cadogan, I beg." And to Anna, "We are already planning the celebrations. The entire Palazzo Cinese shall be given over to one long fete to celebrate our glorious victory."

"I..." Anna swallowed. "What about Captain Duncannon?" She could not quite bring herself to say 'my husband.'

"Capt—oh yes!" Lady Hamilton laughed, her pretty face flushed. She had entirely forgotten that hasty marriage. "Oh, they are still busy chasing revolutionaries here and there. But you are safe enough with me. The queen depends upon me most straitly. Does not dare to take a step without consulting me, or the dear admiral, who is, the king insists, to be awarded a dukedom. Is that not splendid? Though no more than he deserves."

"Yes, my lady."

"Now, my dear, I must have you take part in the fete. I want your beautiful voice in a special tableau I have in mind..."

Anna stared in amazement at a pair of miniatures depicting the familiar faces of King Ferdinand and Queen Maria Carolina set all around in diamonds that winked and gleamed with every roll of the ship. This beautiful item sat in prominent display on a little shelf nearby. She was to be reunited with Maestro Paisiello! Joy suffused her.

As soon as they docked, the entire party was swept into a whirlwind of preparation. Parrette ran straight away to reclaim their old rooms before anyone else could try to claim them, and Anna sped across the familiar palace to the theater wing where the maestro stayed.

There she found him. He set aside his pen and advanced with sorrow in his countenance as he clasped her hands. "My dear Signorina Anna. I heard about your good Papa. I am so very sorry."

Anna stared back as she whispered her thanks for his kind words. Could it be that he did not know that she was now a married woman?

Her lips parted. She was about to speak, but a thought stayed her. He ought to have known! He ought to have been there, as Papa's closest friend. Would he be insulted not to have been?

She swallowed down the forming words. Perhaps it was better to wait. It wasn't as if anything had changed, outside of her name.

Once Captain Duncannon returned, they could tell the maestro together, and the captain could explain how it had all come about, something Anna still did not quite comprehend.

He saw her unhappy face, and drew his own conclusions. "I gather you are now under the guardianship of the Hamiltons?"

"Yes, Maestro," she said.

"It is well. Your dear Mama would have approved." If there was a little dryness to his tone, Anna missed it; though he had sincerely admired the excellent Signora Ludovisi, he had thought her passion for England misplaced. Why retain this love of a land she had left when scarcely able to talk, and which had repudiated her own parents' marriage, though made in the sight of God?

"Now you must come every day, and resume your lessons," he said, knowing that the best specific for grief was work. "If you bring to them all your discipline, there is nothing to get in the way of your attaining greatness."

The days slipped into weeks. Anna was grateful to be kept busy, which in part eased the heartache of grief that recurred each morning when she breakfasted alone.

One night, Anna returned to her cramped quarters, exhausted from a long rehearsal in the humid air. The music kept changing, wearing everyone's tempers to a frazzle.

Parrette awaited Anna with a bowl of soup and some bread. "Ah, Signorina!"

For the first few days she had conscientiously called Anna 'Signora,' but gradually had slipped back into old habit, and Anna did not correct her. "Everyone is talking! The king is indeed awarding Admiral Nelson a dukedom."

Anna eyed her maid, whose thin lips were pursed, her head cocked. "But? I hear a but."

"He is to be created the Duke of Bronte."

Anna gasped. "Bronte?" For everyone who read their classics knew that 'Bronte' was a one-eyed Cyclops. That kind of cruel joke against poor Admiral Nelson, whose physical sufferings were painfully visible, was very much in King Ferdinand's style. "Yet the king and queen hailed the admiral as their savior," Anna observed. "And here we are, exerting ourselves to celebrate them! Perhaps Bronte is immense."

"It is. The pastry chef's brother, who works in the stable, says that it lies on the slopes of the volcano," Parrette whispered, one thin brow aslant.

Anna shook her head. "I cannot pretend to know anything about royal affairs. What I do know is that today, we have changed the song four times, and now I am not to stand by the waxen statues at all, but to sing from the gallery above. Instead of patriots in Neapolitan colors, or the English colors, I, and two choirboys, are to sing as angels unseen."

Parrette clasped her hands. "Nom d'un nom, in the gallery? But it is in painting, and not sturdy at all!"

"They promise all will be complete." Anna smiled. "Parrette, we have to practice our English now. As soon as Captain Duncannon returns, we can approach him together, for it occurs me that surely he could be the means of finding your son. Was not Michel taken while at sea?"

Parrette whispered a few words of prayer under her breath, then said, "I would dedicate a thousand masses if le bon Dieu grants me a, how one says, a pook?"

"Peek?"

"Oui! Yes. Even a peek at my son, that he is living, and well."

"I wish I had thought to ask before." Anna could not quite bring herself to say on my wedding day. That part still seemed a mere dream.

The great day dawned.

The English captains chosen by their admiral to witness the celebrations were gathered, hats under their arms, at one side of the magnificent royal dais put together by the harassed royal carpenters. Above, unseen in a much flimsier, hastily constructed gallery, Anna stood with her fidgeting choirboys in the breathless heat.

The central hall of the newly-built palace had a vaulted ceiling, but with this crowd, there was nowhere for the heat to escape. Anna tried to breathe through her mouth, nauseated by the odor of wet paint. Still tacky were the Chinese scenes painted in mural around the smoothly curved walls. The palace wasn't completely finished, but the King and Queen leading the huge crowd below had declared that it would house the celebration, and so it was.

As she dared a glance downward, Anna wondered if the great waxen figures of Admiral Nelson, Sir William Hamilton, and Lady Hamilton—the latter wearing a heavy purple gown embroidered in gold with the names of all the ships that had fought in the Battle of the Nile—would melt before the festivities ended.

Presently the crowd stilled, pressed in an enormous circle well back of the royal family and the three who were to be honored. Anna looked right and left as their accompanist softly plucked a note on her harp. Anna began to sing, her choirboy companions filling in the harmony.

The crowd below hushed, many faces upturned. The English captains, broiling in broadcloth coats, their necks swathed with cravats, and their feet encased in heavy boots, listened or endured according to their personalities.

Henry Duncannon was one of those who listened with deep appreciation to the pure young voice that floated down as if from heaven. If he shut his eyes, he did not see the glisten of still-drying paint in the vaulting overhead, or not-quite-hidden evidence of the scaffolding that held the unseen singers between earth and sky. He gazed through his lashes at the serene blue, unwilling to move as the golden voice soared and drifted, borne upward by fellow angels.

But he could not completely give himself over to the music. He knew he ought to set about locating his wife. There would be no getting near either of the Hamiltons this evening, so how would he find the girl in this great crowd? He had come determined to make certain Jones had gained her understanding concerning their annulment, before the fleet was ordered out again. But there was no moving, he discovered, and so he tried to give himself up to the music again.

He was balked even in this as a pair of lieutenants whispered to one another behind him.

"Will it ever end?"

"Hold hard. When the caterwauling is over, there's to be

speeches."

"Why isn't there something cold to drink?"

Duncannon was about to administer a sharp reproof when the song ended. As Sir William began to wheeze a speech, inaudible at this distance, Duncannon bit back his impatience.

One of the lieutenants observed, "Well, Nelson appears well pleased, at all events."

The king responded to Sir William in an equally inaudible speech, then attention turned to the slight figure on the dais between the voluptuously beautiful Lady Hamilton and tall, stooped Sir William. Nelson leaned forward as little Prince Leopold, impatient to do his part, ran out to place a diamond-studded laurel wreath upon the brow of the admiral's waxen statue.

Nelson burst into tears of joy, causing a surge of applause and smiles.

Under cover of that, the lieutenants behind Duncannon spoke more normally. "Is it at an end at last? We're done?"

"No, there's more to come, but in other rooms."

Duncannon took advantage of the shifting crowd and forged away, leaving the lieutenants looking about for the exit.

"Will there be a noise if we rabbit?" asked one of the lieutenants.

"Craven," joked his friend.

"There you are!" exclaimed a third, in joining them. "The crowd is moving at last. I'd as lief be sitting in the Nile again, waiting on the French to fire. Speaking of the Nile, wasn't that Wild Harry I just saw, elbowing his way to escape? Isn't he about to set sail?"

"Duncannon got special dispensation to come on shore tonight," said the first. "From what I hear, he seems to have become entangled."

"The Perennial Bachelor? Impossible!" exclaimed the newcomer.

"True as I stand here. I had it from his own clerk," said the second. "All secret, on orders of the admiral, you know." He laid his finger by his nose. "Arranged by Lady Hamilton."

Gossip was rife through the fleet about the admiral and the fascinating Emma, but that kind of speculation had never included

Duncannon's name. However dour he was in dealing with the fair, he was never behindhand on his quarterdeck before the prospect of a French frigate stripped to fighting sail. And so, though he might be quizzed, it was with respect.

"Entangled?" spoke he who mopped his face again, then lifted his hat and wig for a pass of his pocket handkerchief over his shaven skull. "I cannot see Wild Harry ensnared by some Sicilian charmer. Was it not he who suffered some disappointment in youth?"

"Thrown over. For his elder brother, according to what I heard," said the first. "Hasn't looked at a female since. But he obviously has now. Will wonders never cease!"

"Nothing like that," said the second. "That gabbling rantipole of a clerk insists it was marriage, some connection to an Italian duke."

"Oh, Italian. Italy sports more dukes than rats."

"Is she pretty?"

"Is she rich?"

"Wild Harry has all the luck," murmured he of the wig, who had not managed as many cutting out expeditions and other mad escapades of the sort that Nelson loved most, and who therefore had not as yet earned him that longed-for step to commander, though he was the same age as Duncannon.

"A secret wedding?" spoke the third, who looked about him for a source of entertainment that had nothing to do with operatic hullabaloo. "Ah! Speak of the devil. There he is again. Shall we have some fun?" He tipped his chin to where Duncannon was seen looking searchingly to the right and left, before he was swallowed from view.

The three lieutenants began applying elbows.

Without being aware, both Anna and Captain Duncannon had the other foremost in mind.

Up in the gallery, Anna slowly made her way down the rickety stair behind the scampering boys. Having creditably performed her part, she was now free.

She walked outside to where it was marginally cooler. At least the air was moving. She paused to enjoy the sight of the colored lamps strung along the terrace and in the gardens, reflecting in the rapidly melting ice sculptures central to each table of food and drink.

She was hungry and thirsty, now that the performance was safely over, but she must find Captain Duncannon, as she had promised Parrette.

How to accomplish it? She had scarcely spoken to any strange gentlemen outside of her wedding day, which seemed more dream than real. She had no idea how to seek him out, or where to begin if she found him.

As she turned this way and that, she was unaware of herself as a thin figure in the plain white muslin she had worn for her wedding, a wraith in the midst of the glittering crowd dressed in rich silks and velvets, or the martial splendor of dress uniforms.

Captain Duncannon, looking over the heads of the crowd, spied her there alone on the terrace. He had not been able to recollect much past her tear-blotched brown face, but he recognized that rumpled white gown, and the untidy braids with curling wisps escaping from them.

She spotted him as he emerged from the crowd, taller than she had remembered, his countenance far more forbidding.

"Good evening, Captain Duncannon," she said, dropping a schoolgirl's curtsey, and blushing.

"Good evening—" The word Signorina formed itself on his lips, but he forced himself to say, "Mrs. Duncannon," as he took her hand and kissed the air above the tops of her fingers. "I trust I see you well?"

She reddened the more when he saluted her hand, then gazed up at him doubtfully, the hesitation before the words 'Mrs. Duncannon' not having gone unnoticed.

He returned her gaze, puzzled how to begin. Aboard his own ship, he had rehearsed the most expeditious method of reaching an understanding about the annulment. But presented with those wide, questioning eyes, he was forcefully reminded of his sisters, and the words dried up.

She made an effort to be polite and hospitable. "Are you

pleased with the music?"

His relief showed as he grasped at this straw. "Very fine entertainment this evening. Is the song we just heard from a new opera?"

"It is a cantata that Signor Paisiello wrote for this occasion." Anna was quite proud of her singing, and longed to ask if he had liked her voice, but modesty was the first rule of deference. This intimidating stranger whose name she now shared had yet to acknowledge her singing outside of that single reluctant utterance. If only she knew how to go on!

Her thoughts were echoed by his own; each searched the face of the other in uncertainty.

Captain Duncannon's greatest passion was music, a subject of strife during his early years, and one that had earned him a great deal of quizzing once he went to sea. As a result he confined himself to polite nothings about Paisiello's operas, comparing Nina to Andromaca as he sought for a way to introduce his topic.

Anna half-listened, having known the maestro's music since she was small. She was resolving to take her courage in her hands and introduce her chief concern, when he said abruptly, "But music is a subject I can discourse on forever, and I am not to be a bore. I am to understand you are comfortably situated. Is there anything you require?" he asked.

"Yes," she said thankfully. "I am well, but there is something! That is, if it is not too much trouble. It is my maid, Parrette Duflot, her son Michel, you see, was taken aboard an English ship some while past. I do not quite know how it came about, but I am given to understand that sailors are sometimes…that is…"

"Impressed?" he asked, dismayed at this utterly unforeseen attack.

"That is the word. We have been trying ever since to find out where Michel is. He would be about sixteen. Can you find him?"

Annoyance flooded through the captain, to be instantly suppressed. His first impulse was to resent this girl for saddling him with an obligation before they'd exchanged so much as a hundred words, but hard on that thought came the memory of his own mother, when he was first sent away as a midshipman. At the time he'd been impatient with her tears, her cries of, "But how shall I know if you are alive, Henry, or in need? Letters can take so very long, or become lost!"

He had to acknowledge that he had brought it upon himself; though his question had the intent of a polite nothing, he had uttered the words.

And, he reflected, he need not bestir himself in the matter. It was just the sort of business to keep a wag-tongued captain's clerk busy.

Duncannon took out his pocketbook and carefully made a note. No sooner had he pocketed it again when he spied those same lieutenants who had interrupted the music with their infernal chatter, now sailing on an intercept course. Long experience with their type caused him to correctly interpret their expressions: they were intent on having some fun, and he was the target.

He knew he could thank his gabster of a clerk for that. "I shall see to it," he said to the girl, and bowed. "I cry pardon, but there is someone with whom I must speak." A few long strides brought him squarely athwart the lieutenants' line-of-battle.

Here, he forced the prospective engagement to a standstill, using his superior height and rank to keep them firmly on the topic of the king's entertainment until at last they took their leave, signaling to one another with a shrug and a lift of brows awareness of their having been thoroughly rompéed.

They sailed off in search of more congenial entertainment, leaving the captain alone...and the young lady was nowhere in sight.

He cursed under his breath. He had no idea where in this benighted barrack he might locate her, or whom to trust to fetch her. Once again he had been foiled in his design, and the hour was advancing. The tide would not wait.

He walked out into the night air, determined to shed his ire. The matter could wait a week or two, after all. He was not seriously discommoded outside of wishing the business over so he could forget it had ever occurred. He never intended to marry. The devil fly away with all women and their grasping ways!

'All women' usually wearing one face, and one name: Emily Elstead.

Four

"WHAT DID HE SAY?" Parrette asked, hands clasped tightly.

Anna repeated the entire conversation, and ended with, "He wrote Michel's name in his pocketbook."

"He wrote Michel's name?" At a stroke of the pencil, this man had separated himself out from the generality of his worthless sex, though she was afraid to let herself hope beyond that.

"He did."

"We shall see if that means anything," Parrette said cautiously.

"I must go, for the maestro sent for me," Anna said.

Parrette sighed. Now that the fete was over, the servants faced the monumental task of cleanup. Although, strictly speaking, she, as the maidservant to a lady, was exempt from the worst of the labor, there had been a long time in her life when such labor was expected. She was not afraid of work, and she had found that willingness to turn her hand not only earned goodwill from her fellow servants, but furnished the opportunity to hear vital news.

Anna repaired to the music chamber. She knew from experience not to expect unstinting praise, so she was not surprised to find Maestro Paisiello beetling his brows at her as he said, "You did well enough considering the stupefying heat, and those evil vapors, but my dear Anna, you were weak. You are too thin!" he declared, poking himself in the chest. "Can your sound resonate through so flimsy a frame? Would you perform upon a violin made of paper? No! I want you to sing the angel's part in my new opera, but you are going to have to work on your breathing to lift that voice. And you must eat." He banged his baton on his music stand in emphasis.

Anna left the maestro after her lesson, determined to throw herself into her music. It was the only way to fill in the hole in her life left by her Papa, and to cease the chatter of questions she could not answer about this marriage that felt as substantial as a mirage.

A week turned into a month. At its end she received a summons from the legation. There, instead of being conducted to Lady Hamilton, she was met by the lady's chief maid, who passed her a letter, directed correctly to 'Mrs. Duncannon.'

"It was included in the dispatches for the admiral," the maid said with a meaningful glance whose message entirely escaped Anna. Her thoughts were on this, her very first letter.

The words 'Mrs. Duncannon' made her heart give an odd gallop. She felt very unlike herself, as if someone wished her to play a part off the stage, instead of on.

Aboard the Danae:

Mrs. Duncannon: Pray inform your Mrs. Duflot that I sent out an inquiry, and have today rec'd notice that one 'Michael Deflew' serves aboard the sloop-of-war Pallas. He is about the right age. I have no more to offer than this.

I had hoped to wait upon you to settle our Affairs, but I find I am directed to join Martin in Genoa in support of Field-Marshal Sovarov. When duty permits, I shall do myself the honor of waiting upon you; I trust by then that you will have been called upon by Mr. Jones, who promised to execute our Mutual legal Interests.

I conclude in wishing you good Health and happiness,

Yr. ob'd s'vt, H. Duncannon.

Anna took the letter to Parrette, and handed it over wordlessly.

Parrette made out the letters slowly, for English, with its impossible spelling, was difficult for her to read. Neither Parrette nor Anna paid the least heed to the words about 'mutual legal interests,' legalities of any sort lying entirely outside their experience. Their attention was entirely consumed with the astonishing news that Michel had been found, after years of not knowing.

"Captain Duncannon is an angel," Parrette proclaimed, threw her apron over her head, and wept.

As the days turned into weeks, and thence months, during which no notes followed that first one, Parrette took to winnowing out news through her usual labyrinthine methods. It was she, and not Anna, who discovered that Duncannon had been sent to Minorca to aid in keeping the strait free, and finally to Gibraltar, as Lord St. Vincent, who was gravely ill, had sailed home, to be replaced by Lord Keith. There was no word of the *Pallas*, which seemed to belong to another fleet.

Parrette also discovered through the same sources that the whispers about Admiral Nelson and Lady Hamilton had become general gossip, and further, that Lord Keith was not pleased at all with Nelson, and far from granting various commissions, favors, and requests, had sent orders to the admiral to quit Naples.

Anna was too busy to think about those things, except at a distant remove. The royal family demanded entertainment, and entertainment they must have. The more unsettled the world due to French invasions and various nations fighting back and forth, the more people seemed to want the escape of music, plays, and operas. Anna was happiest singing, with the added benefit that it did not leave her time to grieve. She had a goal, to sing her very first major role, which meant hard work under the maestro's exacting eye.

Then one morning Parrette woke Anna with the news, "Admiral Nelson is to set sail to join Lord Keith."

Anna mentally shrugged. Though she admired Admiral Lord Nelson, as everyone did, she had never been close enough to speak a word to him, and his doings seemed very distant from hers. But she had grown up under Parrette's daily care. She knew all the maid's expressions. "I think you are displeased."

"It is not my place to be displeased or not, signorina. *Mais alors...*"

"*Mais alors?*" Anna prompted.

Parrette had folded her wiry arms in the way Anna had learnt indicated the maid was in possession of an article of news of which she did not approve.

Parrette struggled within herself, and finally said slowly and reluctantly, "It seems to come about due to these whispers concerning the admiral and Lady Hamilton. Lord Keith is reputed to be displeased with the admiral."

Anna looked surprised. "But why? Is he not a hero? Oh, I think I have heard something or other. But I never paid it much heed. Lady Hamilton is kind and generous to everyone."

Parrette understood Anna's loyalty to her benefactress, for she now felt the same about Duncannon. Others might worship Nelson, but he was nothing compared the man who had become *The Captain* in her mind. "I thought it my duty to tell you what is being said, but more important, the result is, the fleet might be sent away for a long period. And if the legate is recalled, because of what is whispered about his wife, you may find yourself in a difficult position."

"But surely the maestro would pay no attention to rumors," Anna protested.

Parrette sighed. "You do not understand. It is the Hamiltons who have arranged for our wherewithal. Maestro Paisiello, while in every way a fine man, a genius, he still must depend upon the royal family for his pension. Do you think they will extend their generosity to you, if the Hamiltons do not take you with them?"

"They did for Papa," Anna said slowly.

"But he was a master violinist. The singers are paid by the piece, and unless you gain a primary role, it is scarcely enough to live on. More to the point, if you were known to be earning even a minuscule stipend, you would be ruined. *English* ladies in good society do not earn their livings in this way, you know that! Your Mama taught you to be a lady."

"Then we cannot depend upon Lady Hamilton?" Anna asked.

"She might not be in a position to be depended upon, if the rumors are true. *Fi donc!* There is nothing to be done except to live very carefully, and wait until The Captain either sends someone to fetch you, or his Mr. Jones he mentioned in his letter arrives to make arrangements."

Anna spoke assent, but mentally added, *And practice my music.*

At first, all problems appeared to be solved when the admiral returned in triumph after having won a spectacular battle against the French man-of-war *Genereux*. But a great portion of his fleet, including Captain Duncannon, remained at sea at the other end of the Mediterranean, and hard on that came the astounding news that Sir William had been recalled to London.

Everybody and everything was in an uproar.

Parrette kept her worries behind closed lips until she was told by the palace steward that the legation was soon to depart, and Anna must either depart with them, or find somewhere else to live. No, there was no Mr. Jones at the legation, and never had been.

Anna, on hearing that, ran straight to the legate's house, where she spent the rest of the day in a crowded antechamber waiting for an interview.

It was very late that night when at last Lady Hamilton's maid summoned her to the lady's powder room. While Lady Hamilton clasped diamonds at her throat and ears, and her personal maid finished arranging her hair, Anna explained what the steward had said.

Lady Hamilton looked sorrowful. "My dear, there is simply nothing to be done! Here, take this." She unclasped the bracelet from her arm, and handed it to Anna. "Alas, Sir William's affairs are all in a muddle, and his health is wretched. This is one reason why the dear Admiral has generously offered to carry him, and of course myself, as his devoted nurse, on a repairing cruise to Malta. Once Sir William has regained his strength, Queen Maria Carolina is pressing him to keep his promise of conveying the royal family from Palermo to Leghorn. We are already too crowded. There is not an inch of room to spare! If you have not yet heard from your captain, why do you not speak to the queen about an appointment? I am truly sorry, but even dear Lord Nelson can do little at present, not with Lord Keith as his most determined enemy."

Anna departed tired and worried. When she reached the palace, Parrette was sitting by their single window with her sewing.

Once Anna had related the news, Parrette said firmly, "You must write to The Captain."

"But he is so far away," Anna said. "And we have heard nothing at all. I have been thinking. It seems to me that he has forgotten." She sighed, then admitted, "I was listening to the talk while I waited, and it seems some of these captains are not all they should be. Who is to say that he has not done as M. Duflot did? Perhaps he already possesses a wife somewhere impossibly far away, such as Scotland?"

Parrette bit her lip. One of the many sins that her wretch of a husband had committed, she had discovered before she left France, was that he had another wife in Marseilles. Anna had learnt that by accident, before her parents discovered how much Italian she understood. "I think you owe it to him to report that the Hamiltons have abandoned you. He made a promise before God. It is his duty to keep it."

"I will write to him, but I'll also talk to Maestro Paisiello," Anna said. "I would as lief work in the theater at any event."

"No," Parrette stated, her arms crossed. "You promised Signora Eugenia you would never stoop to taking wages in the theater. A lady cannot do that, especially in England."

Anna nodded slowly, thinking of the horrid things that she had read in Mama's cherished English newspapers about Mrs. Billington, the great soprano, who earned her living as a singer. Then she crossed her arms, mirroring Parrette's own gesture. "It seems I am not *going* to England. I must live somewhere, and on what?"

She walked in brow-furrowed puzzlement to the music chambers behind the royal theater, where she encountered Signora Paisiello, who was busy stitching costumes.

"The maestro is away getting those new music sheets printed. What clouds the brow of our angel?" the signora asked.

Anna began to relate her bad news. To her vast surprise, she had only got a few sentences in when the signora exclaimed, "So!"

The signora raised her needle, resettled her wig, and leaned forward. "We have been talking on that very head, Paisiello and I, about what we are to do for our cherished students if the French return, especially if the English abandon us to our fate. Money is indeed scarce for those such as us. The king is not to be relied upon, especially with the political scene so unsettled. It is our belief you ought to quit Naples altogether, and go to Paris."

"Paris!" Anna exclaimed. "But…the war, the soldiers!"

The signora waved her hand to and fro. "There is no war in Paris. Even the guillotine rusts from disuse. Why, from what I hear, Buonaparte is soon to declare himself king of France. Think of it, an Italian on the throne of France, ha ha!"

"I thought he was from Corsica?"

"The Buonapartes are Florentines," Signora Paisiello stated with a moue of disapprobation. "He may call himself Bonaparte however much he likes, but I never shall. Bonaparte! Such an impossible name! It will never stick." And, as Anna had nothing to say to this prediction, the signora went on. "It's rumored the family ran to Corsica after the Ghibelline troubles, as did many others. But a leopard does not change his spots, even if he calls himself a lion."

She poked her finger through her high-piled powdered wig to scratch at her scalp. "Here is what is important: Buonaparte loves music. He has written Paisiello a hundred times, saying he still hums the march written for General Hoche's memorial, and promises a fortune if we would come to Paris. Paisiello wavers, for he is deep in rehearsals, with the music near finishing, and the stage near to ready. But you? No such trouble binds you."

"I do not write music," Anna began.

The signora laughed, shaking all over. "No! But you sing! Perhaps it might not have been possible over the past years, for everyhing was revolution, revolution, revolution, I hear, but they say the comic opera is coming back into fashion in Paris. Now, you are yet too young for the great roles, for you are not the equal of the great Mrs. Billington, but who is? There are a great many opportunities for a singer of your talents in a city just beginning to rediscover the arts!"

Anna clasped her hands.

Seeing her flushed, smiling face, the signora went on. "We could send you to Buonaparte's wife with a letter of recommendation. *Lei è così volubile!* They say that she is kind, therefore she must get thousands such. Perhaps it would be better to send you to Constance de Pipelet de Leury. I will write ahead to prepare the way! She is a poet, a rich one, who champions the women of the theatre. *She* might be able to approach Madame Buonaparte, or failing that, will surely find you a place if Paisiello asks it of her."

"A place! But..." Her joy vanished. "I promised my mother..."

Signora Paisiello remembered the Signora very well, and her peculiarly English notions. "When I say 'a place,' it means you must become her guest! And if it chances you perform for a select audience, and they happen to reward you, who is to say anything?"

Anna left shortly afterward, and crossed the palace thinking hard about all she had heard in the past few days. It was plain that staying in Naples was not just a difficulty, but it was fast becoming a danger. The royal family might flee, and they would not care a whit for anyone but themselves.

"I like the idea of Paris," Anna said when she rejoined Parrette. "If I still have not heard from Captain Duncannon, or this Mr. Jones, by the next packet that arrives, it will prove that he does not think of me at all. So I must think of myself, and I am determined to go. Only how are we to set about traveling? We've only a few coins left from the sale of Papa's violin."

Parrette said firmly, "That bracelet Lady Hamilton gave you. I will sell it, and those rubies, and any other jewels you can bear to part with. We will probably never see their true worth, but I can bargain better than you will be able to."

Anna agreed, adding, "I will keep only the pearl ear drops Lady Hamilton gave me when I first sang for her Attitudes, and my mother's trinkets. They would not bring much, anyway."

At the same time that Anna and Parrette embarked on the arduous journey to Paris, on the far side of the Atlantic, Captain Duncannon received word of his promotion to post captain. Overjoyed, he did not mind being ordered to hand over the *Danae* to another man and return to England. He was promised command of a frigate recently bought into the service.

He spared a thought to Naples, trusting that no communication arriving with his new orders meant that matters were in train as promised.

But in Naples, as servants labored to load Sir William's collection of antiquities and art into the hold of a ship, in a small room over an inn not far from the legation, several men labored to sort through a mass of papers. The erstwhile Mr. Jones sat among them, deftly unsealing letters and reading them.

He had made three piles: those to be sent on as was, those to be copied by one of the young clerks at the far table before being resealed, and those he consigned to the fire.

Presently he came to Anna's carefully written missive, which brought memory of the entire affair rushing back.

He set the letter down to consider. Nelson was about to strike his flag and return to England. If Lord Keith had his way, Nelson would never sail again, but in any case his influence was diminishing fast. Troubridge had made it plain that his own portion of the wretched business had ended with supplying a suitable captain. After that it was Whitehall's problem.

Mr. Jones tapped the letter against his fingers, then rose and crossed to the far room, where his superior was instructing a young man carrying a dispatch case. The young man wheeled about and departed.

"What is it?"

Mr. Jones eyed his superior, whose tired, embittered countenance did not encourage speech. In silence he held out the letter.

The senior agent had operated under many names over the years, but none of them were aristocratic. In his secret heart, he sometimes thought that the French had had the right of it, words he would never speak aloud.

He threw the letter back. "What of it? Duncannon is the son of a wealthy baron. Send it on, and let him settle his own affairs."

"With respect, sir," Jones said smoothly. "He is the son of a wealthy baron, as you say, and much cherished by Fremantle. He could raise exactly the sort of stink we do not want, if we renege on our promises."

The senior agent's rancor had originated in what he believed an inescapable truth: that a man of parts could not get ahead because of his birth. That virulence left no thought for those he considered beneath him. "*Lady* Hamilton," he said with scornful emphasis. "We might have supposed no better from the likes of her. Why did we have to make promises at all?"

Jones, scenting the cloud of blame heading his way, said with an earnest air, "We had to act precipitously, with whatever means we had at hand. And we gained the knowledge needed at that moment."

"In a disgraceful caper that ought never to have happened. Folly, sheer folly." The chief agent picked up Anna's letter. "Leave it to me. You will soon be Mr. Simison of Halifax, on the King's business in North America. We will deal with this here."

In relief, Mr. Jones departed from the office, and thence from this history, leaving his chief to scowl down at the letter. Irritation boiled up into righteous anger.

They had carried out their orders, but he understood the ways of the world. If this missive prompted Duncannon to send off a hot complaint to the First Admiral before the new legation and its staff came in, he knew who would catch the blame.

He picked up the letter and stood over the fire. The stiff formality of the wording made it plain that the girl was not in the habit of corresponding with Duncannon — the Perennial Bachelor. He was busy at the other end of the Atlantic, on the King's service, exactly where he ought to be. Post, as everyone knew, was months late as often as not, and regularly lost altogether. As time went by, and he heard nothing, he might consider himself very well out of this trouble. As for the girl, she could find her own level, as thousands had done before, and would continue to do.

The chief agent dropped the letter into the flames, and when it had been reduced to ash, returned to his work.

Five

TRAVEL WAS A NEW and not altogether agreeable experience for Anna.

Whenever they reached major cities, they looked for news-papers in English, in hopes of gleaning mention of *Danae* or *Pallas*.

Consequently, despite summer storms, leaky vessels, armies churning up the countryside and driving up prices of food and lodging, broken axels, lame horses, and grasping opportunists not easily distinguished from outright thieves, they arrived at last in a Paris that exhibited the shocking evidence of a decade of troubles. The smells made Anna's eyes water, and everywhere there was the noise of hammering, sawing, and stone-masons chipping away at stonework, as the repairs ordered by First Consul Bonaparte got underway.

When the *diligence* at last disgorged its crowd of passengers, Parrette refused to even look inside the inn adjacent. She marched out into the street until she found a fiacre to hire. They clutched their belongings tightly as the driver whistled to his horse.

Traffic moved about with a speed and a clatter that caused Anna to shut her eyes until at last they arrived on the street where Madame de Pipelet lived. By then she was certain she would suffer permanent *mal-de-tête*.

But as soon as the door opened to a charming apartment, Anna's fatigue gave way to wonder. She gazed at furnishings evocative of caryatids and palm leaves in the Egyptian style that was fast becoming the very latest fashion.

A beautiful woman, sylph-thin, with heavy-lidded, intelligent eyes, glided toward them in in a cloud of floating draperies to welcome them. With a graceful gesture she led a wondering Anna into a salon decorated with waving palms and faux columns built around a fascinating reclining couch.

"Ah, my little guest, she arrives!" Madame de Pipelet kissed Anna's cheeks, her clothes fragrant with a subtle, beguiling scent. Her profuse curls tickled Anna's chin. "So! The tiresome questions can wait. You must refresh yourself. Tomorrow we shall hear you sing, and plan. Come this way. You shall have my husband's chambers."

"Will he not object?"

Madame laughed. "He is gone. One of the very few benefits from those dreadful days of revolution is divorce has become possible. Oh, the freedom, you cannot conceive!" She paused, then laughed again. "My dear Mademoiselle Ludovisi, you look positively shocked! Do you think me so abandoned? Think upon it. We females are married off as mere children, when we know little more of men than my puppy there." She pointed to the little mop-haired dog whose claws ticked over the marble floor, then added thoughtfully, "Less. I hope and trust that if I marry again, it shall be for life. I am old enough, and experienced enough, to make a wise choice. At sixteen, no one is wise."

"*Nom d'un nom d'un nom,*" Parrette whispered under her breath, and Anna blushed.

Talking on about inconsequentials in her quick French, Madame de Pipelet led Anna by the hand to another room also fitted out with Egyptian furnishings. These Anna found quite peculiar, though beautiful in their way. After washing off the grime of travel, she blew out the candles and climbed into a clean, soft bed. Though the noise of Paris still resounded outside her window, and from below came the rapid chatter of voices and the musical tinkle of fine dishes, she slept soundly.

Next morning, Parrette brought her breakfast on a tray. "Madame lies abed until midday," she said, her eyes wide. "She will ring for you. There is a bath through that room. The servants have just finished bringing up the hot water."

Anna threw off the covers. After a delicious soak, she dressed and went out to discover that the house was still silent. She whiled away the time wandering around the chambers examining the tables with hieroglyphics in gilding down the legs and the pyramidal cabinets decorated with graceful animal heads, then settled down with a book of poems that she found, to occupy herself with what patience she could muster.

It was closer to two when at last Madame de Pipelet summoned her. Anna came downstairs to discover that Madame was not alone. Reclining gracefully in the place of honor was a startlingly beautiful figure dressed *a la Grecque*, her curling brown hair bound up in a silver fillet. Anna took in the daring gown, the silver sandals, the bare toes with silver polish.

"Here, dear child, is my friend Julie Candeille, now Madame Simon, who came to us straight from the Tuileries. She will advise us."

"Ah, Constance." Madame Simon clapped her hands lightly, the gems on her hands sparkling. "She is so young! Let us see what we have."

Anna looked from one to the other. "Thank you for your generous hospitality. Signora Paisiello felt certain that you could tell me how I am to go on."

To her consternation, Madame de Pipelet burst into laughter.

"La la," Madame Simon exclaimed, throwing up her hands. "That accent! Quaint, but oh, it will never do."

Anna was stung to discover that the court French spoken at Naples was preposterously old-fashioned. Her mother had taken care to teach her. Anna said with mock solemnity, "Then shall I speak in *this* manner? It is how Parrette and I spoke while traveling, to hide our origins, in case there were revolutionaries still among the innkeepers and coachmen."

Madame de Pipelet lifted silver-painted nails to her lips as she laughed. "Child! You sound like a flower-seller from Lyons. Which would indeed keep your head on your shoulders during the terrible days of the Terror, but those days are over, and you simply must speak like a Parisienne. But we can amend that. I detect a trained ear. It is well."

She put her finger to her chin. "As for introducing you to Madame Bonaparte, it will not do. She is the kindest of women, but..." She lifted her shoulders expressively.

Anna did not care why. She had had her fill of the vagaries of royal courts. And though Bonaparte had not yet declared himself king, as many expected, she had heard enough gossip to gain an impression of autocracy to surpass even King Frederick's.

"I care nothing for courts," she declared.

Madame de Pipelet laughed again. "Then it is decided. I shall throw a soiree, and you shall sing, *hein?* Only how shall you be known?"

"By my name," Anna said. "As it transpires, I am actually married, so I am not Mademoiselle Ludovisi at all, but Mrs. Duncannon."

"*Milles diables!* An English name? Worse and worse," Madame Simon declared. "You must be Italian, of course. I know! What is your parentage?"

Madame de Pipelet pulled a much-folded paper from a graceful little side table that ended in faun's feet. "Her father was connected to a count or a duke—I cannot make it out, but noble. Ponte San Bernardo?"

"*Alors!* You shall be Signorina Bernardo, the new child singer."

"But I am no child. I am nearly seventeen!"

"What has that to say to anything? On the stage, you can be anything you wish, and as for your age, you look twelve, and everybody loves a child prodigy. If you in truth have as fine a voice as Madame Paisiello claims in her letter here, you will do quite well. Oh, it is just the time to be presenting yourself. Women might do anything, these days," Madame de Pipelet said with a sigh.

Madame Simon sat upright on the reclining couch, and pronounced in a low, thrilling voice, "Only if her reputation remains spotless. Without. A. Spot. I am living proof!"

"But all that is ended now," Madame de Pipelet said soothingly. "With the Bonapartes in charge, surely we shall return to civilization. Only better. Oh, to be young again! If you had only come a few months ago, you might now be singing in Madame Devismes's *Praxitèles*. The *Courrier* is full of praises, and by none other than La Delacroix. Think of the possibilities!"

Madame Simon waved an imperious hand, dismissing Madame Delacroix, the *Courrier*, and related possibilities. "We must hear your voice, so that we might consider what best for you to sing."

Though Anna had not warmed up her voice properly, she moved to the pretty Viennese *klavier*, pressed a chord as she took a deep breath, and began to sing her part from the triumph fete. It felt good to sing again.

"Very, very pure," said Madame de Pipelet when she was done. "Perhaps a little light?" Madame Simon tapped her nails on the little mop-dog's silky head, and its tail stirred. "Will she be heard beyond the boxes and the pit in the Feydeau?"

"*We* shall not worry about such things," Madame de Pipelet stated firmly. "I'll fill my salon with those who have the expertise."

Madame Simon concurred. "Have her sing light airs, classic. Nothing revolutionary. Perhaps a love song or two. And *voila!* Instant success. I wish I could be here to see it."

She soon took her leave, and Madame Pipelet said, "Now, let us get busy."

She was as good as her word. Anna was swept into a flurry of shopping and dress-making. Then she was taken to a fashionable barber, who cut off her untidy, heavy braids. Her hair, freed of that weight, clung close to her head in natural curls. The back was twisted up into a charming Grecian style called *a la Titus*, with kiss-curls framing her high forehead.

After several days of Madame's excellent food, her meager figure and face began to fill out a little.

Everywhere they heard the swift chatter of French, which reminded Anna of bird calls. Her sensitive, music-trained ear enabled her to swiftly mimic the Parisian accent, and then set about making it her own.

Madame de Pipelet, having dismissed with an imperious wave all the coquettes and shepherdesses of current operas, insisted that

Anna must begin her concert with the angel Gabriel's arias from Haydn's magnificent oratorio, "The Creation," and finish with a series of romantic songs by Madame's good friend Alexandrine-Sophie Goury de Champgrand, who desperately needed the income from her music.

And so, while Anna rehearsed in the music room downstairs, Parrette, finding herself with free time in that well-ordered house, wandered about Paris, learning the ways of its streets. She dared to walk into the great square before the Tuileries in order to catch a glimpse of Madame Bonaparte, whose beauty was renowned all over Europe.

Parrette was disappointed of her goal, requiring her to return again and again until one day, a stir among the lounging officers and girls flirting with them indicated that at last she would be rewarded for her effort.

The crowd drew aside for a carriage pulled by no fewer than six caparisoned horses. There in the carriage, seated beside her long-faced daughter, was a woman Parrette's own age, with a beautifully shaped head framed by a profusion of feathery dark curls.

When the carriage door opened, Parrette pressed forward in the crowd to stare at Madame Bonaparte, who wore white, draped so artfully and elegantly that Parrette scrutinized every fold, determined she would find out who made those gowns, and how.

At last came the night of the soiree.

Anna faced a crowd of glittering guests, the women wearing soft silks, thin metallic threads or pearls holding up their hair. They all sat on pretty little chairs, surrounding the guest of honor, the Count Joseph de Salm-Reifferscheidt-Dyck. Anna was at first intimidated by this grand gentleman until she became aware that he was more interested in his hostess than he was in music.

When she was not quite eleven, Anna had been taken to hear the great Mrs. Billington, not long after she dazzled Naples in the opera the great Bianchi had written just for her. Anna and her mother had met her at one of Sir William's private concerts, after which Anna had confessed that she wished to be a singer just like her.

Mrs. Billington had patted Anna on the cheek, stooped a little, and said in English, "I will tell you my secret, little Anna. Always sing with a light heart, and a tight middle." And she had pressed her fist against her ribs under her bosom.

Anna's heart felt cloud-light as Madam herself played the opening bars in accompaniment. She touched her fingers to her diaphragm, straightened another fraction, and sang. She had practiced enough to know how to fill a room with sound, and when she saw chins lifting among her audience, the sure sign of pleasure, joy illumined her being.

In the far doorway, Parrette stood with Madame's maid.

"She will take," the maid said, nodding once. "What is she? I know she is not French."

"Her father was Italian, her mother English."

"English! These roast-biffs, they turn up everywhere. An adventuress?"

Parrette kept her temper. It never did to quarrel with the servants in any house. But she would not accept even the slightest slur against the only woman who had ever been kind to her. "Anna's mother was the companion to an earl's daughter. The family traveled to Rome. When the earl married his daughter to an Italian count, they cast off my Signora Eugenia without a second thought."

"Tchah, these aristos are all alike." The maid lifted her shoulders in a shrug, but her tone was sympathetic. "We are well rid of them! *Et puis*?"

"*Et puis* she returned to Florence, but discovered her father dead of a duel. She met Signor Ludovisi there, who wished to be taught in English. They married. He was very old by then, and she was already thirty. When Anna was coming, they decided to go south to Naples, where Madame Eugenia was hired at the royal palace to teach the children French and English, manners and language," Parrette said. "And he became a part of the royal orchestra. He was a great musician. She was an angel."

"She is one now, *hein*?" the maid asked, smiling.

Parrette accepted that in a spirit of amity, and fell silent as they listened to the lovely romantic songs for which Anna's voice was especially well suited.

When the last song was sung and Anna took her bow, the applause was gratifyingly heartfelt. The guests accepted refreshments and moved about to congratulate Madame de Pipelet de Leury and her protégé. Snips of conversation followed them. "...voice is not large enough to fill the Feydeau, or even the Opéra-Comique...she is young, she will improve...anywhere along the Boulevard du Temple. Ah, yes! In a smaller theater, the women must be young and pretty. We will not get the men in else...a trifle thin, but that is easily amended. More important, she is young, which cannot be amended so easily...charming arms, well displayed..."

Before the last of the guests left, Anna had been invited to sing for a private party given by no less a figure than the sleepy Count, and she went to bed in a whirl of happy anticipation.

The next day she was up early rehearsing.

Parrette, who discovered herself with a great deal of freedom as Madame de Pipelet's house was well run, put her time to good use. She ignored most of the gossip, except that about Josephine Bonaparte, wife of the First Consul. Before long she had gleaned useful information about where the First Consul obtained her fabrics, and who made her gowns.

After that, it was simple enough to visit Au Grand Turc, and look carefully at the clothes on display, or Le Roy's shop in the rue de la Loi. The proprietors were quite happy to display the sumptuous gowns they made for Madame Bonaparte, as they deemed it good for business. They did not know that Parrette, with her rigorous eye, meticulously observed the seams and the drape, as well as the deceptively simple curves and dips of the horizontal bodice contrasted with the pure, slim line of skirts.

She took these observations home, talked to Madame about her ideas, and was advanced a sum against expected gifts, with which to buy fabrics and trim. Parrette was no less enthusiastic than Anna as she got to work.

Madame de Pipelet loved the theater, and maintained boxes at the three main venues. It was here that Anna saw the latest plays and operas. When the First Consul and his wife attended the theater, the entire crowd took note.

So did Anna. But she scarcely glanced at the thin man in the blue and white uniform; her attention was all on Bonaparte's wife. How beautifully she moved! How beautiful she was, seen across the vast width of the theater!

A great commotion brought Madame's party to a standstill in the lobby of the Théâtre-Français one night. Here, Anna glimpsed the famous woman up close. She was quite shocked to discover that Josephine was old, forty at least!

Anna stared as Madame Bonaparte turned her head, a quick, graceful movement, and reached to touch the top of the First Consul's hand as she spoke. Her face betrayed the lines of age, and she pursed her mouth in the way people did who wished to hide their teeth, but even so, especially as Anna gazed at her straight back, at the beautifully shaped head framed by soft dark curls, she understood what Lady Hamilton had said once after her attitudes: "The pose is easy, but getting to it, ah, that's when you must catch their eye!"

In the carriage ride back to Madame de Pipelet's, Anna consciously tried to set her head at Josephine's angle, to move her hands and arms the same way. The muscles of her arms felt different, and she remembered the childhood lessons in dancing that had been given the palace children. "That is what I need," she stated to the lurching canvas wall of the equipage.

"What is your need, child?" Madame asked, breaking off her conversation.

"The First Consul's wife. I wish to learn to move the way she does."

"Ah!" Madame exclaimed, nodding in approval. "If you can succeed in learning *that*, you will be elegant even when you are an old woman. But how does one go about it? Perhaps it is a gift of nature."

Anna had to admit that that might be true. Yet there was the evidence of her arms and back muscles. Only did she really look different?

She kept that to herself, as she had other things to think about. Madame one morning presented to Anna the astonishing news that she was very, very lucky: she had been granted an opportunity to audition at the famous Lyri-Comique.

"But is that not earning a living as a common performer?" Anna asked.

Madame de Pipelet was going to return a tart answer, but she knew Anna well by then, and saw no pride or presumption in her face. The girl was heeding, as best she knew how, the precepts given her by her dead mother.

"Oh no," Madame said. "Not if you audition as a mere student. You might appear on stage, but this is how you gain training that is far superior to anything I can get for you!"

Anna was content.

Like the rest of Paris, the Boulevard du Temple was in the midst of changes. After 1791, when the controls against the numbers of theaters had been lifted, the street had proliferated with stages. Anna soon learned that this was one of the most popular streets in all of Paris.

She stared in amazement at the grand edifices—many in various states of repair or rebuilding—as Madame's carriage took her for her first interview.

She was nervous, her palms damp and her heartbeat fluttering in her throat, but the moment she walked in and was greeted by the manager, she began to understand how very lucky she had been. Her being Madame's protégé seemed to have cleared the way: in a short time she stepped for the first time on the stage, looked over the candles into the cavernous house, then turned uncertainly. "What shall I sing?"

"Sophie's song will do," someone called from the back, and the voice lowered, still audible, "How old is she? Fourteen? Fifteen? If she sings half as well as you say, she will do."

Feeling very much on her mettle, Anna took in a deep breath, and sang.

"Fine voice, but light," was the verdict when she was finished. "She will do nicely in the chorus."

She was given brisk directions about rehearsals and what type of costume she must procure, and by the end of the week she had met all her fellow performers.

By month's end, Anna stood on stage in the heat of hundreds of candles, bringing to life a two-act opera for the dimly-perceived, rustling, whispering crowd in the seats. And at the end, amid resounding applause, 'Signorina Bernardo' joined the rest of the cast in bowing; next time, she hoped, it would be she taking a personal bow.

When she retired to change, she found Parrette with her arms tightly crossed as she stared with furrowed brow at the stool Anna usually sat upon to have her hair done.

"What is amiss?" Anna asked. "Is there bad news?" She looked around the crowded little alcove that functioned as her dressing room, as if the evidence lurked in the shadows behind the flickering candles.

"No," Parrette said. After a short struggle, she said in Neapolitan, "I know you have spoken to few. They think you are a young girl, and innocent, and in many regards it is true. But there is something you need to know."

Anna put her hands up to her ears. "Oh, if it is rumor and scandal about Madame, I don't want to hear it. I hate such things. I will not believe any of it."

Parrette shook her head. "No, no, I have heard nothing ill about Madame, though perhaps a little about her play."

"*Sappho*? That was her great opera."

"No, this is a play, *Camille*, which was to be performed at the Comédie-Française, in the rue de la Loi." Her eyes widened as she repeated this prestigious address.

"She never mentioned a word of this," Anna murmured wonderingly.

"Charlotte says because they refused to do it. She says the true reason is because she is a woman, that the freedoms of the revolution are coming to an end, but that is not what I wished to tell you." Parrette drew in a deep breath as she extracted a bit of carefully cut newsprint from her pocket.

Anna read it in astonishment. The article smugly crowed over the fact that the English frigate of 20 guns *Danae* had been taken by its crew, the officers killed or imprisoned, and the ship restored to France.

"Is Captain Duncannon dead, then?"

"It says nothing about that."

"A mutiny! Like those other mutinies the English had. I remember the Hamiltons talking about it. They said it was because of terrible captains who flogged and hanged seamen on whim. He must have been another such terrible captain."

Parrette shook her head. "Surely a terrible captain would not have written back to you about Michel."

That *surely* silenced them both; there was nothing more to be said. Conjecture was futile for want of fact. But afterward, Anna noticed that Parrette no longer referred to *The* Captain.

Six

CAPTAIN DUNCANNON HAD BY necessity been carried to Gibraltar again and thence northward, after beating against recalcitrant winds for so long that, as often happened, news of events he had left behind him reached London before he did.

He read about his former ship in the English newspapers when he reached Portsmouth just before Christmas. Where the French had been smug, the English deplored, the more in light of the mutinies two years previous.

Captain Duncannon also read the less sensational account in the *Naval Chronicle*, and shook his head over the grim tidings, wondering what his replacement had done to the capable crew that he had left behind.

He did not have time to think about it long. He had exactly two days of liberty, one of which he spent in a fruitless journey to London. There, he set about finding where the Hamiltons were living, just to discover that no Mrs. Duncannon was numbered among the company.

He obtained an interview with Nelson himself, who professed surprise and concern. "Did I not issue specific instructions? But Keith has been my determined enemy, I fear. That must explain it. You must carry your question to the Admiralty," he said, peering earnestly at Duncannon through his one good eye. "There you will no doubt be put in possession of the intelligence that no one has seen fit to report to me."

Duncannon thanked him profusely, refused another glass of canary, and took a hackney to the Admiralty, where he was kept waiting among a parcel of lieutenants and beached captains hoping for placement.

There, he discovered not only was there no communication, but nothing known of his missing wife, much less news of the progress of his annulment. "That sounds like Whitehall," he was told by a senior clerk. "That has their stamp all over it. You must put your questions there."

By now Duncannon suspected what he would hear at Whitehall, but he was determined to carry through the business until it was honorably resolved. He had turned his back on everything connected to his life before the navy, except his good name.

He took another hackney to Whitehall, just to find himself balked, and by so junior a clerk that he knew his efforts were for naught. But he wrote out the facts as directed, was assured that his question would be sent up the chain of command, and he walked out into the frigid air. Darkness had closed in early. He was forced to admit defeat.

He returned to his hotel in a disgusted mood. The next morning, the prospect of quitting London for Portsmouth in order to read himself aboard his new command improved his spirits. He penned a letter to the new legate in Naples asking the whereabouts of his wife, posted it, and then mounted his horse.

By Christmas he was beating futilely against gales as the fleet fought to gain westing enough to round Ushant.

The rest of Europe celebrated Christmas, but in France, this was the month of Nivôse.

The calendar at first confused Anna. This one talked about the Year Eight, that one referred to the year 1801, a third scrupulously recorded the ten-day weeks of the republican calendar. Most, however, betrayed the habit of a lifetime, more frequently reverting to naming the days of the week from the Gregorian calendar, as the mobs likely to string you up from a lamppost for such errors had largely vanished.

Many theater managers insisted on the very latest fashions, which actresses were expected to find themselves. It was easiest when the wealthy leaders of Paris donated their gowns, but there were never enough to go around even if you were able to wangle a way to find out when some might be coming.

Parrette, having foreseen this, had assured Anna's success at select concerts with her gowns modeled on those she had seen Madame Bonaparte wearing.

By mid-winter, Anna had sung thrice in the chorus at the Lyri-Comique, without being invited into the company. She was content, as that was the agreement.

She had also performed at private concerts given by several other high-ranking individuals in the Consulate government, culminating in a spectacular evening at the Chateau de Neuilly at a soiree hosted by Madame Grand, who (it was rumored) would soon marry the Foreign Minister Talleyrand.

Anna was sent back to Madame's in a sumptuous carriage, her arms full of flowers, her ears full of praise. But when she reached her room, Parrette took the flowers to find vases, saying, "Was there any money in it?"

"No," Anna said.

"This is the third such," Parrette said, arms crossed in the way that Anna had learned meant she was keeping something back. "It is a very bad precedent, but what can be done? Perhaps there is a way to secure gifts that we do not know about. They say Talma is always sent back with fabulous treasures, gold, and the like, when he gives recitations for the First Consul."

"That's the First Consul," Anna replied, but she was thinking, *Madame Grand is nearly as high.*

Parrette then said, "I believe you should be trying at the large houses."

"The performers are all professionals." Anna studied Parrette's averted gaze. "Am I to understand that you no longer object?"

"Yes, I object." Parrette lifted her chin. "But I have been considering. I owe your mother my life, and I promised her as she died in my arms that I would care for you as she would wish. And so I have tried to do. And yet I am afraid that Madame de Pipelet is soon to be married, and you know that the Count has no use for music, anymore than he does for Paris."

"That is true," Anna said slowly. Though the Count had obligingly hired her for her first concert, it had been apparent that he had done it only to please Madame de Pipelet.

Parrette went on. "The fact is, English rules are no use to us here—we are not in English society, as there is no English society. If Madame does marry, I do not think the Count will take us, and we must live. I have repaid Madame's loan, but only just, with your earnings, meager as they are."

She made no mention of the fact that Anna was not paying Parrette at all, but Anna felt the pressure of obligation just the same, as Parrette said gently, "Perhaps it is time to think of joining a company. It will be no different than what you do in the chorus at the Lyri-Comique, and you can still live as a respectable woman."

Anna straightened her back and tightened her ribs. She thought about Captain Duncannon with increasing rarity, and never without conflict. Even supposing he had survived, it was true that he had put them in the way of locating Parrette's long-lost son—if Michael Deflew and Michel Duflot were even the same person—but what kind of man would cause his men to mutiny?

"I want to sing," Anna stated firmly. "And that is what I mean to do. And we must live."

When she got up the next morning, the wedding ring joined her trinkets in their box. She consulted Madame about auditions—who promptly agreed, with a betraying smile of relief, as she promised she would do her best to arrange auditions.

Unfortunately, in spite of all the praise Anna heard at the private concerts, her auditions were dispiritingly unsuccessful. At the major theaters, she heard variations on the same judgment: "Excellent range, but no volume," and "Fine phrasing, vocal purity, but inaudible from the gallery."

Finally, after great exertion on the part of her patroness, she was invited to audition before the great Talma. In trepidation she dressed in her finest, walked timidly onto the great stage at the Théâtre de la République and gazed wonderingly out at the tiers of boxes.

She could make out no more than a shadowy form among other nameless faces in the middle of the theater. Below the stage, a violinist and a cellist struck up the bars of the music Madame de Pipelet had chosen for her, from her friend Jeanne-Hippolyte Devisme's *Praxitèle*. "Modern is good," Madame had said—and reminding great people of her friend's opera would be even better.

Sing with a light heart, and tight middle. Anna straightened up, tried to lift her heart and tighten the top of her ribs... and though she could hear her singing was pure, perfectly phrased, true to each note, she felt it dissipating like steam in that enormous cold space.

At the end, she was not surprised when the actor's rich, powerful voice echoed with apparent effortlessness back to the stage: "Thin. Thin person, thin voice. Come back when you've achieved some substance."

Blinking against the sting in her eyes, Anna walked off, the only sound the quiet thud of her footsteps. She made it to the street door before the tears overwhelmed her.

Not two days later, a short, round, balding little man attended Madame's salon, and after Anna sang for the company, he was introduced to Anna as Monsieur Dupree.

"Very fine, Signorina, ah, Citizen," he said, bobbing his head. "I think you would sound well at my theater, the Théâtre Dupree. On the Boulevard, you know. Intimate. My wife is the principal singer, but we need a new young soprano for Madame de Pipelet's *Sappho*. Our Lorette is too old for a soubrette, and at all events she prefers the breeches roles."

Anna had been all along the boulevard by then. She remembered the Théâtre Dupree as one of the smallest, in a ramshackle barn of a building that probably had been old when Louis XIV came to Paris to attend the theater. Old, she knew, meant abysmal pay, but poor pay was better than no pay at all.

She thanked M. Dupree gratefully, and discovered the following day that though the theater was indeed exactly as old as she had feared, its size was perfect for her voice. Madame, taller and larger than her husband, joined M. Dupree in their enthusiastic praise.

Anna had become a professional.

"Listen, Duncannon, the Prince of Denmark appears to be as decisive as a shuttlecock," Captain Fremantle said as they stood on the deck of the *Ganges*, overlooking the smoke-filled harbor at Copenhagen.

Captain Duncannon coughed, blinking his stinging eyes. The smolder from the sea battle and the subsequent fires wreathed them, blurring Fremantle's round countenance, though he stood not two paces away.

"Nelson is to go ashore in the morning," Captain Fremantle said. "I will stay and oversee finishing the burning of the captured ships."

"All of them?" Captain Duncannon asked in surprise. The Danes built beautiful ships. Though one had blown up, and others were severely damaged, that was after fighting every bit as intense as the Battle of the Nile.

"We can't spare people to man the prizes," Fremantle said. "We are stretched thin enough as it is. Speaking of orders, I want you to inspect the wounded taken ashore. I need someone I can trust to sort out the prisoners. Make certain that none of our men are among 'em, and that includes a few rascally French pretending to be ours. We've already caught one son of a Whitechapel bird-catcher trying to talk his way aboard of the grounded *Bellona*, my guess is to get at the gunpowder."

Captain Duncannon had already been awake for most of the night before the day's long, fierce battle. But there was too much to be done for anything more than a bite of bread and a sip of very cold coffee to wet his mouth.

His gig rowed him ashore, where many of the wounded had been landed, Danes, French, and English mixed promiscuously. Out of the chaos appeared a smoke-blackened lieutenant, who hailed him with relief. "You are timely come, Captain," he exclaimed once Duncannon had explained his orders. "Though we're a vast deal better than we were a few hours ago." He turned to a short, thin young man whose black hair was queued in a seaman's pigtail, one arm wrapped in a sling.

"This here is Seaman Dafoe, out of *Bellona*. He fell off the foremast yard when *Bellona* struck. He's been rousting out the Frenchies—speaks the lingo, including all the dialects that I can't make head nor tail of."

'Dafoe.' The name was familiar, but Captain Duncannon could not recollect why, and he was too busy to take the time to reflect.

He nodded at the seaman, and said, "Explain what you have here, and we will go on from there…"

Some time later, they paused at last, no fresh wounded having been brought in the past hour. Someone had brewed up coffee and tea, bringing it around, and they were able to sit for the first time in uncounted hours.

Duncannon was just stretching his aching feet to the fire before the command tent, when up dashed a young officer whose clean uniform indicated he had come from one of the ships held in reserve. "Captain Duncannon," this young lieutenant exclaimed, doffing his hat. "I am finally caught up with you. Lt. Bailey, premier of the sloop-of-war *Dido*. Sir Hyde Parker has been holding me for dispatches for London, or I would have tried to get this post to you sooner. I was handed it along with dispatches from the First Lord," he said, proffering a ribbon-tied sheaf of letters.

As Duncannon took the letters, Bailey added, "I'm told the stained one came out of a packet from the Med, nearly swamped by a gale at the Rock, and then escaped being snapped up by the French by running aground off Malta. It took until spring tide to get them off."

Captain Duncannon thanked the lieutenant, invited him to partake of the wretched boiled coffee, and then, as everyone else seemed busy with other things, bent his attention to the letters. The top two were from Yorkshire.

From long habit he pitched them unread into the fire. The third was from a solicitor whose name was familiar. Curious, Duncannon opened this letter, to discover that a great uncle—a retired admiral—had left his entire fortune to "my only nephew worth a damn."

These words, written in the precise legal hand, caused Duncannon to throw back his head and laugh aloud. Heads turned, and he smothered his mirth, begging pardon. A fortune? That was unexpected, to say the very least!

With heightened expectation, he turned his attention to the fourth, a much-battered, water-stained missive bearing an official stamp from Naples. With a sigh, he recollected the burden of his false marriage, and slit the seal.

The handwriting was a neat clerk's fist, and it said everything he had least wished to see: there was no Mrs. Duncannon anywhere in Naples, within the palace or out of it. No one in the new legate's staff claimed any knowledge of a Mrs. Duncannon. If there ever had been such a woman, she appeared to have vanished, and the unknown fellow had the infernal impudence to sign this missive *Your very obedient servant to command*, before the scrawled name.

The captain leaned forward to lay the letter on the fire, then paused. He had it: Dafoe, *Duflot*. Could this be the impressed French boy that his bride, what was her name? The boy she had requested him to locate?

He got to his aching feet and crossed to the area where the seamen had congregated to eat the salt pork and peas someone had brought over from the *Ganges*.

"Michel Duflot?" Captain Duncannon asked, giving the French pronunciation.

The slim youngster with the broken arm and the black pigtail glanced up, and seeing a superior officer, set aside his mess-kid and rose slowly to his feet, the firelight reflecting in his black eyes.

"Sit down," Captain Duncannon said, and took a seat in a camp chair that a lieutenant vacated. Lowering his voice, he said, "I took you for a Guernseyman, or some such. You are in fact French?"

Duflot said, "I am. But if you are asking if I am a Frenchman, pah!" He turned his head aside to spit. "If being a Frenchman means following Boney. It was he who caused my uncles to die in Italy and in Egypt, and for what? My father, too, though his death was a blessing." His sharp face tightened with hatred. "My father roasts with the devil, but Boney is still alive, sending good men after him. Though I was born in Lyons, I am no Frenchman."

Duncannon rarely acted on impulse, but the youngster had

proved immensely useful—and Duncannon now, apparently, had the wherewithal to allow himself some indulgences, like setting a decent table at last, and collecting prime crew between commissions. "What are you rated?"

Duflot's chin came up. "This year, I am rated able seaman. Foretop, starboard watch."

"*Bellona* is going to be in repairs for a time, and you will be useless for knotting and splicing." Captain Duncannon indicated his sling. "If I am to continue in my present command, I happen to be in want of a yeoman of the sheets, and already you have demonstrated a knack for organization. Shall I speak to your captain?"

"To go aboard a crack frigate, me?" Duflot's grin flashed. "Thank you, sir, I like me that ver-ry well."

Anna's success, while not as spectacular as that of Mrs. Billington or La Catalani, whose fame was spreading faster and farther across Europe than Bonaparte's troops, had insured that she had steady work.

As spring ripened into summer, one morning Madame de Pipelet came to Anna's room, sat on the bed and told her sorrowfully that she was leaving Paris with her husband-to-be. "This is no longer my Paris. It is becoming the Paris of the First Consul, a military capital. Fewer newspapers, and I am told that theaters are being told what they may produce, and what not. There is even talk of licensing again." She shook her head, sadly regarding the strange Egyptian figureheads at either end of the reclining couch. "But what can I do? I am telling you straight away, that you must find somewhere else to live," she finished.

Anna carried the bad news with her to rehearsal at Théâtre Dupree, and asked the rest of the company if anyone knew where she could get a room.

She was aware of a couple of the dancers whispering furiously, as Madame Dupree flung her hands wide. "We have too tiny a house, and so many people in it already."

That, Anna knew already from gossip around the theater. The

Duprees had sent all four of their children to convent schools in Belgium, where there were still convent schools to be found. She was hoping they could give her advice, but they seemed to know nothing about renting rooms.

No one else had any ideas to offer, or apparently any real interest. Anna caught glances from the two dancers, specifically from the thin dark-haired one whose sarcastic comments Anna had already noticed. The dancer stared back at Anna with a hostile expression, a contrast to the dancer with the pretty auburn curls, who regarded Anna with ready sympathy.

Anna kept her disappointment to herself. Parrette would surely find something. She was resourceful. And so Anna turned her mind to rehearsal.

At the end, she was surprised to discover the auburn-haired dancer next to her. "The rooms next to ours are free, just yesterday. The Hôtel Foulon. Don't tell Lise I told you!"

She flitted away.

Anna was tempted to ignore the advice, but when she reached Madame's that night, it was to discover that Parrette had had no luck. "Everything is so very costly, or far away, or there was some man offering in a way I found very evil."

Anna told her what the dancer had said.

"The Foulon? That is near to the Lyri-Comique." Parrette pursed her lips. "I admit, it is a perfect location. If dancers stay there, then it cannot be too costly, for they are worse paid even than singers. I am only afraid what other costs there might be," she said with a dire frown.

Whatever those were, they must not have been insurmountable, Anna discovered the next day, for Parrette said that she had engaged the rooms. "Rooms! It is no more than a closet with a pimple of a box adjoining. Barely enough for a bed, not even a bed and a trunk. But the outer room has a window even if it looks out upon the alley, and while it is right under the roof, that means it will stink less in summer. We shall do very well."

A couple of weeks later, patroness and protégé parted amid tears, Anna genuinely sorry to be losing Madame de Pipelet.

"And I am desolated to be drawn away just as I am to witness your rising star of fame," Madame said, kissing Anna.

By then Anna and Parrette had moved their few possessions to the Hôtel Foulon. Anna soon discovered that the auburn-haired dancer, Hyacinthe, and the thin, sarcastic Lise, lived on the same landing. Hyacinthe expressed delight to find Anna close by, but Lise ignored Anna.

Through Hyacinthe, who seemed to be friends with everyone in the Foulon, Anna discovered the best places to eat cheaply, an affordable laundry (that Parrette oversaw with formidable care) and many other useful details about life in Paris for those living perilously on a pittance. Best of all, how to gain entry to all the theaters to watch, enjoy, and to learn.

Parrette would not say why she distrusted the dancers, but she slowly unbent toward Hyacinthe, to the extent of offering to repair one of her two good gowns when they found Hyacinthe early one morning sitting on the top stair and weeping, the cheap muslin clutched in her hands.

Parrette completely remade the flimsy, badly sewn gown, going to the trouble of adding bits of ribbon that she had acquired in her constant bargain hunting.

The result looked so smart that within a week, an actress who lived on the floor below knocked on the door. When Parrette answered, the woman said, "Hyacinthe told me that you are the one who turned that old India-muslin of hers. Will you do that for me?"

Parrette glanced at Anna, who was brushing out her hair. Then she looked back, straightened her shoulders, and said, "I charge dressmaker prices."

The actress shrugged. "You are a better seamstress than Gertrud," naming the local seamstress.

By week's end, six women had come to her for their gowns to be remade. She began building a tidy little sum.

The beginning of the next week, a brisk knock at the door revealed Lise. She held out a torn gown of cheap silk. "Can you repair that?"

Anna walked past and started down the long flights of stairs. She found Lise rude and unpleasant, but she would not interfere in Parrette's budding business.

As summer storms gave way to autumn sunshine, Anna

continued to model herself on Josephine Bonaparte, viewed from the distant galleries when Anna attended the theater.

One morning she went early to Theater Dupree ahead of the first cool rain of the season. Mornings were when the dancers took the stage for their own practice. Anna had been watching them during rehearsals. Alone in her room she tried to copy their graceful airs, the way they tripped so lightly about the stage, but was frustrated. She felt awkward, and when she set up her tiny looking glass to lean on her trunk against the wall, and looked into it, her heart sank at her clownish poses, all elbows and knees.

Lise talked to the other dancers as they turned their laced hands out and stretched arms and back, apparently ignoring the unwanted visitor.

Hyacinthe, seeing her standing in the wings, came over, her wide eyes greenish in the diffuse light. "Anna! You are early. Is there a rehearsal I did not know about?"

Anna shook her head. "I was hoping I might practice with you girls, before the men come in."

At this, Lise halted the pretense of not listening, and advanced on Anna. Her sharp features flushed; even angry, Lise seemed to float.

"What, do you intend to dance as well as sing, and thus shut us out of our places? Or are you aiming to dazzle Vestris at the Opera? And a lot of luck you will have!"

"No." Anna lifted her arms. "I only want to move the way you do, on stage. I thought if I attended your morning rehearsal, it might benefit me."

"Why should she not?" Hyacinthe asked.

One side of Lise's mobile mouth curled up. "Why, be welcome!" She made an airy movement, and curtseyed mockingly. "But at the back. Out of our way. See if you can keep up," she added.

Lise, though younger than some of the dancers, was their acknowledged leader. The women arrived first, the only time they could claim the entire stage for themselves. The stage was bitterly cold, but they soon warmed themselves, and the air around them, by working hard.

The girls' dance practice began easily enough, with the five positions and repetitive movements that Anna thought must train the foot and the arm. Before long they became more difficult, especially the bends, and the lifting of legs. Anna began sweating, her plain rehearsal gown twisting unpleasantly about her, the seams pressing warningly against her flesh and threatening to rip. Now she understood why the dancers wore knitted hose under short skirts, and loose blouses.

Several times she nearly gave up, but then caught a smug, mocking glance from Lise, which kindled her determination. Lise wanted her to quit. Therefore she wouldn't.

After an interminable time her muscles trembled so much she knew she would have to quit or drop right there on the stage, but then new voices echoed from the side entrance, and there was M. Dupree, rushing around madly as he always did, and mopping his balding head with a snowy linen handkerchief.

The dancers withdrew, obviously ready for the real rehearsal. Anna could scarcely walk. She slipped into the wings, grateful for once that her singing part was small.

Rehearsal even so took all her strength. Climbing those long flights of stairs to her room hurt so much that she had to lean on the bannister to catch her breath at every landing. When at last she stumbled into their room and fell on the bed, her legs twitching with pain, Parrette looked up from her stool by the window, where she was sewing. "What happened to you?"

Anna told her.

Parrette's black brows drew together, reminding Anna of Lise, which caused a bubble of laughter that she was too tired to release. "As your dear mother used to say in English, that girl is no better than she should be," Parrette stated.

"And what is meant by that?"

"Never mind." Parrette sniffed. "I think your idea is good, but you can do just as well without those foolish dancers."

By then the stiffness had set in, and Anna almost cried out with the pain when she stooped to take off her shoes. But she said, "I mean to try it again. I think I might need hose, like theirs, and a tunic. Do you know where to find such?"

Parrette threw her hands heavenward. But by next morning, Parrette had traded for the first, and whipped together the second from Anna's oldest gown.

Anna was there early, though she wondered if her muscles might shred like rotten fabric. She gritted her way through the morning, and each morning thereafter. It hurt so much she moved badly on stage instead of gracefully.

But on the third day, Hyacinthe whispered, "It was that way for us all. And it is worse at the Opera! The great Vestris works them until their feet bleed, every day! You will get used to it." She twirled, light and graceful as a butterfly.

I am going to move in that way, Anna thought determinedly. *If I strengthen my body, surely it will strengthen my voice.*

The days slid into winter and the dancing gradually became easier. Anna also learned that though no dancer had any grand title, and no 'birth' to speak of, there was just as strict a hierarchy among them as in any court. The dancers always took the same places, Philippe, the handsome, mercurial *premier danseur,* and the other two male dancers in front. Until it was time for company dance rehearsals, the men held completely aloof from the women, of whom Lise and willowy, light-haired Ninon were rival leaders.

Lise and Ninon hated each other. They never spoke to the other if it could be avoided. Anna saw that taking the lowest place effectively removed her from the silent competition that existed between many of the dancers. She was safe in their indifference, learning more each day.

Seven

PRESENTLY THE LAST SNOW of the winter sent white drifts scudding down the Boulevard. Signs of spring began to appear. One morning Anna, huddled in her pelisse, became aware that her legs did not hurt. She still was not certain the dancing made her look any better on stage, but at least she could get through the dance practice without aching. And she finished the long day less tired.

That, unexpectedly, created a new problem.

Hearing through her open window the faint echoes of people strolling the Boulevard and having a good time made her restless. The sun was now setting later each day, and all the trees and flowers in tiny garden pots began to bloom. Paris was magical at night, everyone said, but she did not see it.

By 28 Germinal, Year X, or Easter of 1802, when Napoleon restored the churches and Parrette could once again attend Mass without fear of being arrested, once again Paris resounded with church bells — those that had not been melted down to make cannon.

On April 6th, everyone "went to Longchamps."

Hyacinthe invited Anna to witness the parade along the Champs d'Elysées. The dancers put together their scant money to hire a fiacre, and in this they dashed along, gazing at carriages decorated with ribbons and flowers. The celebrative crowd streamed along the road toward the valley leading to the Bois de Boulogne. Here and there on grassy areas other dancers in floating classical tunics danced and posed, wreaths and leaves in their hair, pretending to be figures of mythological times.

Afterward all Paris streamed back to the cafés and theaters. The soft spring air was filled with little lights, and the sounds of music and laughter.

At such times, Paris was magical, and Anna loved it all.

And yet it was not a fairy tale, however much it might look that way at night. Anna had had too many dire warnings from Parrette about wandering alone on the boulevard, much less the streets of Paris. She sat disconsolately on the landing late one evening, while the theater stage was being redone. Anna was going over the music of the new production so that Parrette could spread fabric out in the tiny room.

As she sat humming the music and trying to get it by memory, the door behind her opened. Lise and Hyacinthe, both dressed smartly, stepped past her. Their voices and laughter floated up the stairs as they descended to the street for a stroll on the Boulevard with their friends.

Anna watched them wistfully, then made herself return to her task.

The next morning, when Anna left to go to dance practice, she heard quick steps behind her. She was surprised to find Lise's dark gaze on her. Anna sidestepped so that Lise could pass, but instead, the dancer matched Anna's pace.

"Is Parrette Duflot your maid or your *duègne?*" Lise asked abruptly when they got outside in the brisk wind that presaged rain.

Anna's mother had taught her during the rough-and-tumble days in the royal nursery that part of deflection was to answer insulting questions as if they had been put in a charitable tone. *What are they really asking?* Mother had said. *Answer that, if you can. If you cannot? Deflect, disengage, retreat.*

Why must it always be me who has to run away? Anna had asked petulantly.

To which Parrette replied, *Aside from the question of rank, which cannot be got round, a retreat is not always running away. The smart servants learn to never let the royal children catch them, and never show fear if they do. Their example is their father, who lives for the hunt and the kill.*

So what was Lise really asking? Lise had grown up during the Revolution, when people who had duennas were despised, even murdered.

Anna said peaceably, "Parrette was with my mother until she died. She chose to stay with me even though I was left with nothing. I do not pay her as I have nothing to pay her with."

"Who was your mother?"

Anna drew in a deep breath, considering Lise's accusatory tone. One still heard people addressed as 'Citizen' but 'Madame' and 'Monsieur' were also heard, and also, great people such as Madame Bonaparte no longer hid their aristocratic connections. Did Lise think that Anna was an aristocrat, or merely that she was getting above herself?

Anna walked a few steps, not seeing the muddy boulevard but her childhood, the cozy morning breakfasts with her parents. She would never lie about her birth, but she felt that the circumstances of her family's rank were no longer relevant.

So she answered in the manner of a French professional. "My mother was a governess until she married my father. He was a musician. They are both dead."

"Ah," Lise said, her tone lightening, as Anna had hoped it would. "She is very clever with her fingers, Parrette. She could set up her own shop."

"With what money?" Anna gave the Parisian shrug.

Lise laughed. "With what money indeed? Madame said you once lived in a palace, in Italy."

Anna laughed. "So I did. Parrette, too. Many, many people live in palaces. There are those, such as the royal family, who live in the great chambers and give the orders, and then there are the rest of us who live in the attics, and who carry out the orders."

"Ah."

They walked in silence the rest of the way to the theater. Later, when they left rehearsal, as there was no opera that night, Hyacinthe came to Anna and said, "Will you walk out this evening with us?"

Anna looked past her to Lise, who stood against a painted flat, half-smiling.

"Yes, I would like to, very much," Anna said.

"Wear something pretty." Hyacinthe patted Anna's arm.

Anna skipped back to her rooms, her heart filled with anticipation. She would not be alone, therefore Parrette could have nothing to object to. And she could wear her prettiest gown.

Her first night out was every bit as enchanting as any stage performance. Light spilled from theaters and cafés, and every-where people laughed, flirted, sang, danced. Hyacinthe introduced Anna to a great many people—far too many to remember. They mostly seemed to be other performers, with occasional young men rising in some profession, and then there were the officers in their dashing uniforms.

Paris was in full bloom by then, the theaters and cafés enjoying a busy season. One day they met two young naval attaches who had been sent to Paris with reports. While they were bragging about the speed of their travel, and the importance of their dispatches, they made mention of Admiral Nelson's defeat of the Danes at Copenhagen, at the end of March the previous year.

Nelson! The English fleet! Anna had given up being concerned about Captain Duncannon, but there was still Parrette's son Michel. However, the other girls showed scant interest. Anna tried to think of some way of introducing a question about the names of English ships, such as Michel's *Pallas*, but the subject passed too quickly. She made an excuse to leave early, stopped by one of the cafés that always carried newspapers, and for the first time since her arrival in Paris, sought to find old copies.

She was successful in one place, where old newsprint was utilized in a variety of ways. A young daughter of a café owner, hoping to earn something by letting the crazy woman paw through the stacks in the basement, lingered with a candle as Anna swiftly sorted through a stack.

She found what she sought, paid the girl a handful of *assignats*, and carried the newspaper straight back to the Foulon. As a spring storm roared on the roof above their room, she read them. "I overheard something about Admiral Nelson, the Danes, and last year," she said to Parrette, who stuck her needle in its paper case.

She knelt on the floor beside Anna, the candle resting between them, as they compared accounts in the newspapers.

There was little enough to be gleaned. Anna remembered Madame saying that the number of newspapers had diminished steadily under the influence of the First Consul, and she saw that which was printed was decidedly unflattering to the British.

One troubling item caught her attention, and she gazed at Parrette, whose eyes looked black in the light of the single candle. "It says in here that Nelson's ship was the *Elephant*."

Parrette pursed her lips. "They must have it wrong."

Anna shook her head. "Remember how he shifted out of *Foudroyant*, and then back?"

Parrette's eyes widened. *"Nom d'un nom!* You think Michel is no longer in the *Pallas*, then."

"If Nelson can change ships, cannot sailors, too? I'll ask M. Dupree tomorrow," Anna promised. "He must know—he seems to know everything about Paris that it is possible to know."

But when Anna approached the kindly director and asked if there was some sort of British envoy, where she might find out more recent news, his round, beaming face turned serious. Drawing her aside, he said earnestly, "Don't go pursuing that! Do you want Fouché's *mouchettes* snooping around? I, for one, do not want them in my theater. It has enough problems! Please, my dear young signorina, leave well enough alone."

Anna thanked him, and kept silence until later that day, when she caught the dancers waiting in the wings before the performance. She whispered to Hyacinthe, "Who are the mouchettes? Surely something else is meant besides little flies."

Lise's hearing was at least as sharp as her features. Before Hyacinthe could speak, she pulled Anna aside and in a quick, low whisper explained that 'mouchettes' was the nickname for the spies the sinister police chief, Fouché, employed to root out traitors as well as criminals.

"And traitors," Hyacinthe said, her eyes round, "can be anyone he mislikes the sound of."

"It is just that Parrette's son was taken on board an English ship in impressment. We want to discover, if we can, where he is. If he lives."

Lise lifted a shoulder as she absently flexed her feet while waiting for the call to places. "I am sorry for Parrette's missing son. We all have someone gone missing, either as a soldier or during the Terror, but we have learned to leave well enough alone."

After the performance, as Anna carefully changed out of her costume, Parrette listened soberly to Anna's report of her inquiries. "We must avoid direct questions," she said. "About British ships. But there are other ways of learning, as you did with the attachés."

"By listening," Anna said. "It is easy enough. These soldiers? I find, the younger they are, the more they boast."

Parrette gave a squawk of laughter. "Young! Says the old crone."

Anna laughed, but she reflected on the newest dance apprentices, and two additions to the chorus, both relatives of the Duprees, none of whom were older than sixteen. She was no longer the youngest.

It was an odd feeling because when she walked out with the dancers, she had felt like the youngest. That was because she always returned to the Foulon at night, whereas some of the dancers went riding off in cabriolets with their beaux.

"Life is so strange," Lise said to Anna one night, as she posed before the mirror at the end of the narrow hall on which all their doors opened. Her gown was flimsy silk, tied high, and she'd bound up her hair with a golden fillet. As she spoke, she clasped a diamond necklace around her throat, a gift from her latest swain, and patted it happily into place. "A very few years ago, had I dared to go out dressed so, the mob would have hanged me, *tout de suite!*"

"As it is, a thief will get that necklet, see if they don't," Hyacinthe warned. "You are a fool to wear diamonds in the Boulevard crowd."

Lise lifted thin shoulders, like a bird poised for flight. "And if I do? I shall demand another." She smiled in triumph. "What is the use of having it, if I cannot flaunt it, especially under Ninon's nose?"

Hyacinthe sighed. "If you sell it in the right place, that would house and feed us for an entire winter. Perhaps longer!"

"Eh, if a girl cannot find a wealthy boy to cover that, she deserves to starve," Lise said carelessly, and sashayed off.

Anna felt old and experienced as she listened to the dancers. A great deal of what had been hitherto hidden was…if not completely comprehensible, at least somewhat clearer. Lovers, the dancers all promised, were much better than husbands, as they had to please you to keep you.

Parrette watched with tight-lipped disapproval as Anna went off with Lise and Hyacinthe. It was too much to hope that the girl would manage to stay as unworldly as her parents had in Naples's dreadful court. But now Anna was blossoming into a young woman. She was not exactly beautiful, but she was slowly becoming the next thing to it, with a gliding walk and a graceful turn of head. It was to be expected that she would enjoy the enchantments of the Boulevard with the others, but Parrette did not intend to let her forget that, should she decide she was now a woman, she was a *married* one, until they found out for certain that she was a widow.

Anna sensed this wary disapproval. Having no wish to live on bad terms with Parrette, she spoke less to her about what she was thinking, and more to her new friends.

One morning, the dancers stretched legs and arms as they gossiped about someone's sister, who until recently had danced at another theater. But now she was married.

"A husband?" Lise made a dismissive gesture. "What is the use of that? A husband, you must please, or he will beat you. A lover? If he doesn't please you, you cast him off." She dusted her hands in a quick movement.

"But if a very, very rich man offers to marry you, snap him up," blonde Eleanor said, causing all to laugh.

Anna laughed with them, but she thought about how strange it was to recollect that *she* was married. Ordinarily she only remembered her state when she saw that ring lying among her trinkets.

A week later, Lise's sarcasm increased abruptly, and Ninon

smirked behind her back. No one could do anything right: Lise mocked Anna's struggles to keep pace during dance practice; she mocked the singers. She mocked the other theaters, the noise the returning swallows made, the smell left by horses in the street. She and Ninon were overheard squabbling in the alley, voices rising to shrillness, then abruptly cutting off when M. Dupree went outside to demand silence, as Madame was trying to work on her aria.

Anna looked for a cause, and found it in Lise's bare neck. The diamond necklace had not made a reappearance for days.

During a quiet moment midway through rehearsal, she caught Hyacinthe alone backstage, fetching water. "The necklace," Anna said softly. "Was it stolen?"

"No," Hyacinthe whispered back, looking as affronted as so gentle a creature could. "The corn merchant's wife went to the prefecture, and claimed Lise had stolen it from *her!* Someone told her Lise had it. She had to return it. That is why she swears, no more merchants. Only officers. *They* aren't likely to have grasping wives!"

For a few days following, Ninon went about with curled lip, never failing to drop a mention of diamonds into any conversation.

After that Lise confined herself to the officers—and not just any, but a captain who, it was said, reported directly to Chef-de-Brigade Maurin. This captain, the dancers whispered, was Ninon's property.

For days, the two rivals entertained the company by their efforts to beguile this captain, until one morning Ninon left rehearsal with deliberate parade, climbing into a smart equipage with her new lover riding his splendid horse alongside.

Eleanor sighed, hands pressed to her heart. "Is that not romantic? He is to be stationed in the north as they prepare for the invasion of England, and he is taking Ninon with him. It is said that the officers will live in a chateau. Oh, Ninon has all the luck!"

Lise glowered from the wing, white-lipped with fury.

Parrette was watching from beside one of the flats, waiting with Anna's costume. "Stupid hen," she muttered. "She will be sorry enough when he tires of her."

The gradual outward changes as spring warmed toward summer caused an inward change in Anna. She relinquished any pretense of being a prodigy. She had never liked the false feeling it gave her when she was introduced at private gatherings as one, but now, with the spectacular rise of such talents as Mademoiselle Georges, who at fifteen was performing for the Bonapartes at their private theater, as well as the Théâtre-Français, she felt it was time to drop the pose.

One night, after one of their friends inveigled a cousin at the Théâtre for tickets, Anna and her friends went to watch the new comet blaze across the stage.

"Oh, I wish I could project so effortlessly," Anna whispered.

"You think her good? She's as big as a cow in calf," Lise scoffed.

"There is no music in her voice, true—her breathing's all wrong—but the emotional range!" Anna said.

"She's got ankles thicker than an oak," Lise said.

Mademoiselle Georges tripped across the stage, drawing all eyes to her as she emoted a thrilling whisper that managed to carry, and then as the tragedy unfolded, her voice fell to a low, hoarse moan.

As they walked away, Hyacinthe sighed. "It was so romantic."

"Oh, you love everything, as long as it's soppy with tears. She was stupid," Lise said, and turned on Anna. "The First Consul thinks *her* enchanting? It should have been you."

"But I am not an actor," Anna protested. "I'm trying to learn, because one must, in order to sing in opera, but—"

"You would be better queening over Bonaparte than that lumbering cow, and further, you would not forget your friends!"

Anna glanced at Lise's sharp profile. Though they were different in every other way, Lise reminded her of certain of the Neapolitan princesses, who regarded everything, from decorations on shoes to who got in the pony carts first, as competitions. She returned to the Foulon in a thoughtful mood.

A few days later, Anna was leaving the Foulon to walk to rehearsal, smartly dressed as always, when she spied a grand carriage drawn up in the street. She sidestepped young Pierre Dupree, the owner's younger brother and general factotum, busy talking to a young man in a new livery of green and gold. That was the First Consul's livery, Anna thought, wondering what he was doing at the Foulon.

She'd taken no more than two steps when both faces turned her way. "There she is," Pierre said. "Signorina Bernardo! This man has a summons for you."

Anna's heart began to pound. All she could think of was the Minister of Police, and her questions about British naval matters, as she drew near. "Are you certain you want me?" she managed.

The young man consulted a rumpled slip of paper. "Mademoiselle Ludovisi," he pronounced carefully, "also known as Signorina Bernardo?"

Anna's throat went dry. "That is I."

"Well, then, I am to escort you to the Tuileries." And when Anna lifted her hands, one pointing helplessly toward the Foulon, and the other gesturing vaguely at her bare head, the footman said, "Come as you are. I'm to take you and bring you back. You needn't bring anything."

Bring you back. These words heartened Anna enough to enable her to climb into the carriage, though her legs shook. All up and down the street, people turned to stare as the footman climbed up onto the box next to the driver, and waved his hand. "Clear away! Clear away!"

"That would have netted you a fast trip to Madame Guillotine ten years ago," a wizened old woman called as she walked slowly in front of the horses. She cackled as she looked Anna up and down. "And so would that fine gown! Ha-ha-ha!" She walked off, crowing with laughter.

"Take it up with the First Consul," the footman retorted with a laugh, as the driver touched the whip to his pair.

A short time later, the carriage rolled through the Place du Carrousel and to the Tuileries. To her relief she was not taken any-where near the Consular family's private wing, but to a por-tion of the building from which she could hear the cacophony of violins tuning, and here and there the quick, brassy sound of horns.

A few minutes later, she was conducted into a small office that smelled of wet plaster, where she stood in amazement. "Maestro Paisiello!"

"My dear child!" The maestro threw open his arms, nearly knocking a pile of music sheets from the crowded desk. Powder puffed into the air from his wig as he lunged to rescue the pages. "I need not ask how Paris has treated you, I have the evidence of my eyes! I can scarcely wait to tell Madame. She will wish to see you, but she is at the moment under the care of a physician. You must call upon her when she has recovered from the journey."

"Most assuredly. May I ask what brings you and la signora here?" They had fallen into their old habit of speaking in Neapolitan, which to her was the natural language of music, even more so than Italian.

"You will remember that the First Consul favored me with a commission for General Hoche's funeral march. Well, ever since, he has invited me to Paris. Of course I did not wish to quit Naples until the king himself bade me come hither, as a gesture of friendship toward the First Consul. And so, behold me! I am now in charge of the music of the consular court. Guillard has given me a fine *Proserpina,* which will serve as my introduction to the French *tragedie-lyrique.* As you see, I am in the midst of writing the music."

Anna had not spent all this time without understanding something of how the musical life of Paris went. "He brought you here, Maestro? It is wonderful news, but…"

"Go ahead, shut the door," the maestro said to the waiting footman. "We must talk over the opera. When Mademoiselle is ready to return, you shall see her emerge."

And when the door was shut, he said more softly, "I do not pretend to understand, except that there are politics, dear girl. Politics. They say that the First Consul becomes ever grander, that he even has set his sights upon a crown." He sighed. "No, I shall not say that. I desire nothing more than to stay out of politics!"

He threw up his hands again, dislodging another snowfall of powder from his wig, then bent confidentially toward Anna. "Tell me, my dear. How does Mademoiselle Georges sing? The First Consul expects me to put her in Proserpina, but from anything I can find out, she is a mere child. Is she a prodigy, a Billington, a Catalani?"

Anna glanced at the door, then said truthfully, "She is a very pretty girl, but she is an actress." She stopped there.

The maestro sighed as he took in her averted gaze, and glanced down at the table littered with papers. "You are reluctant to say what we both know. It is not only the First Consul, but his sister, who professes to be my patron, pushing this Georges on me, I expect because she wants to make trouble in the First Consul's marriage."

Anna could not prevent a blush.

The maestro noticed, and patted her hand. "You are still an innocent, then?"

Anna shrugged sharply, aware that she had copied the gesture from Lise. "Who has time for anything else?"

"It is just as well. Just as well," Paisiello said on a sigh. "So. Mademoiselle Georges. It is no worse than royal demands, then, if no better. Oh, that patrons would hand over the wherewithal, and then get themselves out of the way! Do I tell them how to conduct their wars? I do not. If he insists, then I shall have to strengthen the chorus, and give her pastoral melodies. Simple."

He made a dismissive gesture, and bent toward Anna. "And so we come to you. I find you here in Paris, and you appear to have overcome your scruples about employment."

"So I have," Anna said.

"What then is your goal?"

Anna straightened up, unaware of the significant changes the maestro observed in her countenance. "I intend to become the best singer in Paris," she said.

"*Bon!*" He clapped his hands. "That is exactly what I want to hear. I want you as my Cyane. Come into the rehearsal hall. I am relieved to find you have fattened up a little, and I approve the way you carry your head. You are no longer such an awkward little colt, oh my! Not at all—I scarcely should have recognized you! Now I must hear you sing. I trust you have worked on your breathing, for I am determined that you shall work hard…"

Eight

IN FRANCE, THEY WERE now back to the Gregorian seven days, though it was still considered the Year IX, and not 1802.

Anna was busier than ever, between her dance lessons and the ever-changing *Proserpina*, and her occasional private concerts late at night after her theater work in the role of one of Dirce's Handmaids in Cherubini's *Médée*. This opera had been so popular when produced five years ago that it was being staged again at the rickety Théâtre Dupree, Madame Dupree singing the title role.

For a third...there was a very, very handsome officer in the Consular Guard.

As spring ripened into summer, more and more glorious uniforms appeared to be strolling the boulevard.

Paris was taking on a decidedly martial air, but the change was gradual, at least to the young actresses, dancers, and hopeful performers who failed to take an interest in politics or foreign affairs. All their attention was for an admiring pair of eyes above gleaming epaulettes, a debonair pelisse, high, glossy boots encasing a fine pair of legs, and above all, the careless largesse of the soldier who lives for the moment.

During one of Anna's evening walks along the Boulevard, they were joined by a raffish set of young officers who each bought the pretty singers and dancers a rose from a street seller, after which the two groups joined and wandered to a café popular with performers.

As always, Lise took the lead. Hyacinthe and Eleanor did their best to fascinate with the play of eyelash, and shrug of round shoulders. Their tiny puff sleeves drifted carelessly to the top of their pretty arms. Anna, the youngest, was also the quietest; her pleasure was divided between the balmy air, scented with the fragrance of linden, the charming lights set out by all the cafés, the general mood of hilarity, and also those admiring glances from dashing men.

Gradually she became aware of a steady blue gaze. She began to steal peeks at the handsome young officer, until one day their eyes met, and he smiled.

After that, she was aware of him while everyone else chattered on. It was a strange feeling, as if she were alone on stage. As if a candle glowed beneath her skin. When the evening ended, Anna joined those returning to the Foulon, but when she glanced back, the tall blond officer raised his fingers in salute.

Blushing fiery red, Anna turned quickly, but she was laughing as she caught up with the others.

To the whispered delight of the dancers, the front rows of the pit at Théâtre Dupree were taken over by a set of young officers of the Consular Guard. M. Dupree watched them with a nervous air from off the wings, mopping his shining head. The officers were boisterously loud in their praise whenever their favorite girls appeared on stage.

One night, after the officers had been there for five straight performances, Anna stood in the wings behind Hyacinthe and Catherine, waiting for her cue, as all three peered past the footlights at the young men in the first three rows.

"He is very handsome. Very! Such an air, and his mustache, just enough. Not like the monstrous ones some of the officers wear."

Lise drifted up to join them, peeked, then raised her thin, arched brows. "You detest the mustaches, *cherie*? I find them gallant."

"Bah! Have you tried to kiss a man with one? It is like kissing an old goat in the field. Worse, that stinky pomade!"

A careful toss of black ringlets, and a sniff. "Tchah! For diamond ear drops, I will hold my nose against the pomade."

The orchestra struck up the notes preceding Anna's entrance. She straightened her shoulders and took a deep breath, conscious of the tightening of her upper ribs. She was also conscious of her toes pointing, the curve of her wrists, the angle of her head as she took the small sliding steps onto the stage that mimicked the floating grace of Madame Josephine, the First Consul's elegant wife.

From the first row came a shout, "Toast!" and "Brava!"

Anna tried not to smile as she began her opening song, but her mind was less on her breathing then on the surprise gift of pink roses that had arrived earlier and was now sitting in her tiny dressing room, filling the stuffy air with their heavenly scent.

As the performance progressed, she could not resist the occasional glances at that first row, where epaulettes glittered on broad shoulders. Ah, there he was: one of the tallest, his hair gilt in the reflection of the many candles. She shivered when she remembered the roses, and the little card with that delightful inscription: *To Anna, who sings like an angel.*

She was conscious of giving her best performance, smiling all the way through to her bows; her partner in the performance, the newly hired tenor, Jean-Baptiste Marsac, watched her speculatively for the first time.

When she returned to remove her costume, she found Parrette frowning at the flowers. "Parrette, what is wrong? You aren't angry with me?"

"Not at all, me! It is just that this great *thing* crowds us right out," Parrette said, waving at the bouquet. "And no doubt will shed petals all over that I shall have to sweep up."

"I will carry it to the Foulon myself. And put a cloth under it to catch petals." But Parrette's brow was still furrowed. "Surely you do not grudge my singing gaining an admirer?"

"If I was sure it was your singing," Parrette grumbled.

Anna laughed.

After the performance, she carefully laid aside her Greek-styled costume and pulled on a smart new gown of striped muslin, trimmed at the little sleeves and high waist in contrasting ribbon.

She gaily wished Parrette a good night, and when she reached the street, she linked arms with Hyacinthe and Eleanor, making it about ten steps before they found themselves surrounded by a number of tall chasseurs of the Guard of the Consul, resplendent in their tight uniforms gleaming with gold braid, extravagant bear-lined pelisses swaying with martial panache.

"Mesdemoiselles," one cried, and Anna turned.

He was taller than she remembered, his blond mustachio curled fiercely. Half-shut blue eyes gazed appreciatively down at her, sending a champagne fizz through her veins as he bowed over her hand.

His warm lips brushed her skin. "*Ma chère* Anna," he said lazily, "will an angel deign to grace mere mortals with her attention?"

Anna blushed hot all over. She scarcely knew what to say; Lise took her arm, tugging. "Come, Anna! They are holding a table for us at the Trois Arlequins."

Anna had never before had her own admirer. As the chasseurs paired off with dancers and actresses, her tall companion walked beside her, his sword rattling at each step of his high, glossy boots. "You know my name, but I do not know yours," she ventured.

"Auguste," he said.

"Auguste?" she prompted, though in Paris people used first names as often as last. Post-Revolution Paris was inconsistent about honorifics.

"Ah," he exclaimed. "Slain through the heart, hearing my name upon those lips!"

They crowded into the popular café. When they discovered that their favorite spot had been claimed, the chasseurs swaggered to the best table, hands to the hilts of their swords as they shoved the young men in civilian dress away from the little chairs, then bowed with extravagant audacity at their female companions.

The waiters, scenting trouble, hastened to bring the best champagne. Anna, unused to the heady drink, blinked as candlelight gained auras, and tricks of light caught in bright, admiring eyes. Edouard was the tallest; Guillaume the one who sang in a pleasing tenor, though the words were so idiomatic Anna didn't quite catch them all. From the way the men laughed, she suspected Parrette would not translate for her.

Then Piers called for yet another bottle.

"…the bad old days," Edouard said, as he began pouring more champagne all around. Anna stared fixedly at the golden liquid, the tiny bubbles rising, then puffing into air, causing a faint smell that tickled the inside of her nose. How could it do that? It seemed like magic The entire evening seemed like a fairy tale.

"…but the worst were the names," Piers said, his face flushed. "Do you know what my mother changed my name to, after the Declaration? Eh? Fevridor. Yes, Fevridor, I ask you! Not even a month I prefer! My youngest brother had it worse, though: Dix-Août."

"My cousin is Crainte. There is not much romance in 'Fear'! He goes by Luc, now."

"That's nothing. The butcher at the end of our street? He named his twins Droit de l'Homme Tricolor and Mort aux Aristocrates. 'Right to a good beating for being intolerable,' and 'Death to patience,' that's what we called those brats!"

Everyone laughed, and Guillaume pounded the table with his fist. "Wager! I'll lay you hundred my sister has it worse. She was born in the Year IV. Amour Sacré de la Patrie et le Constitution, is what our mother called her! Now, if any part of that name crosses your lips, she swears a fate most sanguinary!"

"I've met her. I'll not take that wager," Auguste said, and everyone laughed.

Anna found their laughter so funny that she was still fizzing with giggles when she felt Auguste's strong hand slide around her waist. Her blood heated. She blinked downward, enjoying the sensation of being held by a man, but why were his shirt cuffs so frayed beneath the splendid blue coat with its brave gold braid?

The evening came to a summary end when, pooling their last coins, the men could not come up with the price of another bottle. At first it looked as if there might be trouble, but the waiters, long experienced, had assembled in a mass, outnumbering by a factor of four the tipsy soldiers. Finding themselves surrounded by brawny young men in aprons who carried kitchen knives or cudgels, the chasseurs each linked arms with their fair companions and Edouard led the way out.

Talking and laughing, the party strolled back along the boulevard. Anna, reaching fresh air at last, found to her dismay that the world was slowly revolving, and her lips had gone numb.

She liked the feel of Auguste's steady arm holding her upright, and when he pulled her close and kissed her, the candle beneath her skin flared to firelight. She did not even mind the smell of pomade.

But the dizziness made her stumble. "I need to go home," she slurred. "I feel sick," she added, as the dizziness made her weave on her feet.

When she hiccupped, and pressed a hand to her middle, Auguste smilingly turned her over to Hyacinthe, who was no steadier on her feet. "L-l-l-la," Hyacinthe slurred. "How I ador-r-re the cafés in summer!"

"Me, too," Anna murmured, and hiccupped again. "But perhaps not so much champagne." She hiccupped a third time.

Hyacinthe did not notice. "Lise wants a fiery lover, but I! I love to sip, and to flirt, and the lights..." She bit her numb lips, then said carefully, "Lise laughs at me for being a bore. But some day I want a husband of my own. In a tiny house. With a garden. I shall grow my own cabbages. But not yet! Not while I am young!"

Anna paused on the stairs, swaying. "That is my own sentiment. Except I cannot marry."

Hyacinthe blinked. "You cannot?"

"I am already married."

"You are? Married, and not a widow? For I do not see Citizen Spouse."

"I know not if I am wife or widow." Anna thought this very funny, and laughed.

Hyacinthe laughed because Anna was laughing, and each leaned against the other for support, laughter begetting laughter until Anna hiccupped, and sucked in air. "Oh, I am dizzy. I think I am going to be sick."

"Not upon me!"

"Oh-h-h-h," Anna sighed.

"Then he must be in the army," Hyacinthe said, as they struggled up the stairs together.

"Navy. A sea captain in the English navy," Anna corrected,

and she found that funny, too. Hyacinthe laughed with her, until Anna frowned with difficulty. "Oh. The English, no one likes them. You must not tell anyone."

"Me? I am silent as the tomb."

It took a very long time to mount the endless stairs, where the scandalized Parrette bustled Anna out of her new gown and forced her into a cold bath.

"You should never let yourself be weak," Parrette scolded in Neapolitan, as the walls in the Hôtel Foulon were so thin. "This is exactly how foolish women get themselves into trouble!"

"There was no danger," Anna mumbled. "And I returned with Hyacinthe."

"She! She could not protect you from a rabbit, nor herself either. Look at you! This gown, it reeks of champagne. And so drunk that if one of them decides to attack you, you cannot even walk!"

"They wouldn't. The chasseurs were so very gallant..."

Blissfully unaware of Parrette's continued scolding, Anna fell asleep in the middle of having her hair brushed out.

The next morning her head ached abominably. It seemed that every little noise Parrette made stabbed through her ears into her brain. Her stomach revolted, but Parrette, pitiless, forced her to rise, and to eat, for there was rehearsal.

"I won't dance this morning," Anna mumbled.

"Morning? Tchah! It is near one. Time for *opera* rehearsal. It would never do to lose your position with the Duprees."

"I was very good last night—did you not hear the acclaim? I can miss a rehearsal, I think!"

"I heard a lot of men who want one thing," Parrette stated. "And if they don't get it, will move on to the next set of fools whose heads they can turn with flattery."

Anna blinked owlishly at Parrette. "You hate men."

"I hate the way men will behave," Parrette retorted.

"You know nothing of love."

"I know much about what silly girls think is love. Listen, Anna. You did not listen to me when you married, and I understood, for your heart was with your good Papa. But you had better listen now. I was not quite fifteen when my father proposed I marry Duflot to settle a debt. I took one look and liked him fine, his curling black hair, his strong white teeth, the way he strutted down the street. I tumbled straight into love. Or so I thought, until two days after my wedding, when he first took a stick to me because another man had beat him at cards. I soon learned I knew nothing about love, *nothing*. And that was *before* I learned he already had a wife!"

She paused and eyed Anna, who tossed her head and smiled at her bouquet.

Anna was remembering those blue eyes looking down at her so admiringly, and the strong arm around her, and sighed at the faint echo of warmth through her, in spite of the throbbing of her head. "Now I understand the songs I sing."

"Faugh." Parrette threw up her hands. "There is no talking to a head full of clouds!"

That night, the first row contained more soldiers than before, which caused M. Dupree to look thoughtful.

Anna was cast down. All she saw was that Auguste was not among them. He had lost interest—she had done something wrong—she was no good—the world had gone gray and bleak.

Her performance reflected her mood. After the first act, M. Dupree looked into her face, asking, "Are you ill? Let me fetch my sovereign remedy," and bustled off to pour a small amount of neat whiskey into a glass.

Anna understood that her singing was bad, and pride roused her out of her gloom. The whiskey burned her throat, making her shudder. She straightened her back and sang better. After the performance, M. Dupree, at least, was happy. "It always works," he said smugly, nodding at his hoarded bottle.

She left directly after the performance and made her way back to the Foulon, weary and feeling sick. When she sank into her chair, Parrette was waiting. She took one look at Anna's listless face and gave her little nod. "Just as well."

That roused Anna to anger. "Why do you hate him so?"

"Because he, and the rest of them, when they get you girls drunk, they want one thing, and when they tire of it, they will move on."

"No. No. Not Auguste. He loves my voice. He said my interpretation of the Handmaid is the best he has ever heard."

"Can you not see that as the most atrocious flattery?"

Anna spun around in her chair. "Now you are saying I am a bad singer?"

Parrette sighed. "Anna, you are very good, but you have so little experience of life. You do not know the terrible things…" She gazed into the slowly whirling dust motes around the single candle flame, and shook herself. "Remember what happened to Marguerite Lisle down the hall, when she went off alone with them after they had been toasting her? I hear she is still recovering all these months later — might never regain her health."

Anna grimaced. "But those were soldiers. These are officers."

"They are men. And they can do most anything they wish in this city — Junot loves them all. The First Consul looks upon them as favorites." Parrette took a deep breath. "Also, you are a married woman."

"Tchah! He is a paper husband. He is probably dead."

"Anna, listen to me. Who are Auguste's people? The old ways are not completely thrown over. When people want to marry, they still go to their families. If he means well by you, then he will use his influence to find out if your husband lives, and if so, get your marriage annulled, and do everything properly."

"Auguste might not be back," Anna said sullenly. "He has forgotten me already."

But the next night, more roses arrived, and when Anna joined those crowded at the wings to peer into the audience, joy suffused her when she caught sight of Auguste's fine profile in the very center of the first row. The group of officers was larger than ever, looking splendid to the young females, and worrisome to the director, who saw past them to the increasingly empty seats.

That night, Anna sang better than ever. After the curtain closed, the new tenor, M. Marsac, turned his beautiful brown eyes to Anna. "You were superb, Mademoiselle Bernardo."

The new tenor had until this moment been polite but aloof, and though the dancers all admired his height, his slim body, his abundant curling hair, and his excellent clothes, he had scarcely given anyone in the company a glance outside of the requirements of the performance.

His interest sent another flush of warmth through Anna. Men

admired her performance! Was this how Mrs. Billington had begun her great career? "Thank you, M. Marsac."

"Jean-Baptiste."

She smiled and passed by as Jean-Baptiste Marsac observed the grace of her walk, the gentle sway of her hips that seemed utterly unconscious.

After the performance, Auguste greeted Anna with a kiss that made her head swim. The others roared approval as he swung her around, his saber rattling, the tassels on his sabretache swinging, his furred pelisse brushing her cheek.

They walked in a laughing group, Auguste punctuating his compliments on her singing with kisses. Those kisses were better than champagne, Anna thought happily. They spread warmth all through her, dazzling as the many candles glimmering like golden starlight. Even the thin rain that began to fall could not douse the enchantment of the evening, as they ran laughing for the nearest café. Anna was charmed that the men ran, too, not wanting their splendid uniforms ruined in the wet.

They found an empty table. Piers began banging with his fist and shouting for champagne.

Anna whispered to Lise, "Must we? I hate the way my head hurt last time, and my singing was terrible the next day."

Lise threw back her head, complacently taking in Edouard's hot gaze lingering on the slim line of her throat, and her rounded, dimpled shoulder peeping from the little puffed sleeve that was slipping down. "So? We are only young a short time. Live!"

I live through my music, Anna thought, but here was debonair Auguste proclaiming his admiration for all the world to see. He might not be the First Consul, but he was very important, and oh, those strong arms, those kisses!

She did not refuse the champagne outright, but took the smallest of sips. As the evening progressed, she could not help noticing puzzling things as she raised her glass with the others: how the men exchanged meaningful glances over the heads of their in-amoratas as they spoke their extravagant compliments; how they made private jokes that only the others could understand, and which provoked a low kind of laughter that only they shared. Then there was the puzzle of Auguste's frayed shirt sleeves, and the way Guillaume plunged his hand into his pocket to chase a stray coin.

It came to her that, in spite of their importance — and she could see their importance in the way that all the other citizens deferred — they always seemed scant of funds. *It makes their generosity all the more charming*, she told herself when they reached their last bottle and the group began to disperse in twos. She felt very wise in making this observation.

Auguste held tightly to Anna, though this time she was not the least dizzy. She stood on her tiptoes to lean her cheek against his shoulder, laughing when her temple bumped against his epaulet.

"Come, love, it has begun to rain. Let us find somewhere dry to celebrate your beauty," he whispered, brushed his lips from her eyebrow to her jaw, then down her throat to linger in the hollow of her collarbones.

The champagne fizz in her veins heated to urgency. She knew now what this was — what he wanted, and she delighted in the strength of her own desire.

But she was sober enough to say, "I am married."

"The devil!" Auguste laughed. "You are full of surprises, *ma petite*. I fear Edouard has won a hundred, from me. He has eyes, the dog! But we shall not tell him. Come." He slid his arm around her, and urged her on.

"I tell you I am married," Anna said, stepping back to tug on his hand, her eyes imploring.

"And what of that?" Auguste's smile was tender. "Monsieur le husband must be far, far away, or you should not have such freedom, I am guessing."

"He is—" Anna was reluctant to come right out with the captain's nationality. "In the navy."

"Aha!" Auguste threw his head back and laughed. "I guessed right. Most conveniently far away, and yet so fine a man as to marry you, *hein!* I salute him!" He made a military salute, with an air. Then he kissed her again. "There is no doubt in my mind that he is looking up and seeing this very same moon." He pointed upward where the clouds had parted. "At this very moment, and with a pretty girl on his arm. And if he could see us, he would be wishing us a very good night, for you know that tomorrow there may be a stray cannonball, a horse who balks, the chance en-counter with a bayonet, and *c'est finis,* he is snatched away to hea-ven!" He kissed his fingers and flung them out in a debonair gest-ure.

Live in the moment, that was what Lise said. Anna's heart lifted. Ah, what a sweet idea, to surrender to pleasure now, and the future? It could take care of itself.

And yet she hesitated. What would Parrette say? Anger suffused her—she resented Parrette's scolding, her incessant warnings. "But what if something happens?" she hedged.

"How would he know?" Auguste lifted his shoulders in a shrug, the gold in his epaulettes shimmering. "Bonaparte is open-ing the churches again. If a brat results, you hand it off to the nuns."

Anna was shocked by this callous answer.

He saw it at once. "Oh, my Anna," he whispered. "You are tender, I can see it. And women should be tender!" He dropped feather-light kisses all over her face.

She drowned in sweet sensation, but even in willingly permitting the waves to close over her head, she made one last reach: "I want an annulment."

He stepped back. "An annulment," he repeated, as if she had said she wanted a horse, or a crown. Then he opened his hand in a broad gesture, palm up, the light from a nearby lamp gleaming along his regimental facings and gold braid. "Then you get one. It is easy enough."

The question in his eyes, the hint of impatience, doused her ardor more thoroughly than the rain starting up again. A thousand curses, Parrette was right. This man did not have marriage in mind.

Still she wavered, thinking, *What can be so bad, if everyone else pays no attention to those stupid old rules?* But she could hear herself making that promise before God, and though her Papa had said after Mama's death that religion was a pack of lies, that God—if he existed—cared nothing for this sorry world, at the very end, he had sent for the priest.

Even stronger was memory, her mother's warm embraces every night, her whispered, "God loves you."

Anna had always believed that God had to be a mother. Perhaps her mother was watching her from heaven at this very moment. Would she be smiling to see Anna happy, or looking sorrowful because of those vows?

Lost in this reverie, Anna was unaware of Auguste gazing down at her as the rain increased. The reflected glow of the nearby windows highlighted the raindrops in the curls that framed her heart-shaped face, the enticing curves in her flimsy dress that clung so tightly, the tender, wistful downward curve to her mouth, and he exulted even though he intuited her doubts. He loved the hunt; the prize would be no less enjoyable for a little *ruse de guerre*.

"Come, cherie, you are wet, and that beautiful voice must not take a chill. I will see you home."

Nine

Summer was upon them. One hot, humid day, there was trouble with the machinery backstage, so rehearsal paused while M. Dupree oversaw the repairs. The thick air rang with sharp voices. Tempers rose with the heat.

Madame Dupree sighed as she fanned herself vigorously. She seemed to be sitting down a great deal—everyone had noticed.

"Lazy," Lise whispered.

"Who can blame her?" Eleanor said practically. "If I could marry a theater director, I would not even be here. I would have a carriage. Two! And a salon."

She cast a glance under her lashes at the tenor Jean-Baptiste Marsac, who, it was whispered, was ambitious enough to want one day to own his own theater, and who was talented enough to get it. He never paid the dancers the least heed.

Today, Madame looked positively ill. She kept blotting her face with a dampened linen, at last saying fretfully, "We need a larger theater, but Anton says we've not the money. How can we get more money if we haven't more seats, I say? Anna, you have been singing better than ever; if only your claque of admirers would pay for their seats!"

She got heavily to her feet and walked away to summon her maid for more hot chocolate, as Anna frowned. "The officers do not pay?"

"Who would dare to gainsay them?" Lise said, shrugging, then she gave Anna a meaning look. "Just do not string him along. They mislike that, oh, much."

"Especially when they send gifts," Catherine said, with meaning. "It is not so bad if you turn down a merchant, or even an *avocat*. But the soldiers?"

"So true!" Lorette, older—nearly Madame Dupree's age—made a spitting motion. "They rule France now, and think about it! When they were boys, it was, displease the crowd, and voila, off to the guillotine, or to a lamppost, whichever was nearer." She made a gesture like hanging herself. "You young things do not remember, but I do. Women, men. Even the poor dogs, one terrible season. Nobody was safe from the mob, ten years ago. Less. And they all remember it, how no one could stop the mob. Now, it is known that no one can stop the soldiers."

"Alors! The days of the mob are gone, at least," said another, laying her hand on her breast. "Bonaparte took care of the mobs! His officers are all lovers, and they must answer to their commanders."

"Tchah." Lise laughed. "Here is the truth, my dear. Argue, call them devils, be haughty or sweet, as you wish. The one thing you must never do is make them look foolish. They will never forgive you."

"That's true for everyone," Hortense said, as she restitched her worn practice skirt.

Catherine patted her hand. "And so it is. But the days are gone when a woman can challenge a man."

Lise's features sharpened with impatience. "Good riddance! Let us talk of pleasant things."

Catherine crossed her arms. "I am a citizen. I have the right to speak my mind."

"Not for long," Madame Dupree said good-naturedly, and as everyone turned quickly, she rejoined them, sitting down with a sigh. "Not if Bonaparte has his way. We shall be back to curtseys and bows, that is what I predict."

Her words had the effect of breaking up the group a moment before M. Dupree appeared, beckoning impatiently. "I want to try something new in the first act."

And the rehearsal began.

Anna said nothing to Parrette, but so intense was her inward conflict that Maestro Paisiello, when she went to him for her private lesson, stopped her a few bars into her first piece. "Are you feeling ill, child?" he asked.

Anna flushed with remorse. She knew that he was having trouble with his audiences, who could be difficult for so many reasons that had little to do with music. His opera *Nina*, once immensely popular in Paris, had not been performed since the Revolution, when it was condemned as elitist for having been written in Italian, which "the people" could not be expected to understand.

Complaints about it had resurfaced, and gossips had it that *Proserpina* had been set back a season, some said because Mademoiselle Georges was being coached in singing, others because of the reception of the Maestro's last concert at the Tuileries.

As she looked into the maestro's careworn face, Anna regretted her selfishness. "It is, oh!" She blushed. "It is only heart trouble."

"You?" he exclaimed. "Handsome you have become, but you are yet a mere child!" He lifted his wig, patted his handkerchief over his head, then plopped the wig down again in a cloud of powder as he peered at her more closely. "Perhaps you are not so young, then. Oh, to have small problems! But they are large to you. My dear Anna, permit an old man to stand in for the father you loved. I know what he would say if he were here, for we were great friends. He would warn you that hearts are tender indeed, full of the fire of love, but hearts have not eyes, nor a brain."

"But Auguste is so handsome," Anna protested. "I want to become his lover, but..." She hesitated before mentioning Parrette's disapproval.

"But you are devoted to your music," the maestro stated with an expression of approval.

Anna agreed, remorseful because she had not been thinking of her music at that moment. Her ambitions *did* stand in the way of love far more than the existence of a piece of paper stating she was married. "If he does not understand, if he places himself in the way of your success, perhaps it is not love he professes, but something far more ephemeral. The heart is fickle, for it is made for love, and it will overwhelm you with the enticement of attraction at the flash of a smile, a handsome profile, at a shower of the pretty compliments you most want to hear."

Anna's cheeks burned.

He saw her expression, and his tone lightened to gentleness. "The falsity comes in a man saying what you wish to hear so that he can gain his own ends." He lifted a shoulder. "In this city, they will say La, that is Paris in modern times! But I have traveled much in my years, and I've seen all the variety of human nature. This behavior one finds everywhere. So, to you: if you want something that endures, then you must use your brain as well as your heart to determine if he is saying what he truly feels. There! I have stood in for your dear Papa, and you have been angelic in permitting an old man this liberty. So, let us begin anew, and this time, pianissimo only for the first eight bars, then that little breath, and — glory. *One, due, tre...*"

When Anna returned to the theater, Lise gave her a narrow look. "Where were you?"

"Tuileries," Anna said wonderingly.

Lise sighed and marched away, her thin shoulder blades poking the flimsy muslin as her shoulders twitched in ill humor at every step.

"What happened to her?" Anna asked Hyacinthe.

"Oh, Consular Guard is gone on maneuvers. It cannot be helped!" Hyacinthe threw her hands up. "Why she insists that her lovers have to be in regimentals?"

Anna murmured something sympathetic, but she was aware that her own sense of disappointment was mitigated by a sense of secret relief. She would not have to decide right now about Auguste, lovers, annulments, or anything having to do with the heart.

M. Dupree interrupted them, his usually mild voice surprisingly pettish, "Are you here, then, Signorina Bernardo? Or did you leave your voice back at the Tuileries?"

Anna apologized at once, and willingly threw herself into rehearsal.

To M. Dupree's relief, the front rows in that night's performance sported no chasseurs, but their regular audience was not back. He still did not know for certain if the chasseurs were chasing away custom with their noise. There was nothing he could do about it if any soldiers caused trouble, but forewarned was forearmed, that he had learned during the days of the mobs.

So he took his younger brother Pierre aside, saying, "Find out what you can."

The dry, hot winds died down after two days, but the humid stillness that set in afterward was not considered an improvement. Summer in Paris could be punishing, with brilliant light reflecting off streets, walls, and every bit of metal.

Tempers flared during rehearsal. Props seemed to break with irritating regularity, and even Madame and Monsieur, usually the most genial of couples, quarreled when she missed yet another rehearsal while he was trying to change the staging.

"I have to lie down," she said. "This stage, it is airless. I cannot sing if I cannot breathe!"

"If you were not sick every day, perhaps we would fill enough seats to warrant moving to a larger space!" he retorted.

Madame whirled around and stalked off.

Her husband mopped his face, then said dispiritedly, "We shall rehearse the farce, and the *entr'acte* ballet. Perhaps Madame will return refreshed by afternoon, for we really must restage the entire second act. Musicians! Come, come. Places!"

At the end of a trying day, with everyone struggling through a lifeless performance before a half-empty theater, Monsieur Dupree gathered his company and declared that this week would see the last of *Médée*. "It's simply too hot for the tragedy of the Terror. We shall bring back *La Caverne*, or another reliable republican opera."

The night of the new staging, Anna reached her dressing room, which—being high up, almost directly under the roof—was hotter than an oven, to discover herself nearly crowded out by three bouquets. The heady scent of flowers, the beauty of the blossoms which were still miraculously fresh, and above all the extravagant romance of the gesture succeeded in banishing Anna's ill-temper.

Then Parrette appeared, and, with arms crossed combatively over her spare bosom, muttered, "So he is trying to buy your favors with flowers?"

Anna's good mood vanished like a candle snuffed. "That is so hateful!"

"Or is he in on the wager?" Parrette retorted, and stepped closer, lowering her voice. "Pierre Dupree admitted to me this morning that they are wagering hundreds upon Auguste's success with you. Double if they hit upon a specific date."

Anna's lips parted as she drew breath for a denial, then she remembered Auguste's careless words. He had even admitted that they had already had a wager about her. She frowned at the innocent blossoms. Surely, if Auguste loved her the way she loved him, he would not make wagers over her, or was that the way all men behaved?

She decided to ask Lise after the performance.

"We cannot move about in here," Parrette said, regarding the bouquets askance. "I will take them downstairs. In this heat, they will be wilted before the first act is over."

"Thank you," Anna said stiffly.

Parrette gave her a long look, picked up the flowers and went out.

There was the last performance to ready for, the more exasperating as Anna's costume clung to her sticky flesh. Everyone was in a temper, she discovered when she gathered in the wings. Even the orchestra seemed to play a half a beat too fast, and a quarter-tone sharp. Or maybe it sounded wrong in the humid air.

The curtain opened, and there were the chasseurs, resplendent as always, filling the front rows. From the smell of wine on the heated air, they had been fighting the summer heat in their own manner, and as the performance began, rustling, clanking weapons, and not-very-muffled laughter caused some of the others in the audience to whisper and cry, "Hush."

"Hush yourself. Or step outside and hush me up." That was one of the chasseurs.

Anna's entrance followed on raucous laughter.

"Shut up, now," Auguste said audibly. "That I may worship my divinity."

More laughter. Anna straightened her spine, inflated her ribs, and sang with more power than she ever had.

At the close of the act, the chasseurs stomped and called "Brava!"

Madame Dupree looked impatient as she took Anna aside. "Filling the hall is good, if the upper galleries had anyone in them. Not so shrill."

Shrill! Anna knew she was not shrill. Her temper flared. The house seemed hotter than ever, the smells irritating; even the candles gave off a singe that seemed to burn the throat.

Anna clipped her lips tight against a retort, turned away so abruptly that she trod on her gown. R-i-i-i-p!

It needed only that.

Parrette was there at once, needle ready — but then her arm sank down as she sagged in dismay. The simple gown had ripped to the arms, and in the next act, the Handmaids participated in a frenetic dance. Hasty basting would never do. "There's bound to be a gown in Adelaide's trunk," she whispered, naming a dancer who had had to quit due to a bad fall. "I'll fetch it."

Tears burned Anna's eyelids. She knew how much work her moment's fit of temper would cause. And though she could assuage her sense of guilt by offering to do the sewing, she knew very well that Parrette would refuse. No one made tiny, exquisite stitches like hers.

She slipped away as the actors rushed to take their marks for the beginning of the next act; at least she had a few measures in which to blot her eyes and get control of herself. She wandered into the farthest storage area with its jumble of ancient painted flats, broken props, and stacks of old wood waiting to be reused.

She walked without aim, wiping at her eyes lest they get puffy. She sneezed three times in a row, the stinging scent of candles set too close to wood sharpening into the acrid stench of smoke. There was no light. The air blurred oddly. Anna blinked, her eyes stinging. Alarm prickled the back of her neck, and she peered into the thick darkness. Horror flashed through her when she spied a murky red glow.

In that brief flare, she discovered billows of smoke reaching upward from pale licks of flame outlining an old three-legged chair.

"Fire," she whispered, and then, running back to catch the arm of the curtain boy, "Fire!" She pointed with shaking fingers.

The curtain boy dashed up to M. Dupree, his voice cracking on the word, "Fire!"

He had not spoken that loud, but from Anna's vantage, it appeared that the first two rows had been listening for it. As she watched in astonishment, the chasseurs rose almost in a body, and surged through the surprised musicians, knocking several of them over, then stampeded onto the stage.

"To the rescue!" Auguste roared, waving his sword.

The music ended in discordancy. The performers either froze in place, or backed away hastily as the soldiers rushed off into the wing, half of them straight for the fire, and the rest running to this or that pretty young dancer or singer.

Auguste reached Anna in half a dozen great strides, then swung her off her feet. "You are safe!" he cried, as backstage, the chasseurs made a hullabaloo as they grabbed at the buckets of brackish water that all theaters kept against frequent fires, and splashed it about.

Anna squirmed in her admirer's arms, and he set her down.

She ran a few steps forward, the truth borne in on her through the shock and amazement. At the sight of M. Dupree's pale, drawn face, anger seared Anna, every bit as bright as the flames. *Defer and deflect* were forgotten before the glory of righteous indignation.

"That fire," she cried. "*You* set that fire! You could have burnt us alive!"

Her regal gesture took in the 'rescued' dancers, some of whom were laughing, and others kissing their supposed rescuers.

"Come now, love, all is well that ends well," Auguste said, white teeth flashing as he advanced toward Anna, hands out-held in appeal. "It's too cursed hot for caterwauling. Let us go celebrate your surviving a terrible danger!"

"Caterwauling?" Anna backed away toward the performers' door, more truth unfolding like a terrible black flower. His compliments about her glorious voice— "I thought you loved my voice. That you loved *me*," she cried, trembling from head to foot.

"I do!" Auguste flung his arms wide. "I will! For at least an hour!"

The soldiers burst into laughter, followed by many of the cast, though more of the men than the women.

Auguste looked around, never more handsome than when he was flushed with triumph. He laid his hand on his breast in dramatic style. "For a soldier, an hour is forever."

Her singing was nothing to him! Anna whirled away in her torn dress, spied the three bouquets lined up by the door, and snatched up the closest. "*That* is forever!" she cried, and hurled the vase at Auguste. "And that!" The second vase followed.

Greenish water splashed his splendid regimental coat, as flowers cascaded over him. M. Dupree struck his palm over his eyes, and Anna gave vent to a hysterical laugh.

The rest of the chasseurs howled and hooted with mirth. Auguste smiled, his teeth showing white and strong, the enormous pupils in his blue eyes reflecting tiny flames from the overhead lamps as he said, "*Mes amis!* We must scour the place, and make certain there is no more danger from fire!"

He stalked off, heels ringing on the warped boards of the floor, the last of the roses streaming off his pelisse. The chasseurs gave a great shout, and dashed hither and yon.

Sick with dread, M. Dupree followed, trying to apologize, to remonstrate, but Auguste gave him a one-handed shove, knocking him spinning into the painted flats. The nearest came crashing down onto the stage.

"Get out, get out," M. Dupree cried hoarsely, as he struggled to rise from the ruined canvas. "They are going to run wild."

Anna stared. "But—"

"Go to the street, Mademoiselle Bernardo," M. Dupree said gently, then he, too, ran off, his voice rising as he called for the backstage workers, who stood about with the buckets emptied.

The laughter had ended. The deserted dancers streamed off-stage, talking excitedly, with many backward looks.

Anna started for the exit, then stopped. *Parrette,* Anna thought, looking around. She remembered the costume—Adelaide's trunk, in the attic even farther away from her dressing room!

She ran for the stairs. The lantern was either out, or had been taken by the soldiers, whose raucous voices could be heard dispersing through the theatre, calling mockingly to one another. The stairs were entirely dark.

On her hands and knees, Anna groped her way up the narrow stairs, banging her head at the sudden turning.

At the top, a lantern still burned; grabbing it, she lit her way along the narrow catwalk, choking on the thick smoke. "Parrette! Parrette!" she croaked, coughing as her lungs burned.

After what seemed an endless time, a figure appeared out of the smoke, a bundle of cloth clutched in her arms. "I cannot find Adelaide's trunk, but I did discover two—"

"Fire," Anna cried, then bent double in a burst of coughing. "We must go." She straightened up.

"Anna!" Parrette's horror-stricken eyes gazed past Anna, whose nerves chilled as she looked behind her. Smoke boiled up the stairway Anna had been on moments before, flames eating greedily at the second landing below.

"Back stair," Parrette said tersely, flinging the costume down.

They ran down the catwalk past the little alcove dressing rooms to the storage attic, and beyond that to the oldest portion of the attic, damaged in a fire during the Terror. There was no railing, and the floor creaked horribly, but M. Dupree had caused a ladder to be put there. It was still intact, though it only descended one floor, as its landing abutted the back of the stage.

Anna trembled in terror as she followed Parrette down, the swinging lantern in her hand making the shadows leap and writhe like ghost-fires. The edges of the stairs shifted with the light, and Anna had to feel her way with her toes. She dared not trust her burning, blurred eyes.

At the landing, Parrette threw herself to her knees, and groped for the ladder to the backstage. "Here! Here it is," she cried. "Go first."

"You go. I'll light your way."

Parrette nearly flung herself down the ladder, and Anna tried not to step on her fingers as she followed, one hand clutching the lantern, the other gripped tightly to the splintery wood.

Whirls of smoke obscured the backstage floor. Ruddy flickers glowed hither and yon. The once-familiar area was strange now, its proportions changed to nightmare by smoke and fire.

Terror sharpened every sound, every sense, rendering the flames, the grain of withering wood, the cascade of evilly glowing sparks with a dream-like clarity.

Anna gasped for breath, heat searing her throat as she groped toward distant voices. Ten steps felt like a hundred, a thousand, until they fell through the door into the street, where the entire company stood aghast. Flames licked from the windows, sending towering billows of smoke up to blot the stars from the sky. All up and down the boulevard, crowds streamed out of the cafés and even from some of the bigger theaters to take in the free show.

Anna watched the old theatre consumed by flames, as frantic workers from the theaters at either side worked to keep the blaze from spreading. The roar, the heat, the groans of old wood caused cheers to go up, more enthusiastic than the best performance Médée had ever inspired.

Slowly the discrete details assembled into a whole, and Anna saw that the chasseurs were gone, their laughter echoing behind them. Lise, Hyacinthe, and a couple of the younger dancers had gone off with them, arm in arm, as if to a party—sixteen-year-old Marie-Claude giggling admiringly up at Auguste.

Anna's body ached from temple to heels from the knocks she hadn't noticed in her escape. Gradually the truth forced itself into her consciousness: there would be no rehearsal tomorrow. Auguste had not loved her, he had probably not even liked her singing. Everything had been a sham, for a wager, an hour's tumble.

And the Théâtre Dupree was no more.

With a thunderous roar, the building collapsed, sending fierce heat boiling out. The spectators scrambled backward, shouting and cheering as sparks spiraled upward toward the sky in phoenix brilliance, but unlike the phoenix, the fire was not reborn. It was soon reduced to fitful tongues of flame here and there, and gradually the crowd dispersed.

Anna turned away, her eyes burning. It was the smoke, she told herself fiercely. She would not weep. She would shed no tears for a worthless liar.

She and Parrette walked in silence back to the Foulon. When they reached their room, Anna stripped out of the ripped, ruined costume. When she breathed out, she smelled smoke. She sank down onto the floor, becoming aware for the first time of her head aching.

"Anna?" Parrette said gently. "You saved my life. I would still be in that attic, if you had not come."

"Then I did one right thing today," Anna said, her throat raw. "In a catalogue of many stupidities." She lifted her head, and tried to laugh. It came out sounding more like a sob, so she drew in another painful breath. "*Scélérat*! All I will say is, falling in love resembles the smallpox. But I am now well inoculated," she finished bitterly.

Ten

ANNA WOKE TO THE sound of a thunderstorm rumbling overhead. She lay still, her head pounding, her eyelids aflame. Every bone and muscle ached. She would have to send a message to Maestro Paisiello, for her throat was too raw for singing.

She sat up slowly, appalled at the dark bruises marring her arms. She didn't remember getting a one of them in that terrifying escape from the burning theater.

The smell of fresh bread reached her. She had to be dreaming.

She turned her head to discover Parrette gently closing the door, a basket on her arm.

Parrette advanced into the room and set the basket down. As Anna watched listlessly, Parrette set out a fresh tart, some excellent cheese from the north, and a spray of plump berries. "Come. Eat up."

Anna winced. "Oh, I smell of burned wood."

"We'll go to the baths—the Vigier. I will pay." Parrette's voice was unwontedly soft as she named the finest bath in the first arrondissement. "Once you eat. Pierre was by, and he told me to tell you that Monsieur Dupree is calling a company meeting at midday."

"To blame me for the fire?" Anna groaned. "I know it is my fault."

"It's that yellow-haired satyr's fault," Parrette said with a shade of her old spirit. Then she lowered her voice again. "Anna, you saved my life. You could have left me there."

Anna sat up the rest of the way. "But you saved me again and again when we crossed the mountains and came into France. I think I should have expired but for you."

Parrette said, "That was for us both, and my promise to La Signora Eugenia, your dear mother." She frowned down at the fruit on the little cracked plate. Then she looked up. "Trust comes hard to me. Looking out for myself is..." She shook her head. "I am saying it wrong. I think, Anna, what I mean is that I always see you as a girl, and of late I know I have scolded you as if you were fifteen."

"I think I have behaved as if I were fifteen," Anna said, her entire body prickling with shame.

"That's as may be. But I see you differently now. I think La Signora would be very proud of you," she finished, and then, as if she felt she'd said too much, she poked a finger at the food. "Eat now, before it all goes stale in this heat. I think the storm is passing by. All I hear now are drips."

The rain had cleared off. With good food inside her, and her outside considerably improved by a thorough soak among the lofty pillars of the Vigier, Anna felt measurably better when they returned to the Foulon. She still smelled smoke when she breathed out, but the repaired costume had been sent to the laundry, and Parrette had brushed her shoes thoroughly.

At length she said, "What do you want to do?"

"Sing," Anna stated. "More than ever. But first I believe I owe it to M. Dupree to face whatever it is he has to say. You can blame the chasseurs all you like, but it was I who flung those flowers in Auguste's face, and that after being warned not to trust them."

"Very well," Parrette said. "But I will go with you."

They found Pierre lounging against a scorched tree before the ruined theater, watching as a gaggle of urchins poked about in the ashy pools among the charred ruins. When he saw Anna, he smiled. "They are all at the Egalité café. M. Dupree is waiting."

The café was farther down the boulevard, the aproned servers busy putting out chairs as Anna and Parrette threaded through the outside tables to duck through the door.

Inside, they found most of the company gathered, including all the dancers, Lise looking puffy-eyed, and Hyacinthe yawning.

M. Dupree came to meet them, as the others chattered.

"I am so sorry," Anna said as soon as M. Dupree reached her.

"I am, too, but it was going to happen." He lifted his shoulders fatalistically. "Madame was even counting the days. Ah, and to have it happen not from an untended candle, or a dropped spark, but as a result of such a magnificent gesture against those beasts!" The impresario kissed his fingers and flung wide his hands. "It was a privilege to witness."

Anna gazed at him, and Parrette sensed a little of her guilt easing. Parrette's private conviction was that M. Dupree was accepting the destruction of his theatre with publicly-expressed panache, which would impress the men. But she decided not to tell Anna that, as she did not want Anna's self-blame to smother her ire against those villainous soldiers.

Anna apologized once again, looking pretty and sorrowful, as she was watched by Jean-Baptiste Marsac. He, in turn, was watched narrowly by Lise, who had been trying unsuccessfully to catch his eye.

"Everyone knows that." M. Dupree lowered his voice. "And so many richly enjoyed the story of that arrogant young dog getting his uniform ruined. But we also know that Bonaparte's pets can do what they wish in Paris—the *Gros Talons*, the Cuirassiers, are even worse—and the First Consul will look the other way." He wiped his handkerchief over the gleaming dome of his head, and then smiled fondly across the room at his wife. "The old place was a ruin anyway. Sit down. I have a plan."

When he had taken his place again and laced his fingers with his wife's, he addressed the company. "Remember what Portiez said: 'Man is born a spectator.' As some of you know, young Nicolet has been wanting to run his own offshoot of the Gaîté. My theater was old, yes, but the location is excellent! What I propose is that I lease the land to Nicolet for three years, during which we tour the country." He patted his wife's hand. "In the country, no one will care if Madame is in the family way, for it has been many years since they have had anything from Paris except marauding soldiers."

"The country?" Lise exclaimed, arms crossed. "As well be dead!"

"What does it pay?" Lorette asked.

"Who knows?" M. Dupree lifted his shoulders. "Whatever it is, we share equally, like good republicans. It will be the better as we cannot take the full company. Almost all the clowns refused to leave Paris, so you dancers will all have to act in the farce. You know it is not difficult. Philippe has been promised that the tumbling clowns will gain a bit extra, as it is a double role. All I ask is that you think it over. If you wish to travel with Dupree, be here tomorrow at midday. I will know more then. I go to Nicolet from here."

The crowd began to disperse. Anna and Parrette turned away, Anna stunned by this sudden change.

Hyacinthe caught her arm. "Do you think to go, then? What will he say?"

"He?" Anna said blankly, thinking of Auguste.

"Monsieur le husband, of course."

"He is the last person on earth whose words I would heed." Anna tossed her head, too indignant to notice M. Marsac gazing at her with an arrested expression.

But Lise noticed his sudden interest.

"What are you thinking?" Hyacinthe asked Lise, whose brooding gaze rested on the enigmatic tenor.

"Of them all, only Jean-Baptiste will ever make something of himself," Lise said slowly. "He never talks about where he comes from. He never talks at all, beyond what is necessary. Yet out of the entire set of men, it is he who knows effortlessly how to strut like a prince on stage, how to command a room as pharaoh. But he despises us." She dipped her chin toward the rest of the dancers. "And so, to go with these imbeciles into the country? Faugh. I will never leave Paris. It is time, perhaps, to see if my cousin Minette can be flattered into getting us an audition at the Feydeau."

Anna was sorry to hear that, for she had come to like both dancers. But she shrugged at Lise's observations about the tenor. She was done with men, and welcomed the chance to leave Paris. She had her singing to think of, and if the soldiers were to tarnish her name in the way that Madame de Pipelet had whispered had happened to her friend Madame Simon, perhaps it was better to get away.

As soon as Anna and Parrette reached the street, Anna shaded her eyes from the heat waves shimmering off the new pavement, and said, "I am going to the Tuileries to consult with Maestro Paisiello."

"Go," Maestro Paisiello said an hour later, as thunder reverberated across the sky.

Anna was dismayed that he did not even pause to consider.

"Go," he said again. "Use this opportunity to work on your stage presence. I have taught you enough, I believe."

"Have I so disappointed you, then?"

The maestro looked from those earnest brown eyes to his music, to hide his thoughts. By her own effort, she had emerged a butterfly from the promising chrysalis, but it was a common butterfly after all. She had a beautiful voice, she moved beautifully on stage, but in the end she was not possessed of the voice of genius and power that he sought and so rarely found.

However, he believed that the opera was her passion, as it was his, and he could not find it within himself to hurt her. "It is not you, it is politics," the maestro finally replied, as lightning flared in all the windows. He sighed. "I am beginning to think that the *Proserpina* might not be ready until next spring. I cannot tell you how much trouble…but then, you have troubles of your own, so I will keep my peace!" He sighed again, and shook his head, sending up a little snow storm of powder.

Anna walked slowly outside, as the first big raindrops splattered in the noisome mess in the gutter down the center of the street. The stench was terrific, the flies maddening. She ran as quickly as she could, reaching the Foulon breathless moments before the storm burst in earnest.

She found Parrette haggling with a dancer over some stitchwork. Parrette looked up, her face flushed. The dancer tried to twitch the garment out of Parrette's fingers.

"Not unless you pay," Parrette said fiercely.

The dancer ran downstairs, her feet thumping. Anna sat on the little stool, peeling off her muddy shoes as she gulped in the thick, humid air.

"And so? The maestro, he says what?" Parrette laid the costume on top of Anna's trunk.

"There is nothing to keep me here. What is your thought?"

Parrette wiped her brow with her apron. "Madame Dupree's dresser refuses to leave Paris. While you were at the Tuileries, she tried to hire me away from you. I said no. She promised me my own earnings, if I will become a sort of costume mistress."

"Does that mean you are now to do all the sewing?" Anna asked doubtfully. "No one person could manage all that work."

Parrette shook her head, her mouth compressed, but Anna sensed pride in the angle of her chin, the cock of her elbow as she rested one work-worn hand on a bony hip. "Only for the dancers, if they cannot do their own, and I can charge them, though it would only be a pittance. The dressers are to come to me, and I will show them how to make the gowns smart. Everything I have learned? They noticed. I have gained a reputation." She permitted herself the smallest smile.

"One you have earned, twice over," Anna stated approvingly.

Later, they met Lise on the landing. She tilted her head and leaned insouciantly on the rickety wooden stair rail. "So you decided to go?" On Anna's nod, "Perhaps it's wise. Auguste talked wildly about raising a claque, though there was not much enthusiasm."

Not knowing what to say, Anna decided silence was best, and shrugged as carelessly as she could.

"Still. There are other theaters. The chasseurs do not go to them all. There is nothing outside of Paris. Nothing." Lise yawned as she straightened up. "And you are young and so stylish that people think you are beautiful. You could snare a general, with a little effort."

Anna hid her surge of revulsion. "But all these new uniforms, the talk of new regiments, what if they march to war?"

Lise waved a hand to and fro. "Don't you listen to anything? There is peace, now. The officers have little to do besides look resplendent on a horse, and spend their money on us. Go if you must! Go lose yourself in the country. You may as well be dead. La!" She yawned again, went inside her room and shut the door.

Two things happened before the Company Dupree left Paris.

First, M. Dupree thought Anna would make a capital Séraphine in Le Sueur's *La Caverne*, which was relatively easy to mount in spite of the fact that they could probably not offer the split stage that *La Caverne* had made famous.

Second, a short time after they gathered at the Egalité for last instructions, everyone looked up in surprise when a tall, elegant, light-haired figure walked in.

"Ninon!" Philippe hailed with obvious relief. "Now at least I'll have one danseuse worth the name."

Ninon's lip curled.

Most of the female dancers looked appalled, and a few mutinous.

Catherine said, "So your general tired of you, eh?"

Ninon turned slightly, whipped her arm around and slapped Catherine so hard she fell off her bench.

"*Zut!* I want no broken bones," M. Dupree said, waving his hands. "I will not have mob behavior in my company."

Ninon shook back her honey-colored curls. "Then tell this imbecile to shut her mouth."

Blonde Eleanor helped her cousin Catherine up. Both shot angry looks at Ninon, who sat down beside Philippe, her little smile triumphant. Lise might be gone, but her rival had returned to take her place as leader.

M. Dupree sighed. Dancers! But one must have them: it was said that the common man would not come to the theater if he did not have pretty girls to look at. He finished his instructions.

Two days later they set out in a cavalcade up the Seine, Madame Dupree in a coach that had been taken from some aristocrat during the Terror. It had been furbished up a bit, the coat of arms on the panel scratched out and the tri-colors painted over.

Behind that rolled an ancient berline shared by the female singers, and another by the men. After that followed a series of carts carrying props and clothes. Parrette rode with the latter, so that she could oversee the disposition of the baskets, bags, and boxes.

Madame Dupree's uncle's second cousin, in the army, had

been stationed in a chateau abandoned by aristocrats fleeing the guillotine. M. Dupree leased this chateau from the local Prefect, which was no longer in use by the army now that there was peace. The company—severely reduced—planned to work up a suitable repertoire, while Madame recovered from those sickly early months of pregnancy.

They reached their chateau ahead of a thundery sky. Everyone had expected fine furnishings and comfort, but discovered the shell of a once-beautiful building. The tapestries had been hacked and stabbed, and most of the fine furnishings used as firewood. They slept on discarded mattresses and even folded tapestries, set directly on the beautiful parquet floors grooved by the cavalry's spurs. The next day they had to scrounge for furnishings.

The third day, the diminished orchestra caught up with them, and they were able to begin work. In the morning, Anna joined the dancers as always, careful to remain in the back.

Ninon led the morning practice at a smart pace, her comments excoriating. Anna struggled all over again, and was not surprised to feel the familiar ache throughout the rest of the day. Ninon, Anna realized, really was a better dancer than Lise.

Anna felt the immediate benefit in heightened awareness, gauging space the way the dancers did. Anna was the only singer who never tripped up her fellow singers, banged elbows, or got in anyone's way.

The fourth night, some of the dancers asked for a cart so they could visit the local village.

Anna was surprised when Jean-Baptiste Marsac turned to her as they were putting their music in the trunk. "Were you going to join the others?" he asked. "There might be dancing."

Anna shook her head. She knew from the dancers' gossip that many were going not to see if there was entertainment, but to flirt with the locals.

"Another time?" he asked with a winsome smile, his gaze steady.

Anna smiled back, aware of the warmth of attraction. The instinct to smile, to bridle, to encourage him to smile back had to be squashed, squashed, *squashed*.

She said politely, "Perhaps," and excused herself, resolving grimly to avoid him as much as possible.

After the Revolutionary government had rescinded all the old licenses and controls, stating that every citizen had the right to start a theater, any works by authors five years dead had been declared free to be staged.

But as many discovered, wanting to be on stage and doing it successfully were two very different prospects. The French performers shared grim memories of revolutionary audiences who had voted their disapprobation with baskets full of rotten vegetables (if not worse), or even stormed the stage to entertain themselves by ripping apart the props and chasing the performers off.

Good performances met with wild enthusiasm, especially in the country, which had been starved for real entertainment during the long years of armies shooting and looting up and down the countryside.

Summer faded into autumn, M. Dupree offering free performances to the villagers in trade for foodstuffs. *La Caverne* proved as popular as ever, but so also did Paisiello's *Nina*, which the older members of the company all knew, and of course Anna had been trained in.

After the last performance of *Nina*, a satisfied M. Dupree called the company together and said, "By week's end, we will begin our travels."

The tour began as a resounding success.

The Company Dupree had engaged to stay in Amiens for only a week, but proved to be so popular that they were held over for a month. They could not charge much—and there were a great many citizens who managed to get in without paying even an *assignat*—but the seats were full, and the audiences appreciative.

And a steady stream of would-be entertainers clamored to be auditioned: these M. Dupree had to make time for, lest he be slandered as an elitist, but he took care to hold auditions in the common room of the local inn. There he could rely on the patrons, ever ready for free entertainment, to express their derision for those who had more ambition than talent.

By the end of the year, they had advanced triumphantly all the way north to Lille, word running ahead and guaranteeing an excellent reception. While the company rehearsed, Parrette went about the city, talking and listening: here, so very close to England, she expected to get better news of Admiral Nelson's fleet—and perhaps her son's ship, *Pallas*—than had been reported in the Paris newspapers.

She was told by a friendly cheese-seller to ask the fisher folk. A morning at the dock furnished the dispiriting news that Admiral Nelson was rumored to be living in a palace in England, and his fleet scattered, everyone having opinions on where.

She reported her lack of success to Anna.

"At least there is peace," Parrette said as she sewed, tucked, draped, hemmed.

Anna agreed, as always, talking in Neapolitan whenever the subject was England or English matters. "While it is true that Michel might be anywhere, at least there is less chance he is being fired upon by cannon."

Neither brought up the obvious question: how long would that last? The docks had also been full of rumors about Napoleon's plans for an invasion flotilla, abandoned only temporarily, some insisted.

At year's end (Nivôse, Year XI), M. Dupree called his company together. "After all these auditions, I have, at last, found a pearl hidden in the midden."

The company laughed, having witnessed some of those terrible auditions. "A new soprano. This is Therese Rose. She has been singing in the cafés for a year or two, and so she needs to learn our ways. I know you all will help her."

With abundant, curling black hair and dark eyes, Therese Rose was arrestingly pretty. She looked down demurely, her long eyelashes casting extravagant shadows on her smooth cheeks. *She looks no older than I am*, Anna thought. *Maybe younger*. It was an odd thought, to no longer be the youngest singer.

Therese moved to the farthest chair and sat down modestly as M. Dupree ran his hand over his shiny bald head, and continued. "So. We have reached the farthest northern point. We have done well, eh? But now it is time to turn south, and I ask you, my fellow citizens, artists all, east or west?"

"East," said the older soprano, Lorette, who had relations in Bretagne.

"West," Jean-Baptiste Marsac murmured, with a faint, apologetic smile at Lorette. "East, all the rumors have it, the Corsican is going to war, either Holland or Austria or Italy once again."

Of all the company, only M. Dupree recognized Marsac's aristocratic upbringing in that use of 'the Corsican' for Bonaparte. But as always, he kept his thoughts to himself.

"I agree." Philippe tossed his long golden hair back and set his fists on his narrow hips. "I've now lost two brothers to Bonaparte's adventures in Egypt, and I do not intend to follow. If we go east, we risk falling into the hands of the conscript officers, and I for one have no wish to come to a sanguinary end in a foreign grave."

"*Peste!* It is too true," declared Paul Bisset, their baritone, who favored parts that required powdered hair to hide the fact that his own was thinning. "Three times have I been spoken to by officers looking for recruits." Though he was on the far side of forty, Paul, son of a line of blacksmiths, was a fine figure of a man.

"I hear they have two good theatres in Caen," Therese said, then blushed and looked down at her lap.

"Go on," Madame Dupree said encouragingly. "Tell us more?"

"I don't know more. But Caen is said to be beautiful in spring." She cast quick glances at the men at either side.

"So it is," Paul said, smiling back.

"I've heard that." Philippe gave her the pleasant nod he reserved for beauty.

"Very well," M. Dupree said, picking up a music score and using it to fan his round, red face. "I do not want half my company recruited for cannon-fodder. West it is. I have bespoken transport; I will instruct Pierre to obtain maps along with fodder. We leave on the morrow."

They parted to pack. Anna found Mademoiselle Rose walking

next to her. "I trust *you* will show me the way." Long eyelashes lowered over beautiful dark brown eyes, and the newcomer looked down shyly. "M. Dupree says you are a genius!"

Not knowing how to respond to that, Anna murmured what she hoped sounded encouraging.

Therese smiled, clasped her hands, then uttered a stream of questions about Anna's impressions of the cities she had seen so far. Gradually her questions became more particular — and Anna's responses correspondingly general.

They parted at their lodging, Anna entering her chamber with an uneasy expression.

Parrette looked up from packing their trunks. "What is amiss? Are we delayed?"

"No," Anna said. "It's this new soprano. She seems friendly, but the way she asked about the company." She made a face. "Is it gossip, to say that I think she wanted gossip?"

Parrette shrugged. "Short of suspecting a worse motive, maybe she wants to understand the people she has come among? Does she want the guidance of a friend? Madame Dupree tells me she is just turned eighteen."

"Then she *is* younger than I." Anna moved to the window, and looked out at the stretched lines crossing the tiny courtyard. Washing flagged in the sunny breeze. "I never thought of myself as a guide."

Anna wandered away, thinking for the first time about friends. Her mother had encouraged her budding friendship with the Wynne sisters at legation parties. They had been great fun — much preferable to the royal children — but they had gone away again, just before Mama died.

The closest Anna had come to friendship since then had been Hyacinthe, who was kind to everyone, and in a sense Lise. Now they, too, were gone.

A friend would be welcome, Anna thought wistfully.

By the first of March they'd reached Caen, where they took over a small hotel in trade for informal entertainment, to bring lagging custom to the common room. A couple of the younger dancers were happy to dance and flirt, and Paul had a repertoire of bawdy sea songs that had proved to be immensely popular.

Anna and Therese Rose began a habit of walking to rehearsals together, singing their scales together, and rehearsing together, as Therese was to begin as understudy, as well as singing the very minor female roles.

Therese seemed to hang on Anna's opinions. "I am by nature so modest and retiring," she often said. "And you are so brilliant! I can learn so *much* from you!" And then would come the confidences. "I prefer your voice, oh, to infinity, to Lorette's or, hush, even to Madame's." She touched her finger to her lips and smiled winsomely.

Gradually, as the days fled by, her confidences began to broaden to include the rest of the cast. "Do not tell the others, but I would die if I strode about with my arms swinging, in that peculiar manner Lorette has. I know it is a breeches role, but..." Or, "Don't you think that Madame is a little shrill in the upper range? Perhaps my ear is odd. You, with your *perfect* ear, probably think I am much worse." And she'd lay out for compliments that Anna readily gave, for Therese sang as prettily as she looked.

Their performances in Caen promised to be as successful as Amiens, until the night M. Dupree came banging on Anna's door.

She struggled out of bed, her heart beating in her throat. All she could think of was fire. Without even pulling a wrapper over her nightrail, she opened the door to find M. Dupree outside, his candle flame flaring wildly, throwing extravagant shadows over his distraught expression.

"Madame is lying in early," he exclaimed. "The babe is on the way. You must sing *Nina* tomorrow. We cannot possibly postpone. We desperately need the money to replace the lame horse. It is criminal, how much they are charging for the oldest, lamest nag. It's the cursed army, snapping up everything with four legs..."

Anna nodded, but she didn't hear the pent-up stream of words. Her heart continued to thunder, but from a different cause. To lead! For the first time in her life, she would sing a major role!

Parrette appeared, candle in hand. "Go back to bed," she ordered Anna, after M. Dupree departed. "You are going to need your strength."

Anna obeyed, but sleep evaded her until she fell into restless dreams: walking on stage just to realize she had no notion which act it was—she was wearing her old dance hose and skirt, and the audience roared with laughter—she opened her mouth, but no sound emerged, and the crowd roared its scorn.

It was a relief when the sun at last rose. Very soon after breakfast, M. Dupree, even more tired than Anna, called for a hasty rehearsal. "Not you," he said anxiously to Anna. "Only warm your voice. Preserve it for tonight."

Anna was so excited that she did not perceive the implied warning. For the first time, everything on stage revolving around her.

M. Marsac, as her lover Lindoro, was tender and solicitous; the truth was, he found Anna increasingly interesting. As she drifted gracefully about the stage, he recalled overhearing that she was already wed.

Good. He would take no woman to the altar unless her blood matched his in purity. A married woman, especially one whose ambitions and talents matched his, could make no demands, and might divert him in this tiresome existence while he waited for the proper order to be restored.

That morning he used all his energy to encourage Anna, and the rest of the cast followed his lead.

Everyone wished her well, Therese Rose the most enthusiastic. "I will do anything to support you, I would *die* for you," she exclaimed. "We shall rehearse every note together."

"But I am to preserve my voice," Anna murmured.

Therese threw up her hands. "Shh!" She brought them to her mouth, her eyes wide. "I forget. Everyone laughs at how empty my head is! Do not sing, do not even speak! I will remain by your side, and answer for you."

Anna thanked her, but felt she would be better resting, and retired. She managed to sleep, but by the time she had put on her costume and began humming to warm her voice, her wrists and knees had gone watery with apprehension.

The clock inexorably advanced, and Anna first walked upon the stage as principal singer.

As soon as the violins began the familiar overture, assurance settled her nerves like the first fall of snow. *Light heart, tight ribs*, she said to herself and filled her lungs.

She began to sing. One by one the company joined her, everyone alive to cues...but as the opera progressed, she was aware of a sense of strain. She fought to keep her notes pure, but she sensed that she failed to reach the far corners of the gallery, and indeed, before long she perceived whispers and restless rustles that sounded to her louder than pistol shots.

In desperation, during the mad scenes she flung her arms wide, and began to dance wildly. The rustles ceased, and she caught sight of Ninon in the wings, brows raised and mouth pursed. Anna knew that she was not a great dancer, but nerves drove her to a frenzy and she leaped and twirled as if movement could furnish the lacking sound.

The audience quieted again—and then she discovered the cost: she had lost her breath. Desperately she sucked in breath and pressed her fists to her ribs, aware that at least it was a proper motion for the character. But her voice was flagging.

She sensed the other singers moving in closer and bringing their voices up, until at last it ended. The audience applauded, and she bowed, breathing hard.

The curtain fell, and Philippe sighed with relief. "At the least they didn't throw dung."

"We'll have to remember to move further downstage, hein?" Lorette asked, patting Anna kindly on the shoulder. "Perhaps less dancing?"

"Beautifully done," M. Marsac murmured, taking Anna's hands. "I never expected to play Lindoro to so accomplished a Nina."

He smiled down at her with extra meaning, and once again the warmth of attraction bloomed behind her ribs. "Truly? Oh thank you, thank you. Are you certain I was not weak in my aria? And what about the second act..."

"It was all quite lovely. You have earned a fine supper. I located a little café that miraculously has survived the ructions. I would be honored if you would accompany me."

Her nerves chilled. It was flattering, but was this going to be

Auguste all over again? "I confess I am so tired I cannot keep my eyes open anymore," she said.

"Another time, then," he said, and saluted her hands with his lips, light as a butterfly touch.

"Oh, that is so romantic," Therese said, approaching as M. Marsac walked away. "What did he say? I can never get him to talk to me, or even to notice me."

"He was very kind," Anna said, aware of her tight throat. "But as I told him, I am very tired. Good night."

"Sleep well, and dream of besting la Catalani, who I am sure you will be replacing." Therese kissed her fingertips to Anna.

Anna walked away, still a little giddy. But then she stopped. Would they be rehearsing again in the morning?

She started back past props and stage paraphernalia, slowing at the sound of voices. She caught her name. Therese was saying, "...wonderful, as graceful as a swan, but oh, M. Dupree, I cannot but hope her voice might be stronger. It was so weak, they were cupping their ears right below us in the second row. If she needs to rest her voice, I could gather my courage and—"

"You are not yet ready, Mademoiselle Rose," M. Dupree said as Anna froze where she was. "You still betray bad habits, or bad teaching. If Mademoiselle Bernardo cannot carry through the week, we will have to transpose the two arias for Lorette, who cannot reach the upper registers..." Anna backed up two, three steps, whirled, and withdrew, a sick feeling gnawing her inside. Why could Therese not have said those things to her face?

Perhaps—a horrible thought—she was busy entrusting 'observations' about Anna to others. Was friendship impossible?

Her mother had taught her deference, Mrs. Billington had taught her to be light, her father had taught her to love music, and the maestro to sing it, but no one had ever taught her about friendship. For some, it seemed as easy and effortless as breathing. For her, it was as elusive as a rainbow.

Eleven

BY THE END OF the week, she felt the beginnings of strain in her throat earlier each day, even though Jean-Baptiste Marsac led the other singers in uniting to support her flagging voice.

Anna was not aware of how much the elusive tenor was gradually gaining influence over the others. He made an effort to hide his origins, but the habits of youth are not easily overcome. His fastidious care to his clothing and person, and even his aloof countenance, fascinated the company. The more the women admired him, the more interest the men took in him.

Not everyone felt that influence. Anna was entirely taken up by the burden of her leading role, and even if she had not been, she remained wary of male attention.

That wariness now extended to Therese Rose. Despite Therese's showers of compliments, Anna could feel how eagerly and avidly she was watched, and when she glimpsed Therese talking to Lorette or one of the others, Anna wondered if some of her utterances began with, "Do not breathe a word, but..." followed by pungent observations about Anna.

She tried to shrug off her sense of hurt and exerted herself to act toward Therese exactly as always, but she no longer felt any desire to share her opinions. Therese was pretty, and sang well, and could be good company, but Anna no longer trusted anything she said.

At the end of the week, they set out as the snow began to melt. Anna rejoiced in the hills and valleys showing the first fuzz of buds, and the swoop and dive of swallows returning for spring.

The first sign of trouble was a burned village, the unrepaired ruin and relatively fresh gravestones the more shocking amidst the green shoots of spring.

Within a month they knew that the west was a mistake. The destruction of the Vendee was far worst than any of them had conceived: everywhere were the signs of poverty. Common folk made shift to live, and few were merchants, burned shops with broken windows marking village streets like gaping holes between teeth.

Nobody seemed to have money for rebuilding, much less for entertainment. M. Dupree's auditions dwindled to those desperate to live, then quit altogether. Shelter became increasingly difficult to find, and one by one their musicians began to melt away, until they were left with two violins and two woodwinds, all four relations of someone in the company. Tempers were short.

Late one day, they were turned away for the fourth time from quarters that even little Helene, daughter of a laundress, would have scorned back in their Paris days, a storm broke over-head.

M. Marsac pushed to the first carriage, stuck his head in the door, and shouted against the roar of the rain, "A local says there is a chateau nearby." He pointed up an adjacent road.

M. Dupree was too distressed to wonder why no one had offered him this information, though he was the one soaking wet from getting in and out of the carriage. "We will try to find it," he said. "Tell the driver!"

The chateau had once been magnificent, but had been used as target practice for artillery, and the entire roof had collapsed. However, the stable had largely survived. Once they discovered this, M. Dupree took one look at his weary wife, his infant son in the arms of the newly hired nurse, and said, "Settle in. I will ride back to the village and offer entertainment in exchange for food."

There was one area of the stable that was somewhat less filthy than the rest, where the lambs had once been sequestered. This was taken over by the Duprees, and the rest had to make shift as best they could.

Marsac looked around the stable in distaste. He was not about to reveal that he had once visited the place as a boy; by indirect suggestion he got the men to brave the chateau in hopes of discovering an outbuilding left intact.

The women elected to remain in the stable, in spite of the rustle and scratching of rats in the dark corners, rather than brave the storm in the fast-gathering darkness. When the men departed with the last of the lanterns, they shoved their trunks into a rough square barricade, and set four of their precious candles on the trunks at each corner.

Darkness closed in as they shared out the scant remains of stale bread and drying cheese. For a time there was general chatter, but as the long night stretched out ahead, some fought yawns: the squeaking from beyond the candle nimbus made Anna shiver.

"I will not lie down," Parrette said, sitting bolt upright on her trunk with her worn winter cloak pulled tightly around her, and her voice thin with disgust. "I will not have rats eating my fingers or attacking my face in my sleep."

"I will never shut my eyes again," Eleanor proclaimed dramatically, and was fervently agreed with by Catherine and Helene.

Anna silently agreed. Yet as time wore slowly on, measured only by the melting candles in their pools of wax, her eyelids burned and she caught herself nodding.

Each time she pulled herself upright the effort took more strength.

Midway through the night when the air was coldest, Ninon rose. "*Peste!* Let us rehearse the changes in the dance," she said to the other dancers, cast a sidelong look Anna's way, and turned her back.

Anna had no intention of accepting that silent rejection. But when she joined the others in the candlelit square, Ninon turned on her, hand upraised. "Sit down."

Anna, cold and cramped, protested. "I have always practiced with you. No one minds. I stay in the back."

"You can stay away altogether, unless you start to carry your share."

"My share?" Anna repeated, and several of the dancers looked confused. Others smiled privately, a sign that warned Anna of something unpleasant that had been discussed in secret.

Sure enough. Ninon tossed her artfully curled golden locks, crossed her arms, and said, "If you want to dance with us, you can take your part in the farce now and then, just like the rest of us."

Anna stared at her in surprise.

What was this really about? The farces were ancient, everyone knew that, always bawdy, the details merely adapted to the times: these days, the cuckolds and butts of the jokes were invariably aristocrats. The females were still coquettes, only their dress had changed from hoops and silk and feathers to republican rags or the extravagant costumes of the Merveilleuses.

Anna knew what Ninon really wanted. The acting was easy. Not much was required in the way of dance in the farce. The women were on stage mainly to act as objects for the male clowns' lascivious buffoonery.

The problem came afterward. While the male part of the audiences had no problem believing that the male clowns were playing roles, they seemed to regard the females as coquettes whether on stage or off. The singers were able to get on and off stage without being molested, perhaps protected by the grandness of tragedy. The dancers, especially those in the farces performing their roles within arm's reach of the audience, had to guard against pinches and fondles, or being grabbed and kissed.

Even though the Terror had ended when Monsieur Talien took his mistress's dagger to Robespierre, the easing of Thermidor had not reached all parts of the country. The shadow of the Terror lay in the dancers' minds when they had to fend off unwanted advances from drunken butchers, farmers, carters, and the like. Everyone was afraid of being shouted down as an elitist. They knew that mobs could form between one heartbeat and the next.

Anna studied the dancers' faces as the candles wavered and streamed in the stuffy slow-moving air. *Who are you to be spared our hardship?* those unblinking gazes seemed to ask.

Anna faced Ninon. "Someone will need to walk me through the part."

Ninon's eyelids lifted, revealing her surprise. *So she thought I would cry off,* Anna thought.

"Helene can do that," Ninon said. "It is simple enough."

"In the morning, then?" Anna turned to Helene.

The younger girl yawned and nodded. "Easy."

Ninon lifted an ironic hand, and Anna took her place at the back. Counting softly, their footsteps rustling over the dusty ground, the dancers began their daily routine. Anna sank gratefully into the familiar rhythms. All night they danced, and when they tired, sat and talked about anything and everything. Nothing of consequence: mostly reminiscences, beginning with the delicious seafood at Le Procope, laughing visits to the cafés with dashing men, and then walking back in the hour before dawn, and buying fresh, hot bread from street vendors just starting their day. When their voices got hoarse and their limbs heavy, they forced themselves up, which would cause the advancing rats to scatter. Nerves jangling, they would dance again.

When dawn's light began to send pale shafts down through the broken roof, the rats vanished back into the corners, and they retired to sleep.

Parrette shook Anna awake just before noon, when M. Dupree returned with a laden cart. "Why did you agree to that? It is a terrible comedown. Your mother would grieve to see you demean yourself in those farces. They are low," she whispered fiercely.

Anna sneezed at the dust. Her eyes ached, and every prickle of hay was like the prod of a sewing needle in the back of the neck. "Because it is no more than they are required to endure."

Parrette, aware of her own conflicted views, said nothing to that. While she understood the justice of Anna's view, she had promised to see the daughter of her beloved Signora Eugenia firmly established in the rank that the loving mother had always desired for her daughter. Acting in farces was the latest, and the worst, step down the road away from that goal, and Parrette saw herself as foresworn.

But Anna was no longer a girl. She made her own decisions. Parrette bit her lip, striving to keep her turmoil hidden.

After M. Dupree passed out bread that seemed to be made of more sawdust than flour, and some very withered turnips and cabbages, they set about readying for the promised performance.

"Perhaps if they like us, they will be more generous," someone observed wryly.

As M. Dupree went through the props with the prop master, Helene, impressed with her new responsibility, exhaustively talked Anna through the simple role. Helene's motivation, Anna could not help but notice, seemed an act of unstudied friendship, and yet there were Therese's derisive eyes watching.

When Anna turned her way, Therese's gaze shifted quickly and she began briskly brushing her hair.

Anna did not have to perform that afternoon, but Ninon saw to it that Anna's chance came at the next village. M. Dupree expressed surprise that Anna was willing to appear in the farce, but as her appearance in the opera was not until later in Act One, he did not occupy himself with the matter.

Anna wore a low, coarse-woven blouse and a skirt shared among all the dancers. It was not particularly clean. She followed Eleanor into a heady atmosphere of wine in the stuffy, heated air.

The farce went much as they usually did, received with roars of laughter and ribald commentary. They performed in a cleared space at what had been the local church, ruined by the revolutionary soldiers. The narrowness of the altar area had kept the performers on top of one another, after which the players had to pass down the chancel in order to get out through the transept perpendicular. Here the audience had crowded in with no organization. Anna followed Eleanor out again, picking her way with arms akimbo in hopes of warding off the hands of vinous men young and old, who clearly thought that grabbing at them was the best part of the festivities.

Despite her best efforts, Anna was not as skilled at sidestepping as Eleanor; she found herself cut off by a would-be swain, a sizable man wearing a tanner's apron.

Before he could finish his blunt proposal, a small figure thrust her way between the men gathering in hopes of further fun.

"There." Parrette pointed over their heads at huge Marc Gris, who played an extra in the farce and operas, and who also managed the horses. Jean was at that moment overseeing the shift of props to the performance area for the opera. "That is her husband," Parrette declared in the rough street accent of Lyons. "If she smiles at you, he will beat her black and blue."

"The devil," roared the tanner.

"*After* he kills you!" Parrette finished, hands on her hips, a sparrow squaring off to a bantam cock.

The other men roared with laughter, and let them both pass.

"Thank you," Anna said, breathing in relief that the ordeal was over. "I never thought of lying."

Parrette grumbled, "Better you were not here at all."

Anna did not reply, but inwardly she was committing Parrette's word and accent to memory as the dancers saluted her, exchanging their own unflattering comments about the men in the audience.

Anna glanced as usual past M. Marsac, who watched her from the side, his lip curled faintly, and his head tilted back at an arrogant angle. He had no idea why Anna Bernardo, who reputedly had been raised in a palace, would so demean herself as to associate with that dancing rabble.

There was another person whose reaction to Anna's acceptance by the dancers was more thoughtful: Therese Rose.

As the company had worked their way southward from Caen, Therese had let drop hints about her past, or rather, the past she wished others to attribute to her. A fine mansion—a music master from Germany (though apparently not familiar with opera, Madame said privately to Lorette)—exalted relations, alas, who did not survive the guillotine.

Therese Rose admired M. Marsac above all, setting out to emulate his fastidious habits and his avoidance of the dancers. Her long, careful toilet of the morning had kept her from learning about Anna's dancing until they were on the road, and she began to wonder if the whispers about Anna and her palace, and ducal relation, were embroideries of the sort she had added to her own life. Those dancers were little better than *canaille*.

But as food and quarters became more scarce, it was certain among the dancers, having survived starvation on the streets of Paris during the years of the Terror, who vanished quietly among those rough villagers, returning later with baskets of extra offerings. These the enterprising dancers shared among themselves — and with Anna, who in turn shared with Parrette.

Therese began to wonder if she had made an error. She attempted to insinuate herself into ballet practice one morning, to find Ninon standing arms crossed before her.

Therese knew that Ninon kept discipline among the female dancers, using not only her sarcastic tongue but her ready fist. She took one glance at those strong arms, those narrowed eyes, and beat a hasty retreat.

In the days that followed, Marsac treated Anna with a hauteur that surprised her a little, but that she accepted with an inward shrug and a sense of relief.

She had other things to think about, such as her discovery about trust. The dancers, who were the lowest in the hierarchy, and who had the least of material value, possessed a mutual trust so naturally that no one seemed aware of it.

On stage, they trusted one another in their movements, so quick and potentially dangerous: they relied on each other to know where to be, and where not to be. They trusted one another in the little tricks of survival, sharing what they had, and banding together whether to ward off marauding men or rodents.

Trust, Anna was coming to believe, was stronger than riches.

They headed inland at last.

"I will say this much for Anna," Ninon commented as they packed up after another village performance. "She doesn't prance about like some duchesse."

"Her voice is purer," Helene said admiringly. "Like a silver bell."

Eleanor yawned. "Do you think it's true, what Lise said about her being married to an English sea-captain?"

Behind the dancers, Jean-Baptiste Marsac paused in folding his stage cloak.

"English?" two dancers exclaimed, and behind them, Marsac echoed silently, *English?*

Ninon shrugged. "I don't believe a word that she-devil Lise

ever spoke."

"Lise got it from Hyacinthe," Eleanor said defensively.

"Hyacinthe!" Ninon threw her hands skyward. "An idiot as well as a blabbermouth! Far more likely Anna's husband was captured or killed *by* an English sea captain. If she is even married. I wouldn't trust anything that pair of reptiles ever said."

The dancers hefted their baskets and moved away, Ninon predicting what she hoped was Lise's lack of success in Paris, as Jean-Baptiste retreated in the opposite direction, his expression thoughtful.

They traveled inland toward Burgundy, and as they began once again to see real theaters, Anna was finding it more difficult to ignore Jean-Baptiste Marsac.

They often performed together; his performance, if rarely inspired, was never less than note-perfect. From a safe distance she admitted admiration, for in spite of the dire travel conditions he always managed to stay clean, his nails beautifully trimmed, his clothing fresh. But there was a new appraisal to his glance, a lingering caress in his touch that caused her heart to thump with interest — and with warning. Admiration was not trust.

"There is Lyons!"

A city! At last! Pierre Dupree rode ahead and found them lodgings at an abandoned cloister now owned and run by a consortium made up of former washerwomen. Pierre brought with him the latest news, the first item of which was that the First Consul was going to war against England.

Anna had noticed Parrette's silence as they approached her birthplace.

As they settled into the dirty, nearly-bare cell where once a nun had lived and prayed, Parrette looked about her, hands on her hips. "Disgusting. This place has obviously not been cleaned since the last postulant was murdered by that devil's hind-end Fouché." She made a spitting motion with her lips.

Anna ignored that. "Parrette, if you want time to seek your family, I can look after my costumes."

Parrette shrugged her bony shoulders. "They are either dead

or long gone. Nothing here for me but memories, and most of those are bad."

At least the old damage was being cleared away. Lyons, the former City of Light, had begun a massive reconstruction campaign, on the direct order of the First Consul. Pierre brought back news that in Paris, Bonaparte had recently ordered Corneille's *Polyeucte* resumed at the Theater Français.

Theater was popular again. M. Dupree found himself besieged by no fewer than three theater owners, and Marsac was able to secure private bookings as a soloist for select company. What's more, the principal violinist found a number of musicians who had been more or less in hiding since the bad days of the Revolution, which meant they would have a full orchestra again.

The only shadow on their happiness was the martial tread of conscripts daily progressing down the main boulevard: Bonaparte had caused an order for 60,000 conscripts to be raised.

Everyone knew what that meant.

M. Dupree, successfully interpreting the trepidation of their male members, at the end of autumn once more took the company to the road, promising them a milder winter in Provence, at which time they would consider what to do next.

Everyone in the company, from the old prop master, M. Dupree's uncle, down to the babe, was tired of bad roads, bad food, bad beds, and the never-ending struggle against rodents and lice. But M. Dupree had leased the land under his burnt theater for three years, and they had two more ahead before they could expect to return to Paris.

Pierre Dupree found them winter quarters at the abandoned university in the beautiful town of Avignon. One night, as the mistral blew ice over the ancient monuments, M. Dupree burst into the former library. With its huge fireplace almost warming the room, it had become a salon for the company.

"Look what I have achieved!" He brandished a carefully wrapped package.

As everyone started up, he declared, "It is the libretto and score for *I riti d' Efeso!*"

Exclamations all around—Farinelli's *dramma eroico* had debuted in Venice the year before, and they had all read reviews.

Now they would hear the actual music.

Under cover of the noise, Jean-Baptiste Marsac said to Anna under cover of the general hilarity, "May I beg the interest of an Agenore in whether you will sing Argia?"

Therese was right there. "Oh, would she not be *perfect* in the *travesti* role, Clearco of Macedon?" And with all the enthusiasm of one who had been harboring all the ambition of an Argia, Therese clasped her hands. "Anna, you are so wonderful that I believe that you are equal to anything."

"I shall sing whatever I am asked," Anna said in her politest manner. "Whether King of Macedon or maid." After which she found an excuse to leave the room.

When Jean-Baptiste made a motion to follow, Therese stepped in his way. Asking him what he had heard about *I riti,* she gazed up at him from under her lashes.

The next day, M. Dupree announced that he and Marc Gris had hired some new clowns for the farce roles, whom Marc would be training. This news raised a general cheer. As for the new opera, Lorette would sing the *travesti* role, and Anna would take Argia. Therese was still doing tiny roles and understudy.

When spring brought balmy air over the Mediterranean, the company arrived in Nice. Parrette promptly went out to buy newspapers and fashion periodicals. The former she brought back to peruse in private, in her never-failing hope to read something of Michel's ship. In her secret heart, she also hoped to discover the whereabouts of Captain Duncannon: until he was known to be dead, he was Anna's husband.

The fashion magazines were shared generally, sparking a great deal of discussion, for under the First Consul's direction, fashion was changing again.

"Silks! Silk, lace, everything made in France," Madame exclaimed.

"Everyone says Bonaparte is going to crown himself King of France at last," Lorette put in.

Some scoffed. They had been hearing that for ages, but Pierre said, "It's true. What's more, the rumor is passing around the military, and *they* always have the latest."

Madame frowned into the middle distance, and then rose briskly. "Do you know what that means? It means that *Nina* is going to require restaging. The Count must look like a courtier!"

Of them all, only Jean-Baptiste Marsac was silent, shock pooling into chill in his heart.

How could these fools not notice the most important piece of news? Bonaparte had secretly sent soldiers to cross the Rhine and capture the Duc d'Enghien, hope of the royalists. They brought him back to the Château de Vincennes, where they shot him.

Marsac looked around grimly at his fellow performers. Commoners all, they did not pay this astounding item of news the least heed. Their only interest in politics was as it impacted the stage.

Jean-Baptiste was exactly the same age as the duke, thirty-one; they had known one another when youths, learning military matters under the Commodore de Vinieux. Until now, he had been content to while away his days in the guise of a performer. He played a role in life as upon stage, always expecting the upstart Bonaparte to be thrown out and the Bourbons restored at last.

And he had expected the Duc d'Enghien to be leading the army of restoration.

There would be no stopping the Corsican upstart now, Jean-Baptiste thought, barely able to contain his bitterness. There was no recovering lost land, lost revenues, lost titles. It was time to quit looking no further than his own idle pleasure, occasionally earning extra here and there to augment his need for shirts and shoes and hats.

He must begin planning for something larger, something suitable for a man of birth and blood—as much as was possible in this new, benighted France.

He gazed across the room at Anna, who sat upright, her curly head and graceful neck outlined against the window. Whatever her reason for demeaning herself in those farces, it was apparent that she still held herself aloof from hairy butchers and garlic-breathing cobblers. She was clever, finding strength in numbers, as the democratic rabble had.

Perhaps he had underestimated her.

Twelve

THE NIGHT OF THEIR opening, as they peeked out at the audience, one of the dancers pointed at the nearest box. There sat a very imposing personage, judging by the orders and medals decorating the broad sash he wore over the breast of his splendid coat, and the gold braid on his uniform.

"Who is that?" Eleanor whispered to Catherine, who spread her hands.

Madame rustled up, fanning herself. "Did you see?" she asked, eyes wide. "That is the elder brother of Prime Minister Godoy! He is on his way back to Spain from Paris."

Excitement was high: a new piece, a new city, and a very distinguished guest. Everyone gave of their best. The company took four bows, and as the curtain came down, they saw M. Dupree enter the royal box, bowing repeatedly.

Very soon he came backstage and, heedless of various states of undress, assembled the company.

We," he announced proudly, "are summoned to perform in Madrid, before Prime Minister Godoy, and the king and queen!"

Reactions divided quite sharply, to M. Dupree's surprise. All of the women, from Madame with her fractious son to little Helene the dancer, loathed the notion of leaving France.

The men were enthusiastic at the prospect of getting farther away from possible conscription. This included the new musicians, who were grateful to be playing after all the ructions of the past ten years.

Jean-Baptiste considered the matter coolly. Perhaps there might be a place for a company directed by a French aristocrat in Spain, especially one who had performed before their king? That was a possible future, at least until France regained order.

M. Dupree said to his wife, "Once we do return to Paris, would not our name gain considerable luster if our placards could state that we had performed by invitation before King Charles of Spain?"

Madame stood before her husband, arms crossed under her considerable bosom. "Perhaps. But in that case," she stated, "we *must* all have new clothes. We simply cannot wear muslins before their majesties. It must be all silk, with real lace. And velvet against winter."

Lorette sighed, and the dancers all exchanged looks. If Madame had given in, they had no hope: to Spain they were to go.

The journey to Madrid started with several sharp disappointments, beginning with the discovery that the invitation did not come with the wherewithal to travel.

Second, M. Dupree had assumed that everybody in Spain spoke French, the way he had been told everyone else in Europe did, even the English *roas' biffs*. When they climbed aboard the Spanish-owned boat that was to take them midway along the east coast of Spain, it was to discover Spanish being spoken all around them.

One of the sailors spoke Italian. Due to most operas being written in Italian, M. Dupree knew enough to question the fellow, bringing the third disappointment, a strong recommendation to hire guards as well as a translator.

"Banditti," the sailor said succinctly.

But it was too late to go back.

When they reached the walled city of Castellón de la Plana, the warmth of the sun was most welcome. Madame Dupree assembled the company in the coffee room.

"I have been thinking about the news. Clothes in the new mode are very well." Madame turned to Anna. "But! Mademoiselle Bernardo, it is said that you grew up in a palace. The days for hiding such antecedents are over. Crowns, court, curtseys are to be the custom again. *You* can teach us. It is also true that the king of Spain is brother to the king of Naples. Surely the etiquette is the same?"

"Oh, how exciting," Therese exclaimed, clapping her hands. "You never whispered a word about being an aristocrat."

Anna had been playing so many roles that she no longer knew how to define herself. But the question did not concern her identity, it concerned her knowledge. Ignoring Therese's interjection, she said slowly, "I remember all my lessons in court etiquette, but we were told that Spain's courtly protocol was much more rigid than that in Naples."

"I cannot believe this!" Ninon would not have spoken to M. Dupree, but she felt safe enough in her position as first dancer to protest to his wife. "What is the use of bowing and scraping to these Spaniards? We are *French!* We can hold up our heads to anyone."

Philippe tossed his mane of hair back. "In this, I agree."

Anna was unnerved by the intensity of M. Marsac's gaze, his unreadable expression. She looked away from him as she said, "If it is true that the First Consul is about to crown himself king, that means court etiquette will be the new mode in France, too. In, fact, I expect that this very day at the Tuileries in Paris, Madame Bonaparte's ladies are lined up, just like you, about to practice their first curtsey."

"Exactly what I was going to say!" Madame Dupree exclaimed. "We do not have to bow and scrape to the Spaniards on the streets, but what they do at the Tuileries, they will expect to see on the stage, will they not? It will only be to our advantage if we return to Paris well practiced in how to move in a room, how to line up according to rank, and how to manage court trains."

Eleanor burst out, "We will not be forced into those terrible panniers that my grandmother wore?"

"Or the absurd wigs?" Catherine cried. "My father was a *perruquier*, and he used to tell us that those grand ladies wore whole ships upon their heads, complete with sails, and feathers beyond that! They used to have to kneel on the floor of their coach, and crawl out like beggars at the gate, lest they disturb their heads."

Madame Dupree laughed. "Do you really believe that Madame Bonaparte, the most elegant woman alive, would suffer a headdress the size of a chair upon her head, or skirts wider than a coach?"

No, they all agreed, and, at a wave from Madame Dupree, Anna demonstrated the court curtseys and bows. She was glad of her dance lessons as she demonstrated over and over. Except for Marsac, the singers were loud in their protests at the strain in their backs and legs. None managed the dip and rise with any grace.

At the end of that session, everyone separated. Anna was grateful to get away from M. Marsac, who *stared* so.

Ninon led a party of dancers into the city to seek entertainment. They returned at midnight. Most of the company was still awake, unused to the heat. "We went to the Spanish opera," Ninon declared.

"Spanish opera?"

"They have such a thing?"

"It must be—"

Ninon waved her hands. "The opera itself is boring. Mostly speeches, and we could not understand a word, of course. But the dancing!" Her eyes widened. "*Las labradoras de Murcia*, it is called—"

"No, that is the opera itself. The dance, it was called za, zar, something," Eleanor put in.

"Guitars like thunder. Tambourines. Little castanets." Ninon drew herself up in a compelling pose, brought her knee high, flashing the hem of her skirt. Then she slammed her heel onto the warped flooring, as she snapped her fingers in counterpoint. "It is *not* ballet."

"At first I laughed," Helene admitted. "It looked so, so wild." She flapped her hands. "But it draws you in, and you cannot stop watching. The men especially."

Philippe, who had been silent, crossed his arms and looked down his chiseled Greek nose. "I will see this za-za dance of yours."

The next day, while the luckless M. Dupree ventured out yet again in hopes of hiring an escort, Madame ran the rehearsal.

They incorporated the simplest of courtly etiquette into their stage movements, and that night all the dancers went out. They returned, most thoughtful, Philippe rigid with disgust. "This is not dance, it is the shuffle of..." Habit caused him to suppress any comment about clod-hopping peasants. "There is none of the purity of ballet."

"I know now why the Spanish believe our ballet to be boring," Ninon retorted with spirit. "I am going to learn this Spanish dance, me."

The next morning, when Anna woke, she found the dancers already at work, Ninon having sweet-talked some of the younger musicians into playing for them. Ninon and Eleanor led the others in trying to incorporate Spanish dance elements into their own ballet, as the musicians experimented with new rhythms and melodic sounds.

When Philippe came downstairs, he protested with such vehemence and passion that M. Dupree came at a run.

He listened to both sides, then mopped his head. "I see your point, Philippe, and I agree that nothing in the world reaches the height of art as taught by the great Noverre. But!" He turned to Ninon. "We are in the kingdom of Spain, which has its own tradition of dance. I traveled here once, when I was a boy. I know the *zarzuela*. I was here when Boccherini introduced his famous *Clementina*. And so I say, if you can adapt some of the Spanish dance to our opera, I think we shall be the better received." As Philippe began to curse, he added in haste, "The male solos may be preserved intact, *naturellement*."

"*Naturellement*," Philippe declared, arms crossed over his magnificent chest, and rehearsal commenced.

The third day, M. Dupree's efforts were at last met with success, and the company set out two days later, crowded into hot, stuffy carriages, perched on the baggage carts, or riding mules. It seemed that mules were as ubiquitous as olive trees in Spain.

As they traveled inland, the spring of Spain felt to the French far more like the summer farther north. The inns were long, rambling buildings, often with swallows' nests in the attics, the birds' song as unceasing as the rasping rhythm of cicadas. The company fretted about the mules, the heat, the unfamiliar noise and smells, and M. Dupree fretted about the fact that he not only had to pay his impressive escort, but to house and feed the men and their animals.

Most daunting of all, M. Dupree had assumed that mention of the Godoy name would go a ways toward giving them what ministerial largesse had not. He was astounded to discover that the Prime Minister was not universally loved in the country.

After days of dispiriting travel, everything changed when they reached Teruel, whose towers and arches were decorated with carved stone that looked to French eyes like lacework. The town was small, as was its main inn, but not long after they sat down, dusty, hot, and thirsty, their guide reappeared with a young fellow in beautiful livery.

"This is an equerry from the marquis," the guide explained. "Is it true, that you perform the operas of Italy?"

A marquis? Though his purse had grown disturbingly flat, M. Dupree swallowed a couple of times, then offered to perform for his excellency the marquis, if it would please him.

It was the right decision.

After a hasty rehearsal, they hired the inn's cart and gig to carry them to the castle of this Spanish grandee. Here, they discovered a complete stage as fine as anything they had seen in Paris, if on a smaller scale, and a full set of stage hands waiting to serve them, all wearing the livery of the marquis. They could hear the rustles and whispers of a considerable crowd from the other side of the curtain.

The marquis had invited not only his entire household, but all the local persons of rank. Marc Gros was able to set up the stage very swiftly, with all that willing help. As the sun set over the shimmering landscape, the company musicians struck up and the performance began.

And here they made a happy discovery that went a long way

toward reconciling them with the heat, the dust, the terrible roads, the strange foods and the lack of a comprehensible tongue: the Spanish were opera mad.

When the curtain fell, the marquis handed M. Dupree a purse filled with golden ducats, and delivered a long and flowery speech of thanks.

Thereafter, M. Dupree sent Pierre riding ahead not only to secure accommodation, but to apprise any local grandees of their presence. At the performance end, Philippe changed his mind, and threw himself into adapting the more militaristic flourishes of Spanish bolero, to enthusiastic success.

Early in May, the travel-worn company crossed the heat-shimmering flat plain, which seemed endless, until at last they spotted the beautiful bridge over the Manzanares, the first sign of civilization to come.

Presently there was walled Madrid itself, with its forest of spires, domes, and towers. Pierre was anxiously watching for them from the gate of the Fuencarral over the grand boulevard of San Bernardo.

The Prince of Peace had assigned a functionary to Pierre, who joined him at the gate to meet their party. The company looked in wonder on the rich, crowded streets, the air filled with the fragrances of tobacco. Once they had been conducted to the customs house for a cursory search through their belongings, now liberally sprinkled with red dust, they proceeded down splendid streets as the functionary gave Pierre a list of royal Spanish expectations.

During his wait, Pierre had taken care to obtain the latest French newspapers, brought in by a constant stream of couriers. These were awaiting the company as they traversed the beautiful buildings of Madrid to the narrow street where they were to be housed.

He pointed out the assigned accommodations and then waited in resignation for the expected lamentations.

They were not long in coming. "What is this? My room has no

windows?"

"Mine looks directly into a wall!"

"At least you found yours. Mine seems to be up the stairs, and then down another set, and through a closet!"

"Yes, and my chamber is that very closet!"

"Is this a deliberate insult?" M. Dupree asked his brother.

Pierre stroked the air between them, as if gentling a nervous horse. "No, no. This is merely what they call a *casa a la malicia*. The city is full of them, due to a royal decree generations ago, that the citizens must all house palace functionaries and guests in their second floor. So many of them built these terrible rooms. I assure you, Anton, there are worse!" He spread his hands. "At least this entire house is owned by the Prime Minister, so we will not be subjected to the exigencies of resentful citizens."

Madame reappeared. "It is still intolerable. No room is on the same floor as another. We must find a hotel."

"This is a very crowded city." And Pierre bluntly named the going prices.

M. Dupree squawked as if he had been stabbed. He mopped his shiny dome, and then sank into a chair. "At least we have our performance date?"

"That, yes," Pierre said thankfully.

At that, some of the company settled down to read, or rest, and the younger among them set out to take in the sights. Presently the angelus was rung, a sound that reached into infant memory for many. The Spaniards paused in their business, parade, flirting, and when the last shivering bong died away, resumed their preparations for the evening. To the French it seemed that the great bell demanded a universal pause, a moment of quiet during which all that was heard amid the dying echoes were birds, and the hush of the river.

As for those gathered in the main salon with the newspapers, meeting their astonished eyes was the news that France was now an Empire. Bonaparte would be crowned Napoleon I by winter.

"And the creation of all these marshals?" Pierre predicted, making motions as if tearing out his hair. "There is to be war and more war. What else have marshals to do? And you know who is to fight these wars, if we return? You and me, that's who!"

"We can do nothing about it at this moment," his brother stated. "Come! Dispose of your belongings as best you can, and let us get to work. This must be our best performance yet."

There was time to attend both Madrid theaters. At La Cruz they found an odd adaptation of Moliere, awkward and uninspired to the French, except for the dancing; the *bolero*, which Philippe had been driving his dancers to master, was astonishing. As was the slower, more expressive *fandango*.

They had an entire day to arrange the palace's private theater, so that they would be ready to perform when the royal party arrived that evening. The King of Spain's palace, a massive white-stone building festooned with arches, windows, pilasters and a riot of decorations, stretched out to either side to a considerable degree, looking loftily over the surrounding plains and distant hills. They were led down corridors that seemed to stretch into infinity, past busts and marbles, tapestries and magnificent paintings of enormous size, their subjects often larger than life—all the ornamentation that had been stripped away from Paris palaces, and carted off or sold on street corners.

The theater was elaborately decorated, with a fine royal box that by nightfall was full of people in glittering costume. The company spotted military figures whose chests were laden with sashes and medals, women with high-dressed hair and low-cut gowns that were partly obscured by beautiful carved fans and ex-quisite lace mantillas draped in graceful folds over their shoulders.

The dancers knelt low, peeking out and trying in whispers to determine which was Prime Minister Godoy, the Prince of Peace, and which the royal family.

Anna peered over their shoulders, curious to see how the Neapolitan princess she had known in childhood appeared. Now married to Prince Ferdinand, the heir, she looked sulky and heavy; Anna wondered if the princess was pregnant or merely ill.

The royal prince looked like a dullard in his diamonds and silk, and Anna backed away from the curtain, reflecting on how they both had been married off summarily.

As least I am well rid of mine, Anna thought, looking at that pouting prince.

The signal was given to take their places. The curtain opened, the violins wailed...and the company nerved themselves to the best performances of their lives, suitable for royalty.

Unfortunately this exalted company was far more interested in their own conversation than yet another dramatic presentation. The queen chattered to the Prince of Peace, the royal prince scowled from under heavy brows at anyone who addressed him, his wife whispered behind her fan to the ladies behind her.

Only the king seemed to be interested in the performance, but when they took their bows, he confined his enthusiasm to an idly lifted hand.

As the company made their way back through the long corridors of the palace, M. Dupree muttered, "At least we can say we played exclusively for them. I shall use their names with profligate indiscrimination."

By the next morning, M. Dupree had recovered his spirits. His new plan? "We shall travel southward to Badajos, and thence to Toledo, everywhere there are wealthy grandees. And we can resurrect all the great aristocratic operas on which we were all trained."

They reached Toledo before the height of the simmering Spanish summer. Here, the French women acquired beautiful lace mantillas with which to protect their heads from the relentless sun.

In every city, Parrette's first purpose was to obtain English newspapers, if she could get them, and *Les Costumes Parisiennes* in order to stay *au courant*.

They continued to adapt to local custom, designed to keep one as cool as possible in the dry, blazing heat. Parrette and Anna swiftly picked up Spanish.

The only point on which the women were adamant was their adhering to French fashion. Though they liked the mantillas, and put a great deal of energy into acquiring the exquisite cashmere shawls that in Paris could only be afforded by the likes of Madame Bonaparte, little else about Spanish fashions appealed. French fashions in gowns were still regarded as the smartest.

Some of the wealthy Spanish ladies who came night after night to fill the boxes sent their maids to request patterns, and Parrette earned substantial sums on the side, dress-making for the wives of grandees.

Sometimes Parrette earned more than M. Dupree did. While their performances were generally well received, some grandees apparently felt that it was reward enough to be permitted to perform before their blue-blooded selves and relatives. All they got was the loan of a stage, perhaps a meal, and florid speeches of gratitude.

At the end of summer, M. Dupree gathered his company. "We shall go west," he said.

The oppressive heat made it nearly impossible to respond. Dull faces stared back at him as he said, "We are desperately short of money. West is where French soldiers are being brought in."

Paul said heartily, "Of course! We must surely have a greater success among our French brethren!"

The republicans all agreed, and Marsac curled his lip.

Success in the west became as sparse as the countryside. The massive influx of Spanish and French soldiers resulted in a scarcity of horses, food, water, and patience. The peasants, bearing the brunt of the insatiable appetites of many thousands of soldiers and sailors, did not welcome the prospect of more French people, and as the towns and villages got poorer, so did their reception.

One blazing October morning, they woke up to discover that their guides—paid to take them all the way to Badajos—had absconded with their horses and mules.

When M. Dupree went to find someone in authority to complain, he discovered a strange, hostile silence. The women clustered worriedly inside the rough *posada*, the typical Spanish inn. Some of the men remained with them, others stood outside, oblivious to the glare-bright sun, as they argued about what had happened, what they ought to have done, and what was to be done now.

The French voices rose on the somnolent air, Spaniards nowhere to be seen. Local headmen wouldn't speak to them.

Anna had been sitting disconsolately at a worn table into

which some long ago patrons had carved initials, and here and there idiomatic phrases. She was too dispirited even to use her new fan, carved from aromatic wood. All it did was stir the hot air, without cooling or refreshing.

She looked about wearily, until she noticed a sympathetic glance from a young girl, daughter of the innkeeper. The girl peeped out from the low door leading to the kitchen.

She got up and went to the door. The girl peered up at her, and in an excited whisper, "Mamacita says, you must go straight to Don Alejandro, who is nephew to the Duke of Medinaceli, Don Luis Fernández de Córdoba y Gonzaga." She said the name softly, as if so exalted a personage could hear from a great distance, and pluck her straight to prison for not speaking with respect.

Then she took a step closer, so that Anna could smell the fresh olive oil that the maid had been cooking with in her mother's kitchen, and whispered, "It is said that the English dogs have destroyed our treasure ships. There is going to be a terrible war, Papa says."

Anna thanked her and ran outside, where she discovered M. Dupree, his head red and shiny, his arms waving as he exclaimed passionately, arguing with a stone-faced Spanish man armed to the teeth, whom he had found approaching the nearby stable.

"For that price, I could buy the coaches, yes, and all the horses too! It is unconscionable!"

"That is the price. Take it or leave it, Frenchman. I advise you to take it."

M. Dupree turned away, groaning. Then he spied Anna. "What is it, Mademoiselle?"

Anna told him what she had heard.

M. Dupree did not speak until they were all shut inside their airless, superheated chamber. "That explains the insults I've heard. They are angry with us, their allies. How could we have known the *roas'biffs* would turn pirate? Why do they blame *us*?"

They all stared at each other, stunned, horrified as only people can be who have woken up and found themselves regarded as criminals without having done anything to warrant it, while upstairs the baby wailed fretfully, in the grip of another fever.

"I suspect it is because they see us as foreigners," the clarinetist said morosely.

"Surely they can tell the difference between us and the English, who everybody knows are all mad?"

A violinist nodded. "My cousin, who used to trade in wool, said that your Spaniard hates everybody, French, English, Italian alike, and the Portuguese worse than all three."

"I refuse to go to Badajos," Madame said fiercely. "If it is just thieving, brawling, stealing soldiers, it is the worst of the revolution all over again, but in another land where we are the foreigners. They are not going to give us a theater, and gold. I demand we go directly to Cadiz, and seek the first ship for France!"

"If I may respectfully demur," Jean-Baptiste interjected, with an elegant gesture toward Madame that emphasized his aristocratic training. "I believe we would do best to seek this marquis, if you wish to avoid soldiers. And Cadiz being also filled with war ships, there might not be even a rowboat for hire."

M. Dupree looked around the peeling plaster of the walls, the shutters closed tightly against the heat waves wavering off the tiled square, and finally to the crucifix over the door, as if any of these sights would offer an answer. Except that he had his answer in Marsac's commanding gesture.

Aristocrats had power. And in Spain, at least, they loved theater. "We shall go to this duke."

The next day the entire company either rode upon donkeys, or in donkey-pulled carts, as they wound up ancient trails, past ruins ranging from Roman to medieval times. The dust was thick, obscuring low, tenacious plants dotted with bright pink or purple heron's beak, and partly obscured by occasional stands of scrubby oak. Around them rose the scent of the spiky sharp cedar, none of which afforded shade to speak of.

Anna dutifully noted the countryside as their guide pointed things out, but she rode with her mouth covered by her handkerchief, and her pretty lace mantilla covering her bonnet so that her skin would not blister in the sun, though sweat trickled down the back of her head to pool at the base of her spine.

By nightfall they reached a fine walled city of the sort they were becoming used to, at its center a plaza with a cathedral and opposite it a beautiful palace. Pierre, who had learned a great deal of Spanish by now, was sent to request an audience with the don.

A very short time later he returned, a splendidly dressed young man with impressive mustachios with him. "A French opera company, in truth? And played before the king? The very thing to cheer us, after so treacherous an attack by those cowardly skulking English...my friend Lucien Bonaparte—his brother soon to be crowned Emperor, did you know..."

Talking volubly in accented but clear French, the don grandly invited them all inside, and within a day they found themselves housed around a small plaza at one end of the vast palace. The theater was nearly a stone's throw away.

Life had taken an abrupt turn for the better, Anna thought.

She had forgotten all about her paper-husband, but no more than he had forgotten her.

While she stepped onto yet another Spanish stage, he and the fleet were tacking wearily in form, one after the other, off of the coast of Spain.

Thirteen

CHRISTMAS FOUND THE COMPANY Dupree in Merida, playing in the splendid Roman theater.

From there, they proceeded to Zafra, where they stayed in an Austrian-style palace as guests of another noble Medinaceli relation, and from thence to Seville, site of operas by the great Rossini and of course by Mozart.

By now Pierre had become as fluent as Anna, and expert at finding lodgings better than the ubiquitous *posadas*. He had learned to scour the inner city for pieces of paper tied to the edges of balconies, which was the Spanish way of advertising that a house was to be let. In Seville he discovered a fine house near the theater, built around a central patio.

The company had become adept at moving their things into new quarters and swiftly making them homelike. Anna followed the servant carrying her trunk, but instead of going into the room she had been assigned, she paused in the patio, and looked from the handsomely carved doors to the cool tile floors to the shady trees and roses in pots. There was even a fountain, which could be seen from the gallery running all around the upper story.

She knew there would be a little time to explore before they were expected to gather in the theater to rehearse, a prospect she faced with no particular joy.

She bent over the fountain, gazing down into the ripples of water sparkling in the sun, and considered her emotion: there was no joy in the prospect of singing. When had that happened?

She began to walk around the patio, and thought back. It seemed to have been vanishing bit by bit, ever since... Caen? Was it because she had not become a second Billington?

No, that was not it. Anna knew she was good...enough. Would genius make her any happier? She splashed her fingers in the water, then cupped them to watch the droplets cascade down. She had heard stories enough about Mrs. Billington's sicknesses, her tantrums, to wonder if the joy had gone from singing for her, too.

Anna poured out another handful of water. For the first time, she thought past today's rehearsal and performance to tomorrow, and next week, and next year. The next *ten* years. She contemplated the idea that she must do this every day, or most days, and was appalled at the emptiness in her heart.

Not long ago, she had overheard Madame Dupree saying to Lorette, "When we return to Paris, I shall retire, and never sing another note, unless I wish."

Anna had attributed that to the heat, to the dreariness of travel. Perhaps to Madame's age, for she was six-and-thirty. But now she understood the real emotion.

She scolded herself mentally. She knew she was lucky, for she had witnessed both starvation and desperation as the results of war.

Anna turned away. Yes, she was lucky. She would not be forced to travel back to Italy and attempt to beg for a place in a world that was pretty much indifferent to her existence. She had made a place among these people. It was not the ideal place, but it was good...enough.

And that gave her an idea.

She touched her wet hands to her cheeks to cool them, and walked up to her room, where she found Parrette busy unpacking Anna's gowns to air them. She let out a squawk of disgust as she picked up one of the coarse blouses the dancers wore in the farces. "Anna! You are not lowering yourself to the farces again!"

"Naturally not!" Anna heard the sharpness in her own voice, and bit her lip. She tried to breathe out her exasperation: Parrette knew very well that the last farce Anna had danced in had been before they reached Lyons. She forced her voice to a lower tone. "It must have slipped in there with the other things drying in the sun, before we packed."

"Good. That was such an act of madness. You could have—"

Anna clapped her hands over her ears. "If I have to hear about being a 'lady' I shall scream. The first thing I must do when we reach Paris again, if this new Civil Code is still in force, is get an annulment. It ought to be easy enough, considering the other party is a devil-dog Englishman!"

Parrette's frown became a scowl. "You ought not to joke about such things, Anna."

"Very well, very well," Anna said soothingly. Parrette must be feeling exactly as hot, tired, and dispirited. Anna refused to start an argument when Paris lay so far in the future. "I might see if anyone wishes to walk out to look at the Alcázar, which Pierre said is a famous Moorish palace."

Anna pulled her mantilla around her head to ward the sun, and walked down to the room Therese shared with Lorette. When she knocked, Therese opened the door.

Anna invited her along on her walk. Therese blinked her long eyelashes, smiled her false smile, and professed herself very ready to explore.

Anna waited until they reached the street, then said, "I wanted to talk to you myself, Therese. There is something I think you should know."

Therese Rose flushed, then passed a hand over her magnificent bosom, and her middle, which would be plump if she were not encased resolutely in stays. "You mean in *embonpoint*," she said, flushing. "It is this olive oil in all the food."

"It is no such thing. I wish to talk about singing," Anna said firmly. "This theater is enormous. You know how I strain in large spaces; I cannot maintain both purity and volume. I believe we ought to ask M. Dupree if you can sing Argia in *I riti*."

"You would do that?" Therese's wide gaze narrowed. "What do you want in return?"

"Nothing untoward," Anna said. *Deflect and disengage.* "Merely that when we come to a smaller theater, where I know my own strength, that I resume the role again."

Therese's smile of triumph lessened a degree. Anna sensed

that Therese still believed she was destined for greatness; she did not seem to hear the truth of M. Dupree's admonitions about shrillness on the high notes, or sloppiness of tempo.

"Very well," Therese said, and began to gush about how they would always be friends, and how great Anna was to think of her.

When Anna made no answer, Therese said a little less airily, "Perhaps we might explore the Moorish palace another time, and find M. Dupree now. He might be busy later, rehearsing the orchestra."

They both knew she meant, *You might change your mind.*

But Anna was not going to change her mind. They went together, and as soon as it was done, she felt a curious lightness of heart.

The rest of the cast heard of the switch that afternoon. Most accepted it without interest, a few with mild surprise.

Jean-Baptiste Marsac waited until rehearsal was over, and fell in step beside Anna. "Why did you relinquish your role? Has she some hold over you?"

She glanced up at him in surprise. "Surely you have heard how much effort I expend in a great theater like this? I do not want to strain my voice."

"Surely," he retorted with good humor, "you can employ any of your pretty little tricks to draw the audience's awareness away? I speak as your friend. You must see how stepping aside for such a person as Therese Rose is to lower your status in everyone's eyes."

"Such a person as? What does that mean? She has improved immensely, and she is pretty."

He said gently, "She lived behind a mansion, not in one—I saw her sing in Lille, and discovered at the prefecture that she was a runaway cook's apprentice. M. Dupree was taken in by a pretty face, but that is his affair. Can you not see how stepping aside for her is unwise, given your place in life?"

"My place in life?"

He turned his wrist up in a way that recalled expensive lace in embroidered satin sleeves. "Madam—oiselle, if you wish to perpetuate that little ruse—Mademoiselle Bernardo, with Bonaparte having crowned himself emperor, I believe the pretense of republicanism can said to be well and truly over. I have hesitated against speaking until now, but you have demonstrated in a thousand ways your gentle birth, for I have been observing you."

They had reached their street. The patio was empty. Anna paused beside the fountain. He smiled down at her, his curling brown hair touched with gold in the sunlight, a smile of expectation in his handsome face. He was beautifully dressed in a fine new coat of blue with silver buttons, worn over a waistcoat of ivory silk, and camel pantaloons above his fine shoes. She knew that her mother would have agreed with everything he said. If he had been English, she might even have thought him perfect. And yet Anna was aware of a pulse of resentment.

"I have noticed your interest," she admitted. "I did not understand it."

"Then you must be the only woman who does not," he retorted, his humor unimpaired. "Permit me to speak as a disinterested admirer, then. This impulse of yours really is unfortunate, though perhaps it can be spoken of as a tribute to your sex. Generous, giving, as a woman ought to be. And yet, even these days, especially these days, I believe it behooves those of us born to a rank to set an example."

The words rolled out as easily as if he spoke on stage. Perhaps he had practiced them before a mirror, she thought as he gestured again, turning his palm toward her. "I believe that you would grace a company I am considering forming. I am minded to tour the capitals of Europe, where refinement and order still abide. My company will be made up of those of gentle birth, for the *true* aristocracy recognizes good blood. It is the way of nature."

"A company?" Anna repeated, only half-aware of the words that followed. She had to laugh at herself—here she had been dreading a declaration like Auguste's. But he wasn't thinking of that at all!

"Surely you did not believe I would remain with this rabble of blacksmith's sons, cooks' daughters, and the rest of the spawn from the back alleys of Paris!" He extended his hand to sweep around the balcony, then with his other, took her fingers lightly in his grip. "Dupree has taught me how a company is run. When I assemble *my* company, we will perform only at royal theaters, in Vienna, in Berlin, in Prague, in Stockholm. Wherever there are kings." He pressed his lips softly to her fingertips. "And you would, I am convinced, grace my life as well."

Oh. So she had *not* been wrong. "You know that I am married," she said gravely, freeing her fingers.

"What of it?" He spread his hands. "I have gained the impression that you are related to a ducal family, though at a distance, is it not so?" And when she nodded, "If you were single, the duke's daughter, and came with a dowry, things might be different. But under these circumstances, we could arrive at an understanding—"

"I am married," she said, and though she knew herself for a hypocrite, it was the fastest way to get out of a conversation she did not at all wish to have. "So I must honor my vows. I made them according to the laws of God and man."

"To an enemy of the state?" he retorted, his smile less complaisant. "As for your laws of man, they appear to change with the seasons, these days. And finally, as for God, if he even notices us anymore, I have yet to be convinced of the evidence."

Her resentment flared. She itched to slap that smug smile off his face, but memory of Auguste stayed her hand. He had been full of soft words until she crossed him, and then he set the theater on fire. Men could do what they liked; they had the strength in their hands.

But that did not mean she ought to throw away her wits.

"I am honored," she said therefore, dropping a curtsey. "However, I have no ambition beyond singing with the Company Dupree."

Anna walked up the stairs to her room.

Jean-Baptiste watched her straight back, her uplifted chin as she retreated. His first reaction was a laugh of astonishment. He had imagined gratification, even gratitude, perhaps the blushing pretense of coyness to which women were so prone. That she would dismiss him so cavalierly took him utterly by surprise.

He waited for her better sense to bring her seeking him, but the days turned into a week, and the weeks to a month. She sang the smaller role in the great theater, she danced every morning with the canaille, and she went out shopping for fans and mantillas and cashmere shawls with the former cook's apprentice Therese Rose.

His amiable generosity turned to disgust. Presumptuous coquette!

⊰⊱

One day Pierre came around before the siesta period was properly over, summoning them all to the theater.

Weary and overheated, the company gathered. M. Dupree bounded in from the recesses of backstage, his bald head shinier than usual. "Don Alejandro is back," he announced. "We have received a special invitation to perform in Cadiz."

"Cadiz?" several repeated.

"Is that not where the army is gathered? It will be like Badajos all over, no horses, bandits..." Madame waved her hands limply.

"No, no army. That is, I believe there is a garrison, but it is the *navy* that is gathered there. Our horses should be in no danger."

"Ah, the navy. Well, that is different," Madame said, thinking privately: *That means ships, which in turn means we are that much nearer to France.*

Others agreed with satisfied nods and murmurs.

"Don Alejandro has been appointed adjutant to a French admiral, and particularly requested us. It seems this admiral is just returned from a hard chase to the West Indies. Don Alejandro says he needs diversion, and what could be better than a French company who has also met with success among their Spanish allies?" He smiled.

Paul Bisset thumbed his chin, and observed hopefully, "A French admiral would have the ear of Bonaparte."

"Exactly!" M. Dupree clasped his hands. "If we are successful, who is to say we might not be put in the way of something better, something *imperial?*"

"We could go home to Paris," Madame murmured aloud, and this time, no one demurred.

"So we shall finish our contracted time here in Seville, and I will send Pierre ahead to make arrangements," M. Dupree said, beaming at his company.

Pierre soon reported that the easiest way to travel to Cadiz would be down the river by sailboat. It would be speedier than overland, "but there is no accommodation on board. And the

153

travel might be at most three or four days."

With Don Alejandro's help, they were able to hire a series of barges, on which tents were set up. The women had one to themselves.

Glad to be at this distance from Jean-Baptiste's cold looks, Anna found it restful to sit under a tent and watch the Spanish countryside slip by, but though she had made peace with her diminishing ambition, she brooded about the future once again. *What do I want?* she thought. *Women seldom get what they want, even wealthy women of rank, these days. Princesses are sent off to dullards who happened to be born princes, and duchesses get their heads cut off. What am I willing to settle for?*

She sighed in the hot, humid air. Sliding sweetly along this river like Cleopatra of ancient days made her feel as her life were slipping away along with the Spanish scenery.

At last they drew near the sea, and there were other things to think about. From the Isla to Cadiz, the road was raised on a causeway, the foot of which was washed by the waters of the bay on one side, and by the Atlantic on the other. At the end of the causeway stood the diamond-bright city of Cadiz, dominated by an enormous fortress built at the highest point.

Cadiz was built after the Moorish fashion, with high parapets, frequently castellated. The bone-white walls of the houses were blinding in the September sun. They stood in rows carved into the side of the palisades, affording a magnificent view of the Atlantic.

The streets were very narrow, the balconies all painted green, many decorated with flowers. The streets were quiet, which the tired, travel-worn French took for peaceful, though there were a great many guards with helmets and pikes and muskets about.

Accompanied by men wearing the livery of Don Alejandro, the company was conducted to the theater, and pointed to their lodgings nearby. Completely unaware of the tensions between the recently formed Combined Fleet, M. Dupree and his flock assumed that the Spanish were as well disposed toward them as they had been in Seville.

The sea breeze, sweet-smelling as it ruffled over her damp face, prompted Anna to forgo the usual siesta, and to walk past the colorful booths in the marketplace on the narrow street below. She might venture all the way to the ocean.

"What are you about?" Parrette asked when Anna picked up her mantilla. "Are you not going to rest? You know the performance is to be this evening."

"I need fresh air, and movement. It will be infinitely more refreshing than another hot, stuffy room."

"Then I am coming with you. You cannot go alone," Parrette said in a scolding voice.

"I see women alone here and there. There is one directly below, carrying a basket of fish."

"Common women. And they live here. Besides, I want extra thread. Surely I will find some in one of those market stalls."

Parrette did not find her thread, but they did discover an amazing array of colorful lace, embroidered cloth, straw hats, boots, shoes, elaborate horse gear, and of course fans.

Anna carried out her plan of walking all the way to the point, where she stood gazing out at the forest of masts heaving gently in the bay. She loosened her mantilla, the better to feel the salty breeze carried over the water from the sea. So many ships! How it reminded her of Naples!

"Look at the sun," Parrette said suddenly, indicating the fiery ball sinking beyond the Point. "And the docks are filling with soldiers. We had better get back."

It was true. Patrols marching purposefully this way and that tramped along the docks and the wharf. The two women pulled their mantillas tightly about their faces and toiled hurriedly back up the hill to their lodgings.

It was a relief to shut the door; a tension she had hitherto been unaware of loosened the back of Anna's neck. She began humming her scales to warm up her voice as Parrette rearranged her hair and pulled out her costume.

The theater was small and beautifully appointed, built for a select audience. M. Dupree called, "Places!" for a quick run-through, no more than measuring the stage and warming their voices.

Anna turned toward her mark, startled as Therese stepped forward confidently at the same time.

M. Dupree looked at her under his brows. "Mademoiselle

Bernardo will sing Argia this evening," he said. "We will put forth our very best for our countrymen."

Therese bit her lip and flushed, for she had counted upon something very different. Then she smiled her false smile. "Here am I, always ready to do what I am asked!"

A short time after, Anna peered out from behind the theater's curtain at the rows of officers in their splendid coats, gold braid, and glittering orders. The audience seemed to flicker like the river waters. It was the constant, gentle movement of the ladies' fans.

"Which is Villeneuve?" someone whispered.

"There."

Anna directed her gaze back to the row of men in dark blue coats. She was not certain which was Admiral Villeneuve, Commander of the Combined Fleets, but she thought he might be the one in the center. He looked odd, as if someone had pushed in his eyes, or maybe that was the bruised color of exhaustion. His mouth seemed pinched.

Above and around him, the Spanish ship captains, dons all, wore coats of satin and silk in a dark blue nearly black, very different from the faded blue of the French, made even more glorious with sashes and orders proclaiming their ancient lineage. She became aware of two distinct currents in the quiet hubbub of conversation, Spanish and French. The lighter coats and the dark sat in knots, with little or no interweaving.

Then the orchestra struck up the overture, and everyone tiptoed hastily to their stage marks.

Among the French, Villeneuve, exhausted in mind and spirit, closed his eyes, his pleasure derived mostly from the French-accented Italian. It awakened his longing for home, though a home that was forever gone. Reality pressed in, memory of Bonaparte's latest dispatch, superseding all his previous orders. He had begun to dread each new arrival carrying the imperial seal: Bonaparte, though a genius upon land, knew nothing of the sea, and every new set of orders demanded yet a new impossibility.

The opera came to its end. As the applause died away, M. Dupree was called out. He accepted the thanks of the dons in his broken Spanish, and the audience got up to leave.

Villeneuve also rose, but gave in to impulse. He waved an aide to bring Dupree to him, and asked, "You are French?"

"But yes!" M. Dupree spread his hands, as if anyone could doubt.

"Will you come to our lodgings in the castle, and give us something French?" When he saw the doubt in M. Dupree's face he said quickly, "I care nothing for your stage settings. I long for the refreshment of my native tongue."

"We could give you *La Caverne*," M. Dupree said.

"*La Caverne*." Villeneuve shut his eyes. "Ah, one of my favorites. Yes. Please."

M. Dupree bowed as the admiral departed, then turned to Pierre and began issuing rapid orders. So absorbed was he that he was unaware of the surly expressions of the Spanish honor guard detailed to conduct the French naval officers back to their temporary lodgings.

However, several of the others noticed, and looked about, their reactions characteristic: Therese still irritated that she had not made her promotion to Argia permanent; Paul Bisset skeptical, Madame and Lorette uneasy, Ninon shrugging, and Jean-Baptiste with his expression shuttered. He listened to the rapid conversations as he walked away, his childhood grounding in Latin having aided him in grasping the Spanish language almost before anyone else, though as yet he had seen no reason to admit it.

He could see that all was not well between the supposed allies.

The next day, in a hall that had been cleared to accommodate the French commander, the company performed *La Caverne* to the gathered French officers and a few favored guests. Afterward, the entire company was invited to a repast.

The air filled with French conversation. The emperor—the beautiful empress—Paris—all passed under review, no detail too exhausting, as often happens among people a long away from home.

Drink flowed freely, and presently, Villeneuve, still oppressed by Napoleon's latest impossible orders in spite of the glasses of excellent *tempranillo* he consumed, was approached by one of the opera singers, a man whose carriage and accents did not quite hide his aristocratic origins. "I perform under the name Jean-Baptiste Marsac," he said, and Villeneuve knew he had surmised correctly.

Villeneuve was glad to be diverted from his worries. They spoke of wine, each appreciating the other's knowledge, but when Marsac was reaching to refill their glasses, Villeneuve sighed. "I ought not. Tomorrow I must carry out an inspection, and it will be even less agreeable with an aching head."

"Your ships, they are in readiness?" Marsac asked.

"The Combined Fleet is neither combined nor ready," Villeneuve said bitterly, to the empty glass in his hands. "We cannot careen the bottoms, which are still full of seaweed from the West Indies. Some have no extra sailcloth. Others suffer rotting futtocks, and we cannot get replacement timber. Even the dons have had trouble, although their king has just given them a letter of credit. Will that do *us* any good? No."

He looked up, trying to blink the glaring halo away from the lanterns. He spoke bitterly, quickly, anything to get away from the danger of mentioning Bonaparte's name. "The worst of it is these dons have little interest in this war. The wharves are alive with English spies, more numerous than the rats, but the Spaniards don't do anything about them. They are too busy brigging my own seamen, who merely show their resentment of the murder of their mates by these Spanish dogs."

"English spies?" Jean-Baptiste repeated.

"Everywhere. The English have been blockading for years. I am convinced they know every cove and inlet better than the dons, and they land their devils by the hundreds. If I could but catch one, no doubt I would obtain a better list of our weaknesses than I will ever get marching around on inspection, where every captain strives to hide the worst."

Marsac had entered the conversation in hopes of sounding the French admiral about the possibility of a letter of introduction to Bonaparte, but the mention of spies prompted a malicious impulse. "One of our company is secretly married to one of your English captains," he said with a confiding air.

Villeneuve sat upright. "What?"

It was only an idle impulse, but the commander's reaction, his searching gaze and angry tone, made Jean-Baptiste almost wish he had not spoken. Almost. "One of the women. You heard her sing this very evening—she calls herself Anna Bernardo, though I have no notion what might be her real name. Married to an English sea-captain, though she keeps it to herself."

"How does she communicate with him?" Villeneuve asked, frowning so terribly that Marsac sat back.

"I don't know."

"A woman." Villeneuve sighed the word. "No one would suspect. A million devils! I will talk to this woman," he promised, his fury finding outlet at last.

Jean-Baptiste shrugged. He knew very well that Anna Bernardo was no spy. But she was a smug little coquette with her preposterous *honor my vows*. Let her get a little fright. It would do her good.

Fourteen

EVER SINCE THEIR ARRIVAL in Spain, after each performance Anna had begun drinking a glass of wine mixed with water. Consequently she was just finishing, as Parrette shook out a gown to air for the morrow, when they heard the rhythmic clump and clatter of a patrol marching along the tiled hall beyond their door.

Parrette started, her mind going back to those terrible days in Lyons, then she snapped the gown out, mentally scolding herself as she waited for the patrol to pass.

But the footsteps stopped directly outside their door. Anna and Parrette stared at each other, each about to speak, when a gauntleted fist rapped heavily.

Parrette whisked the gown into its trunk, then opened the door.

"Where is Madame Bernardo?"

"Here." Anna set aside her wine glass and rose to her feet.

A thin young officer in an ill-fitting uniform stood stiffly, blocking the doorway. He said in wretched French, "You must with me come."

Parrette backed away, aghast. This was like the revolution all over again: one day life is as normal, the next day the unthinkable occurs. That mighty hilltop castle that they had seen all the way from the causeway had looked from afar like a Spanish Bastille.

"Why?" she asked, standing in front of Anna.

"Espionage," said the young officer.

Anna gazed witlessly. "Impossible!" Parrette tried to block the pike-bearing men who tramped inside the little room. "You cannot! You must speak to M. Dupree—he will tell you that is absurd."

"I am a performer," Anna said. "For whom would I spy?"

The men ignored Parrette, one handing her off impatiently. The other took hold of Anna's arm.

"I will go with you," Parrette said fiercely.

"The immediate orders only concern la Senora," the officer said stiffly. He had no relish for arresting a terrified young lady, or her protective maid. "Wait here."

The patrol closed around Anna, who nipped up her mantilla from its hook by the door, and swung it around her head so that at least it obscured her face. It was bad enough to be arrested, but to be stared at compounded the horror.

And she was. Through the filtering of the lace, she saw faces peering between cracked doors, and through shutters as they wound down the beautifully patterned tile steps, across the private plaza, and then through the gates into the city.

She was not marched up to that forbidding fortress of Santa Catalina, but down a narrow road to the building where earlier she had sung so light-heartedly. They rounded the great hall, going up a narrow stairway to a series of offices under the guns of fortress.

Here, Anna was locked into a room bare of anything but a bench. One of the patrol left a lantern sitting on the deep inset window sill before he went out, and she heard the clink of a padlock.

She sat down to wait, her heart beating rapidly. Her tiredness had vanished. Endlessly her mind insisted on repeating questions she could not possibly answer, and what she ought to say, around and around and around. Her head panged; finally she leaned it back against the stone wall and shut her eyes.

She began to doze fitfully, waking with a start when a key rattled in the lock.

The lantern had burned out. The door swung open, candlelight flaring, the shadows dancing crazily over the wall in elongated distortions as a group of men entered. Her eyes widened when she recognized the one in the center: none other than Commander Villeneuve, still in his blue uniform coat with gold-embroidered sleeves, though he had removed the sash and the medals.

An aide set a chair facing Anna's bench, and he sat down, hands on his knees, and stared at Anna from under furrowed brows. His eyes were narrow, with dark circles under them. Guards took up stances on either side of him, and farther away, an ensign sat with a lap desk, another aide holding a lantern over his head. The ensign began writing, his pen scratching. Then he looked up enquiringly.

Admiral Villeneuve nodded shortly. "Madame, please state your name."

"Anna Maria Ludovisi," Anna said. Then she remembered the 'Duncannon,' but gave her head a tiny shake. It had no meaning.

Villeneuve leaned forward, his elbows jutting out. "You say 'Maria' the English way. Murr—*eye*—ah." He growled the 'r' sound deep in his throat in his exaggerated pronunciation. But it was recognizably the English pronunciation.

"My mother was English," Anna said. "She said that was her own mother's name. My papa's mother was Anna Elisabetta, which accounts for my first name…" She was aware she was talking too much and stopped abruptly.

"They said you claimed Bernardo as your name."

"It was my performance name. Italian singers are popular, these days. In the way of La Catalani."

"Who is Italian," Villeneuve observed, and then, with an edge of sarcasm, "Mrs. Billington did not see fit to alter her name. And yet she has managed to be successful."

Anna was frightened again, but she was also aware of impatience. The situation was entirely mad. "My patroness, Madame de Pipelet—a Frenchwoman—thought it best. 'Bernardo' being from Ponte San Bernardo, my father's birthplace. His cousin is the duke."

Villeneuve lifted the back of his hand to Ponte San Bernardo and its duke, a quick, violent gesture that made her jump. "I have spent most of this night questioning this company of yours. It seems you have forgotten to mention your marriage *to an English sea captain.*"

Anna sat upright. "How did you—" She let out her breath in a sharp sigh. "It is true. But I never think of him. I have not seen him for more than five years."

"How do you communicate with him?"

"I don't. Oh, I wrote before I left Naples, but I never received an answer."

"Naples?" Villeneuve repeated. "Five or six years ago…that would be when Nelson was marauding all over southern Italy. You are married to one of Nelson's captains?"

"It was an arranged marriage," she protested. "We saw one another exactly twice, and never again."

"Twice, and never again," he repeated, "and yet you stayed faithful, honoring your vows? I must request you do *me* the honor of not assuming I am stupid."

"Honoring my vows," Anna repeated, flushing in anger. "You can only have got that from Jean-Baptiste Marsac, who made me a dishonorable offer. In refusing, I said those very words. It must be spite. I cannot imagine why he would even tell you!"

Villeneuve let out his breath in a sharp, hissing sigh. "Your maid refused to speak to us, and we have her locked up elsewhere for further questioning, if need demands. Three others of your company all attested to the fact that you are married to an English sea captain. They also said," and he touched his fingers on each point. "You came to the company in Paris, where you consorted with soldiers. Then you traveled with the company to the north coast, the west coast. The south coast. And all over Spain, the kingdom of our allies. For an innocent singer, you seem to have happened most extraordinarily upon all the sites about which Nelson and his friends in London would desire most to gain firsthand reports."

"But I never—"

Another finger. "I am not finished! In each of these places, you and this maid of yours sought newspapers. It was not in French that you spoke to one another. Sometimes English, sometimes Italian. The maid was seen on the north coast questioning mariners, and again on France's coast. They said you walked out to inspect the garrisons of every Spanish city you visited."

"I did not." Anna spread her hands in appeal. "I visited

164

cathedrals, and castles, and marketplaces. Why would I go to a garrison?"

"To inspect the strength of our allies," he retorted. "And yesterday you and your maid, upon arrival, walked directly to the wharf to spy on our fleet. Do not deny it—you were seen by my own men!"

"I walked down to breathe the fresh air," Anna began.

Villeneuve raised his hand to stop her. With his other, he pinched his fingers between his brows. "In a very few hours, I must inspect the fleet. That cannot wait. We will question you later, as vigorously as is necessary. I am very sorry to have to say it. Making war upon women turns my stomach; it is perhaps as well that Minister Fouché is not here, for he would, from all accounts, enjoy nothing better. But I will do my best," he promised heavily as he rose to his feet. "Because it is my duty, and the devil knows we are hard put enough as it is. As you no doubt saw on your tour along the wharf. *Bon soir*, Madame Sea-Captain."

The last word was spoken with heavy irony, and the door shut behind him, leaving her in the darkness. Anna stared in the direction of his empty chair, for a time too sick and too numb to react.

Exhaustion caused her to doze fitfully until the crick in the angle of her neck, and her dry mouth, woke her. Pale light, the color of dirty milk, emanated from two tiny windows set up high on either side of the cell's door. Through them light filtered, enough to reveal dirty stone. In the corner was a bucket, not even decently covered. Against the far wall, unseen until now, was a narrow cot covered with what looked like rotten sailcloth. Anna shuddered, her gaze wandering past to the three-legged stool at the cot's foot, on which sat a cannikin. She got up and looked into it. She smelled water.

She tasted it cautiously. It was stale, but no more than one got in most inns, and tasted slightly metallic from sitting in the can, but she knew good well water when she met with it.

Anna drank half, forcing herself to ration it. Who knew when she might get any more.

She returned to the bench, her arms wrapped around herself tightly. Tears burned, but she would not let them fall. She had done nothing wrong. She had to find a way to convince the admiral, and letting herself weep and wail would not help her to think.

But her mind revolved in circles, impelled by questions she could not answer. Gradually she became aware of occasional puffs of air through the tiny grated windows, and she closed her eyes, trying to imagine the endless sky as seen the day before, the seabirds diving and cawing, the restless green waters.

Now the dancers will be warming their limbs, she thought, and she got to her feet. First stealthily, jerkily, she began the well-known patterns, and soon found a small measure of comfort in the movements. She did not have to think. She stretched and arched and danced, aware of the kinks and tweaks smoothing away.

At the end she stood in the middle of the room, her throat aching. Now she would have been warming her voice with scales. She found middle C, and discovered it was comforting to sing her scales softly, almost under her breath. When she had finished, her throat was ready, and her blood pulsed through her veins. Sorrow flooded her heart, overflowing into song.

Berenise's "Da Torbida Procella" poured forth as she sang down mighty Pharaoh.

She sang aria after aria, songs of sacrifice, loss, and passion.

She had finished Gluck's "Je t'implore" from *Iphigenie en Tauride* and was beginning Purcell's anguished "When I am Laid in Earth" from *Dido and Aeneas* when once again she heard the rhythmic tramp of feet.

She flung herself back on the bench, her breath held in terror. Again, the patrol halted directly outside her door. It was unlocked, and to her amazement, the soldiers were not in the blue of France, but white and gold, the livery of one of the dons.

"Senora," spoke a tall officer with a ferocious mustachio. "By the orders of Admiral Federico Carlos Gravina y Nápoli, you are to be conducted to the Castillo de Santa Catalina."

And so it was the fortress after all.

Blinking back tears, Anna pulled on her mantilla and stepped out, and stared not over the ocean, as she had imagined, but down into a plaza alive with seamen and officers and guards. Most of them were motionless, faces upturned as they gazed at her. She looked away, glad of the relative shrouding of the mantilla as she followed two tall guards, one bony, one stout, their necks brown from the sun below the polished edges of their helmets.

When they reached the end of the gallery and turned through a gate, she glanced up in trepidation at the fortress with its jutting points overlooking the bay. The massive honey-colored stone building shouldered above her menacingly.

The patrol escorted her up a narrow switchback that gradually widened, until they passed through iron-reinforced gates, under ugly cannon jutting between the castellations.

They crossed a vast parade ground as the smell of stables wafted on the cool breeze, and into the stone building. Anna clasped her hands tightly, terrified. But the patrol did not march her down into a noisome dungeon. Once again they climbed tiled stairs.

Up and up, until at last they stopped outside a thick double door beautifully carved with biblical scenes. The guards in white and gold at either side stood stiffly, as one of her guards opened the door.

The mustached officer lifted his hand to indicate she must go inside. Anna's knees trembled as she stepped tentatively in a beautiful room with whitewashed walls, a brilliant rug covering the floor and fine carved chairs and benches arranged around a table with curved legs ending in lion's feet. An enormous epergne of silver sat upon it, framed by solid silver candelabra. An intricately wrought crucifix hung on one wall, and on the others gold-framed paintings of men in stiff, jewel-encrusted armor and sashes, either mounted on rearing horses, or standing in what appeared to be marble rooms, surrounded by the accoutrements of war.

At the other end of the room a second, even finer table had been set, behind which sat a swarthy, handsome man wearing a tightly fitted black coat with crimson lapels embroidered in gold, and a crimson sash. His epaulettes looked to be made of real gold. Over the front of his splendid coat extended a green and white silk sash, and on his breast a great medal whose diamonds reflected light from the open east windows. The reflections caught the streaming sunlight and threw rainbow splashes against the white walls.

The young officer clicked his heels and announced in a hieratic voice, "His Excellency, Don Federico Carlos Gravina y Nápoli, Admiral of the Spanish Fleet. Senora Duncannon."

"Thank you, Captain. You may withdraw," the admiral said in the lisping Spanish of the don.

When the door had shut, a pair of narrow dark eyes searched Anna's face, then the admiral spoke in Neapolitan. "I understand that we are countrymen?"

Anna was so startled to hear Neapolitan she gazed witlessly for a heartbeat or two. Belatedly she remembered her curtsey, and performed it with grace. When she rose, she thought she detected a slight easing, almost a smile in the hard face before her.

"Your Excellency," Anna said. "I am not a spy. I do not know how this comes about."

"It appears to originate in the surprising fact that a young Neapolitan lady, living in France, appears to have somehow annexed an English sea captain as a husband. Before we proceed to recent events, you might tell me how this came about?"

Anna bit her lip, and decided that half-truths were worse than useless. And she would scorn to lie. "Well, the origins begin in political affairs in Naples. Your Excellency is surely familiar with those?"

"I left Naples as a lad of twelve, but consider me tolerably well informed."

"I did not quite understand it at the time, but rebels having taken Naples and proclaimed a republic, my father's man knew many of the ringleaders..."

Out it all came, including Anna's own lack of awareness of what her father had traded in order to gain Anna a place, exactly as Parrette had later related.

She finished, "...and so my father was *not* a spy. But Beppe had heard this information through his friends among the *lazarones*, and my father only sought to see me established, since there was no one else. My mother being dead."

Admiral Gravina said suavely, "I am sorry to hear that. God rest her soul."

Uncertainly, Anna went on. "There is little more to tell. I was married to Captain Duncannon, who I subsequently saw exactly once, after a fete, and then never again. The English fleet sailed away, and when Sir William and Lady Hamilton departed Naples, I was left to my own devices. Maestro Paisiello—"

"A great man, a very great man," the admiral interrupted, the first real expression she had seen from him. "I myself have traveled great distances to hear his work."

"Yes, he is! He gave me an introduction to a lady in Paris, a great patron of female musicians and singers. When Madame de Pipelet remarried and quit Paris, I was hired into Company Dupree, and I have been with them ever since. That is the truth."

"And yet you do not explain your maid questioning mariners on the north coast, and so forth? Or did your company all tell lies?"

"There were no lies. But misunderstandings, yes." And Anna told the admiral about Michel Duflot, ending with, "So you see, with revolutionary feelings being so against the English, we thought it best never to mention Michel. But we always hoped to find word of his ship, at least."

The admiral moved a diamond-handled gold letter opener from left to right upon his desk, placing it as if getting the correct angle was of monumental importance, then he looked up. "My men have been calling you the angel of sorrow."

"I don't understand, Your Excellency," Anna said.

"Your singing," he replied, lifting a hand toward the window. "Perhaps it was not intentional? They could hear you through the grating in what was actually a winter pen for donkeys. We had to clear those cells out for the French, as we are very pressed for space. My prison," he added with a faint tone of irony, "being crowded with unruly and outright criminals who call themselves French sailors. But you must have observed these troubles between what are supposed to be allies."

"I truly didn't," Anna said unhappily. "That is, I might have if someone pointed it out, but I was not looking at sailors and the like. I wanted to see the sea and the sky, my first glimpse of the great Atlantic. It has been so very hot, much hotter than it ever is in Paris. I don't know how to convince you or Admiral Villeneuve that I am not a spy."

"Then you probably do not know that until fairly recently, I was in fact an ally of the English," the admiral went on.

Not certain how to respond, Anna made a little gesture, half of appeal, then dropped a quick curtsey again—long-inculcated habit from her days in the royal palace, when curtseying and dropping one's gaze was often the safest answer.

He observed her bewilderment, the unhappy quirk to her brows, and went on, watching carefully, "I spent time in England studying their methods of maritime warfare, and I was honored to serve alongside Admiral Lord Samuel Hood at the siege of Toulon."

From all the reaction Anna made to 'the siege of Toulon' he might as well have been discussing events at the Antipodes. He made his decision; she was only aware of his continued irony as he said, "But our Prince of the Peace decided that Spain must throw in with the French republic, specifically with the new Emperor of the French, and so..." He lifted the letter opener. Light gleamed along the golden blade. "I am placed under the command of Admiral Villeneuve by royal decree."

Anna curtseyed again.

"I am not without sympathy for the admiral. Both fleets are, let us say, in dire need of many specifics. Admittedly the harbor is rife with spies, many of them former friends of warrant officers, traders, and seamen. They talk in their cups. The English, though standing well to the south, seem to know everything there is to know about our movements. Consequently my esteemed colleague's rage is, perhaps, if no more pardonable, at least understandable, when he is presented with an apparent spy."

Anna's dismay and perplexity were so plain that the admiral set the letter opener down and reached for a tiny silver bell that tingled sweetly.

The door opened at once, and the admiral rose, speaking in Spanish once again. "Madame, I beg of you, permit the captain to conduct you to quarters I have specified. Admiral Villeneuve has been informed of the change of venue; perhaps he will be relieved to regain badly needed space." Admiral Gravina bowed slightly.

Anna understood that the interview was over. Further protest was useless. She curtseyed again and followed the captain out.

Instead of going downstairs to some dungeon, they proceeded

along a tiled hallway to a wing on the far side of the command quarters. Here they came to a plain wooden door, which was opened by an armed guard stationed there.

The captain bowed slightly, and Anna passed inside an airy room with two broad windows. The whitewashed walls were bare except for the expected crucifix, and opposite that, a picture of a woman in a stiff gown with a ruff and a pearl headdress on another. A rug of blues and golds lay on the floor, on which was set chairs and a table, with fine candlesticks on it.

There was a door on the other side. As the entry door was shut and locked behind her, the inner door opened—and there was Parrette!

"Oh, I am so glad to see you. The French admiral said they questioned you," Anna burst out.

"And so they did. But I refused to tell them anything. The very idea. Spies! Whom would we spy for? I demanded to know who accused us of such a thing, but they would not tell me. However, an orderly did say they would bring us something to eat," she said, drawing Anna into a bedroom with two smaller rooms off it.

At one side stood a monumental bed upon a platform, with a canopy over it fit for a queen. On the other side, a narrow alcove gave way to a garderobe, decently closed off. Anna recognized her trunk against the inner wall. "And hot water to bathe in is on the way," Parrette finished with triumph, as if restored amenities also restored order to the world.

Anna quickly related the gist of her interview with Admiral Gravina, then said thoughtfully, "There was no one writing our words down. I wonder if that was a good thing or not."

"I would not dare a guess," Parrette answered. "But this much I've learned, mostly through overheard curses and slanders, the French are not very popular in Cadiz. Ah. That must be our tray." The sound of the salon door unlocking caused her to cock her head. "Come. Eat and drink something. Then I will repack our trunks. Who knows what these men will be at next. Whatever it is, we ought to be ready."

Anna slept through the rest of that day, clean, fed, and resting in a comfortable bed. The next day, she rose betimes. She had finished her dance stretches before the sun came up. Then she prowled the salon and discovered an ancient trunk in a corner, the carvings on it peopled with women in high coned hats and long trailing gowns, the men in short tunics, with hose on their legs and odd pointed shoes with the tips tied back to their ankles in what looked like chains.

She opened the trunk, and caught her breath in pleasure: books! She had not been able to read since her long-ago days with Madame de Pipelet in Paris.

Many of the books were in Spanish or Latin, with fragile leather covers. But she found a small stack of newer French novels, and even more amazing, three in English: a book of Pope's poems, a novel by Samuel Richardson, and a book of travels by Daniel Defoe.

The novel by Richardson, tied up with tape, was a seven volume production in octavo. Anna opened it first.

Clarissa was slow going initially. Anna had not thought in English for so long that she struggled to recall the meanings of words. She set it aside frequently, resorting to either the poems or entries in the travel book, but she discovered that rereading sentences, or trying them out loud, sometimes shook loose the meanings that had been buried in memory.

Gradually the humor was borne in upon her, and she began to read with more pleasure, thoroughly hating the arrogant, presumptuous Lovelace, though admittedly he wrote with wit. All of the characters spoke in a style that strongly brought Anna's mother to mind—she heard Clarissa's letters read in her mother's voice—and so the hours, and then days passed, broken only by meals, and by Parrette being permitted to attend Mass, accompanied by one of Admiral Gravina's guards.

That Sunday, Parrette returned with an air of excitement. As soon as they were alone, she said in a whisper, "You will never guess what I have learned."

"Come into the bedroom," Anna said, casting a doubtful look at that wooden door, beyond which stood an armed guard.

Parrette led the way to the bedroom, her eyes wide. "Hah! I

met Pierre at the early Mass. As Madame and some of the others go to the later one, he was free to talk to me, to say farewell. The Company Dupree is ordered to leave on the morrow. The Spanish have said that there is no place for French actors here."

"They are leaving? Without us?" Anna asked.

Parrette spread her hands.

"But what about my earnings?" Anna asked.

Parrette uttered a back-street imprecation that shocked Anna. "There are no earnings. That is, Therese Rose offered to bring them to you a few days ago, Pierre said. She said she had obtained permission to speak to you."

"But I never saw her."

"Well do I know! She never returned to the lodging. And that is not all. It was none other than that devil's spawn Marsac who said you were a spy."

"So I thought," Anna said. "What I don't know is why."

"Helene told Madame Dupree, who told Pierre that at the special performance for the French officers, it was noticed that Marsac remained behind, talking to Admiral Villeneuve, then la la! A short time later, they were all swept up for questioning, not just us. But they were kept in the large room, and let go one by one when the questioners had done with them. Pierre begged me to tell you that Helene, Ninon, and the others were very sorry, that if they had thought, they never would have said as much as they did. They thought their recollections would prove your innocence, for none of them believed you were a spy."

Sickened, Anna briefly described the offer Marsac had made.

"I wish you had told me," Parrette said fiercely. "No, no, of course I could do nothing. Say nothing. About that. But I always hated him. He was the worst kind of aristocrat, born well, but hiding behind republican words to escape the mobs, and profiting thereby. Yet whenever he deigned to take notice of me, it was to drop his sewing in my lap, as if I existed only to serve. Even little Helene asked me with politeness when she needed something delicate mended."

"I never noticed that," Anna said, unsettled.

"His habit was to bring his ruined things to me in the mornings, when you were dancing. Not that it was often. He is very careful with his things. It was his manner, and I saw no reason to mention it. You could do nothing. But!" A valedictory finger. "There is a hint of justice, for M. Dupree turned him away. He said that after such a thing, no one would trust him again, and so he could seek another company. And so he left, some thought for Paris. But after, it was noticed that he had taken more than his own trunks—you remember, he had three. That of Therese Rose was also gone, they saw, after she did not reappear from her supposed visit to us."

Anna shook her head. "She always admired him. Or he could have threatened to turn her over to the French as a runaway." She told Parrette what Marsac had discovered. "Though he despised her, I could see him using her for his own convenience."

"Despicable! She will get what she deserves, and as for him, I pray that he gets snapped up by the conscript officers," Parrette said. *"Spies.* Tchah!"

She jabbed her needle vigorously into cloth, indicating the subject was closed.

At the month's end, Parrette returned from Mass with astonishing news: "Everyone at the cathedral was whispering that Nelson has arrived, and joined the English fleet."

"I wonder what that means," Anna murmured.

"If it is even true, who knows?" Parrette opened her hands. "What it means for us, that remains to be seen," she finished on a dire note.

Later that night, as they went about getting ready for bed, they were surprised by a quiet but insistent knock upon their door. Anna entered the salon as the door opened, and the young captain with the mustachios performed a quick bow. "Gather your wraps, please, ladies. You are to be transferred."

"To where?" Anna asked nervously.

There was no answer. The captain silently directed a couple of burly men to the inside, where they fetched the trunks that Parrette had kept packed and ready.

Then they wrapped themselves in their cloaks, and out they

walked into night air that had become surprisingly brisk. Excitement warred with spurts of horror: at every turn Anna dreaded a dank entry to a dungeon, or worse, French soldiers sent to take them back into custody for that promised hard questioning.

But they bypassed all these, instead twisting down back stairs at a dizzying speed, until Parrette was breathing hard, and Anna's leg muscled twinged, in spite of all her dance.

At last they were led through a gate past silent guards, their eyes gleaming in the lantern light. The smell of brine was sharp: they had reached the seaside!

The lanterns were doused. A cluster of dark figures, barely discernable against the endless black of the ocean, turned their way. In a low, rapid voice the captain held a quick exchange, and then he said, "God go with you, senoras."

One of those shrouded figures drew near, and a hand took Anna's arm. She pulled back with a breathless cry.

"Shush now," came a voice — speaking English. "We'm here to fetch ye, on the admiral's orders, but quiet like, or there'll be the devil to pay with Johnny Crapaud."

"I—" Anna moistened her lips, trying to think in English. "I do not understand."

"He'll explain it all anon. Come away cheerly."

The hand tugged insistently, but not harshly. Anna hesitated. If she screamed, would the French or Spanish hear?

"Bear a hand, mates, every second them frogs could happen on us, and they'm likely to shoot first."

Anna had to agree. She and Parrette were escorted by two burly figures to a waiting boat, and motioned to a central bench, where they sat shoulder to shoulder, both shivering, as men climbed in around them to take up oars. Their trunks thumped softly in at either end. Three figures shoved at the boat with soft grunts of effort, causing it to hiss over wet sand, then bump into the low breakers inside the bay.

As Anna watched, slow-marching clouds briefly revealed the moon, faint and silvery, shedding blue light over the world. The sense they had entered a dream ended abruptly when the boat reached the breakers, jolting horribly. Water splashed in, swirling coldly about their slippered feet, but neither made a sound.

"Stout 'uns," a quiet voice whispered approvingly. "Not a peep, now. We're all a-taunto, though she's going to skip about a trifle. Just bide tight."

Anna could barely understand the man's accent, and Parrette could not make out more than two words. They pressed together, glad of each other's presence, as the boat juddered from one wave to another, propelled in surges by the rhythmic movement of the oars.

One thing was clear: for whatever reason, they were about to be handed over to the English. *Well, there is one thing I can do,* Anna thought, and reached behind her. Not two feet away was the familiar contours of her trunk. She worked the latches loose, wormed her fingers inside it, as Parrette looked on wonderingly, her face pale in the moonlight.

At last Anna encountered her trinket box, and let out a satisfied "Ah." She withdrew her hand, refastened the latches, and brought her fingers around to the front.

Parrette's expression altered when she saw Anna slide something onto her ring finger. "It was Admiral Nelson who got me into this situation," Anna whispered in Neapolitan. "I fully intend that he shall get me out again."

"And then?" Parrette asked.

"And then they must set us down somewhere, well away from their war, I trust, and we will figure out where to go next," Anna breathed, though she had no idea.

But it would come. Her earnings were lost, but she had her belongings, her wits, and her talent.

After an eternity of rowing, there was an indistinct mutter from someone at the back of the boat. At once two or three figures moved, rocking them alarmingly. Anna and Parrette clutched each other as these men did something at the bottom, sending splashes of brine everywhere, then raised a pole with a sodden mass of sailcloth attached.

"Duck down, now, so the yard don't take you over the side."

Anna and Parrette bent over obediently, as with a muffled rumble and then a snap, the sail caught the wind and bellied out. The boat lifted and plunged, dashing through the waves. Spray splashed liberally over them all.

Anna straightened up slowly, and dared a look behind her. High overhead, a gleaming row of lights marked the impressive fortress. They had come a considerable distance already. Beyond the point, a part of the bay curved, the lights of Cadiz winking like a necklace of glowing gold.

Anna had begun to doze while sitting up, until a voice startled her. The command was incomprehensible, but clearly there was no longer any fear of being heard. She straightened up, surprised to find a ship towering a few yards away, ruddy light from square spaces along the hull glinting off the cold iron mouths of cannon.

"Bosun's chair abaft your elbow, mum," someone said, touching Anna.

Once again, rough-palmed hands took her arm insistently, turning her toward a canvas arrangement suspended between ropes.

She discovered to her horror that she was expected to sit in it. "Oh, no."

"Just clap onto them ropes, now, and hold tight. We'll boom you up in a trice."

Strong hands pulled her inexorably into the contraption, whose slimy ropes she gripped with all her strength. Her body swayed sickeningly in the air, then hands closed around her arms again, and she let out a shuddering breath of relief. She opened her eyes to discover a deck under her feet. Relief suffused her as she let the slimy rope free. She did not want to wipe her hands on her gown, so she stood there, fingers spread like starfish, as she looked around dazedly.

Then the figures around her parted, hands to forelocks, and here and there the lifting of enormous cocked hats as a tall figure approached.

The swinging lantern light revealed a remembered hawk-nosed face staring grimly down at her.

It was Captain Duncannon.

Fifteen

THAT MORNING, HENRY DUNCANNON had received the signal to report aboard the flagship, where Nelson received him, handing off a note sent by the Spaniards under flag of truce:

> *My Lord Nelson, I make myself the honor to inform you I have*
> *in the company here subsequent to the musicale fete the lady*
> *wife of Captain-of-warship Duncannon, I am given to*
> *comprehend is honored to number amongst the English fleet.*
> *Due to the unfortunate nature of events we are to transpire I*
> *take the liberty to offer to restore the lady to the captain with the*
> *good will of you.*
>
> *Your very obedient servant to command...*

Shortly thereafter Duncannon had been ordered to part company with the squadron of frigates watching Cadiz from a distance, to dispatch his trusted coxswain directly under the guns of the enemy.

Now here was his longboat returned with a problem he'd thought lost years ago.

The first one over the rail was set down. He took in a French lady, elegant from her ordered curls to the hem of the fashionable gown whose style was scarcely marred by wrinkles and splashes of sea water. He forced his gaze away, searching for the blotch-faced little weed he had been forced to marry six years ago. But the next one over the side was a scrawny, needle-nosed French maid-servant. Strange, how so many of these southern French looked a bit like birds, with their beaky noses and scrawny arms and legs.

The next object boomed up was a trunk, followed by a second — and then the sailors began the process of bringing up the longboat. No more passengers? Had their scouts managed to find the wrong women?

He discovered he had nearly crushed his best scraper under his arm, and consciously loosened his grip as he brought his gaze back from trunks to maid to lady. Was she familiar? He took a step toward her, trying to find in that elegant countenance any sign of the wretched girl he'd so briefly seen only twice.

Wind-tousled curls blew about a heart-shaped face in which a pair of wide brown eyes stared back at him. The sodden gown revealed a graceful form. Stepping past his first lieutenant, he saw her stiffly spread fingers. The light from the binnacle gleamed on a ring he remembered sliding onto a thin finger.

He swallowed, and took in that wide gaze. It, too, was familiar, from that hot summer's night on the terrace after Nelson's fete when she begged him to locate Michel Duflot.

Aware of every single pair of eyes aboard the ship, he extended his hand. "Madame. Welcome aboard the *Aglaea*."

"Captain." She did not say *capitaine*, but she might as well have: her accent was decidedly French. She dropped a curtsey, and then staggered as the ship gave a lee lurch.

He sprang to take her arm; her muscles were rigid. Anger or fear? Could they possibly be more awkwardly situated? He forced himself to smile, and to say as pleasantly as he knew now, "Permit me to conduct you to the cabin, where my steward will make you comfortable. Is that all your dunnage?"

"*Dommage?*" she repeated, looking round-eyed with worry. Her pupils were huge and black; it was impossible to see the color of her eyes.

"*Dommage?*" he repeated. What did that even mean? His French, never great at the best of times, had completely escaped him. From her expression, it meant something terrible. "Your traps. Trunks? Yes." Acutely aware of the avid interest of his midshipmen, a parcel of pranksters unless strictly governed, he shut his mouth against saying anything further to entertain the ship's company, and led her down into the cabin.

Anna was aware of two things: the horrible way the ship lurched around her, sometimes shifting between one step and another. In a way, it was worse than the little boat, for the movement was slower, making her feel a little dizzy.

The second thing was the grip of that hand on her arm, fingers cupped firmly under her elbow. She would have fallen into these oddly curved walls but for that hand. She tried to grasp the fact that he was still alive. So he *had* survived that mutiny!

The captain led her into a spacious suite whose floor appeared to be a tacked-down canvas covered with white and black checkers.

She blinked, the salt crusting her eyelashes stinging unmercifully. She tried to make out the proportions of the rooms, but the movement and the blur masked the unexplained odd shapes, defeating her.

There appeared to be a suite of small, oddly-shaped chambers. The one she was conducted to had two broad, inward-leaning windows that opened directly over the sea. Dominating the space swung an odd-looking bed, shaped like a candy box, suspended from ropes. Its sides appeared to be made of canvas. A bench lined the back of the room under the windows.

She sat on the bench, shivering in her heavy, wet clothing, as Parrette narrowly watched the sailors stow the trunks between two curving pilasters. They departed under the direction of a grizzled man with one sound leg and one that appeared to be made of wood from the knee down.

"We'll have hot water up in three shakes," this man said to Parrette, his accent so thick that she gazed back uncomprehendingly.

The man then touched his forehead and withdrew, his uneven *thok*-step, *thok*-step nimbler than either Parrette or Anna with two sound legs apiece.

Duncannon appeared in the doorway, and cleared his throat. "This is my sleeping cabin. You shall have it. I will take the after-cabin beyond these bulkheads." He nodded at the curving wood projections that Anna had taken for pilasters. "Are you hungry? Thirsty?"

"I would welcome some water, thank you," she said, enunciating carefully. He, at least, spoke clearly.

"May I suggest tea in its place?" he asked. "I fear that our water is casked, and if you are unaccustomed, it can be disagreeable."

She remembered her mother's tea from her childhood; to Duncannon, her shuttered expression turned wistful before her eyelashes lowered. "Yes. Thank you."

"Perkins, my steward, will see to it. I must get back on deck to oversee our return to station. If you require anything, Perkins will fetch it for you."

He bowed again, and left, aware of his cowardly retreat. He knew that Nelson would eventually be signaling for a report, at the least, but he trusted to the thousand greater demands on the admiral's attention. He could not seem to think past the shock of seeing her again, and finding her so different from the girl he'd so briefly glimpsed in Palermo and Naples. Gratefully he lost himself in a swift flow of orders.

For Anna, sitting uncomfortably in the cabin, there was nothing but questions no one could answer until the welcome arrival of the tea. Anna drank it down gratefully, and discovered a secondary effect of the beverage. It eased the unpleasant sensations in her middle caused by the continual pitching of the ship.

She had finished a second cup when the hot water arrived, great canisters carried by sweating mariners under the direction of a blushing midshipman. The moment they were gone, Parrette held the door open to get rid of the lurking steward, and on his egress, smartly shut the flimsy door. Then she marched around the cabin pulling the stern windows firmly shut, and the curtains drawn, as Anna regarded the gently steaming water.

"Now, you tidy yourself while I brush that hanging bed. I am tempted to use our own sheets, though in truth this oddly shaped room seems very clean," Parrette said.

There was a single pier glass suspended at a slant between two of what the captain had called bulkheads. In the light of the swinging lamps, Anna was startled to see how dirty and bedraggled she had become. With a brief resurgence of energy, she shed her grimy, stained gown and washed thoroughly, then brushed out her tangled hair. By now she seemed to be sinking under waves of exhaustion, but she was afraid to wear a nightdress. The captain might return.

"You put that nightrail on, and climb into that...object," Parrette said. "You are going to need your wits about you come morning. I will sit up a bit longer, to make certain you are not disturbed."

Though it took some effort, Anna figured out how to mount the swinging canvas bed. It smelled odd, like canvas, and under that a masculine scent that was not unpleasant.

"Now, tomorrow, you must be the great lady," Parrette said.

Anna shook her head. "Tomorrow, I expect I will need to convince Captain Duncannon that I am no spy, before we even get to whether I lowered myself to earning a wage. At all events..." Anna yawned fiercely. "There should be no trouble annulling the marriage. You saw. He could not get away fast enough."

Parrette sighed. "Spies! I spit upon your future grave, Marsac."

In spite of the constant swing and sway of the canvas box bed, Anna fell into a fitful slumber until the insistent ringing of a bell — *ting-ting, ting-ting, ting-ting, ting-ting* — following which a voice bawled "All's well!"

The cabin was dark. The ropes holding up her bed creaked. She listened to those, and to unfamiliar noises farther away: the groan of wood, the hum of rigging, the muted thudding of sails. Footsteps overhead. She could not determine if she was alone or if Parrette lay somewhere in the cabin, and she was afraid to look, lest she fall out of this swinging bed.

She skimmed the surface of sleep, dreaming of being awake and trying to explain her history to a parcel of blurry-faced, tall men in naval blue coats. Central stood the tallest, with a hawk nose and narrowed eyes with tiny lines at the corners, lines incised by either anger or laughter, she could not determine which...

As she slid at last below the surface of sleep, in the next cabin over Henry Duncannon lay awake in the hammock slung for him, listening to the song of the ship's timbers and rigging, sails and wind, counterpointed by the *splash-slap* of water against the hull, as he considered the peculiar note he had received from Gravina.

In company. What did that mean? How was he to get a purchase on this situation?

While Gravina was everywhere respected as an honorable man as well as a fine fighting captain, his English left much to be desired.

"Duncannon, what does this mean?" Nelson had asked, as all the captains stared.

"I have no notion," he had been forced to admit, and then, itching with embarrassment, though he could not have said why, he said, "If you remember, sir, I came to you in London some time after Captain Troubridge honored me with a request to take part in an arranged marriage, when we were at Palermo. But she vanished, and I was never able to find word of her."

Before the interested gaze of Captains Fremantle and Hardy, Duncannon held back his own request for annulment.

"Palermo. Naples," Nelson responded with a sentimental sigh. "How happy we were there."

Duncannon had remembered only the fighting, the heat, the illness, the hanging of that miserable scapegoat Carraciolo, but such was his respect—reflected in the faces of the other officers— for Admiral Lord Nelson that they all smiled, and no one brought up the name 'Lady Hamilton.'

"I remember that," Hardy exclaimed, fists on his knees. "Troubridge arranged it, just as Duncannon says. The girl's father connected to an Italian duke, mother a gentlewoman living at the palace in some capacity before she died, the girl left alone. The father, Ludovano, no, Ludovicci, Ludovisi, something of the sort—"

"Little Anna Maria Ludovisi?" Fremantle exclaimed. "No one told me about this! She was thick as thieves with my dear Betsey and her younger sisters at the Hamiltons' parties, in '97. Lord, I remember their shrill gabble, like a parcel of parrots. They were just girls, the age of our smallest reefers. Heyday, however she got there, we cannot leave her stranded in Cadiz!"

Before Duncannon went over the side with his orders to fetch her, Collingwood had pulled him to the leeward rail, where the wind would sweep their words over the water unheard. "You know the admiral. As canny a fighting man as we could ever hope

184

to see, but romantical in the article of ladies. Especially ladies from Naples, d'you follow? I make no accusations, I insinuate nothing, but I urge you to determine that she is all she should be."

Duncannon had climbed down, aware of an added sense of burden.

Anna Maria Ludovisi. He had forgotten her name.

She woke with a start, vaguely aware of that persistent bell having rung intermittently through the night. The most recent had been followed by the deck above her shuddering to the thunder of many running feet.

"Is it war?" Anna asked, sitting upright so fast the bed swung and jiggled.

"I believe it is their mealtime." Parrette came to the side of her bed, glancing over her shoulder as she fingered her hair back. "I think they are wanting in. Or wanting you to come forth," she whispered. "I have the rosebud muslin laid out."

Anna tried to climb down from the hammock, but fell to her knees when the bed hitched up behind her at the same moment the floor slanted away. She picked herself up, her knees smarting, and hurried into her clothes, breathing easily only when she sat on the trunk so that Parrette could comb her hair into order. Parrette had scrubbed most of the salt from her slippers, but they were still unpleasantly damp as she slid her feet in.

"Do you want your half-boots?" Parrette asked.

"No. Those heels might make me slip. I scarcely notice the wet."

They looked at one another, and Parrette drew in a deep breath, her expression anxious as she said in Neapolitan, "These English, they will turn against you if they think you are not by their lights *comme il faut*. You *cannot* tell them that you earned your wage singing in theaters."

Anna's eyelids stung as if gritty, her toes were unpleasantly cold, and her middle churned with unpleasant urgency. "And if they do? It will only get me the annulment the faster, no?"

"Your mother," Parrette uttered in a low, guttural whisper,

"would turn in her grave for the shame. I *know*, me. You were per-haps too young to take note, but I heard how those English talked, when I accompanied you and your sainted mother to their church, and their parties, and I had to wait for you to come forth. They did not think I understood—none of them knew your mother taught me English. If they think you are little better than an opera dancer, then that is how they will regard you. And you will be treated so."

Opera dancer. Anna thought of sweet-natured Hyacinthe, prickly Lise, dear, generous little Helene, curious Eleanor. Catherine, so adamant about equality and freedom for all. Even Ninon had been honorable in her own way. "I hate to hear you talk about them as if—"

Someone scratched insistently at the door, and a man said loudly, "It's nigh on eight bells o' the morning watch. Capting sends his compliments, and breakfast is served."

Parrette's head turned quickly, and she grasped Anna's wrists. "Listen! It is not I who have this regard. The English are beasts, *beasts*, with their good birth and their cold manners! You cannot tell them the truth. Promise you will not." Her grip tightened. "On your mother's heart, on her soul, *promise*."

Anna longed to shout, to turn away, but Parrette, to whom she owed so much, was in desperate, even deadly earnest. And so she felt herself take a step into the lies she hated. "I promise."

Parrette loosened her grip, rubbed her much-pricked, rough thumb over the red marks she had made on Anna's thin wrist, and muttered, "I beg pardon. But I could never hold up my head again if I failed your mother now."

"The marks will fade. What is another lie? Should anyone ask, I will say you caught me before I fell," Anna retorted, knowing it was unfair, but she was indignant enough to step past Parrette, her back straight and her head up, as she opened the door.

The steward had his hand raised to scratch again. His glower changed to relief, and he said, "This way, Missus. It's just a step."

The dining area was indeed scarcely more than a step, a small cabin on the other side of the bulkhead from where Anna had been sleeping. She braced herself in the doorway against the pitch of the ship.

And so husband and wife met once again, each anxious to

understand, and determined to be understood.

Captain Duncannon, waiting within, saw her framed there. The elegance he had perceived so dimly in his sea-drenched—guest? *Wife*—struck him with all the force of sunlight now. Bathed in the pure glow streaming from stern windows behind him, she was more graceful than she had looked the night before.

Artfully tousled curls framed her face. Her gown flattered her shape with its gently scooped neck under the delicate line of her collarbones, set between little sleeves. Embroidered rose leaves started at one straight shoulder and curved over her bosom like a court sash, trailing slantwise between her hips and down to the flounces around her little slippers. There was nothing vulgar in the way the intermittent rosebuds enhanced her form—the very opposite of vulgar—but the overall effect was so...so *French*.

He reined his gaze hard, and kept it somewhere above her curly head as he advanced to welcome her; she stood there becoming more apprehensive with every heartbeat.

He looked so...so formidable, as he paced toward her and held out his hand, as if he had already condemned her as a spy. She put her fingers in his, her heart beating in her throat—what was to come next?—but he merely escorted her to the place of honor at the right of the head of a very long table.

"Good morning, Madame," he said as he pulled out her chair himself. "I trust you slept well?"

"Yes, thank you, Captain Duncannon," Anna said, with more politeness than truth. She was thankful that he had seated her to his right, rather than at the far end of that long table, though what did it mean?

I am a guest. That must be it.

Parrette was correct. She was being given the treatment of a lady, though she was not seated where a hostess would go. She must recollect all the little rules she had once been taught.

As he took his seat, he cast a quick glance at her face. He could see by the shadows under her eyes how well her sleep had been. Overhead eight bells rang, and she started.

"I apologize for the rudeness of your wakening," Captain Duncannon said with a smile he hoped would set her at ease. "Seven bells is the time for up hammocks. Eight bells has just rung, and it is now the forenoon watch, that is, eight o'clock in the morning. I am afraid that our shipboard life is very much ruled by our clocks." He indicated the open casement behind him, and the open sea beyond, on which another ship could be seen a short distance away. "If you should care to listen from the stern window here, you will hear the same sound all up and down the line."

"Line?" she asked. Her diction was careful, her accent as French as her gown, and the little curls around her face. "The ships sail in a line, not togessaire, ah, togetaire?"

His lips twitched at her attempt to correct her English. "Two cables apart, back and forth. I was part of the frigates watching Cadiz, but the Admiral has requested us to join the ships of the line. We lie well out of sight of the harbor, in hopes of drawing out the French at last..." He saw complete incomprehension in her face, and mentally set aside his questions about her presence in Cadiz. Odd, he felt so callow, like a reefer at his first captain's breakfast. But the situation was so devilish strange.

"And so a battle is to begin?" She cast a frightened look at the stern windows, as if she expected cannon balls to smash in that very moment.

Perkins, hovering with a pot, poured out tea into fine china cups. Very aware of his listening ears, the captain said, "Why, that will happen only if the Combined Fleet obliges us by coming out of the bay. But I expect that before that does happen, my tender will have returned from Gibraltar with supplies, and we can then send you to safety."

She relaxed incrementally at this, and turned her attention to the dish full of a lumpish, grayish soup the steward set before her.

"I am afraid all I have to offer you is burgoo, but it is well salted, and you may help yourself to sugar. Some say it adds to the taste. Most of the midshipmen's berth would heap it in by trowel, had they the means. I can, however, promise you a much better meal if the admiral invites us to dinner aboard the flag, as I expect will happen."

As he spoke the steward lifted a silver cover shaped like a bell, revealing the remains of a sugarloaf that reminded her of a near-burnt candle. She picked up the sugar nip and took a small piece.

The captain ate his burgoo with every evidence of appetite.

Heartened, she tried a small spoonful of her own. It was not as terrible as it looked. She navigated around the black spots, which she could not determine were insects or burnt bits, and found it surprisingly easy going down.

"It is much better with milk," the captain said. "But that has not been possible these four months—our Nanny-goat died during a hurricano in the West Indies, and we cannot get milk from the bum boats this far out."

The questions he wanted to ask—that had seemed so sensible during the night watches—had evaporated with the first rays of the sun. She sat within reach, her head a little bent, her fingers holding the cup daintily, a tiny pucker between her straight brows as she tried not to spill. She ate neatly, one wrist pressed discreetly to the table when the ship gave a particularly skittish lee lurch. He could not bring himself to interrogate her as if she stood before the Court of King's Bench.

So what could he say? He had never been good with polite gabble. Emily had twitted him on it, so long ago. From long habit he shook away the thought of Emily, and ventured a question: "Have you been acquainted with Admiral Gravina long?"

She looked surprised. "Oh, no. I only met him in the once."

Her tone seemed genuine, and he mentally reevaluated the few facts. "I am given to understand that you met, then, at a musical performance?"

"It was after," she said, and mindful of her promise, bit back the words *we performed*. "The occasion was *I riti d'Efeso*, for the Spanish and French commanders and their guests."

"Farinelli," he exclaimed, his furrowed brow clearing. "I envy you that. I was able to see his *Il Cid della Spagna* when we touched at Venice. It was admirable, admirable, though perhaps my memory is better than the opera deserves. It was entirely due to Farinelli's Don Diego, a tenor named Gaetano Crivelli. He had not even the premier role, but he was splendid. One of the best I have ever heard. Did you chance to hear him before you left the peninsula?"

"No, I have not," she said, uncomfortable again. Surely his comment presaged close questioning about where she had been.

He had been thinking along a parallel path, but with far less intent than she dreaded. Gravina, Naples, what could be more natural than Queen Maria Carolina sending a young friend of Lady Hamilton to royal relations in Spain when the French threatened yet again. Didn't those royals pack their extra females to convents reserved to the high born?

He said, "I take it you have spent time in Spain? They are not known for their opera, though I protest against your thinking me an expert. I have never been in Spain."

"Yes. I have been. Spain is not known for the—one might say, the creation of opera," Anna enunciated carefully. "Except in the form of the *zarzuela*, which is, one could say, more, ah, speak? Speech?"

"Recitation," he offered, smiling.

"Like the French! I ought to know this, me. The early *zarzuela* is more recitation than song, with a prodigious amount of the Spanish dance. The last opera presented in Spain, I was given to understand, was *Clementina*, by Boccherini, and that twenty years ago."

He nodded encouragingly, secretly as amused by her French accent as by the quaintness of her English. Some of her expressions reminded him of his parents' generation, from the days of towering wigs and satin coats. "But," she continued when he made an encouraging gesture, "the Spanish are passionate about opera, even so. The theater in Seville is monstrous vast, beautiful, and prodigious well attended. Even in summer, when there was not so much a breathing of air." Again she strayed near the truth, and forced herself to halt.

"You have been in Seville, I collect?" he asked.

"Yes. A much, ah, most beautiful city. One apprehends the palace as the beautifullest one has ever seen."

So she'd been sequestered in Seville? He rather thought he had the gist of it, and without coming it high-handed, without sounding like a prosecutor in wig and robes. Collingwood must be satisfied. Even the French fashion explained itself, for were the two nations not allies at present?

And as for his personal interest in the matter, he could stand before any archbishop and swear the truth, that their marriage had been unconsummated. Perhaps he was going to scrape through this affair with far less trouble than he had feared twenty-four hours earlier.

His mood eased considerably on this comfortable thought. She, seeing that smooth brow, felt less oppressed and they finished breakfast conversing, if not with ease, at least with no awkward silences as the subjects of music, favorite composers, famous actors and singers heard and seen, all passed under review.

They had both heard Mrs. Billington, though at different times. He was impressed by Anna's knowledge, but then she had been bred up in Naples, where it was well known that the great Paisiello had charge of the royal entertainments. Of course she would possess a high degree of musical refinement.

As they brought the meal to a close, he made a mental note not to embarrass her with his customary quartet; their awkward adaptations of Bach's string quartets for clarinet and flute would only be laughable to so knowledgeable an ear.

When they rose, he said, "Should you care to take a turn in the air?"

He had to get to his tasks, but knew the lengths his crew would go to catch a glimpse of the mysterious Mrs. Duncannon. This was the best way to go about it, under his eye.

She would much rather have retreated to her little cabin, but she was afraid that such behavior might make her look uncooperative, and so she said, "Thank you." And then remembering her mother's long-ago admonitions, she added, "I haven't a bonnet. We have been used to the Spanish custom, wearing mantillas. May I fetch mine?"

He assented and she sped to the sleeping cabin, where Parrette sat upon one of the trunks, her hands clasped anxiously. "And so?"

"He was very polite. We talked about music and Spain. But he mentioned a dinner with the admiral. Perhaps that is when I shall be questioned," Anna whispered in Neapolitan as she whipped her mantilla around her head, and tucked it secure with her decorated comb. "Now I am to take the air."

"It is well," Parrette said, breathing easily at last. Perhaps she could find whoever was in charge of mending and repair, and in offering her aid, learn what she could.

When Anna reached the outer doors to the captain's cabin, she stepped back, startled by the sight of a marine standing there in his red coat, a musket at his side. She was going to retreat into her cabin, afraid they were prisoners after all, when the man touched his oddly shaped hat to her, and said, "Gorton, mum, marine sentry. I'm to show you the way to the quarterdeck."

She thanked him breathlessly. "Is there always a sentry?" she asked, turning huge brown eyes inquiringly up at him. "Or must you stand there because of us?"

Gorton chuckled. "Bless you, Mrs. Capting, the skipper of a frigate rates a sentry. Was you to attack him, why, I must come to his defense." He clashed his musket to the deck.

Anna peered up into his weather-beaten face, and discovered a broad smile. The man was joking. She uttered a breathless laugh, more relief than humor, and made her way up to the quarterdeck, where she was surprised to find a small number of officers standing about, in addition to seamen busy at their tasks.

Duncannon had, during the long months of chasing to the West Indies and back, permitted a modicum of informality in the article of dress, but ever since Admiral Nelson had rejoined the fleet, coats and hats were required on deck.

However, once word had spread that the captain had a missus and that she was coming aboard, a general interest in cleanliness had fired the crew from First Lieutenant Theophilus Sayers to the smallest of the ship's boys in their watchet-blue jackets, and Master's Mate d'Ivry had scraped his few blond whiskers off so assiduously that the lower half of his face was quite red.

The captain presented Lieutenant Sayers first. Anna felt as if she were playing a role on stage to hear herself referred to as Mrs. Duncannon; she peered shyly at the smiling first lieutenant, who doffed his hat with an air, revealing a shock of nearly white hair above tufted white eyebrows. Eyes of a startling blue gazed at her out of a sun-browned face.

"Mum," he said, or that's what the word sounded like.

She took it as an honorific, and curtseyed. Next was another lieutenant, a thin young man with golden hair neatly queued back, called Lieutenant McGowan. The last introduction was to the blushing d'Ivry, the officer of the deck. His voice cracked horribly on the single word, "Mum," and she heard a muffled snicker somewhere on the lower deck behind her, and someone else muttered, "Stop your gob, mate."

But when the captain glanced that way, there was instant silence, except for the groan and creak of wood and rope, the clatter of blocks, and the wash of water down the sides.

The captain then said, "I beg to apologize, Madame—" He said it the French way. "—but I have a great many tasks to attend to. With your permission, I shall turn you over to my clerk, Mr. Leuven, who is ready to conduct you on a tour of the ship, if that would please you."

Anna was getting used to his speech by now. His words were clear, his voice as deep as she had remembered. She curtseyed again, intuiting what was expected of her, and turned to the sallow-faced fellow with unruly black hair waiting expectantly behind the captain.

"If you'll come this way, mum?"

She took her place beside this young Mr. Leuven, who appeared to be somewhere between boy and man. He launched into a stream of gibberish, delivered with a self-conscious, pompous air. Midway through an impossible-to-understand description of the difference between a sheet and a halyard, the sea gave one of its sudden lurches, nearly pitching her into the waist of the ship.

He caught her, and blushed furiously as a watching topman whistled high above.

"One hand for yourself and one for the ship, is what we say, mum," Mr. Leuven murmured with an anxious air, freeing her and backing a step as if he had been shot. "Clap onto the rail anytime you like, and steady on."

"Thank you."

"The sea is kicking up a bit," he offered apologetically, as she experimented with bending her knees slightly, and taking the sway in her hips. That seemed simpler than trying to stand stiffly upright.

He squinted upward, then observed, "Cap'n will have the royals off her in a shake, see if he don't. It would never do to encroach on the line, never."

They had scarcely taken ten steps when there was an

incomprehensible shout from the platform they had recently left, which Mr. Leuven had explained was the quarterdeck, reserved to officers. Mr. Leuven thoughtfully drew Anna back a heartbeat or two before a party of pigtailed sailors stampeded along the gangway past her, and then scrambled aloft so rapidly it made her dizzy to watch.

Sails flapped with thundering noise, loosened, and were gathered in as Mr. Leuven conducted her to the front of the ship, which he called the forecastle. There he painstakingly instructed her in the differences between starboard (right) and larboard (the left side of the ship), windward and leeward. The mighty spar that slanted up in front was the "jib" and the three masts also had names. The masts were actually in segments, she discovered.

"Oh, yes," Mr. Leuven said, smiling broadly. "You don't want t'gallant masts on her in a real blow, without you expect to be dismasted altogether. Why, when we chased off to the West Indies, we all, the frogs too, had to win miles of sea room against one of them *hurricanos*, which we ride out with only a scrap of sail, and pray we don't broach to."

Anna shivered, which gratified Mr. Leuven mightily, and commented that she could not understand how such a heavy object as a ship did not sink even in relatively benign waters. He thoroughly enjoyed her French accent, and could not suppress a glance of triumph at a pair of midshipmen glaring at him from abaft the mizzen.

He then took her down the forward hatch and conducted her along the upper deck, pointing out the galley, the midshipmen's berth in the forepeak, the waist—from which she could look up and see the gangway where she had walked shortly before—and there were the doors to the great cabin. Down they went again to the lower deck, and through the wardroom (which is where the senior officers messed, he said briefly, without explaining who they were or what "mess" meant) and on through to the gunroom, directly below where Anna had slept.

Here, he pointed out where cutlasses, boarding axes, pikes, and the like were mounted on the bulkheads, between which were stretched canvas walls on which doors had been painted. These minuscule spaces were the cabins of the junior officers, Mr.

Leuven explained.

To her surprise he cast a furtive look about him as if to make certain they were truly alone in the low-ceilinged space, and then uttered a garbled string of words, his expression intent.

He paused, his expression a comical mix of pride and apprehension. Belatedly Anna caught a badly-pronounced word amid the stream, 'giorno', the Italian word for 'morning.' She said, "You speak Italian, Mr. Leuven?"

The apprehension vanished, and Mr. Leuven grinned proudly, his homely face red to the ears. "My grandmother, m'mother's mother, was Eye-talian. She taught me some things when I was a nipper. This being my first chance to try it out, as it's my first cruise, on account of my grandfather being the ship's surgeon."

"Your first?" she asked, aware of some disappointment. She had been trying to think of a way to ask about the mutiny, though she did not know what she would do with the information. "And your position one of importance, I see?"

"Very," he said, and then quickly, as if he might be overheard showing away, he added in a lower voice, "m'mother sent me to Grandfer Leuven, and thinking I'd be kept safe, conditioned for captain's clerk, on account I write a neat hand. She would pipe her eye was she to know that, if we come to battle, why, I'm right there next or nigh the skipper, taking down notes." He laughed heartily. "And don't I wish we may! Those mids come it the high and mighty, don't you know it. A brush with the frogs *and* the dons would put us all square."

As he spoke, he conducted her along the length of the lower deck, showing her where the crew's hammocks swung in the night watches, and where they messed. Next was the manger and sickbay, and then down again to the main hold. She tried to hold her breath against the oppressive air, as Mr. Leuven rapidly pointed out the magazine, the shot lockers, the spirit room, and the stores. She peered obediently at dimly lit barrels and boxes, as little light from the gratings reached this far below.

By the time they attained the sweet air of the deck once more, the sky had changed dramatically, a low layer of clouds turning the blue sea to grayish green. There was no sign of land in any direction.

The swell rolled deliberately, but she found that if she loosened her knees in a manner that reminded her of certain dance motions, she was able to balance more easily.

She was so absorbed with remaining on her feet that she had no time to think about how she looked, and of course she was unaware of the intense interest of men who had been long months away from the company of women. The only female on deck, she drew the eye with her straight back, her curls blowing under the frothy lace mantilla, and the thin gown outlining her form. But she was the captain's wife — a fact that had pretty much stunned the entire crew — as well as a lady, and so she moved about in a kind of invisible shield, the avid gazes sliding away if she approached.

Over the remainder of the day, it seemed that every time she turned around she glimpsed crew members busy with some task. She was not to know that the midshipmen and the junior officers all — with a wary eye captainward — found some sort of work in the vicinity of the captain's lady so they could get a good look.

To each introduction, from Midshipman Corcoran's hideous stammer to Second Lieutenant McGowan's mellifluous, and rather studied, French, she returned a polite, friendly greeting. How did each wish to be perceived? *Royalty will take what they want to support their dignity, but others, like you, if you give respect freely, they will like as not give it back*, her mother had said. In Paris, 'dignity' had still been a dangerous concept to those who could remember the mob and summary hangings. With these English, she was cast back to her mother's quiet morning lessons.

The framed sporting prints she had glimpsed in the great cabin, the weapons mounted as decoration in the gunroom, the continual rumble of boots, the deep voices hallooing — this was a man's world. She was an intruder, not just because of her sex, but because of her origins. She was not English in the way they understood. But they used the English rules of behavior, and she did her best to respond in kind.

Before the sun set, the midshipman in charge of the flag signals presented himself to the officer of the watch, and thence to the captain, conveying the expected invitation to dine aboard the flagship on the following day.

Sixteen

ANNA HAD A NIGHT to dread the prospect of being brought before Admiral Lord Nelson, about whom she had heard so much over the past six years: wild admiration from the English at Naples, wild hatred from the French.

She had seen him from afar just once, the day she sang at Lady Hamilton's fete. She remembered little beyond a slim figure of medium height with a sleeve pinned up, diamonds flashing on his medals and in his hat.

After intense discussion, she and Parrette settled on the gown she had worn upon the stage in Seville. It was her finest, made up of watered silk with a bodice of lace applique, with a Greek tunic over-dress in eggshell blue, caught under the bosom with embroidered laurel leaves. Since she had no hat, she wore her longest lace on her head, Spanish-style, anchored with a filigree comb. The top corners of the lace attached to her wrists in flowing drapes, the rest hanging down to the back of her skirt.

"I have made this over into a boat cloak," Parrette added, producing a voluminous garment with a triumphant air. "You must do The Captain credit on Admiral Nelson's ship. Here are your mother's gloves. You see I have kept them. They ought to fit. You are much of a size."

"Gloves! It is not cold enough for gloves," Anna protested.

"It is English custom," Parrette said. "You will wear these

gloves, but not to eat in. At least, I remember your mother used to leave off her gloves at meals."

"Where do I put them?"

"In your reticule."

"I did not think I had to take one, for I am not shopping, am I?"

"You must have a handkerchief in it, and you put your gloves in it until you need them."

Anna sighed, then inwardly chuckled. 'The Captain' was back. She wondered what Parrette would call him once he turned them off in Gibraltar like so much unwanted lumber. *And it cannot be too soon*, she thought, looking at those white gloves, which she knew would be a bother to keep clean.

The steward scratched. She left her cabin, and found The Captain in his best coat, waiting with a gold-laced hat clasped under his arm. It was going to be a longish journey past two or three other ships of the line, and they must not be late to the flag.

She shrouded herself in her new boat cloak, and pulled the gloves on. They were tight, but fit, and the old thrill of sorrow purled through her at the idea of her mother's fingers once warming them.

She was startled from her reverie by the clash and stamp of the red-coated marines and the bosun's wailing signal. Captain Duncannon escorted her to the side. She held her breath as she was lowered carefully in the bosun's chair. The captain clambered nimbly down the side and stepped into the boat, watching as his coxswain assisted her as gently as if she were made of glass.

The gig's crew all wore jackets they had made themselves, their caps embroidered with *Aglaea* on the fronts, the seams of their trousers worked with ribbon.

"We all look very fine," Anna said, smiling around at them.

The sailors vouchsafed nary a word—she did not know that they were to row in strict silence—but she caught smiles and becks from them, before Captain Duncannon gave the nod to his coxswain, who roared, "Stretch out!"

They left the ship behind them. Captain Duncannon cast his eyes from long habit at the set of *Aglaea*'s sails, the clouds, the color of the ocean, and the motion of the current as they rowed away. It gave him time to think.

It was not her fault that this false wife of his had turned up in his life again at the worst possible moment. He glanced at her tightly gripped hands. This situation could be no easier for her. "Are you comfortable, ma'am?"

"I am become accustomed, thank you," she said, proud of the remembered phrase.

He nodded. At least she tried to make the best of things, unlike some he could mention. Perhaps he ought to mention? "There are scarce suitable women for you to meet in company, but what we have, I am to tell you that the admiral has invited on your behalf, to be better company at dinner and so you will not be alone in withdrawing after the covers are removed."

Covers? Anna thought, groping mentally for meaning. Was that the cloth upon the table that she recollected from childhood, or the items set upon the cloth?

"There is Lady Lydia Neville, daughter of the Marquess of Oversley," Captain Duncannon went on, hoping to convey a sense of the honor Lord Nelson was doing her, without being oppressive. "She recently married George Neville. You might recognize the family — they are very distinguished, long service, though he's a third son. Captain Neville of the sloop-of-war *Mermaid*, very fast in stays, will run dispatches if we come to battle. Then there's the wife of Lieutenant Fellowes, from *Polyphemus*, of 64 guns. Mrs. Fellowes has charge of the ship's boys; her father was a headmaster of some northern school, and she is famous for her shining parts. She has been sailing with him these three years. And finally, though perhaps in respect to age I ought to have mentioned her first, there is Mrs. Porter, wife of the premier of *Sirius*, 36..."

He was acutely conscious that he was chattering. Did she comprehend any of what he said? Though she kept glancing at the ships they passed, and at the mild sea, the cant of her head, her tightly gripped hands seemed to indicate her listening closely.

And she was. 64? 36? Why these numbers, after he named a ship? She did her best to distract herself from how very close by he sat. He was so very, oh, so very tall, his legs in their white breeches so much longer than hers. She looked away from the curve of his thigh as if she had been caught in personal trespass; her clearest emotion was a dread of severity. Would not a mutiny be caused by a very great degree of tyrannical behavior?

"...He is even older than Captain Prowse, but a fine officer. It is a vast shame that he has little in the way of influence, and so he is still a lieutenant at sixty. However he is much cherished by captains who know him, so there is no danger of *him* languishing on the beach with half-pay. I understand she's crossed the Line some eighteen times, in course of following him. It is understood in the service that they always sail together."

As he spoke, they bumped and jolted past a ship larger even than the *Aglaea*. It was imposing, with its gleaming black hull layered by row upon row of yellow bands, which were in their turn broken by gun ports in black squares. The effect was a great checkerboard of menace. Anna stared past the sinister round mouths of the cannons, and glimpsed people moving about. Incomprehensible hails passed between someone high on the ship and the coxswain, and then they left that ship behind.

Unaware of the protracted silence, she gripped her hands a-new in her mother's gloves as they bucketed over the ship's wake. The men rowing paid the bumps no heed, so she shut her eyes.

He checked his pocket watch when the *Victory* was in view and he gave a satisfied huff of breath.

The ceremonial for boarding the flagship was even grander, as the Captain ascended the side with an ease that nearly made Anna's heart stop. The ceremony was solely for the captains, she saw, as another followed on Captain Duncannon's heels from the boat that had come up behind them.

She sustained this unsettling sensation that she was invisible, excluded from the arcane customs and language reserved exclusively to men. The very way she soared easily into the air in the canvas seat, and was set gently on the deck, seemed to underscore her strange position, not within their ordered world, but not altogether shut out as she curtseyed to this staring mass of officers with orders, medals, sashes, epaulettes, gold lace in their cocked hats, which they swept off as they bowed.

From the leeward side, without her husband (being a mere lieutenant, not invited) Lady Lydia Neville watched jealously as the naval blue and marine red coats parted. Only four months a bride, and already old—uninteresting—and who was this Mrs. Duncannon anyway? When Lady Lydia's mother had tried to convince her not to marry dear Charles, she had pointed out that these naval men married pot-house women, flower sellers, anything with a pair of pretty eyes, and she would be forced to give way before such if the husband had a higher rank than Charles Neville.

At that moment the wind whipped along the quarterdeck, blowing open Mrs. Duncannon's boat cloak. The men stirred; Lady Lydia caught her breath at the lady's grace, from the fascinating curve of her Spanish headdress down to the little French slippers. She embodied *le bon ton*, she was *beautiful*. Lady Lydia eagerly read every French fashion newspaper; she would take an oath that exquisite gown had come straight from Paris.

And every single man stared at *her*.

Thoroughly intimidated, Anna dared not look anyone in the face as she performed her curtsey. Then there *he* was—it could only be he, the famous Lord Nelson—holding out his left hand.

She proffered her own as she gazed into a pair of blue eyes, one with its black pupil larger than the other. There was no mistaking the sweetness of Admiral Lord Nelson's smile as he uttered words of welcome; she said something disjointed and tried to marshal her wits as the mass moved past white-gloved marines and orderlies to a beautiful suite much, much larger than Captain Duncannon's.

They paused as Nelson quickly performed introductions. Lady Lydia appeared to be about the age of the dancer Helene, no more than seventeen, with diamonds flashing at her neck and in her headdress. Mrs. Fellowes was tall and thin, her gown dove-colored. Last was Mrs. Porter, a smiling gray-haired lady who touched Anna's arm and said, "The cloak room, and what will pass for our own parlor, is here in the Admiral's day cabin."

Day cabin? This turned out to be a ship's cabin rich with white wainscoting gilt in squares, with portraits on the walls. Anna glimpsed a framed silhouette that called Lady Hamilton to mind, as the other ladies removed their cloaks.

A pigtailed sailor with white gloves took the cloaks and effaced himself, leaving the women alone. The youngest lady cast her reticule and gloves carelessly upon Lord Nelson's fine carved desk, and covertly studied the new Mrs. Duncannon. Why, taken separately, her features were no more than ordinary: a pair of brown eyes, a straight nose, a firm chin, a broad forehead under those artful curls. What did the French call them? Kiss curls. Lady Lydia would adopt them. She was sick of frizz.

She turned away, satisfied that this new bride was really no prettier than she was, in spite of that fabulous gown, and the way she held her head. She wore no diamonds, and as for that ring, it was the merest trumpery.

Lady Lydia glanced complacently into a pier glass, then exclaimed in a high voice, "I knew it. I said it would be so. Mrs. Duncannon, you will have to forgive me for my wretched appearance—a thousand pities we must venture out in this gale. But you will forgive me, I know."

Mrs. Porter said, "You look charmingly, as always, Lady Lydia."

Lady Lydia bridled, casting her eyes skyward. "You are too kind, Mrs. Porter."

Mrs. Fellowes turned Anna's way. "What pretty lace! Is that not the Spanish style of headdress?"

"It is," Anna said. "Thank you."

"But your accent is French," Lady Lydia cried. "And here I was just thinking that your gown must have come straight from Le Roy, if it wasn't for this vile war. Lady Bessborough made us all die a million deaths from envy when she wore her French gowns the season before last. Or was it two seasons ago? Oh, my head." She fluttered her fingers. "She could talk of nothing else but Le Roy, though she never met Madame Bonaparte, now an empress, as she took against Napoleon. I don't suppose *you* met Bonaparte's wife? Oh, but you was in Spain, I collect?"

The white-gloved sailor stuck his head in again. Glad for an excuse not to answer, Anna said, "The officers, they wait, is it not so?"

The sailor touched his forehead. "Which the bells is about to ring the watch change, if you please."

"And we know the entire fleet would sink if they were a stroke past the hour sitting down to their dinner." Mrs. Porter chuckled. "Shall we join the gentlemen?"

"I must lead the way," Lady Lydia began, rustling toward the door, then she paused with a dramatic start. "No, no, it is Mrs. Duncannon who is the guest of honor—"

Whatever she was going to say next was lost as the ship's bell rang. The ladies only had a few steps to walk. The sound caused all the officers to be in motion. Once again there was the dazzling display.

This time Anna was able to take in more details: young and old officers, fat and thin. Most of the younger ones, like Lord Nelson, wore their own hair fairly short, but several of the older captains wore beautifully powdered wigs, and one wore his own hair queued and powdered; snow dusted his shoulders from the wind.

Lord Nelson himself escorted Anna into the dining room, which was dominated by a long table ablaze with light. Golden candelabra gleamed richly down the middle, between two rows of exquisite china dishes.

Anna was seated to the admiral's right. She was relieved to see the other women placed at her end of the long table, each with an officer on either side. Lady Lydia was highest up, across from her. Another thought: how was she to be addressed? Was Lady Lydia the informal use, like the French *tu*, reserved to intimates and children? She tried to recollect the tangle of titles and usages her mother had taught her; she was fairly certain she had the exigencies of birth rank straight, but what happened after marriage? Was this young bride properly addressed as Lady Neville, or was she Mrs. Neville?

In Paris, all the rules had been topsy-turvy, and they had never been quite the same as her mother's careful lessons in English, that much Anna remembered from her childhood. Oh, yes: the Captain had referred to her as 'Lady Lydia Neville.' All right, she could remember that.

As they were served, Lord Nelson turned to Anna. "And so you were born at Naples, Mrs. Duncannon?"

"Calabria, sir."

The admiral did not hear, lost in fond memory. "Ah, the beauty! You were acquainted with Lady Hamilton, were you not?"

"A little," Anna said, and, catching sight of the glitter on her finger, reflecting the light from the candelabra, "This is her ring."

Lord Nelson's smile was brilliant. "Ah, so kind, so generous! A toast to Lady Hamilton."

"Lady Hamilton," the officers said, raising their glasses.

With genuine good will, Lord Nelson leaned toward Anna. "And so you ended up in Cadiz. Music, was it? Did you chance to look into the harbor?"

"I walked down the very first day, to take the fresh air," Anna said. "It was a very hot journey down the river."

"And what did you see in the harbor? Did you observe how many ships of the line were gathered?"

Anna's brow puckered. "It was a forest of tall poles, so many. Some of the ships were very big, oh, I think there was one prodigiously greater than this one we sit in. But I could mistake. It is difficult to tell from the wharf, and I was mostly looking out to sea. It was my first sight of the Atlantic." She became aware of the entire table listening to her, and glanced uncertainly. "I beg pardon. I am so ignorant of these things — for many years I have seen no ocean at all."

Lord Nelson laughed. "No one expects a lady to give an exact accounting of warships. Let us turn to a subject you must know well. What was the great Paisiello working on when you left Naples? What have you seen in Spain?"

Anna could talk knowledgeably about that! Without admitting that she had performed in some of them, she began to name operas, but scarcely had she progressed beyond *I riti* and *Nina* before others exclaimed that they had seen this, or heard of that.

The conversation turned to London theater — famous performances — famous performers — no one wrote opera like the Italians, except for that fellow Mozart — Englishmen couldn't write opera anymore than Dutchmen.

Mrs. Fellowes was resigned to another long naval dinner. She had no ear for opera, and disapproved of its stories, which always seemed to be about disreputable, if not immoral, persons. For her, the point of the evening would come after the ladies retired. She hoped that Mrs. Duncannon was a reading woman. Otherwise, the evening would end in dull female chatter about fripperies.

Mrs. Porter was the most comfortable, content to enjoy the sight of the captains enjoying themselves, and Lady Lydia the least. She tried very hard to regain the attention she had come to expect as her due when a new bride, and she made a little business of joining the toasts with what she thought a daring, dashing air.

As the meal wore on, the gentlemen spoke much too rapidly for Anna to follow, using expressions she did not understand. She watched their faces instead, the ruddy cheeks and bright glances that threw her back to the Paris cafés with the soldiers. She shook off that memory, and listened to the deep buzz of men's voices. Was there an English word for it? The *frémissement*, the *bourdonnement*, a sound felt as strongly as heard.

She was not used to wine, except watered. Though she only sipped, the jacketed, gloved servants behind each chair kept her glass filled, as they did the men's. She noticed that Lady Lydia began by tossing hers off with an arch look. Mrs. Porter only lifted hers to her lips when they toasted the King, then put it down. Mrs. Fellowes never touched her glass, and Anna left hers, relieved.

The food came and went. Anna had long since sated her hunger. Still the men talked on, faces flushed, laughter louder and more broad, their conversation utterly impenetrable as they talked about ships, parts of ships, armaments of ships. The only French words were names of ships and commanders, and places like Toulon. She could not descry what *polishing Cape Sicié* meant, but it caused a general roar of laughter.

Anna looked down at her hands in her lap below the gilt rim of the china dish, thinking how very strange a turn her life had taken. She did not see Vice-Admiral Collingwood watching her narrowly as the talk wound on, touching now and then on Lord Nelson's strategy should Villeneuve come forth. He shifted his gaze from Anna with her downcast eyes to Duncannon, halfway down the table, whose attention to his wife was no more than polite.

Anna was deep in reverie when some signal occurred that she had missed: the men were stirring, the plates vanishing rapidly. Lord Nelson turned her way and said with an earnest, confiding air, "If Villeneuve brings them out, your station will be in the orlop, in course. Remember, put the knives to heat. The poor wretches will take it kindly. I shall never forget the horror of a cold knife cutting into my flesh." He tapped the pinned sleeve and then rose.

Anna had no idea what to say. He held out his hand and

kissed her fingers, then turned a little as he let her hand go, as if he expected her to do something. She raised her eyes, seeing the women all standing. Mrs. Porter looked at her with a significant smile, and Anna remembered her mother telling her how English-women withdrew after a meal.

She followed Mrs. Porter, consciously moving against the pitch, unconscious of her grace, though all the men were watching.

As soon as the door to the Admiral's day room shut behind them, Mrs. Porter whispered to Anna, "They *will* serve wine to us. I assure you they are all very well brought up, but custom in the service is impossible to overcome, and so they will talk across the table like perfect hobbledehoys. However, we forgive them. Especially before an action."

A scratch on the door caused her to pause. In came one of the stewards with the long sailor's pigtails, bearing on an embossed silver tray a beautiful tea service.

Lady Lydia cast herself in an armchair and lay back, groaning. Mrs. Porter said to her, "Come, dear, some tea will set you right up." And to the sailor serving as steward, "We can pour for ourselves. Thank you."

The man set the tray on the desk, knuckled his forehead and exited.

Mrs. Fellowes sat down beside Anna on the bench that ran under the bulkhead, her back straight. "I promise, Mrs. Duncannon, the gentlemen know what is due to us. Their manners are rather more nice when they are on land."

Lady Lydia pulled fretfully at her reticule resting on the nearby table. "They were so bor-ring." She extracted a beautifully embroidered square of linen, and pressed it to her lips before saying, "I thought it would never end, this ten ages at least. Neville will stare when I tell him how rude they were, so unlike during summer! It is this war at fault. All they think about is the Nelson Touch, all they talk about is the Nelson Touch, until I am brought to the brink of extinction from *ennui*."

"Drink this, dear." Mrs. Porter held out a cup and saucer, balancing nicely on the long roll.

Lady Lydia sullenly took the cup and saucer, sipped, and wrinkled her nose. "Ugh! Simply scalding." She faced Anna and said in stilted, heavily accented French, "One was given to expect to have civilized talk, one was promised." And then in English, shrill and indignant, "Who can expect civilization when they will make anyone a captain? Berry no better than a merchant's brat, Prowse the son of a collier or cook, Conn the same, or worse, and Irish as well."

"Drink up your tea," Mrs. Porter said soothingly. "I have blown upon it. There is no scald."

Lady Lydia gulped her tea, and hiccupped.

"You must remember not to empty your wine glass, without they water it first. It is not what you are used to," Mrs. Porter murmured.

"But it was so *tiresome*. Four months ago *I* was the toast of the fleet. Everybody was agreed, it was the romance of the new century." She turned to Anna. "I met Charles at a ball, and Cupid's dart struck us at exactly the same instant. It was fate! I carried my point against the entire family—Charles said no one could have more courage—and married him on my seventeenth birthday. I came away with him—we could not be parted an instant. I knew I would die if we were. But men are so fickle. Here I am, old and forgotten in four months, and I must warn you, do not look for anything better. They will drop us in an instant for their war."

She hiccupped again, then closed her eyes. "Oh, I am so very unwell."

A body of sound echoed through the thin walls, *Hear him, hear him!*

"Dull, dull, dull." Lady Lydia put her arms on the table, and laid her head on them. "I am dull as a nightcap."

"That's right. Rest your head. The gentlemen will be at their toasts for a time," Mrs. Porter said comfortably.

She paused as the cabin rolled, then with a step and a turn, neatly for so stout a woman, she sat at Anna's other side. "Now, tell us how you met—what happened. We have only heard that it was sudden, and in Sicily, very like Captain Fremantle's romance."

Mrs. Fellowes said seriously, "You cannot conceive how surprised his friends were, to discover Captain Duncannon married. He never spoke of it, but he never speaks of anything of home, or family, or friends. One only sees him come alive when he is playing Bach with certain of his officers."

"A disappointment in youth has been spoken of," Mrs. Porter whispered, as a moan emanated from Lady Lydia's folded arms. "He was used to be against women on board. Would sit apart at balls, if he even attended. Could only be got ashore for musical events. They say he has never been home, not even when his father died, and his brother Northcote succeeded to the title."

"Have you met Lord Northcote, his brother?" Mrs. Fellowes asked, her expression one of extreme reserve. "He goes up to London every season."

Lady Lydia groaned and murmured something in which the words 'Lord Northcote' could barely be made out. Then she subsided.

"I have never been to England," Anna began. She had expected interrogation from Lord Nelson—and indeed, she had thought it begun at the dinner, but he had not followed that first question with anything about war, or ships, or the like. But here were these women and their questions.

Well, she could ask questions, too. "Captain Duncannon, when I heard last, was captain of the *Danae*. But was there not a mutiny?"

Mrs. Porter sighed and shook her head. "It would have been better for those poor souls on board, was Captain Duncannon still in command, but he was given his step and promoted into *Aglaea*. *Danae* was given to a man known as a hard horse captain, a real Tartar." She leaned close and whispered, "There was indeed a mutiny. The crew killed all the officers, and deserted to the French. A terrible thing, terrible!"

Mrs. Fellowes, tired of old naval news, got to what interested her. "I take it you are a well-educated woman? A reader? Captain Duncannon is known all over the fleet for his interests in music."

Anna turned her way. "I was educated at the royal palace in Naples—I do not intend *forfanterie*, what is the English word?"

"Bragging," came a muffled moan from the table. Then another hiccough.

Three heads turned that way, then back as Anna continued. "I cannot tell you if that is 'well' or not well. It is all that I know, do you see? Reading, I read everything that comes in my way." She smiled suddenly. "It is perhaps well that I recently discovered an English book, *Clarissa*. It helped me in a prodigious way to recollect my English, because it is many years since I spoke it, so. The book is so very long that I had to come away before I finished."

"*Clarissa*, a profound tragedy," Mrs. Fellowes said approvingly.

"A tragedy? Never say so! It is so light, so *débonnaire*, but perhaps this Lovelace is the worse ignoble?"

"I haven't Richardson's books," Mrs. Fellowes admitted, "but I can find them for you, somewhere in the fleet. I could also make you a package of books to read, if you would care for that."

"Oh I would be so grateful! I can hear, my English is much out of the practice. At dinner, I comprehended one word in fifty."

From the cabin beyond men's voices boomed: *His Majesty, George the Third, God rest his soul!*

Mrs. Porter cocked her head. "And that will be the end of it." She rose, and moved to gently shake Lady Lydia, who sighed, moaned, and sat up. "Come drink this off, quick. It will help you get overboard. At least you haven't a long pull ahead of you."

"Charles said he would come under *Victory*'s lee," Lady Lydia mumbled. "He knows what is due..." Her voice died away as everyone pulled on gloves, hats, and cloaks.

Out in the main cabin, the men were also in general stir. Vice-Admiral Collingwood waited for an opportune moment, and pulled Captain Duncannon aside, abaft the wheel outside of Captain Hardy's quarters. "Nelson," he murmured, "is as you know as shrewd as he can hold, except when it comes to a certain lady, and Naples."

Duncannon assented with an inquiring look.

Collingwood whispered, "Unlike these others, I happen to know what Troubridge was about when he bustled you into that marriage. She might be as ignorant as she appears, or she is very practiced indeed, but we shall not put ourselves to the trouble of answering that. You are to keep her on board, using whatever excuse you wish, until we have been brought to action. After that, you may do what you wish with her: whatever knowledge she possesses will be irrelevant."

Collingwood did not wait for an answer, but moved rapidly away to where Nelson stood with Fremantle, Pellew, and Hardy in close conversation.

Captain Duncannon turned from him to the lady, his—no, the word 'wife' would not stick in his head—his responsibility standing with the other women as a couple of sailors got Neville's tiresome bride into a bosun's chair. In contrast to Lady Lydia's affected airs, Anna moved with a kind of style that caught at his heart, and he shifted his gaze, appalled at himself. The very last thing he needed in his life now was a wayward, useless *tendre*. He had no use for beauty: it was false, at best, dangerous at worst.

He waited until she was let down into the gig, and gave his coxswain the nod. Once the boat was some distance from the flagship, he asked, "I trust you were pleased, ma'am?"

Which of her many emotions to share? She had at least rid herself of her fears about the tyrannical captain who could cause a mutiny. "Admiral Lord Nelson was everything that is most kind. And such a beautiful ship."

"I apologize if you were sadly bored by the conversation. It cannot be helped. We must always get onto the details of our professsion."

"I could understand but little," she admitted. "It was entirely to be expected, and there is no fault. Indeed, Mrs. Fellowes promised to share some books with me, that I may better my English."

"A laudable idea," he exclaimed. "What do you read? There are books to be had aboard *Aglaea*. Not an entire library, in course, but between my officers and me, I fancy we could accommodate you, if you do not object to mere novels."

"It is novels I am most partial to," she said. "Though I think I would read anything. Books in English have been rarely met with. For example, before I came away, I was nearly to the third volume of Mr. Richardson's *Clarissa*."

They were both glad to find in the other an unexceptionable subject of which they were genuinely fond, and it was therefore the topic of books that occupied them for the remainder of the journey back to *Aglaea*. By the time they climbed aboard, they had made the shift to music. Duncannon gave in to impulse, and invited her to listen to the quartet who habitually met in the cabin.

Seventeen

THE MIDSHIPMEN OF THE *Aglaea* held their captain in the highest respect, but when they talked over chaps with good humor, Captain Duncannon's name was not the first to come up.

Yet soon after dawn lightened the horizon, the lookout called down when he spotted a familiar topsail nicking the horizon. The midshipman of the watch duly reported it to the captain. "Tender, sir, off the starboard beam."

This news would be generally approved, the midshipman knew, because the tender would be laden with much-needed supplies (the midshipmen's mess was always short), and possibly even post, but never before had the arrival of the tender caused the captain to lift his brows, and utter a short laugh.

Altogether it had been a week for surprises, the midshipmen were agreed when the watch changed.

In their cabin, Anna and Parrette were woken by the rhythmic grinding sound of the waisters holystoning the deck. This sound began daily well before dawn, but until this morning they had been so exhausted that neither had been aware of it until now. Consequently they woke betimes, and so were ready for the day well before the thunder of feet presaging the change to the forenoon watch.

They were consequently waiting for the bell when there came a scratch at the door. They were both taken by surprise when a muffled man's voice spoke: *"Maman?"*

Parrette flew across the checkered canvas deck and flung open the door to a wiry young man with curly black hair worn in a long sailor's queue, and black eyes very like her own.

"Maman, it *is* you," he said in French, but he got no farther because Parrette had hurled herself into his arms, squeezing his breath out.

"Michel, my little cabbage," Parrette exclaimed in the accent of the streets of Lyons. "Ah, not so little anymore!" She stepped back to smile tenderly up into her son's face, an expression Anna had never seen and would have thought alien to Parrette's nature. Her eyes filled with unnoticed tears as she asked, "How is it that you are *here?"*

"We're just come aboard this minute, and the captain sent me to the cabin. I'm a purser's mate now," he said in English, a note of pride in his voice. His French accent was almost gone; he had absorbed the accent of Wapping with his seafaring duties. "Mr. Gates, he's the purser, sent me and a crew to Gib for supplies."

"Michel," Parrette said, wiping her eyes. "You are alive, *le bon Dieu* be thanked! How did this come about?"

Michel blushed, crushing a shapeless hat in his hand. "The captain found me in Denmark, after our brush with the Danes. Brought me aboard, and I went from topman to yeoman of the sheets. My being a dab hand with numbers, the skipper promoted me Michaelmas last."

The bell rang then, and he looked past his mother to say hastily to Anna, "Ma'am, I am to ask, would you honor the captain with your company for breakfast. He is waiting."

"Go, go!" Parrette pushed Anna through the door.

Her heart light with gratitude, Anna walked into the dining area to find the Captain standing courteously.

"I wish to thank you," she said as he seated her. "Oh, such a prodigious surprise! Michel Duflot, alive—and here! Parrette is *aux anges."*

Through the thin bulkhead came the sound of rapid French, mixed with happy laughter.

Anna hazarded a quick glance, but the streaming light from

the windows rendered the captain in silhouette. She could not make out his expression.

He watched her face turn his way. One moment she gazed at him, brilliant pinpoints of sun in her eyes, then she lowered her head, her eyelids shuttered, the blue veins delicately traced.

He had let a silence build. "I was happy to oblige," he said. "And in fact I need no extraordinary thanks, as it was entirely by accident that I encountered him, and though it was impulse that brought me to hire him, he has proved to be so excellent a crewman that there is scarce credit in keeping him by. With his facility for languages he has preserved my pursuer from being practiced upon by foreign dockyard sharps, and I expect to see him a purser, or even a quartermaster, should he desire to give over sailing, before he is much older."

The steward had served the food and poured out tea. On his departure, the captain said, "What is their story? When I first found him, he was still learning English, and said only he had been pressed from the French army. He had been just a boy."

"Parrette Duflot would not object to your knowing, as you have done her so very great a favor. She was married off, oh, so very young. Duflot proved to be a drunken, gambling brute, who scarcely could find work, he was so troublesome. He led her a life of the most dismal, and that was before it was discovered he had already had a wife in Marseilles."

"I am sorry to hear that," he said, distracted by her hands, the way she ate so neatly, so daintily, that absurd ring winking and gleaming on her finger. It did not fit, and she sometimes flexed her little finger to right it. He considered how to broach the question of how soon she might rid herself of it altogether, as she laid down her fork, and, with her fingers supported her cup against the pitch of the ship.

She went on. "You know there was terrible destruction during the Revolution. When his first wife came to Lyons to find him, Duflot threw down his tools and went off to the Vendée, taking along Parrette's son. He was a little boy."

"We heard that the Vendee was a terrible slaughter."

"So it was! In Lyons, Parrette was left with his debts. The first wife quarreled very much with Parrette's family over Parrette's bride price. Then Fouché began committing atrocities of the most sanguinary in Lyons, the entire street was destroyed, and with it, their livelihood. They all fled the city. Through Duflot's relations, Parrette discovered that Duflot went off to Italy with his corps, and she followed, wanting much to get Michel back. When she at last finds—found—them, it was that her husband was killed in a brawl with a sailor, before their ship fell into the hands of the English. The prisoners were told, choose impressment or prison. She found the prison, to discover Michel chose impressment, we thought to get away from his father."

"How did she come to your family?"

"My mother discovered her penniless and abandoned in Calabria. She hired Parrette as a tire woman, but soon promoted her to personal maid. Parrette was devoted to my mother, oh, much, and after she died, she was like a mother to me."

The sun had gone behind a cloud, dimming the strong sunlight. When she glanced up, her eyes met his. She dropped her gaze to his hands, clean, with well-kept nails. "She never gave up hope of finding Michel."

Then a new thought occurred to her. Michel had come with the supply ship. It was here.

She glanced out the stern windows, and made out the uneven line of Spain on the horizon. They had left the great ships behind, and were now closer to land. "Are we to expect to be sent to Gibraltar, then? Our trunks can be made ready in a moment."

Captain Duncannon bowed slightly. "My sincere apologies, but my orders from my superiors will have to supersede my offer. The tender shall be required to run dispatches. I beg your forgiveness, and I promise we shall do our best to accommodate you as we can."

She was spared the necessity of expressing her disappointment when there came an insistent scratch at the door. A small midshipman came in, hat squashed tightly to his side. He flushed scarlet when he saw Anna. "Sir, the officer of the w-watch s-sent me t-t-to..." He lost his breath, shut his eyes hard, and let out the word, "Signals."

"Thank you, Mr. Corcoran. I shall be on deck directly."

"S-s-sir."

The captain rose and reached into a trunk behind him. He came out with a small stack of books, which he handed to Anna. "I took the liberty of making up a collection, between Sayers, myself, and the surgeon's mate. I must return to duty. Will you honor us with your company at dinner?" And then, "I mentioned our musicians. Perhaps I ought to warn you that we must rely on ourselves for entertainment, and so you are not to be expecting expertise. It would be perfectly understandable should you object to hearing music written for strings tootled on winds."

Anna did not know what to make of this grand statement, whose effect was somehow overpowering. She knew him too little to detect the signs of embarrassment, even guilt for the necessary lie to cover his orders.

She spread her hands. "I am happiest hearing music," she said. "Any music will do." She curtseyed, then picked up the books. She meant to whisk herself out, but she had scarcely made it two steps before the ship pitched sharply.

Her hands being full of books, she teetered. He sprang to her side and set his palms along her arms. His breath stirred the top of her hair. She felt the heat of a blush from her cheeks to her toes and sped into the little cabin next door.

She set the books on her trunk, relieved to find herself alone. She brushed her fingers over the top of her head, and blushed again, but at least no one was there to see it.

Dinner was enlivened by the presence of three of Captain Duncannon's officers: the tall, gaunt surgeon's mate, Mr. Jorgensen; a spotty-faced, gangling midshipman named Mr. Jones, who seemed lost in his uniform; and pale-haired Mr. Sayers.

Initially, Anna could see how constrained they were by her presence. Every remark occasioned a quick glance her way, often with another peek at the captain as if to see how he judged their words. Only Mr. Sayers and the captain spoke easily, their accent very alike — even the rise and fall of their voices, their phrasings, so similar that Anna suspected before the captain mentioned it that they had known one another in school.

"Even then," Mr. Sayers said to Anna, "the captain was your great musician, though only in the fourth form. I was inspired to take up the flute because of him; you may either congratulate or condemn him after we have played for you."

Anna had never seen Captain Duncannon smile like that. There were attractive shadows outside of his mouth, small ones that made him seem young as any of the boys, though only for a moment. His smile was quick, there a moment then gone, a grace-note. Mr. Sayers smiled steadily, his eyes narrowed with good humor.

"Though I was always partial to music, learning the clarinet began entirely as a subterfuge," Captain Duncannon admitted. "I was ten years old, and discovered that the headmaster gave extra leave to those who went into the village to an old Italian music master who had retired there, teaching several instruments. I would do anything to get out of school on long spring and summer afternoons, and I thought the clarinet would be easier to learn than the violin. The joke was on me, as it became my boyhood passion." He turned to Mr. Jones. "You said you found the flute easy, I recollect."

Mr. Jones flushed. "Only because I'd first learnt trumpet—" His voice broke. He flushed even redder, abandoned whatever he was going to say, and gulped his wine.

Anna was relieved that Captain Duncannon had occasioned only two bottles of wine to be set out, and there was tea as well as water. Mr. Jorgensen, it transpired, did not touch wine. Anna was able to water hers, and confined herself to a single glass.

She noted that the captain only refilled the boys' glasses once, and the rest of the second bottle was split between him and his first lieutenant.

When they drank the health of the king, the meal was deemed finished—and she was not expected to go sit alone. Instead, the captain told her they would set up for music, and she might watch if it would amuse her. The steward brought in a couple of his mates, the table was knocked apart into pieces with a couple of smart blows from a mallet, and then tidied away in the matter of a minute, as the four musicians took out their instruments and readied them.

Grog was brought out, a tankard set by each music stand, and then the mates departed.

The four tapped the checkered deck, watching each other, then struck up the well-known Bach air "Wachet auf." It was odd, hearing it played by wind instruments rather than violins, but then Anna had also heard it on the harpsichord as well as the fortepiano. Though the musicians varied in skill, she rather thought that Maestro Paisiello would approve of the arrangement.

Oh, Maestro Paisiello! She hoped he was well in Paris, writing great music now that he had an emperor as patron.

Paris. She did not miss Paris as much as she missed the maestro, or maybe it was really that she missed those warm days in Naples's summery weather, the smell of orange blossoms drifting in the open windows while she was singing her scales. Looking out upon the lacy fig trees and myrtle hedges as she practiced her first arias.

She recollected how fervently she had promised never to slacken her studies, and she resolved to find some corner of the ship where she could at least hum, to warm her voice and work on her breathing. Perhaps she could recapture the old joy.

Her reverie ended with the Bach air. The players went straight into the "D Suite," to which she unconsciously tapped her foot to the strongly marked time, gazing out from under the low ceiling of the quarterdeck into the golden afternoon sunlight. The music carried beautifully, and in this, the first dog watch of the late afternoon, those not on duty gathered on deck to listen, to make and mend, and a few sailors on the forecastle used the beat to dance hornpipes. One young upper yardman dared the capstan, twirling and kicking nimbly without missing step in spite of the roll of the deck.

The captain's outer doors standing open, Anna was drawn out by degrees to observe, until she heard an adolescent snort of laughter, and caught sight of two midshipmen bumping a third, a very small boy, in her direction.

She recognized instantly what was going on, from her days in the royal nursery: the older ones were using rank, or size, or both, to propel the younger one into doing something he was reluctant to do. She recognized little Mr. Corcoran, who couldn't have been more than twelve.

Catching her eye, he paced stiffly to her, bowed and made his leg, then said with a kind of desperate formality, "Will you honor me with a dance, mum?"

She held out her hand and said, "Why yes, thank you."

And with her toes pointed, and her hand held high, she minced with the gratified Mr. Corcoran to a small space in the waist between two boats, and they pranced out the measures of a minuet.

She rejoiced at her ability to perform the dance without falling. *Men have strong legs, sure*, Lise had said what felt like a lifetime ago. *But their balance is all in their shoulders. Watch their turns, it is always shoulders first. But us? The secret is to lead with the hips.*

And so Anna let her hips sway with the yaw of the ship. In the slanting rays of afternoon, with the light airs abaft the beam in the frigate's happiest point of sailing, sailors—the most superstitious beings alive—universally regarded her smiling, graceful presence as a lucky omen.

At the end of that piece, the bigger boys summarily thrust aside their junior, and each brazenly offered to dance with Anna. She enjoyed the air and the exercise, and smilingly assented to each.

The quartet played, and she danced, until the *ting-ting* announced the second dog watch. The music ended. The thunder of feet on the gun decks meant cannon drill. Most of the rest of the great cabin vanished as summarily as the dining table had, revealing carronades housed in the stern. Only the little cabin assigned to Anna remained, and she perforce retreated to it so as not to be in the way.

Parrette was still absent. Anna guessed she was with Michel, and picked up the top book, *Splendid Misery*, by one Thomas Skinner Surr. She sat on the stern window bench to read by the fading light, but she was distracted by the rumble and bump of the guns being run out and back. Her thoughts drifted from the sound to the man who commanded such effort.

She had never seen Captain Duncannon smile before this day. The contrast was marked. It demonstrated how very reserved he had been.

"I suppose I am a burden to him," she thought, tucking her feet under her, the book open upon her lap, as she gazed out at the ever-widening wake.

In a sense it was just, for she had found him a burden, too. False marriage—false expectations on the part of others—even the false conclusion about his ship having mutinied against him—she could not blame *him*. It was the awkwardness, the unsettled sensations that she disliked. Balked of being conveyed to Gibraltar, she could not plan her life until she was quit of him. No doubt he felt the same.

Promptly at eight the watch changed again, the din of running feet now caused by the bringing of hammocks from the netting to be slung between the guns, as the great cabin was put back together again. The ship gradually quieted as much as it ever did, and she ventured out to take a last turn upon the deck before retiring for the night.

She spied Mr. Leuven, who tipped his hat courteously. He broke into a broad smile when she greeted him in Italian, and they made their way, laborious on his part, through a stilted conversation about the weather (*bello*), the music (*bella*), and the ship (*bellissima*) before he went below. She did not correct his errors; she thought he would learn the faster by hearing her phrasing.

She had reached the bow, and was turning to walk back when she was surprised by a party of midshipmen who had evidently been lying in wait.

Once again it was little Mr. Corcoran who approached. "Please, mum," he said, doffing his hat and making a leg. "Do you know any French songs?"

"You wish to learn French songs?" she asked.

"Not in the way of singing *French* songs," he began, looking left to right. "By that I mean, not their words."

The tall, handsome blond master's mate, his uniform better made than the others, pushed impatiently past. "My name is d'Ivry," he said with an air of expectation, his cleft chin raised. "If you please, will you accompany us to the cockpit—that is, to our quarters? Our question is in the nature of a..." He glanced quickly around, as if worried about being caught. "Of a *privileged* nature."

"But of course," she said, hiding a spurt of amusement at the covert nudges and shifty glances exchanged between the boys.

She remembered the stuffy little hole that the captain's clerk had shown her. It was exactly as stuffy as she'd remembered, smelling strongly of adolescent boy, though the small, oddly spaced shape was scrupulously tidy. The trunks had been shoved together in the middle to form a rough-and-ready table for the boys to eat and work at, and shelves fitted into the walls and even overhead, into which were stored plates, glasses, newly-brought loaves of sugar, clothes brushes, boots, cocked hats, dirks, writing desks, and even musical instruments. In the far corner sat sacks of potatoes, containers of sea biscuits and other comestibles belonging to their mess.

Five of the six midshipmen gathered around the trunk-table, on which sat a single candle and a plate of butter; one boy was missing, being on watch. "You see, Vesuvius Jones, here, is a poet as well as a capital flute player," d'Ivry began, indicating the boy with the spotty face — the latter rolling his eyes to convey his silent opinion of his nickname.

"We have been putting together a review, for the ship," d'Ivry said. "The seamen put on a play aboard *Victory*, you know, and we aim to top them with a better. They sang the same old songs. Jones writes new words to songs."

"In the way of 'Yankee Doodle,'" another midshipman put in, a thin, earnest boy with spectacles flashing on his nose, and a somewhat pedantic manner. "Which all the crack in our fathers' day. Started out as 'Lucy Locket,' you know."

"Stop your gob, Gilchrist," Bradshaw muttered. "You and your fathers' day." He yanked the younger boy back.

"But it's *true* —"

"Oh, stick a macaroni up your —"

"You don't *stick* macaronis, you *were* one," Gilchrist said painstakingly. "My Uncle Timmons was a macaroni —"

It looked to Anna as if Mr. Gilchrist was going to be choked out of having his say. To prevent what looked very like impending murder, she turned to him. "What, pray, do you mean by macaroni? I know another meaning, in Italy, a food made of durum."

Thus addressed, Mr. Gilchrist was summarily freed by Bradshaw and Jones. As he put his spectacles right and straightened his jacket, he said, "It was a fashion, you see. 'Call it macaroni' refers to a fashion. My uncle was a famous one. Never spoke anything but French, wore great ladder toupets, and painted his lips red."

"They all painted," Jones put in. "Men *and* women."

"But not in pictures," Mr. Gilchrist returned.

He was thrust aside by d'Ivry, who said, "At all events, ma'am, Bradshaw has the way of it. We make new songs, to sing in the fleet, to old tunes. We thought it would be capital if we might put new words to French songs. But we're keeping it dead secret, see. It will be so much better if we spring it on 'em."

"Ah," Anna said, thought, and then quickly, softly, sang "*Ça Ira*."

The boys instantly took to the catchy tune. "Might I trouble you to sing it again, please?" Mr. Jones asked.

"I will take you through it in phrases."

Anna pitched her voice to carry no further than the room, and instructed them the way she had been taught, phrase by phrase, with the result they not only got melody and words, but they were reasonably on pitch. She was less satisfied with her own voice. To her sensitive ear, she sounded lamentably rusty. She must at least find a way to do her scales, she promised herself, as the boys complimented her on a thumping great song.

Seeing how pleased they were, she gave them "*La Carmagnole*," which they liked even better.

They fell to putting together their own phrases, calling out to Jones for rhymes. Anna left them to their poetic afflatus, and made her way along the deck, enjoying the fresh air. She acknowledged every knuckled forehead, every lifted hat with a smile and a dip of her head, as polite to the one-legged cook's mate as she was to the first lieutenant, standing on the windward side of the quarterdeck as she passed below into the cabin.

Parrette had returned. "Michel took me aboard the little ship," she said. "He was given a day's liberty, that we might catch up." She wiped puffy eyes; she had apparently been weeping, but Anna knew better than to take notice. "Oh, I am so happy. So happy!"

She added with a hint of her old ferocity. "Though I would be happier if we could but leave in Michel's company before this threatened battle that they all anticipate with such joy. Men! Shall I lay out your night things?"

"Not yet. I am going to read for a time."

Parrette gave a short nod. "So I shall repair to the gunroom. Michel sits there, and I have offered to make myself of use. I will mend anything I am asked."

"Michel!" Anna exclaimed. "Surely he has told you his history?"

Parrette's lips thinned. "He has begun to do so. Even though he was given liberty, he was interrupted, oh, so much! And we wandered down many other paths. His memories of Lyons, what happened there. We talked in circles," she finished, with evident satisfaction. "It will take many days to relate it all."

"I would very much like to hear it," Anna said.

"So you shall. Michel will tell you himself, when things are settled." She did not further define 'settled' but left the cabin. Anna curled up into the bench below the stern window, between two lanterns, and opened Mr. Surr's novel.

But it was not the novel that claimed her attention. Her eyes skimmed over the words, the sense escaping her. She began a page three times before setting the book on her lap.

She knew what it was. She wanted, for the first time, to converse with the captain. There was no urgent question. It was just that ever since she had heard his music, and begun to know a little about his crew, she longed to ask about it all. How long had they been playing together, was it always Bach? Did he hire crew, or were they assigned in some way? Did he seek musicians?

Innocent questions, she hoped, scarcely impertinent, or encroaching. And yet she was hesitant to take the ten short steps to the door, and to poke her head out, though she could hear him moving about directly above her; there was the rumble of his voice through the skylight above his dining cabin, on the other side of the thin false walls.

No one had told her to confine herself to this cabin. She went to the door, opened it, and looked out. The great doors to the cabin had been replaced after the gun exercise. She stepped out at the same moment the door opened, and here was the captain himself.

He checked at the sight of her, as the marine guard clashed his musket on the deck.

"Good evening, Mrs. Duncannon," he said, his voice dropping self-consciously a note on the name that neither was at all accustomed to. He glanced to the side and then back, and said, "It is our customary time for supper, and while in general I cannot recommend stale, weevily ship's biscuits, or the other heel taps we have been obliged to eat, thanks to the return of the tender, we now have fresh hardtack and cheese to go with it. If you would care to join us, we would be honored."

The smell of toasted cheese had already traveled along with the steward bearing a heavy tray. With suddenly awakened appetite, Anna thanked him.

When she entered the dining cabin, the easy chatter stopped as the officers rose. Anna saw the subtle signals of the constraint. To call attention to their sudden restraint would only worsen it. If she wished to banish it, she must find a topic that would circumvent it. And that, she thought, meant finding something that would not keep her at the center of conversation. "I enjoyed, oh, very much, the Bach quartets. But I asked myself, why the violins thus arranged for wind? Are there not many fine pieces written for winds?"

A quick exchange of looks, then Lieutenant Sayers said with an apologetic air, "Mine is the blame, ma'am, if blame there is to be. It is a favorite exercise, transposing them. If the lady will indulge me with what might be a tedious explanation..."

"But there is nothing tedious about music," she said. "It is my favorite topic."

Lt. Sayers flushed slightly. "Then with your permission: I believe there is a strong affinity between music and mathematics. The purity of the one translates to the purity of the other. While our esteemed Lt. Abrams here maintains that the two have little in common beyond the numbers of notes and bars."

He indicated the stout commander of the ship's Royal Marines, whose bristling red eyebrows clashed oddly with his neatly powdered hair.

"No, no," Lt. Abrams said genially, hands upraised. "I grant you more than that. I do, and no mistake. But the element of *sensibility*, now that, I think it fair to say, no, mathematics cannot touch. You cannot make a claim upon the point of sensibility, one might say emotion. There is no equation for that, is there, gentlemen?"

"On the contrary, if you will forgive me, Abrams," Lt. Sayers said mildly. "On the contrary. If one wishes to evoke sensations of sorrow, of reflection, what better than the *andante* count, which is to say, a numerical—mathematical—quantity?"

"I cannot agree," the marine lieutenant exclaimed. "A sprightly song played slowly is lugubrious. A dirge played fast becomes a farce. These counts are incidental, that is to say, more than mathematical quantities. They are bound to emotions: no matter what language, or even if a man cannot count, he understands that 'allegro' means merry, that it raises sensations of joy, of cheer, in the breast."

"Allegro," Lt. Sayers admonished, "is a strict count, 120 beats to the minute.

Anna knew nothing about mathematics; in ballet 'allegro' referred to the steps of elevation, the *sautes, soubresauts, changements,* and *echappes,* and so forth, but she remembered Philippe's admonishments to lift the heart, to express joy. *It is universal*, he had said. *The emotion raised when ballet is done well is universal.*

She would not speak. She listened to the ensuing debate with a fair assumption of interest, her smile entirely due to her sense of triumph. They were talking again. If not with their former ease, at least they were not sitting mumchance, laboring to find topics suitable for the intruder into their wooden world upon the sea.

She stayed long enough to eat a bread-and-cheese, and at the first pause in the conversation, rose to excuse herself.

Instantly the constraint was back. "Is there anything you need?" Captain Duncannon asked. "You have only to mention it."

The impulse came from nowhere; she hadn't really thought about it. "Actually, there is," she said slowly, and viewed the waiting faces, the curiously blank faces. What did they expect her to demand?

She smiled. "You will say, I am frivolous, and I will not deny it. But when we were aboard the *Victory*, I saw that the other ladies all wore hats. In Spain, we did not."

Captain Duncannon said with a conscious air, "I beg leave to apologize, but the tender will not be returning to Gibraltar."

"Yes, so I was told, and I remember, me. But I was thinking that nothing would make me happier than to make one for myself. I saw some men working with sennit earlier, and I wondered if there might be a little extra. I would pay for it, if that is the custom—I would not ask for anything to be given me that is not my due. I could plait the brim myself, and the rest is easily got from my own things."

The waiting faces all relaxed and smiled once again.

"Why, nothing would be easier," Lt. Sayers exclaimed heartily. "First thing in the morning watch I'll have a word with Mr. Gates. We will rouse you out whatever you need. We carry plenty of sennit, more than enough for our needs."

"Thank you, Lieutenant Say-*airrrs*," she said, doing her best to get his name out right, without being aware of how delightfully her accent fell on English ears.

The men rose and bowed. She curtseyed and left.

There, she thought as she let herself into her cabin. The men's voices, punctuated by laughter, carried on, the words muffled by the intervening wall. They were enjoying themselves, clearly. Perhaps the better without her there?

She shifted the lantern to the hook above the bed, and paused, distracted. This was *his* place of rest. She wondered if the captain must regularly read himself to sleep.

It was strange to think that this was his bed, that he regularly looked out this window, or up at the deck just there. What did he think when he saw those scratches? Did he think about her climbing into his bed, she wondered as she settled herself and pulled the hangings to admit the lantern light, but shut out the rest of the cabin. There was a curious sense of intimacy in it all.

She read until the flicker of light caused by the constant movement tired her eyes. She blew out the light, shut her eyes and slipped into dreams, as in the next cabin over, the guests departed and Captain Duncannon dealt with the last of the official post that had been brought by the tender.

He was finishing that up when Lt. Sayers returned after his last round of the deck, and asked permission to enter. The lieutenant glanced at the desk, reflecting once more on how nearly every reading man in the ship (and some of those who didn't read) had in expectation of battle been writing or dictating letters home, except the captain.

Duncannon looked up expectantly, and Sayers gave a succinct report on the state of the sails and sea. They talked a little of ship's business, and the lieutenant prepared to leave.

The captain raised a hand to halt him. He officially took no notice of his midshipmen's maneuvering to put together their review, a fact of which they remained blissfully unaware. When they weren't squabbling among themselves, they were a good set of youngsters, attentive to their duty, and their determination to outdo the other ships' attempts at theatricals kept them busy.

But he would not permit them to disturb the lady.

Out of long habit against the listening ears on the other side of the skylight overhead, Captain Duncannon said, "*Pueri numquid domina fatiga?*"

They both knew that their schoolboy Latin was wretched. But their former masters were not here to be shocked at their mangled ablatives, and Sayers understood the captain's concern that the boys might be pestering his wife.

"*Eorum antics,*" Sayers said carefully, as the captain translated to himself, *Their antics.*

"*Oblectandi eam.*"

Amuse her. And Sayers nodded firmly.

Very well, the captain thought, he need not interfere. He was aware of a surge of gratitude toward her, even of good will. No, he had to be honest, if only within himself: he was beginning to look forward to their conversations.

That could lead to nothing good. He had been made a fool of once, and he had vowed to be done with women and their ambitions. He did not know what this one wanted, but he was certain that if he asked, he would not hear the truth. Women were never straightforward the way a man was. He would avoid her at breakfast—easy to do, as there was plenty of ship's business always awaiting his attention.

Eighteen

THE NEXT MORNING, PARRETTE brought in tea, waking Anna. She said in Neapolitan, "I would have told you that ladies do not make hats."

"But my mother taught me," Anna exclaimed as she rolled out of the swinging bed. "I remember it so well. We plaited together as I sang for her."

"So it was." Parrette tipped her head to the side. "But only when you were alone, that no one could see. Her own mother taught her, and she used that skill to make your hats because money was always so scarce. But the English at Naples thought she bought them."

Anna said, low, "I had no notion."

"Eh, *toutefois*," Parrette said as she pulled out a fresh gown and gave it a vigorous shake. "I have learned that English ladies will sometimes *trim* their hats. And also, there is a lady in the fleet who made trouble wanting naval ships to go off to buy her new hats, as if they had nothing else to do. A marquis's daughter? And so, you, making your hat? There is general approval."

"I did not look for approval," Anna said, laughing as she shrugged into her gown, and the hem fell about her feet. She reached for her sash. "But I do require a hat, if I am expected to appear properly English. I wonder if hats are in fashion again in Paris, now there is an emperor?"

"Who knows? We are not in Paris." Parrette shrugged as she carefully unwrapped the edging of a hat brim. "I went ahead and started it, while I was waiting for the hot water."

"The most difficult part," Anna acknowledged, and thanked her.

"Now, let us get your hair brushed out. What if The Captain expects you for breakfast? You know how they are ruled by these bells, tingle-r-r-r-ringle, tumble-r-r-r-rumble."

But when seven bells started the tumult of "hammocks up," Perkins arrived with a tray at their door. The captain, it seemed, was busy elsewhere in the ship.

Consequently Anna ate alone, then picked up her sennit and brim, and made her way to the deck.

The air was cool, the sun's fiery rim crowning the headlands above Cadiz in the distance. She could make out the silhouette of another frigate against the horizon, but they were no longer in that long line of battleships, as far as she could tell, and she wondered if that meant the danger of war was over.

Heartened, she took a turn about the deck and hummed through her scales. When she reached the prow, the little boy in the overlarge uniform came her way, grinning. He made a correct leg, lifted his hat, and then ruined the effect of this debonair politesse by looking around furtively.

"Should you care to hear what we have, ma'am?"

"I would very much!"

Though he could scarcely get out a sentence without his tortured stutter, for some reason Mr. Corcoran could sing. His high treble was even true to pitch as he quickly sang "Johnny Crapaud" to the tune of "Ça Ira." The words were typical of boyish humor, scurrilous rather than genuinely humorous. She had heard the same sort of song sung on the streets of Paris by urchins there, and took it in much the same spirit: she wondered what might happen if the boys from either country met one another in circumstances outside of war. They might find humor, and games, in common.

She hoped that would happen, that the war would vanish like the morning mist as she gave him the nod of approval that he was plainly expecting, before he was summarily elbowed aside by the stout, black-haired Mr. Bradshaw.

"I wanted to ask, ma'am, have you been in Barford Magna recently?"

"I have never been there at all," she replied. "Am I to know where this is?"

His eyes rounded. "Why, it is the captain's home. That is, he lives at the Manor, I mean, his family is from there. The Lord Northcotes have been barons there forever. But if you don't know it, how could you be married?"

She could not prevent a smile. "The marriage happened elsewhere."

"Oh," he said.

His look of acute disappointment was easily interpreted: this sturdy, rough-and-tumble boy missed his home. "Tell me about Barford Magna," she said.

He smiled, but it was soon clear that the question, though gratifying, was too large to compass. He did not know where to begin. He made a helpless gesture, and began in an important voice, "It is a very large parish, ma'am..."

"Did you know the captain there?" she asked, hoping to help him along.

His eyes widened. "Oh, no! He was gone as a middie before I was breeched. And I wouldn't be acquainted with the family in any case," he added scrupulously, though in a low voice. "My father being a bookseller. But I live right there on High Street. And I've seen the baron twice. The new baron," he added. "The old baron being dead now. The new baron is a capital whip. He drives two pairs of matched bays." His voice dropped on the word 'two' and he held up a pair of fingers for emphasis. "He drives a curricle, a capital set-out. Right through the village, at a smashing pace up the middle of High Street itself, sending dogs barking and chickens cackling!" His blue eyes widened. "He wears at least ten capes to his greatcoat. You cannot conceive – the completist thing! In any case, we haven't had post from home in a thousand ages, at least a year."

"Mr. Bradshaw."

The boy straightened up guiltily, pulling his hands from his pockets as Mr. Sayers appeared. "It seems you have nothing to occupy you, unlike the rest of your watch. With your permission, I believe we will remedy that. The captain wants a party made up to sort the rusted balls."

"Yes, sir," was the resigned reply, and Anna was left to finish her walk. She tucked her cloth-covered package more securely under her arm, and began to look about for a place to settle down. She had just passed the waist when she encountered a big sailor. "Might I put a question to you?"

"Yes, mum." He knuckled his forehead. "Finch, gunner's first mate, mum."

She turned her smile up to his enormous, unlovely face. "Good day, Mr. Finch. Where may I sit, and be out of the way?"

It was shortly before noon that Captain Duncannon finished a long inspection of the shot locker. He emerged on deck to find the lady sitting decorously on a cheese of cannon wads. She had chosen her spot on the lee side of the quarterdeck, well away from the holy weather side, reserved to the captain or his representative when he was not on deck. So quickly she seemed to have grasped the invisible but iron-clad rules.

She sat quietly working on plaiting her hat, her fingers slow and careful as she smiled up at little Mr. Corcoran. From the sextant in his hands, and his gestures up toward the sun and out at the horizon, the captain surmised he was stuttering his way through an explanation of the noon sighting, the most important part of the ship's day.

He moved away to the windward rail, and lifted his telescope to sweep the headland.

The captain was thus in profile to Anna, the strong morning sun outlining his face. Her attention was caught by the shadows emphasizing the strong line of his cheeks, the severe lips as he peered at the land so far away.

The sun lit the tips of his lashes, turning them to gold.

She looked away, to hide the cascade of sensation in her heart. She knew this sensation, as if a rose inside her had softly unfurled a petal. She had rejoiced in this feeling once, with Auguste, and as a result was nearly burnt to death. She had begun to feel it with Jean-Baptiste Marsac, who had betrayed her.

Captain Duncannon was no mad chasseur, and no smiling traitor like Marsac. He was a good man, so far as she had seen, but she had also seen just as clearly that he had no use for women. No use for her. This ship was his life, and she would soon be off it.

So she must simply keep out of his way, before the rose could unfold and dig its thorns into her heart. She laid the hat in her lap, debating whether to go below and work on it, or remain there until the sun was too high and strong, but then a man called from on high, "On deck! Signals!"

Jones, the signal midshipman, dashed by, and Anna listened as the sailors and officers exchanged quick, cryptic remarks, everyone gazing off in one direction. "It's the *Euryalus*," came Mr. Jones's excited voice as he dashed up to the captain to salute. "Sir, *Euryalus* signals, 'Enemy have tops'ls hoisted.'"

"They're coming out!" Mr. Bradshaw shouted, and then looked aghast at his captain.

Duncannon's mouth twitched, but he did not move from his position. After a long breath, he said, "Mr. Bradshaw, I commend your enthusiasm, but perhaps you may put your enthusiasm to use at the foremast-head. You may watch the shore, and as you do, contemplate the matter of ship discipline."

Anna looked after the crimson-faced Bradshaw as he scrambled upward into the complication of ropes and sails, vanishing from sight. Everyone straightened up, alert, their smiles reminding Anna uncomfortably of the similar looks on the faces of the chasseurs when they came over the lip of the stage and stampeded to the back of the theater. It was anticipation of game, dangerous game.

She picked up her pile of sennit, carefully folded her half-plaited brim, and retreated to her cabin. Parrette was there, hanging chemises on a line across the cabin to dry in the air from the open stern windows.

"What is it?" she asked when she saw Anna's face.

"They received a signal, something about certain sails. I think it must mean something dire."

Parrette gave a short nod. "One cannot disturb the officers at their duty, but I can ask below." She whisked herself out, and returned almost immediately with Michel, who glanced at the line of washing, blushed, then turned his back on it.

He ducked his head in an awkward bow to Anna, and then, crushing his cap in his hands, said, "It means the French are coming out. I will tell you as soon as I know more."

"Good," Parrette said, and Michel ducked again and took his leave.

An hour, two, three passed. Anna forced herself to return to her task, though at first her fingers trembled. Every time she heard feet running about on the deck she braced for the terrible sound of cannon.

Michel reappeared in the early afternoon. "The admiral has given orders for a general chase to the south-east."

"Does that mean there will be battle?" Parrette asked.

Michel's thin lips curled. He looked very like his mother in that moment. "First we have to see 'em. I have to go. Gates will want me by."

Anna and Parrette were left staring at one another. Anna forced herself to sit down again, and resume her hat, carefully tightening each strand as if she could weave order into the world.

She assumed she must stay in her cabin, and was surprised when the steward Perkins scratched to invite her to dinner. She touched her hair and straightened her sash, and walked out to discover all the officers waiting, lieutenants, marines, and midshipmen.

Today, she was placed at the foot of the table. Though the gentlemen scrupulously saluted her as hostess, that was the last time she had any part of their attention.

They talked nothing but war: Nelson's daring plan of attack, who had the honor of following *Victory* and *Neptune*, where the frigates would be stationed; what the French might do first, Villeneuve's terrible record of battles, and Gravina's good one. What if the weather turned bad? There were signs of storms ahead.

Voices sharper, eyes brighter, laughter loud enough to hurt her ears, they were all excited. Captain Duncannon, sitting opposite her at the other end of the long table, smiled genially, looking more like a young man of twenty than a man near thirty as he toasted, and laughed.

It was a relief when it was over, and the captain remembered her at last, inviting her to take a turn on the deck.

Here, she was surprised to find the entire ship's company present. There would be no music; most of the sailors not actually tending the ship sat about chipping and knocking at round, evil-looking balls of iron. The deck sounded like a demented band of tinkers as rust and bumps were smoothed off the cannon balls as lovingly as if they made pieces of art.

She encountered Mr. Leuven standing with a knot of warrant officers with their spyglasses, staring at the coast in spite of the sun still being relatively high in the sky. He approached her to initiate a conversation in Italian about the expected triumph and glory to come. From the scornful glances of the older midshipmen, it appeared that this obviously rehearsed speech had not impressed them the way it was intended.

When they returned to duty, she passed along the gangway, stepping aside for a party of sailors carrying a long worm of rolled sail.

Forward of the mainmast, a young gunner's mate smiled at her as he passed a ball back and forth between his hands, his fingers gently fingering the ball for smoothness. She smiled back, unable to comprehend the good will here—good will about something that was deliberately intended to be lethal to the unseen French and Spanish sailors, who were without a doubt employed the very same way aboard their ships.

She paused at the ladder to the upper deck, caught by the sight of the captain standing on his quarterdeck as the rising wind rippled through his blue coat and tousled his brown hair. He moved with easy grace as the ship slanted upward and plunged through the mounting waves, sending splashes high to each side. He did not see her, that she was certain of. His mind was on another plane altogether, alert and intense, perhaps bordering somewhere on happiness. She knew that plane—it was the same one her mind went to when she first trod to her place as the orchestra tuned their instruments and the stage hands held the curtain pulls, waiting for the signal. But though an opera performance might depict war and tragedy, everyone knew he or she would rise again when the curtain fell: it was art.

Did the captain think war was art? It was strange that he should seem so pleased at the prospect of the ship surging straight toward the terrible cannon of the enemy.

She turned away, slipped below, and abandoned plaiting, as it gave her too much occasion to think and to worry. She picked up the book she had tried so many times to begin, and concentrated upon it until her eyes burned with tiredness.

Her sleep was restless, partly from apprehensive dreams, but also from an unaccustomed violent sway of her hanging bed. She woke to a gray world: sky, sea, and bands of thick rain.

"They have lost sight of the French," Parrette said abruptly when she appeared with Anna's tea. "I am also to warn you that when the orders come, they will be striking down our cabin. Our trunks are to go in the hold with the rest of the captain's things."

Anna set her cup down. Her stomach had closed. "Perhaps I had better wear my sturdiest travel gown."

Parrette said, "I am of the same mind." She moved about in the little space, busy straightening, patting, and tucking.

Anna, knowing her well, sensed that there was something else. "What is it?"

Parrette turned. "I learned in the gunroom that I am expected to aid the surgeon. Women are put to work as nurses. You are the captain's lady, so no one will say anything unless the captain does."

"And yet, I think it is expected of me, too," she said, remembering Nelson's horrible words about knives, so kindly spoken. "I will request an interview with the surgeon. It will give me something to do. This waiting is terrible."

"Fighting," Parrette said in French, low and rough, "will be worse."

There was no answer to be made to that.

Anna quickly finished the dish of burgoo. She heard no noises from the other side of the bulkheads, surmising that Captain

Duncannon had been on deck since the very early hours.

Parrette went ahead, having become acquainted with Mr. Leuven senior after taking meals in the gunroom. She returned soon and led Anna to the lower deck, all the way forward to the dark, dank, stuffy area where the surgeon worked. Little air made it through the gratings this low in the ship.

Mr. Leuven waited in the low-ceilinged space, his head bent, for he was a tall man. All around the perimeter narrow pallets had been set out below a few hammocks. Central was a table, with instruments lying at one end. Steel instruments, the sight of which caused Anna's stomach to churn. The closeness of the room was not helped by the heavy scent of spirits. Was the surgeon drunk?

"Mrs. Duncannon," Mr. Leuven said, his pouchy eyes alert. "Mrs. Duflot." A gnarled hand swept in a circle. "I thank you heartily. Here is our action-station once they beat to quarters. Permit me to explain my system, my own system."

He pointed out the bandages, the needles for sewing, and rested his hand on a barrel. "I am not a certificated physician, but I have been practicing surgery upwards of thirty years. You may leave the surgery to me and my mates. If we get anyone coming below, they come quick, especially if the enemy uses canister or chain-shot. But even a ball making a shrewd strike will send splinters flying."

He raised his palm upward. "You know that the sick berth is on the deck above us, starboard side. But you will not be carrying. If the men are not ambulatory, we set them in the cable tiers until we can shift them to the sick berth."

Anna found her mouth was dry. She looked away from the cold steel instruments waiting on the surgeon's chest, and the row of bottles.

The surgeon, catching the direction of her glance, said, "We will not be concerning ourselves with physic, or the usual run of diseases exhibited by seamen. It will be torn flesh, not diseased, that will be our concern. And I have a singular practice, not at all accepted among my colleagues, but one day I hope to publish my treatise. What I do have is experience."

He tapped the barrel. "The men know my method. In here is the finest whiskey. The men will beg or plead for it. Seamen in battle long to get drunk, or they will insist they require its medicinal properties. There are no internal medicinal properties. It is all external: that is, when properly exhibited in a severe wound, it acts upon the nerves in the exact same way as a cauterizing fire. The sensation is burning. But the flesh is not burned. You will put a dose of this into each wound before wrapping it."

"Spirits, in wounds, Mr. Leuven?" Parrette asked. "Not lint? How does more liquid sop up the blood?"

"Spirits, sew, wrap," the surgeon repeated doggedly, as if he had held this argument many times before. As indeed he had. His manner convinced his listeners that he was not to be moved from this strange course, and as neither Anna nor Parrette knew much of nursing, he was able to go on. "We save the powder of basilicum for superficial wounds. Use the lint if we run out of powder. You can see." He lifted the tightly fitted lid on a wooden bucket. "I am very careful where I get it. There are quacks and cranks a-many out there who will sell you powder of lead instead, they will practice upon the gullible, and so I am careful. We have thus not been able to fill it. Gibraltar runs low as soon as they acquire it."

He took in the wary disbelief in the women's faces, their tight mouths as they looked at his barrel. "Five and thirty years have I practiced," Mr. Leuven said. "It was an old infantryman when I was a lad, who told me yarns about his mates dousing their wounds with wine and spirits during the campaigns on the colonies, the War of Jenkins' Ear. He was much scarred, but had all his limbs. When I experimented, I discovered that his tales were largely true. I have since then been formulating my theory…"

While he went on in exhaustive detail to the silent women, in the cabin, the captain was finishing a consultation with the gunner and bosun. Lt. Sayers paused in the open door, and on being beckoned in, listened to the last of it.

The bosun and carpenter having been dismissed, Lt. Sayers said, "We have hawsers laid along, against the wind freshening."

Captain Duncannon replied, "The signal midshipman just reported: *Euryalus* has spotted the French again. They are indeed out."

On receiving the captain's nod, Sayers slid his hand into his coat, and withdrew a sealed letter. With no more than a heightened color, the lieutenant said, "You have my letter to my father, still." On receiving another nod and a gesture toward the locked desk, he continued. "If it becomes — if it is necessary, would you do me the honor of seeing that this also goes out?"

Captain Duncannon accepted the letter, glanced at the direction, and recognized the name of Lt. Sayers's betrothed. "I pray that it does not come to this, but you have my promise."

The lieutenant hesitated, and Captain Duncannon knew why, but he forbore saying anything. There was no letter to go home from him, and Sayers knew it.

Earlier in the year, when they had been at the West Indies chasing the French, the news that the packet carrying their post — an accumulation of post going back to Christmas and before — had been swamped, the captain alone had been unmoved. In their years of sailing together Sayers had only seen Henry Duncannon write one letter, to his mother, after they read of the death of his father in the newspapers half a year after the fact. He would not write home now. As far as Captain Duncannon was concerned, a line in a newsprint article reporting his death in battle would suffice.

The lieutenant glanced at the door. No one was in view, beyond the musket of the sentry stationed at the other side. Trusting to the noise of the rain pouring on the deck overhead, Lt. Sayers said apologetically, "The lady?"

Captain Duncannon also glanced at the door. "Where is she?"

"She and the maid are both with the surgeon, learning his ways. If…if it comes to me to direct her movements, what are your wishes?"

Captain Duncannon felt an unwonted, and entirely undeserved, pleasure, as if he could take credit from her creditable gesture. He deserved no such credit. Her merits were entirely her own; if anything, his personal resentments, which owed nothing to her, were such that he had not given a thought to her eventual future should anything happen to him.

He felt, in short, rather like a scrub.

The idea unsettled him. He was impatient with himself for weakness. This pride in her gallantry, his pleasure in her neat ways, her grace, even the sound of her voice, it was nothing more than mere animal nature—as ephemeral as morning mist and every bit as obscuring to the clear sight he must rely on shortly.

Collingwood had kept her aboard the *Aglaea*, but after the battle, his scruples would have no basis. A spy, absurd! She must go back to Naples, or wherever she called home; he could make arrangements when she was comfortably established.

He was startled to find Sayers waiting for an answer.

The captain took his letter and locked it in his desk, then he said, "Should anything happen to me, she will in course have my fortune." It had been so many years since he had let himself think in these terms it felt very like opening a door into an attic long closed off. He nodded. "That will leave her comfortably off. Exert yourself to see that she gets safely home," he added, thinking of Naples.

Then he returned to his desk, and the lieutenant went out. He had come to like and even to admire the captain's lady, though it was apparent that the marriage was only on paper. They each slept alone. It filled him with inexplicable sadness: he was old for a lieutenant, because his family had no influence at the Admiralty. He longed for his step, for were he to be promoted to post captain, he and his Mary, waiting patiently in Sussex, could wed.

He longed for his step, he longed for money, and he longed for his Mary. His old friend Henry Duncannon possessed the first two, but even with what anyone might consider the perfect wife right at hand, he had not the third, which, in some ways, was the most important of all.

Nineteen

SIGNAL FLAGS FLUTTERED UP and down the lines on both sides.

Out at sea, boats plied to and fro, conveying officers to meetings and dinners. Captain Fremantle hosted a splendid meal for his fellow ship-of-the-line captains, far astern of the frigates strung out to make certain the French did not slip back into port.

But Admiral Villeneuve had no intention of regaining the harbor at Cadiz. He had obtained warning that the emperor had issued a fresh set of orders contradicting all previous—and that these new orders were being carried by his replacement.

His signals directed his fleet into readiness, and the instructions he sent out were to prepare for Nelson's throwing away the old line-of-battle rules in favor of cutting the line. "Use your own initiative," Villeneuve sent to both Spanish and French captains. To try to form the unwilling allies into a cohesive line, he insisted they form up interweaving, one French ship, then one Spanish.

On the *Aglaea* Captain Duncannon invited his officers, including warrant officers, to a crowded, high-spirited dinner, and made certain that the hands were given their Sunday duff as dessert.

Anna dined once more with the officers. The talk began with former battles, those the men had survived and those they had heard about, and the meal ended after a lengthy review of every shot of the Battle of the Nile, at which Captain Duncannon had earned not only a medal but his promotion to commander.

After the meal, they dispersed to Sunday leisure, though there was no relaxed atmosphere. Anna, walking the deck, surprised many furbishing up uniform coats and accouterments as if for a general inspection. Captain Duncannon seemed to be everywhere at once, dealing with an unending stream of questions, while always checking the sky, the sails, and of course the signal flags fluttering from the next frigate up in the line.

Presently Anna became aware of Mr. Jones, the lanky midshipman with the large Adam's apple and the spotty face, lurking forward of the mainmast by the hatch. He appeared to want to speak to her.

She drew near, and when the boy made his leg and doffed his hat, his gaze darted about, and his hands dove into his pockets, yanked out hastily, then rubbed together. "I know Bradshaw, my particular mate, well, he'd take snuff if he thought I'd talked to you, but if...Jupiter, this is hard, this sounded better in my head. If anything goes amiss with Bradshaw. If you or the captain would carry the news to his family. Don't let 'em find out in the newspapers. He tried writing a letter, for in case, you know, but d'Ivry said something about sentiment, and Bradshaw got angry and threw it out the scuttle. Now he regrets it, but time's too short to pen another."

"But surely you will be below, you and the little boys?"

"Lord, ma'am, the reefers command gun crews, those who aren't on deck, and the boys will be running powder and the like. Even that pompous goat Leuven will be on deck next or nigh the skipper, taking notes for the official log."

Anna looked into that pimply face, the earnest brown eyes, and said, "I promise, should anything happen, I will do what I can. But I am going to pray that nothing bad happens."

"Thank you, ma'am, if you pray nothing bad happens to us, but I'd as lief God smites the froggies and the dons right, left, and center," he said, grinning. A flick of his hat, and he was gone.

Anna and Parrette slept in their plainest, sturdiest clothing in case they were wakened early for the ship to be readied for battle.

And so it was. Scarcely had they been roused by lantern-bearing shadowy figures than a party of seamen entered with mallets and began banging away.

Anna walked up to the deck, peering out to the east. The stars still twinkled, remote and glittering. There was only the faintest lifting on the horizon. Close by, someone stamped, coughed, a low-voiced, "By your leave, mum," and here were the afterguard, ready with their holystones and buckets, preparing to scrub the deck by lantern-light. Even impending battle did not warrant an abatement of the naval passion for cleanliness.

Someone brought hot tea to the deck, and Anna stood at the rail with it in her fingers, as the cool breeze lifted her hair. Life seemed unreal at that moment: the peace of the night, so quiet, and so false with the promise of violence by day.

A tall, slim male silhouette joined her, with a respectful tip of the hat. "Mr. Sayers," she said. "Has it been an anxious night?"

"The Admiral has been preoccupied," he admitted. "The captain has been summoned to the flag—all the frigate captains. As soon as we have light, the boat will be in readying. We cannot let the French by."

"If it should happen?" she asked.

"Why, then Boney will have his invasion at last."

"Invade England? *Why* should he invade England?" she asked, and then shook her head. "I confess, I have no head for politics, not at all. I cannot understand what he is about. He was First Consul, he brought about a cease of terrible civil war in France. He is now emperor. Why does he not decree an end to fighting?"

Lt. Sayers smiled. "When the Peace of Amiens was concluded in the year two, that was what we all expected, even to Boney's making himself king. But the very next year he broke out—slandered the British ambassador—sent armies on the march. We are told that Talleyrand, who, whatever else they say about him, seems to understand that France would do better with peaceful relations—is cast down, and Boney wants not only Europe, but will not stop until he sees the Pacific Ocean under his command. But first, he must rid himself of us." He struck the breast of his best coat, the buttons shiny. She noticed in the swinging light that there was even fresh lace in his hat.

"Good morning, ma'am. Lieutenant."

They both turned, and there was the captain, his coxswain behind him. Captain Duncannon took his hat off to his wife, noting the simplicity of her dress, her tight shoulders. "I have given orders for cold bread and meat to be served out, that the galley fires need not be lit. I doubt the admiral will keep us long."

Already the eastern horizon had paled, touching the waters to a deep, serene blue. Blocks clacked, ropes creaked, as the captain's gig was hoisted over the side to splash down.

One last glance upward—Anna saw his face turned toward her, or toward the lieutenant, she could not tell in the uncertain light—and then he settled into the boat, and the coxswain, a deep-voiced, powerful man, called out the order to ready oars.

They watched the captain's boat diminishing in the direction of a cluster of silhouettes emerging from the gloom, their ship lights a galaxy of yellow stars below the celestial blue-white.

Presently the watch changed, the rolled hammocks were brought up, and it seemed to Anna that they were packed with extra firmness into the shrouds; time began to flow, faster and faster, a flow from which she caught individual moments.

The sun rose at last, and there appeared what seemed an infinite line of ships—great, towering ships—rolling on a slow, building Atlantic swell. But it was not an orderly line. Some sailed close together, others seemed to be maneuvering in front of or behind their neighbors.

Voices seemed distinct, sharp. Bits of conversations:

"We're in for a blow, or I'm a Dutchman!"

"That one has to be the *Santísima Trinidad*."

"Shift over, mate. Your dad warn't no glazier. A man can't see through you, and I want a glim at them frogs."

"They're drunk as Davy's sow, ha ha!"

"They appear to be wearing in succession," Lt. McGowan called down from the masthead.

"'S that what they call it?" a deep-voiced upper-yardsman hooted, amid much laughter.

Lt. Sayers called, "Quiet fore and aft."

The noise died away to soft-voiced mutters here and there.

Sights: little Mr. Corcoran, his voice shrill as a girl's, as he shouted imprecations at a party of seamen. D'Ivry with his head bowed, his face absorbed as he listened to that little boy Gilchrist, his hands gripped tightly together. Then both lifting their heads, quick as startled birds, as the lookout hailed, "Captain's gig two points off the stern."

The officers all wore their best, as if they were going to a ball. The marines as well, their cross-belts pipe-clayed white, red coats neat, hair thickly coated with powder. Their sergeant walked along the gangway, the brass gorget on his breast throwing back the strong sunlight. Some of his men stood at the sides of the ship, muskets ready, others climbed into the tops with their heavy bags of shot and powder, where Anna glimpsed them taking up a station on the mastheads.

In contrast to them, the seamen grouped around the guns, now cast loose on the bare deck, were simply dressed. Many had bared themselves to the waist, tying handkerchiefs around their brows; she had not seen half-naked men since she was a child running about the harbor at Naples. Some of the men worked away at polishing their cannon to a gleam. On the forecastle, the armorer and a party of burly sheet-anchormen polished cutlasses.

There was Captain Duncannon, his hat clasped beneath his arm, his Nile medal worn on his coat.

He climbed with ease over the side, his gaze turned upward as he checked the sea, the sky, the rigging and sails—the Union Jacks at foretop stays, the peak, and the mizzen so that they could be identified in the smoke—and then he swept his gaze over the netting spread above to catch falling debris, down the deck, along the guns gleaming in the low sunlight, the gun ports open wide. He took in the fire buckets, and the sand sprinkled on the dampened decks. The racks for the cannon balls had been filled. Lanterns were lit, water casks opened, powder boys for once still, each with his box filled and ready.

All was ready.

He turned, and started when he saw Anna, so very out of place in this setting. She returned his regard with a steady, troubled gaze, and he was aware of his heart stirring. There was no room in him now for resentment; he wished suddenly, almost violently, that he had made the time to talk to her. But what would he say?

"Good morning, ma'am." He doffed his hat.

"Good morning," she said, gulping in a breath to still the tremor in her voice. "Pray, may I ask—those swords in sharpening. Is it expected that the French will come aboard to attack us?"

Captain Duncannon's smile was brief. "Bless you, ma'am, have no fears on that score. Did no one explain the rules?" He kept his tone measured, aware of all the listening ears.

"Rules?"

"There are even rules to war. Though in truth the French have not always honored 'em. But we expect the Spaniards to lead by example: the ships of the line do not fire upon frigates, unless we fire first."

"Yet the cannons are out, and those tubs of smoke, is that not for shooting cannon?"

"We have to be ready for any eventuality, which includes coming to the rescue of any ship who needs us. And if we do catch stray balls, why, we send 'em back post-paid," he said, and sure enough, the old joke brought laughter rumbling all along the curving deck of waiting gun crews.

"Come." He cupped her elbow to draw her to the taffrail, aware of the trembling that she tried valiantly to hide. "Here is the *Victory*, nobly leading the vanguard. Is she not the grandest sight? And *Neptune* given the honor of following directly after. Ha-ha, there is the signal flying, *Neptune* is too eager, she must luff up a little. The admiral will have the honor of going before all."

Anna looked at that sinister line of ships slowly bearing down. "But will not all those ships fire upon her?"

"They will," Captain Duncannon said gravely. "Look your fill upon *Victory*. Take courage from the sight. Ah, there is the signal for *Mars* to lead the larboard division. Pray observe her well, that you will always remember her. Then, with your respect, I suggest you go below. The time has come, I believe."

Anna stood at the rail, looking at *Victory* with her brave golden checkerboard, guns at the ready, and above, the towering geometry of gently curving sails, white in the brilliant sunlight. She breathed, her ribs tight, but could not suppress the drumming of her heartbeat.

Great as the ship was, yet she seemed small in comparison

with some of those mighty Spanish argosies, and Anna clasped her hands to her breast. Her throat had dried.

The marines began to thunder the drums, and sailors ran about with purpose. She could not prevent a last, questioning look at the captain. He met her gaze—he had been watching her. He half-lifted his hand, but then, aware of the watching eyes, he doffed his hat to her.

She curtseyed, and turned toward the hatch. There Parrette awaited her, face tense.

As Anna caught up her skirts and began her descent, she was aware of the rap of the captain's boot heels as he crossed the deck and began addressing words to each man. Her throat tightened, her heart hurt, though she could not define why. She only knew she was afraid, for him, for herself. For them all.

Anna descended the rest of the way and found the orlop transformed. Tarpaulins had been laid down, and then spread with sand. Buckets of sand stood under each corner of the table. "For fire?" Anna whispered to Parrette.

"Blood," was the answer.

Anna looked away, to where a portable stove glowed. So the admiral had made his wishes known to others besides her. Of course he had. The mates and the loblolly boy stood at one end, talking in low voices. They broke off at the clatter of a newcomer, who ducked through a moment later. It was Mr. Gates, the burly purser, who turned an empty bucket upside down and sat, fists on his knees. "Signal from the flag," he said. "Anchor at the end of the day."

Old Mr. Leuven grunted. "I told ye, I told ye it was going to come on to blow."

As the men began to argue about the weather, and surmise if the French would be able to slither back into Cadiz under cover of rain, Anna turned to Parrette. "Where is Michel?"

"He will run powder, or aid here, or fight a gun, wherever he is needed most." Parrette's lips had thinned. Anna suspected that her worry was less for herself than for her son.

Anna pressed her arms across her middle. Time had slowed again, each creak of the wood, each slap of the waves against the bulkhead, sharp and distinct. She closed her eyes and softly, softly, began to hum, first her scales, and then the lively "Papagena" air from Mozart, the first she ever learned.

She trusted to the louder men's voices to cover the sound of hers, but Mr. Gates cocked his head, motioned the others to quiet, and then got to his feet. "Ma'am, would it trouble you to tip us that piece so we can hear?"

Anna considered the expectant faces. She saw no impatience. Perhaps they, too, wished to fill the time as best they could. And so she sang for them, there in the fetid murk, and watched the faces relax. Even severe, occasionally sour Mr. Leuven appeared less sour.

So she sang two more arias from *Magic Flute*, breaking off when a cheer roared overhead. Everyone looked at one another.

"Go," Mr. Leuven said to the loblolly boy, but before he could get out, noisy footsteps approached, and Michel Duflot ducked in, grin slashing across his face. "The flag signaled. Nelson says that England wants us all to do our duty, then followed it with 'Engage the enemy more closely.'"

The men in the orlop sent up a hoarse cheer, and Michel vanished, his footsteps retreating—to be lost in a sudden deep boom.

Anna had heard the cannons go off from time to time, in signal. But she had yet to hear a broadside from a ship of the line.

The sound reverberated through the wood, the true note muffled by the water surrounding them. It was followed by another, then another, each sound building on the last. The extra men in the orlop had departed by then, their footsteps lost in the noise.

Each time Anna thought it could not possibly get louder, there came a new tumult, vibrating through bones and teeth. There was no hearing anything the others said: in the light of the swinging lanterns, she could see Mr. Leuven's head tipped back, his mouth moving, moments before the floor abruptly slanted, throwing Anna into Parrette. The two crashed over the midshipmen's trunks lashed together as a secondary table. Anna winced, pain lancing through both knees and one elbow.

The surgeon's mate had been struck by something sharp, and the first blood of the day dripped down his arm as he and the others picked up the surgery tools that had slid off the table, all while standing with one foot against the slanting deck, and the other against the hull. Another surge, another plunge, a fresh roar, and the ship heeled again. Anna and Parrette pressed themselves against the hull as the men held their instruments in place.

The noise was ceaseless. The smell of smoke drifting down sent thrills of alarm through Anna's nerves. She locked her teeth to keep from crying out, though no one would have heard her.

A shock rang through the ship as above their heads, the guns fired a broadside.

Mr. Leuven's wide eyes, his pale face, revealed tension. His mouth moved: Anna was only sure of the words *fired upon.*

Groaning, crashing, roars…and then in the doorway the extra men reappeared, and here were the first casualties.

One sailor was laid on the table, and another brought to Anna and Parrette. He curled up, rocking back and forth, his side dark with blood. At first Anna could not bear to look at his mangled flesh, but Parrette pulled her insistently, and motioned for Anna to hold their first patient still.

Anna gripped him by the forearm, and as he resisted, she pulled his arm against her thigh. Long shards of wood had penetrated the man down one side. He opened his mouth, teeth showing, as Parrette gripped the worst splinter and pulled it free. Was he screaming? No one could hear over the roar.

When the last splinter tugged free, Anna dashed for the bandages, felt Parrette's insistent hand, and remembered the spirits.

"Do it," Parrette mouthed. She pressed her small, strong hands on his shoulders, holding him down.

Anna took up the wooden cup, dipped it, and flung the liquid into the gaping hole in the man's thigh. He stiffened, then slumped into a faint. Tears burned Anna's eyelids. She hastily doused the rest of his wounds.

Parrette stitched up the wounded flesh where she could. At the end, she and Anna took up a bandage and passed it back and forth as they bound the man's leg.

All right. She could do this work. Remove the cause of the wound, pour, sew, bind. As soon as the worst of the man's wounds were wrapped, the loblolly boy thrust his hands under the seaman's armpits and hauled him off the table as he began to stir and groan.

A terrible grating sound caught Anna's attention. Mr. Leuven was plying his saw on a lower leg as Mr. Gates held down their patient, who uttered guttural groans around a leather thing stuck between his teeth.

Stars glittered across Anna's vision. She gulped breath, shut her eyes, and leaned against the bulkhead.

"Here they come," someone shouted in another lull between cannon booms.

The wounded came so quickly that Anna had no time for anything but the work before her: the world filled with bloody, torn flesh; pleading, shocked, angry eyes; limp fingers; blood-matted hair. Anna swiftly learned to distinguish between splinter wounds, those caused by metal bits, and the nasty round puckers of musket balls.

Once again the ship heeled, and blood washed sickeningly down the canvas deck cover in sluggish streaks. Anna looked away as someone dashed sand into the flow, and then threw down another tarpaulin.

Then came more wounded. The first was Mr. Sayers, shockingly splattered with blood, his face blackened with gunpowder. The hole in the side of his knee kept him writhing, his face twisted.

Anna and the loblolly boy held the lieutenant down as the surgeon's mate plied a long instrument, probing the wound. Tears burned Anna's eyes as the lieutenant stiffened, teeth bared in the extremity of pain.

A push, a twist, a yank, and the musket ball was held up in triumph, then flung into one of the buckets. Anna dashed a cup of spirits in the wound, Parrette closed the pucker with two neat stiches, then bound it, but before the loblolly boy could help the lieutenant up, he shook his head, snatched the cup from Anna's hand and drank off the dregs.

Then before anyone could react, he thrust the cup back into her hands, heaved himself off the makeshift table, and plunged back through the door, to vanish in the direction of the ladder.

The next shock was a crumpled figure carried in the arms of a big quarter-gunner, and Mr. Bradshaw's lanky young form was gently laid in the gore on Mr. Leuven's table. At first Anna thought he was dead, but the surgeon felt the boy's chest, nodded, and motioned to his mates to cut off the mangled remains of one boot.

Two more men were brought down, so Anna did not witness what was done to the poor boy; when she had a moment to look next, he lay pale and motionless, waiting to be taken out as another broadside shook the ship. An eternity, a thousand eternities passed, during which she mopped, held for stitching, bandaged, and bent to refresh the cup of spirits.

Then a crowd of men surged into the orlop, bearing—the captain. Their distraught faces testified better than mere words to the regard they held for Captain Duncannon.

Mr. Leuven motioned for the seaman on the table to be shifted, and the captain was laid with infinite care in his place.

Anna stood, unable to move, until Parrette yanked her by her blood-smeared wrist. The world filled with tiny lights, and a rushing sound replaced the din of cannon. A hand pushed Anna's shoulder down and her legs collapsed under her. She found herself sitting on a barrel, her hem draggling in gore, her head in her lap. She sat up and breathed deeply. She would *not* faint. The lanterns swinging, the remorseless pitch of the ship, above all the dizziness caused her stomach to protest at last.

"...get him into his cot," came a voice.

A voice! She could hear!

"Anna." That was Parrette, next to her. "Drink." The wooden ladle was pressed into her fingers. The pungent aroma of whisky rose, and Anna nearly swooned again. "Just a sip."

Anna forced herself to swallow. The liquor burned the acrid taste from her mouth, burned going down. She looked up, aware again. "I beg pardon. I know not what overcame me."

"Exhaustion, first," Parrette said, the harsh contours of her face emphasized in the guttering lantern light. "I ought to have warned you. But I could never talk about...what I saw. Before I ran to Italy to find my son."

Anna looked down, saw the hem of her gown, and gritted her teeth. A step away, the men began to pick up the captain.

"I can walk." Captain Duncannon's voice rasped hoarsely.

"Handsomely does it, sir, handsomely does it," an elderly member of the afterguard replied, his tone grandfatherly. "Don't top it the nob. Let we'm do our bit."

The captain insisted on being set on his feet, but he staggered. Supported on either side, he was taken out of the orlop and was replaced by another, and yet another, a nightmare of lacerated flesh.

Anna worked on, her brain numb, until she became vaguely aware that sometimes their clothing was wrong, but she paid little heed until a young fellow no more than sixteen rolled back and forth on the table breathing, *"Mon Dieu! Mon Dieu!"* Followed by rapid, idiomatic French.

Parrette paused in tearing sheets of cloth, and both women turned to the purser, who said hoarsely, "They're pulling 'em out of the water, ours and frogs alike."

And the work went on, until at last there was a pause for breath between one wounded man and the next, then a longer pause. Mr. Leuven looked around at last, and Anna's nerves chilled when she perceived the tear tracks glistening in the furrows of his face.

"Get those who can shift into the sick berths," he said. "I want to see Robert first, in case they throw him over the side." And to old, grizzled Perkins, the captain's steward, "Take this cup. Get this dose into the captain. Don't tell him it is laudanum; he will try to refuse, to stand a watch, but he must rest. That wound on his head mislikes me."

Perkins departed, followed by Michel and Mr. Gates with an unconscious sailor.

Parrette put out a hand to stop her son. "Young Leuven?"

Michel's smoke-stained face turned her way. "Killed," he said in a dull voice. "The first one. The splinter that did for him was the captain's first wound." He jerked his head to Mr. Gates, and they moved out with their burden.

Parrette said, "Anna, come into the hold. You must shift your clothes."

"We both must," Anna said, sick at the sight of her ruined dress.

Parrette lowered her voice. "Your work is not done. The weather is worsening. We must get the wounded bound into their hammocks. And you," she added, "must tend your husband."

Twenty

ANNA HAD NO STRENGTH to protest, and what could she say? She did not feel in any respect a wife, but everyone regarded her as one.

Gripping a pail of unused water, she followed Parrette into the hold. She ran her thumb along her fingers, and then peered down at her blood-crusted hand by the flickering light of the lantern that Parrette held high.

The ring was gone. Probably somewhere in that horror of an orlop. She could not bear to return. Perhaps someone might find it, someone inured to the aftermath of war.

Parrette continued into the hold, poking through the boxes and barrels until at last they found their trunks. Each set down her bucket of water. They were alone, though footsteps could be heard above.

They hurried out of their clothes, and Anna gratefully plunged her hands into her bucket. The cold liquid was shocking. Anna scrubbed feverishly over every inch she could get at—she felt could not scrub enough. She left off only when she discovered she was rubbing her skin raw. She scrambled into fresh clothing, as Parrette blocked her from view of the ladder.

Parrette bent to pick up their discarded garments.

Anna said fiercely, "Fling mine overboard. Or I will do it. I will never wear that gown again."

"I will put it to soak," Parrette said tonelessly. "There are other uses for the cloth."

Anna heard no rebuke in her voice, but her throat ached, and her eyes burned with unshed tears. "I beg pardon. I…"

"We both must take food. We will need our strength, and Lt. Sayers said before he collapsed that the captain ordered a meal be shared out."

"A meal." For the first time since the cannon had begun to fire, Anna began to wonder about the wider world—the upper deck, the weather deck, the battle. She forced herself not to blurt questions that she knew Parrette could not answer, and picked up her bucket.

They emptied the buckets into the scuttle, and Anna began to make her way slowly upward. The roar of cannon had gone silent, but the ship was filled with noise: hammering, sawing, the shout of voices, the thump of footsteps. The cry of wounded.

She heard the noise before she saw the shocking aftermath of battle. Where she had only seen scrubbed order was a chaotic tangle of rope, wood, iron, sailcloth. Crimson spatters, streaks, and splashes marred wood, rope, sailcloth.

Lanterns hung everywhere against the dying light, as the boatswain oversaw the most desperate of the repairs. The captain's cabin was still missing, except for his cot, and the checkered canvas deck cover that someone had unrolled. He lay in his cot, the steward Perkins bent over it as he helped the captain drink.

Perkins looked up at her approach. He touched his forehead, and said, "Ma'am. If you'll bide here, I can fetch the portable soup, which the cook has in hand. Carpenters is bringing up the bulkheads as soon as they get the hull patched forward, as it's coming on to blow."

'Coming on?' The wind howled through the rigging, and the ship rose and fell on great swells. She could see through the tangle amidships forward. Men crawled in the rigging, using ropes and tackles to lift and lower spars.

"He's dead."

The voice was almost too soft to hear.

Anna turned. The captain swung in the cot, his dark hair lying over his bandaged brow. "He's dead," he murmured again, and

Anna bent closer. His pupils were so large they swallowed the rest of his eyes, in the indifferent light a color impossible to discern.

"Who is dead?" she asked. "Did you mean your clerk, Mr. Leuven?"

"Nelson," the captain murmured, still in that slow voice. "Neville shouted it over his taffrail. Running messages. From Collingwood. No one could see signals for the smoke. Sharpshooter, he thinks from *Redoubtable*."

"I am very sorry to hear that," Anna said, sorrow crowding her heart. Though she had only met Admiral Lord Nelson the once, she vividly remembered his gentle smile when he uttered those words about instruments. He would feel no cold steel cutting into his flesh now.

"Duff, too. I breakfasted with him and his boy this morning..."

"The little boy?"

"I do not know." He struggled to sit, winced against the bandage that bound his left arm to his side, and fell back. "McGowan. Away in boats. I need to get up. I need to see..." His right hand fumbled over the edge of the cot.

She moved instinctively near, and his fingers, hot and dry, grasped her wrist with surprising strength, but almost at once he let her go.

"I will go find out any news. Pray rest here," she said.

"I can't..."

Perkins arrived as the captain struggled up again. Holding the tray expertly with one hand, the man pushed the captain down again. "Now, capting, sir, the surgeon says you cannot get up this day. You're to eat this here soup, and sleep a watch." He jerked his chin at Anna. "Your missus will cast her glims over the rail, and see what there is to see."

Anna said, "I will do it now."

She turned away, almost bumping into a party of carpenter's mates carrying bulkheads. She ducked around them and ran up to the quarterdeck, her head panging at each step.

When she reached the rail, she stopped in shock. In the fiery, cloud-streaked sunlight she saw nothing but destruction in all directions. Debris floated on the water, and small boats. There seemed to be people in the water as well, some clinging to snarls of rigging and wood, as little boats plied about, pulling them up.

The damage to *Aglaea* had looked terrible to her when she first glanced along the deck, but when she saw the wrecks listing dangerously, some completely dismasted, she began to comprehend how lucky they had been to escape relatively lightly.

"Pass the word for the skipper's wife!"

The words echoed down the ship. Little Mr. Corcoran appeared, almost unrecognizable but for his small size in the uniform much too large. He was streaked with dirt and smoke, his voice shrill. "Come away along, ma'am, it's *Belleisle's* long boat, if you please."

"Why do you require me?" she asked, following him carefully over the debris and the wood and rope being laid out for repair work.

"It's in want of the female, that is, they think she's gabbling French, but it's a kind we none of us can make head nor tails of."

They reached the larboard rail in the bow, where Anna gazed down into a boat crowded with people. She recognized tattered remains of French sailor's clothing on some. At the very front, a bedraggled figure sat, nearly lost in a pea coat that obviously did not belong to—*her*?

"She was in the water, ma'am," a tall, thin lieutenant called up to her. "Someone says you can parse the lingo?"

The woman lifted her head. Anna could only make out straggling dark hair and a pair of bruised-looking eyes. Anna called down in French, "They wish to know who you are, why you were in the water?"

The woman clasped thin hands together. "I am Jeanette Caunant," the woman cried in rapid village French. "I worked aboard the *Achilles*, dressed as a man. I take the powder to the guns. It was so I can stay with my husband, but the ship, he is afire, and they say we are sinking—that my husband is dead—and I cannot swim! That I can stay afloat if I throw off my clothing! This I did, and when the lead was melting, I hurled myself into the water, where a man, blessed by the angels, he gave me an oar to clasp. And so it was I floated on the sea until these English in this boat, they plucked me out of the water, and put this coat about me!"

Anna repeated it all to the lieutenant, who saluted, turned to a harassed young midshipman struggling with a pencil and a damp logbook, and said, "She's off the *Achilles*, running powder, married. She goes to the *Pickle* as a seaman. Oars out!" And as the heavily laden boat labored away, the lieutenant called, "Thank you, ma'am!"

Anna turned away. French again, and that accent—for a moment she did not see the grisly wreckage of battle, but the coast of France in spring, the swallows rustling in the eaves.

But France's coast had also suffered, the shadow of the Vendee behind the wariness, the angry voices, the poverty.

"*Achilles* exploded," Mr. Corcoran said, and in triumph, "we thumped it into 'em, ma'am. We thumped it into 'em good, and we won."

"Corcoran," d'Ivry called hoarsely. "If you are quite done showing away, it's nearly eight bells, and there is the muster to be made, now the shot holes are plugged. Pray summon the men of your division."

Mr. Corcoran bounded over the debris and vanished in the direction of the gun deck.

As d'Ivry spoke to Anna, she saw in his thin face shadows of the lines that would mark it if he lived long enough to become a man. "The captain requests your presence, ma'am," he said formally. "He insists on rising, on giving our three dead the proper send-off, before the weather turns foul. We are in for an uncommon blow." He glanced at the limb of the sun vanishing, blood-red, under tangled clouds of livid crimson and violet.

The entire ship's crew—those not too wounded to rise—gathered in clumps, the lanterns casting a forgiving golden glow along the ruin of the deck. The three dead had been sewn into hammocks.

Perkins had supported Captain Duncannon to the upper deck. The captain leaned heavily on his steward, who had managed to ease his coat over his bandages. Anna was going to join him, but the strict rows of the officers (those able to stand) and the mass of men suggested a ritual, one that bound the shipmates into a whole that did not include her, and so she remained on the companionway, behind the knot of warrant officers' mates.

On the quarterdeck, Perkins helped the captain open his Bible. The ship yawed, the masts above describing an enormous arc against the cloud-streaked sky. Wood creaked and blocks clattered as the ship plunged down and down. Anna watched the company sway with the pitch, then lean as the prow aimed toward the sky, water streaming off both sides.

"Hats off," the officer of the watch bawled.

Every head was bared. The captain read the service, but all Anna could hear from her distance was the cadence of the words, nearly smothered by the wash and hiss of the sea. But those words seemed to comfort those who could hear, before the three were committed, one by one, to the deep.

Another rise of the prow caused Anna to clutch at the pitch-covered ropes behind her, and then the ship dropped into a valley between gray-green waves. The Captain swayed, and Perkins caught him. McGowan and Perkins helped the captain down to his cabin, which had been put together again, though bare of any furnishings save that swinging cot.

Anna followed, one uncertain step at a time. She was unsure where she ought to be, what she ought to do, until Perkins looked round, and his heavy brows lifted with relief when he saw her.

Anna passed the smoke-streaked marine guard, whose stubbly chin and red-rimmed eyes testified to the day's immense labors. His gaze flicked to her, and his face relaxed minutely. Anna tipped her head in greeting, wondering if it was a relief to sink back into order after the chaotic exertions of the day.

"Ma'am," Perkins said. "He needs his dose. We only got half into 'im." He pressed a wooden cup into her hand.

She took the cup, and watched after he ran down toward the galley.

Parrette was nowhere in sight; everyone was busy. The sense of relief, almost a holiday relief, when she first came topside had vanished with the sun, and the disappearance of the dead into the water.

Anna closed the door behind her, to shut out as much noise as she could, and stepped toward the captain's cot, but pitched into the bulkhead when the ship yawed. Her shoulders bumped the carving in the wall as she braced herself, knees locked, her hands tightly holding the cup to keep it from spilling.

The steady swell was building, or maybe it was her own exhaustion. When the floor slanted the other way, she ran the few steps and caught herself against the swinging cot, and did her best to steady it.

Captain Duncannon lay with his eyes shut. The lantern swung behind her, and as her shadow crossed his eyelids, he opened his eyes. He saw her, and turned his head minutely, his eyes narrowing.

"Please drink this." Anna slid her fingers under the curve of his neck, a gesture well remembered from her father's last days. She lifted his head, and in spite of the sway of deck, bed, and light in three distinct parabolas, she held him steady enough to get the rest of the cup into him, sip by sip.

Then she gently laid his head onto the pillow, her fingers sliding through his hair. It was unexpectedly fine, in spite of its tangled state, the grit of brine, of dripping pitch from the rigging, of smoke.

She knew what she could do. "The grit, should you want it removed? This I can do, a simple task."

"Thank you." His voice was soft. He made an effort that she could see, and added, "I confess I couldn't bear the notion of Perkins mauling me about anymore. A good man. But accustomed to the vigor of a polishing cloth."

She smiled in assent. So he wished to talk? "A wounded man is not a silver teapot." And won a brief smile, no more than a quirk of his dry, cracked lips, but she felt it a victory more strong than any battle. That brought a new thought, one that ought to please him, after all his efforts, surely? "Little Mr. Corcoran says that the battle is won. Is this true? The sea, it is filled with burning and ruined ships."

"We are better off than most," he said, his eyes still closed. "Did you follow our movements?"

"I did not," she said, returning from giving the order for water to the sentry outside. "I could only feel, and hear, but saw nothing until the wounded were bringing in."

"Do you wish to hear?"

"If you have the strength to tell me, I listen," she replied.

His eyes opened, and met her gaze. "We remained untouched until we were ordered in, to *Victory*'s aid. She was fairly clawed by the time we neared, and then we could not come at her for the smoke. We took shot, aimed in the smoke—I suspect that is when I gained this splinter wound, but I noticed it not as poor Robert Leuven was cut down. We followed *Neptune* until a pair of French frigates came at us, intending to drive us off. That is probably when a French marksman put this ball in my leg."

He stirred under the bed clothes, and his eyes drifted shut for a moment. Then, "It was warm work, very warm, smoke as thick as fog. We aimed by the fire of their broadside, the only thing visible, and fought both sides of the ship until *Achilles* exploded. Perhaps that is when my head was cut by the debris raining down. We hauled wind after the French, but there was no chasing them in those airs. After that, our task was to rescue those in the water, enemy and friend alike."

A quiet knock, and the water and the cloth appeared. She set the jug between her feet, and wetted the cloth. Then she stood with water dripping down her fingers into her sleeves, for she had put on her second best winter traveling gown, as sturdy as the one she had ruined.

His eyes opened slowly. Once again his pupils were enormous, the effect of laudanum on a sorely tried body. Sorrow flitted through her and away at her remembered motions: only instead of her dear father, his beloved features wasted from fever, here was this much younger man. There was no puffy flesh, but the clean, strong bones of his jaw, the fine ridges of his cheeks. His high, smooth brow, the curve of his temples over his eyes. His eyes, their expression so cool, remote, so alert, sometimes crinkling from laughter inwardly held, and now, barely open, so that only a reflected gleam shone beneath the long lashes.

He lay there in his shirt, the front opened, his free hand loose. The bed clothes had been pulled to his waist. She began with his hands, working up over his wrists above the shirt frill.

"I beg pardon," he murmured. "For my state of filth."

"Cleanliness," she said, "how is it to be expected, given today's events?"

"And yet here you are." His eyelids crinkled in a smile. "How did you manage that?"

"When the last of the wounded left, me and Parrette creeped into the hold like mice, with our buckets of water, while the ship's people must do more duties."

"We have come off relatively lightly," he said.

She finished with his hands, wrung the cloth out extra hard, and began to brush it over the top of his head, getting rid of sticky grit everywhere but the bandage.

"Thank you," he said, low-voiced. "You cannot conceive how well that feels."

"Oh, on contrary," she said, laughing a little. "I know it, much." Her nose wrinkled. "Prodigiously well!"

"Sayers tells me you and Mrs. Duflot labored the entire time in the orlop. I thank you for that."

She smiled ruefully. "But it is expected of the women, this I find aboard the flagship. I only did my part."

"Those other women chose to follow someone aboard," he said, and tried to lift himself on his elbow, but the pitch of the ship, the bed, and the effect of laudanum defeated him. "Confound it! I should have spoken to you before," he said in an urgent tone. "You were taken, I am very much afraid against your will. I find I still do not entirely comprehend whether you were a guest or a prisoner of the Spanish."

"I think," she said, "I was both."

"You will have to explain that, but at your leisure. More important, what was your intention, had you not been brought aboard us?"

This was treading into dangerous territory. Anna wished she did not have to converse in English, which still took so much effort. Mindful of her promise to Parrette, Anna said only, "I had not thought so far ahead."

That much was the truth. She was reluctant to utter lies, and so, to skirt the danger, she laid her finger over his lips. "Do not speak! This ship, how it rolls. I must take ver-ry great care that I do not poke out your eye, and that marine without the door, he must shoot me for mutiny."

He shook with silent laughter, and closed his eyes with such readiness that she knew her labors were appreciated, and not

SHERWOOD SMITH

politely endured. She smoothed the cloth over his hair until it lay damp, and tousled, but clean, upon the pillow.

She could see how good it felt in the way he held his head steady, or turned it for her, and in the deepening of his breathing. She found that she was enjoying it as well, and took her time, dipping and wringing the cloth, then smoothing it again over every plane and curve of his face, tender over the fine skin of his eyes, a stronger motion curving with the back of his neck, and down, following the jut of his collarbones.

She drew the cloth over the visible flesh inside his shirt, along the sling; with a sudden movement, he grunted, shrugged, and the sling came loose. Anna lifted it over his head and set it on the checkered deck covering, next to the jug.

Then she worked very carefully, avoiding the bandages, and at last lifted the cloth to wring it out once again.

He lay very still, his clean hair lying on his brow, his chest beneath the loosened shirt rising and falling slowly. With a tentative finger she brushed the hair off his forehead. It was soft as silk.

The sway of the ship, the cot pressing against her hips, the sough of wind in the rigging, the wash of water down the side, the scent of his skin, each sense sharpened, closing around her protectively. She glanced down at his lashes so still on his cheeks, the shape of his face, his mouth, so stern when he stood on his quarterdeck, so entrancing when he smiled broadly enough to cause those little shadows to wink in his lean cheeks. His lips, so severe, and yet so soft to the touch.

Heady with exhaustion, she gave in to impulse and leaned over the edge of the swinging bed to touch her lips to his, light as the brush of a feather.

Warmth flared through her, as bright as starlight. His eyes opened, and his steady gaze blended with hers: she made herself look away, to busy her hands without having purpose.

A toss of the ship, the slosh of the bucket, recalled her to the cloth still gripped in her hands. "The water is monstrous dirty," she said, a little breathless. "Shall I send for more?"

"I'm an idiot," he whispered. She looked startled, and he could not prevent a laugh, though it was entirely against himself. He had been a captain too long. No one had dared to speak to him, king

260

aboard his wooden castle, no one to tell him he was a fool to superimpose one woman's perfidy over them all.

Anna had come into his life through no merit of his own, and she was nothing like Emily Elstead. That was all he knew, which was entirely his fault; when he thought about how nearly he had come to throwing away this chance, whether by a French cannon ball or by his own pig-headedness, he reached and caught her wrist as if to never let her go.

She stilled, balanced against the cot: it swayed, and she swayed with it. He looked up at her smiling eyes, the tender arch of her lips, the stray curl hanging neglected by one pretty ear, the sweet curve of the neck of her gown below the little hollow of her throat, and he pulled, not insistently, but with question in the lightness of his grip, the pucker of his brow.

She understood the question, and looked about her with her own pucker of question. It might be considered foolish to crawl into the cot, next to a wounded man, but if she could comfort him, who was to gainsay? In the eyes of God and of man they were one. She had never felt like a wife—she was not certain even now what a wife might feel like—but the question, the future, everything else could wait.

Practiced now, she hitched her hip over the edge of the cot, and curved her knee. A slight wince, a grin as he shifted, and they swung together in the cot, the bedclothes rumpled between them. He pulled her close with his good arm, and she carefully fitted herself so that she would not press against the damaged one, and turned her face to his.

Their lips met, and met again. Comfort flared into sweet, ardent insistence; unnoticed, the washcloth fell to one side, his bandage to the other, and then, at length, the bedclothes thumped softly to the deck.

They laughed breathlessly as each made adjustment, question conducted through touch, caress, and then answer in their truly becoming one.

After a time, he laughed huskily, and sighed into her neck, "Ah, Emily."

His breathing deepened into sleep.

.

Twenty-one

EMILY?

She glanced at that sleeping face, wondering if this man she had married — the man who had become her husband now in every way — even knew her name. Or was Emily someone else?

She swung there, listening to his breathing as she tried to sort her emotions. Affront, regret, bemusement, she recognized, and underneath them laughter. That steadied her. How little they knew one another, after all; the captain was full of laudanum, wounded, desperately tired. Though now she believed she had a right to them, this was no time for questions. He needed his rest — as the cot swung more deeply, she recollected the warnings about weather.

Storm. Thirst. One by one the demands of life crowded in, and so she waited until the swing returned and flipped herself smoothly out of the cot. A quick glance back showed the captain still asleep.

She straightened her clothing, picked up the counterpane, shook it out, draped it over him and tucked it down securely. Then she retrieved the washcloth, picked up the bucket, and let herself out of his after-cabin.

She found her own cabin had been restored, Parrette busy folding things into her trunk. She looked up sharply, her gaze traveling over Anna, who blushed hotly.

Parrette smiled, bringing her chin down in a decided nod of approval. Parrette knew very well what had happened, and her nod expressed her sense of the right of it.

But all she said was, "Set that bucket down. Here is hot water waiting in that basin. I thought you might want a wash. This hot water might be all we get before the weather worsens. I will bring your meal on my return."

"Worsens?"

"They say a storm is coming."

"I thought we were already in the midst of it," Anna stated as she leaned both hands against the bulkhead. It felt as if the floor slanted to the pitch of a roof.

Parrette had lifted the bucket of dirty water so it would not slosh. As soon as the pitch eased, she left. Anna busied herself with the basin of hot water. She decided against changing into nightclothes. The coming storm—her own questions—nothing seemed sure, so she put her gown back on, brushing out the wrinkles with her hands.

Parrette reappeared with supper. Anna found she could scarcely eat it. Her eyelids burned with exhaustion, her entire body throbbed. When she could not lift the spoon again, she climbed into her cot, and was not aware of falling asleep.

Two bells in the middle watch, or one o'clock in the morning, Henry Duncannon woke abruptly to find Mr. d'Ivry at his bedside, candlelight flaring wildly over his drenched form in its hooded tarpaulin-jacket.

He was instantly aware of something wrong before the master's mate spoke: there was a high, dangerous note to the wind in the rigging, and the groan of the timbers indicated high seas.

"Sir, Mr. Sayers's duty, but the Spanish barky we're towing is all a-hoo. He thinks it might be sinking."

Pain lanced through the captain's body, but beneath it was a layer of well-being, of a note of happiness so unfamiliar he could not immediately define it. "I shall be on deck in a moment. Send Perkins to me."

"I'm here, sir, I'm here, a-waitin' with the last of the water, and these here clothes," Perkins said as the midshipman darted out. "And a pot of tea. It's in me bosom, right and tight."

While the steward was talking, the captain eased himself out of the bunk to the deck. The wound in his thigh where the nearly-spent ball had been dug out burned as if a hot coal had been put there, and white shards of pain lanced through his head and shoulder.

The water felt cool on his flesh, waking him thoroughly, which brought to the front of his mind brief sensory memories and images—gentle hands, of ardent kisses—of his wife pressed against him. It had happened. He had not intended it to happen, he would have said he had not wanted it to happen, but he smiled at the memory of muffled laughter at her inexpert but eager accommodation as the cot swayed and jiggled and danced, and the intensity of matched desire. He laughed under his breath as he buttoned the shanks on the thick coat the steward held out.

His arm hurt like blazes, but he did not dare try a sling. He knew from the wild shriek of the wind and the slant of the deck that he would need both hands.

He drank off the lukewarm tea that Perkins had worn inside his jacket for at least an hour, then sent the steward forward. Urgent as was the need to be on deck, he had to see her. For the first time, he opened the door to his sleeping cabin. Lightning flared far over the water, lighting the stern window, creating a silhouette of the still form slumbering in the cot.

He smiled to see her there safe and warm, then closed the door soundlessly and forced his way up to his quarterdeck. The wind nearly took him over the rail. He bent double, both hands tight on the man-ropes.

Unawares, Anna slept so deeply that she did not waken until an enormous wave of water smashed the stern windows behind her.

She woke, startled, to see an angry gray-green sea rising nearly as high as the deck above. White foam tore across the top of the swelling billows, and whipped away on the shrieking wind.

What was that beyond the waves? Between one and the next she caught sight of a massive bowsprit rolling, and gasped in fear.

They were being chased by a Spanish ship of the line!

She flung herself out of her cot, and landed on hands and knees in rilling water. Lightning bolts shot through her joints. Every muscle in her body ached.

Her slippers were floating on this thin tide sweeping back and forth. She grabbed them and crawled to her trunk. Her instinct was to fetch out her second pair of slippers, but she looked at the water washing back and forth and her fingers shook as she wrestled the slippers over her bare feet. She ran to the door, then out, pausing when she reached the outer doors to the captain's cabin.

The marine on duty, standing with feet braced wide, said apologetically, "Orders is, you must stay inside, missus. It's too dangerous on deck, even with the man-ropes. We already lost one upper-yardman, insisted on laying aloft with one hand a-bandaged."

"But we are being chased, are we not?" She pointed behind. "I saw one of the Spanish ships."

He looked away. "We was towing it, on Admiral's orders. But it's not swimming, and they're bringing the last of the prisoners over now."

"Prisoners!"

"Yes, missus."

"Thank you," Anna said, and nearly turned back to ask about the captain. But of course he would be on deck, in spite of his wounds.

When another huge wave splashed up to the stern windows, she retreated to sit upon her trunk. She knew if the water crashed in she would be no better off seated on the trunk than in the cot, but that wild sea was too frightening to be near.

Chilled, she wrung out her skirt as best she could, then plunged her hands under her armpits. Her heart thundered with every great rise of the ship, and each downward plunge.

It could have been five minutes or five hours later when Parrette appeared, something wrapped in sailcloth gripped in her arms.

"It's tea," she said. "The cook set the fires for hot water only, for the officers, and for you, captain's orders. He put up a breakfast of sliced salt beef and ship's bread harder than a cannon ball."

She unwrapped her cloth, disclosing the captain's silver pot and a couple of sturdy wooden mugs.

The two of them sat side by side on the trunk, gratefully drinking hot tea and then determinedly gnawing through the tough meat and the stale bread. Anna's thoughts winged back to the long, astonishing day previous, which had begun so terribly and ended... she could not characterize it in her mind, except she smiled. So *unexpected*.

She longed to see the captain's face, to discover what it meant to him, if anything. She stared at her fingers, the nails uneven after the horrors of the orlop, and at her knees poking the skirt of her dove-colored serge gown. She knew she looked no different from the outside, but she was aware of a fundamental difference, a change of state. It might not be real to anyone else—would it be to him?

Thump, yaw! The ship heaved at an impossible slant, then dove downward at such an angle her stomach clenched. She willed each plunge and rise to lessen, but they rose inexorably larger. Anna looked back, down, at the stern windows, and flung herself away—it seemed she was going to fall through the glass into the furious seas.

She and Parrette clung together in terrified silence until rumbling footsteps and a perfunctory thud on the door brought in Perkins with several men behind him. "Mrs. Capting, we're striking down all extras," he said, pointing at the trunks. "Come with us. You're to go below."

"The captain?" she asked.

"Still on deck."

Anna and Parrette were bundled down to the wardroom, where they found the boy d'Ivry, his eyes circled a dull gray with exhaustion. His hair was plastered to his skull as he sat down heavily at the table bolted to the deck. "Well, at all events, it's done," he said.

The purser looked up from playing whist with the gunner's mate. "Them dons is in the hold?"

"We got them all across, near eighty of them."

"Eighty?" Anna repeated, astonished. "For so large a ship?"

Mr. d'Ivry's expression lowered. "Eighty was all they found, after she struck her flag to *Royal Sovereign*." He looked unhappy, as if the day before he had not been gleefully crowing about 'thumping it into them, again and again.' "Many went over the side, and between us all, they got scooped out of the water. Those who could float. The rest drowned."

"Skipper set the marines in double guard on them devils," muttered the gunner's mate. "That's smart. I heared that first boat-load, gabbing away in foreign. Planning a mutiny, most like."

The midshipman lifted a shoulder upwards. "At all events, their lieutenant, the only one still alive, is a civilized cove, speaks English—"

He broke off at the sound of footsteps and voices.

The crewmen rose to their feet, hands to foreheads. The midshipman doffed a hat that was not on his head as the captain limped in, followed by a thoroughly drenched young man in a once-beautiful Spanish lieutenant's uniform, the red lapels leaking color down his waistcoat as if he bled. One epaulette had been torn off, and he had tied a handkerchief around his hand. From the look of it, at least a couple of fingers had been broken.

"Sit, please, gentlemen," Captain Duncannon said, his voice hoarse. "Madame." He nodded at Anna, the corners of his mouth lifting briefly as she curtseyed (she could not prevent a blush), then he turned to the midshipman. "Mr. d'Ivry. I regret that I must rescind your permission to retire. I know this is yours and Jones's sleep-watch, but there cannot be time for sleep. Fetch Mr. Jones, please, and both of you report to Mr. McGowan on the forecastle."

While he spoke the warrant officers and their mates vanished into the much wetter gunroom.

"Please, seat yourself, Lieutenant Suarez," he said in careful French, and holding out his hand toward Anna, "May I have the honor of presenting Lieutenant Suarez? Perkins," he called in English, "please wait upon the lieutenant."

Perkins stumped up to the table. His method of talking to the Spanish officer was to speak very loudly and distinctly, as if the young man were hard of hearing, or slow.

Under cover of their laborious conversation, Duncannon limped to Anna, wincing at every step.

"Can you not take a moment to rest?" she asked.

His head turned in a negation. "Not until this blows out. Sayers is up on deck, a capstan bar bound to his leg. No one will sleep until this squall passes." He glanced at the young officer. "He's very low. Lost nearly all his shipmates. I would take it kindly if you were to talk to him."

"I would be happy to."

He had been leaning against the table with his good hand; the wounded arm came around, and his fingers touched hers. His hand was cold. She gripped his fingers, but dropped her hand when Perkins boomed loudly, "Capting says, no galley fires to be lit."

Captain Duncannon murmured to Anna, "I had better get him out before he talks the wretched man into a calenture." He said, "Perkins, help me to the ladder. I must return to my post." He bowed stiffly to the lieutenant.

Anna approached the Spanish lieutenant. He was not only still grimy from battle smoke, he looked exhausted. She held one hand to the table to steady herself as she curtseyed, wondering what to say. She understood Captain Duncannon's impulse to be courteous, but she hadn't the first idea how to speak to a man who had just lost a battle, and most of his shipmates.

She said in Spanish, "I trust and hope you shall soon be home again."

His dark brown eyes widened when he heard her speak his language, and his head dropped back on the word *home*. "And when I am, it shall only be to be ordered out again to more of this damned, purposeless war, protecting these atheistical French, their souls to the devil. Ordered by the Prince of Peace." His teeth showed when he uttered Godoy's title, his voice derisive.

Then he shook his head. "Pardon me, Senora Duncannon. I ought not to speak so before a lady. How is it that you speak the Spanish? And so very well?"

He was still standing, also holding onto the table.

"Shall we sit?" she asked.

He moved like an aristocrat, but even so he could not entirely mask plain human tiredness as he fell into his chair. His head turned, and she saw that he was probably a year or two even younger than she was — scarcely any beard.

"I have traveled to many cities in Spain," she said, before she remembered that she was not supposed to be a lowly performer.

But either he was too polite to ask why, or more likely he was too exhausted to take any interest in her motions. "My country," he said, "is the most beautiful in the world, and the greatest. But the rot is at the top, and will continue to destroy us unless we attend to it." Again he caught himself, and he asked politely what she had seen.

She described the Roman theater of Merida, the Moorish palace in Seville, the beauties of Madrid, which brought the lieutenant's chin up in pride. For a short time they discussed opera and Spanish dance, but after a remark about how Spanish dance was like the duel, once again he strayed to the war.

And then it came out, what a disaster it had been from the beginning. Everything, from the stupidity of weaving together the Spanish ships with the French ("Because Villeneuve feared we would run. *We!* I was with the admiral at Toulon, as a ship's boy. It was not *we* who have run from battle.") to Captain Infernet's noble, mad dash to rally what was left of the Combined Fleet. "And it might have answered, had the others followed…"

As the lieutenant talked on, Anna remembered Villeneuve's bitter complaints about his allies. She did not pretend to understand the young man's words about strategy, wind, or artillery, but she sensed in his fatalistic language, so different from what she had heard at Admiral Lord Nelson's table, that while the British had fought to win, from commanders to sailors, perhaps the French and Spanish commanders had fought because it was their duty to fight, and those under their command level had fought to live. Who would choose to make a "noble, mad" dash for a cause in which they had no faith?

She was glad when Perkins brought some food and drink. The lieutenant was given one of the captain's best bottles of wine, which he drank steadily as he grimly tried to work his way through a stale biscuit and a hunk of unsoftened salt beef straight from the cask.

After his fourth glass of wine, his eyes actually rolled, and Anna said, "Pray excuse me."

She got up and made her way to the galley to seek water. Perkins and the cook were there. She was given a cup from a barrel, which she drank off while standing there, and when she returned, she found Lieutenant Suarez asleep, his head resting on his crossed arms.

She withdrew to the gunroom, pressing against a bulkhead as the ship gave a violent yaw, water dripping from the working timbers. She nodded at the marine sentry, smoke-streaked still, his hair unpowdered. But his musket gleamed as he stood guard at the ladder.

That was the last conversation for what became an endless stretch of terror as the storm built inexorably into a wild, howling hurricane. Parrette also sat in the gunroom, quietly telling over her rosary, her eyes closed; even the warrant officers had vanished to tend to the ship either on deck or from the hold.

Anna shut her eyes, trying to compose herself to rest until Mr. Leuven, looking old and ill, appeared. "I beg you, ma'am, if you can tend the sick-berth, I can look after the cases coming down with storm-wounds. We are devilish hard-pressed."

Anna made her way into the sick berth, while Parrette went below to lend a hand with the wounded. The space with its close-packed cots and swinging hammocks was thick with a fug tinged with the aroma of spirits. On a chalk slate similar to the one Anna had seen on the binnacle were scrawled directions for the various cases.

There was little she could do beyond change bandages at intervals, dousing each with the splash of whisky. The patients endured this treatment because they were also permitted a dollop of said whisky, eked out with water, in a wooden scupper that they all shared around.

At Anna's appearance, they brightened considerably, the least wounded plucking at coverings to make themselves somewhat decent, and one or two even pushing back filthy tangled hair, and fingering bristle on chins and upper lips that would not be shaved any time soon.

She saw all those eyes on her, some dull with pain and desperation as the room pitched mercilessly, water dripping down, and others shy, or bright with expectation. Midshipman

Bradshaw's eyes glittered. When she reached his cot, she saw that he was flushed with fever, and complaining of thirst.

"He cannot have his dose until the watch bell, and that foot bandage gets changed," Mr. Gilchrist said, one thin hand pressed to his bandaged ribs, several of which had been cracked by falling debris.

Anna's memories of torturous thirst during the relentless heat in Spain caused her to reflect that fever must feel very like, and what could be the harm in drinking? "Then we shall declare the watch change now," she stated. "Since I hear no bells ringing."

She made her way around the beds, not only dispensing bandages and whisky-laced water, but trying to find a part of sheets or blankets not damp, wiping a cool cloth over flushed faces, and listening to fretful comments.

At the end, she groped her way to the stool set by the hatch, directly under the swinging lantern. Mr. Bradshaw, lying nearby, reached his fever-hot hand to take hers. She understood it was comfort he sought, the unspoken comfort that could only be vouchsafed by touch.

"Would you tip us the foreign song?" he asked, seeing her questioning gaze.

"Foreign song?" Anna repeated.

"The bird," someone else said. "You sang it on us, in the orlop."

She protested, "I am very out of voice — out of practice."

"Sing for us," Mr. Bradshaw whispered. "We could have the French ones again, if you haven't a better."

Anna had much better songs. She took a moment to hum her way through a couple of scales, and began softly, to warm her voice further. Simple tunes — "La marie et la mariée," "Aucassin and Nicolette," the lovely "Il fantasma dell'opera," and "Douce Dame Jolie."

When she finished those, she looked around at her audience. Some slept, lulled by melody into a semblance of peace, but the others had turned her way, faces hungry for something that food, water, and medicine could not give. She thought she understood those waiting eyes, casting her back in memory to her early days, and how she longed for the heart-lift of song, so beautiful, so powerful though it could not be touched and held.

This longing was what had motivated her to learn to sing.

Mr. Bradshaw tugged insistently at her hand. "The bird. He said there was one about a bird. Please, mum."

She had to brace her feet wide against the deck, but it felt good to sing again, and better, it kept her from worrying about what she could not help. And so she sang through the brighter, happier arias in *Magic Flute* until one by one they slept.

And then, though her entire body throbbed as she sat on that uncomfortable stool, she leaned against the trunk lashed to the wall beside her, folded her arms, and dozed fitfully until someone moaned and began thrashing.

She jerked awake, and it was time to carry water around again, and to tend bandages.

And so began a long, slow, unending nightmare. Time had become meaningless, impossible to measure: it was experienced in a series of images and expedients, emotions and snatches of nightmare-riddled dozes.

When the sick-berth was awake, they wanted song, and so Anna sang. They were not the only ones. Unseen by Anna, those few who came, or were sent, below-decks crept forward, drawn by the rise and fall of her beautiful voice, a miracle amid the roaring maelstrom.

It lasted until the storm, in a final act of viciousness, brought the foremast by the board. The crew chopped away like madmen lest the spar with all its complication of yards and rigging should drag the ship over and cause it to broach to. It wasn't until the last of the tangle vanished in an enormous green wave that the captain was discovered senseless, an axe still gripped in his one good hand, caught by two crewmen before he could be swept out to sea.

Twenty-two

"HE IS IN A coma," Mr. Leuven said. "Put him in his cot. He must be kept in darkness, and as quiet as can be, with as little movement as can be."

Numb with shock, Anna said, "I will tend him."

Mr. Leuven glanced from her to Perkins, saying, "You must keep him as still as ever you can. Violent movement, a sudden jar, can be mortal in these cases."

Anna stayed beside the captain's cot for the remainder of that dreadful voyage.

It was only a pair of days but time had long since lost its sense of meaningful measure. They had lost sight of the rest of the fleet, but steered for Gibraltar to discharge the load of prisoners. The tender, which alone had sustained limited damage, was sent ahead to report, and to alert the physicians there to the captain's condition.

The exhausted officers and crew relieved one another watch-on-watch so they could all get at least snatches of sleep, and the galley fires were lit again so that the ship's people could be fed properly, though the stores diminished rapidly due to the addition of all those prisoners stuffed down into the hold. At least they had plenty of clean water, for the cook's mates had set out rain barrels as the last of the storm swept overhead.

Once the seas had diminished enough for the regular ship routine to resume, the officers of the watch suspended the holystoning of the storm-scoured quarterdeck. The sailors used swabs to mop what was already clean as nature could make it. Those who were required to stand on the quarterdeck walked softly. Even the evening gun was no longer fired off.

Anna remained beside the captain's cot, steadying it against the sway, and reflected on how the universal expectation of a wife placed her there. Should Anna Bernardo the opera singer have boarded the ship, the expectations due a single woman would have been so different. It would have been deemed inappropriate for an unmarried woman to nurse a man, even a man in a coma.

Yet she was both women, and in her own mind, she was still more the singer than the wife. What, really, *was* a wife? She no longer possessed the outer marks of a wife, the ring, and —

She glanced at the captain's face. It hurt to think of him no longer living, and so she suspended thoughts of the future. There was enough to think about now, she decided as Perkins brought her a meal on the captain's good silver plate. He would never have done that for a mere Miss.

When her eyes burned she steadied the cot against her shoulders and tried to read. In desperation she finally made her way through the novel she had begun so many times. Perkins came to relieve her through the night watches, for which she was grateful. She woke herself before dawn and dressed hastily in the cold air, so that Perkins could retire. As the second day wore on, the ship rolling and creaking under fretful skies, she sat on a stool and steadied the cot against her hip while she finished plaiting her hat, and breathed for him, unconsciously pulling with her belly as if she could will him to waken.

Late in the day she watched the wavering light patterns across the low ceiling and curving bulkheads, reflections of sunlight off the restless waters below the stern window, and observed his face. Where was his essence? Had his spirit departed, leaving only this faintly breathing shell, or did he lie helpless, locked somewhere below the surface, where dreams lived?

She still could not define her emotions: sorrow seemed to hover just outside of perception, as if she could feel the beat of wings. Absurd, she tried thinking. She scarcely knew the man. If he woke, he might wish her away.

And yet there were the memories, so many sides to him: the wounded man who laughed ruefully into her hair when she tried to find a place to fit her elbows, the hot breath of pleasure, the cool commander on his quarterdeck, looking up at rigging and the sky beyond as king over his wooden kingdom. His strong hands, his eyes closed, as he and his quartet wove a musical tapestry with the complicated patterns of Bach as the ship sailed on and on.

She could not but wonder how much of that life would he share with her, given his waking again.

But sometimes she held his hand, in hopes he could feel her warmth; she waited for the slightest twitch or tug as evidence he was there somewhere inside the slowly breathing body.

At last, at last, the lookout shouted "Land ho!"

Gibraltar had appeared on the wild horizon.

She still did not permit herself to believe them secure until they had actually come into the harbor and the thunder of the anchor being let down rumbled through the ship. Her relief at safety—relative safety—so overwhelmed her that once again she could find expression only in music. Softly, softly: it was the aria Paisiello had written for Lord Nelson so long ago, sung from on high in that freshly painted palazzo.

She hummed, her heart so full that tears blurred her eyelids.

She began softly, but gradually, inexorably, the tide of emotion was too strong and she lifted her face and sang with all her power. She was no Catalani—they did not hear her on the quay—but all through the ship the hands paused, listening, and the prisoners being brought up were amazed by light and air and the beautiful sound.

Unaware, Anna sang on.

Because she sang with her eyes closed, she never saw the subtle movement beneath Duncannon's eyelids, as at last his mind, drawn by the heart-lifting aria, drew him up and up through the layers until he floated just below the surface. He remembered that sound, the angels on high under the painted dome of heaven, but this was the real angel, not a palace smelling of paint, with officers shifting and sighing right behind. This was the promised heaven, a realm of infinite peace, and he was alone with the angel, song, heart, spirit perfectly in tune...

"The lieutenant wants you," Parrette whispered voicelessly from the cabin door

Anna stopped singing.

"They want us ashore before they bring out the wretches locked below." And, when Anna cast an uncertain glance at the captain, Parrette murmured, "I shall sit with him. He is not going anywhere."

Anna wiped her eyes, and got to her feet.

Suspended somewhere between memory and exaltation, he was bereft. The angel was gone.

He sank down again into dreams.

Lieutenant Sayers had made the wardroom his temporary headquarters.

He sat on a bench, his bad leg stretched out to rest on a cheese of cannon wads. He steeled himself to ignore the ever-present throb of pain from his ruined knee, an attitude only partly effective.

Tired as he was, he could not sleep well, partly from the pain and partly from his anxious wait for Collingwood's orders respecting the *Aglaea*. Promotion was fairly sure, at least for all lieutenants who had been active in the battle (and had survived it), but what was very unsure was a ship. There would be many more new captains hungry for a commission.

As acting captain, he now had power over the ship, but with it commensurate responsibility. That included attending on the flag the afternoon of his arrival at Gibraltar, when the signal was raised for All Captains.

At this meeting, he discovered the personalities behind the shining epaulettes and the laced cocked hats; most he respected, though he grew to dislike Harvey's constant carping about the victory, and what he would have done in this or that situation. Captain Fremantle muttered as Sayers climbed down the ladder behind him to their waiting gigs below, "That fellow has obviously never served in an action before Cadiz."

Sayers did not know if Captain Fremantle meant to be overheard, or if he forgot and thought that his old friend Captain Duncannon was following him, so the new acting captain kept a prudent silence.

He also did so later that night, when he had himself rowed ashore to execute business concerning the prisoners, where he overheard captains muttering about Collingwood's sometimes contradictory orders.

While he disliked very much the idea of climbing over Henry Duncannon's back, there was no arguing with the fact that the captain lay in the cabin hovering between life and death, and therefore unable to command the ship. Someone would have to take command, and Theophilus Sayers meant to be that man if he could. That meant driving the crew to a peak of efficiency that would impress the new C. in C. with his zeal.

All this was in his mind when the post was brought to him. He had not expected much, as after all they had been brought post only a week or two past. And it proved to be scarcely a dozen pieces of mail. But it was his job to sort it and get it passed to its recipients... and so he stared down at the last of the letters, his mind stumbling to a halt for a time, until roused by the boatswain's tweeting the hands to dinner.

Tucking the last letter under the ship's log, he roused himself to a new set of urgent tasks. He summoned his remaining midshipmen and sent them flying off on errands, some clutching notes. He would mention the letter to no one until he had his arrangements well in hand.

Anna and Perkins traded watches sitting by the captain's cot, keeping it as still as possible. He never stirred except for his slow, shallow breathing.

Late that night, once Parrette had made certain that Anna had hot water to wash, and a good meal inside her before she fell exhausted into her cot, she joined her son in the after-cabin, where the great table had sat empty ever since the captain's injury.

"Perkins says the captain is to be moved to the shore. I am certain that Anna will go with him, and so shall I. Do you come with us?" she asked in French.

"My duty is here." Michel took hold of one of her hands. "I am so glad to have found you again, Maman. But this is now my life."

"You were forced into it," Parrette said.

He shrugged. "I was forced to be a drummer boy, forced to many things when the army crossed Europe." His expression altered to hatred. "I will never go back to France. Even if I did not have bad memories, however they change the laws, I will still not likely have a right to my name."

Parrette's face was grim. "I confessed my part of that sin, and was absolved. I said my vows in good faith, and so even though he was a worthless man, I believe I have a right to his name. And so do you."

Michel shook his head slowly. "Maybe, maybe. But not in the eyes of Boney's laws. And what sort of justice has he brought? Fouché would have murdered you along with the others if he had caught you. And what is the result of his butchery? Boney rewards him." Michel shook his head. "I do not yet know where I might settle one day, but France is dead to me."

Sorrow contracted her heart, though she was not certain that she saw herself as a Frenchwoman anymore.

"This is a good berth," Michel said, seeing her expression. "Sayers is now acting captain. He's as good to us as Duncannon, whose rules are his own. Mr. Gates says, another year or two, and I would be ready to put up my bond, supposing we come across a prize so I can raise the ready. He will give me a good character, and I would like to be a purser. I am good with numbers."

"And that is what I wished to talk to you about," Parrette said. "I have been putting by my own earnings for a shop. But I will put up your bond, or buy a little house for us, anywhere you like, if you wish to give up the sea."

Michel grinned down at his mother. She was so small. In his memory she had been tall and strong, flying between him and his roaring, fist-swinging father, until the night his father yanked him out of his bed in the middle of the night and told him he was going to be a drummer boy for the Revolution. When he tried to run to his mother, he found her lying senseless on the floor. He had thought her dead.

He patted her bony shoulder awkwardly. "I'm grateful, I am. But no man rightly lets his mother do what he must do himself, and Collingwood is sure to give us a cruise, on account of the dons who slipped back into Cadiz. Why, even if we don't earn prize money, there's the head count on prisoners, and in any case we have to clap a stopper over 'em or they're sure to be up to their old capers. You take care of *her*." He pointed with his chin toward Anna's cabin. "She needs you more."

"I shall. That was my promise to her dear mother."

"And when she's right and tight, why, then you go and buy that shop. It could be when I do give over the sea, I'll come join you. I would like to be married someday, and the three of us can live together."

Parrette smiled. "You're a good boy. I will have a Mass said for your safety."

"You do that, ma," he said, but again cast a quick look around.

She successfully interpreted that quick, guilty glance. It grieved her heart that these English seemed to have an animus against Roman Catholics, but perhaps he could be led back to the true church in time. That would not happen now, and she did not want to crab her gratitude that he was alive, that she had found him, that they had reached safety. So she said only, "If we must leave, be sure that when I know where we are settled, I will send a letter to this ship."

"Do. So that I will know where to write back when I know something." Michel bent and kissed her, then they parted, he to vanish into the swarm of activity.

The next morning, Parrette intercepted Anna before she could go to the captain as usual. "Mr. Sayers wants an interview," she said.

Anna had scarcely seen the lieutenant since the burial at sea, as he stood swaying behind the captain with his bloody bandage around his knee.

Sayers looked up at her entrance. "Mr. Jones," he said to the midshipman busy writing at a side table. "Jump to the galley and discover if the cook can put up some punch for us, then see if the launch is arrived."

The boy bounced up, happy to get away from having to copy papers out in fair. "Yes sir, cook, punch, and launch." He shot out of the wardroom.

Sayers nodded at the sentry, who pulled the door shut behind the midshipman, leaving the lieutenant alone with Anna. "Pray take a chair, please. I trust you will forgive my neglect of you. It has not been intentional."

"I quite understand, Lieutenant," Anna said, her expression one of polite inquiry.

To her surprise, instead of coming directly to his point he fumbled with his pen, so for a moment all she saw was his pale hair, and then he reached past his neat stacks of papers to a battered book, and withdrew a sealed letter from beneath it.

Her puzzlement sharpened to worry. She looked down at the scrawled direction on the letter:

To the Rt. Hon.'ble Lord Northcote
Captain, H.M.S. Aglaea

"What does this mean? I do not understand. Who is this person?" Her brow drew together. "Northcote. I have heard this name, certain."

"It is the hereditary title," the lieutenant said slowly, "of our captain's family. Ma'am—Lady Northcote, I understand I should say—by your leave, I think you're the only one who can open it."

"But this is not my letter," she said, not hearing his correction. "And nowhere is mention of his name, his true name. Can it be an error?"

"It is the correct direction," Lt. Sayers said patiently, "if—if something happened to the captain's elder brother, who was the baron, and he had no son to inherit, the title would fall to the captain."

She still looked blank.

He hesitated again, striving to find some compromise between delicacy and making things plain to a lady who, however gallant, was still a foreigner, and therefore ignorant. "News is always sporadic for seamen," he said. "We can go as much as six months, even a year before the post catches up, if we have been on a long commission. Then, there is lost post. The packet carrying six months of post had been swamped in the hurricane that drove us off our stations, for example, and most of the letters in our bag were ruined. One of those was probably for the captain, had we but known."

He paused again.

She still waited with that air of puzzlement. "And as for the newspapers, it is easy to miss announcements without you have the right date."

And she still said nothing.

So he said, "Captain Duncannon, to my knowledge, has not been in the habit of communicating with his family." He could have said, *When we were boys, the only thing I knew about him was that he had one brother, an arrogant blood in the sixth form. And we knew better than to ask questions, these past years.* "Given our present situation, and all that is implied in the direction on this letter, I think it best to tender it to you."

He pinched his fingers to the bridge of his nose, and Anna's heart contracted in a way that had nothing to do with the gentle motion of the ship.

Why was he so short with her, so reluctant to speak? The idea occurred that her situation, her questions, were merely another burden to add to his impossible number.

She said, "Must I open it now, or was there something else?"

"Open it at your leisure," he said, in a lighter voice, clearly relieved to see her take responsibility for it. "There is another matter that cannot wait. Before the battle, the captain made me promise to send you home should anything happen to him."

To Sayers, the word 'home' could only have meant one thing: the place of his birth, to which he longed to return in order to marry his patient betrothed. And so Captain Duncannon's wife — that is, the new Lady Northcote — must of course be sent to Barford Magna, Yorkshire, England, where the captain had been born.

He said, "Captain Neville, who it happens is a particular

friend, awaits you now. He has agreed to take you to England. He is carrying the latest dispatches."

"England!" she repeated.

"It is your home," Sayers said with utter conviction. "Here is a purse. It is his own money, which I know he would want me to surrender to you. It should see you comfortable until you have had a chance to make your arrangements."

He handed her a small purse containing crackling bills. "I feel obliged to say, while there is life there is hope, but I still believe he would desire you to go ahead of him. He will receive the best of care, from the most experienced medical men. The admiral promised that for all his wounded officers—his own physician is waiting for the captain now, once the launch reaches land."

"Is it not my place to remain with him?"

The lieutenant pinched his fingers between his brows again, his voice tense. "I have received word that given the many wounded in carrying off the ships, the hospital here at Gib is overcrowded. There is no place, none at all, for a lady. Please. The arrangements have been made, and the best thing you could do is go ahead and see to his affairs as best you can."

To him that meant all the specifics of the transfer of an estate, but to her it meant nothing whatsoever. It was going entirely too swiftly. But the way he looked away from her and at his desk reminded her that he already had an impossible number of immediate demands on his notice.

She said, "If I may be permitted to bide long enough only to see him safely to the hospital." She spoke the words knowing that there was nothing she could materially do, and further, no one wanted her there. But it seemed the right thing to do. "How will I find out his progress?"

"You may depend upon me for that," Sayers said. "It is no more than he has done for all the ship's people, a task I will take scrupulous care to honor as he did. I shall write to you at this direction." He indicated the letter in her hands.

In those few words everything the letter represented, hitherto lying utterly outside her experience, suddenly engulfed her.

"You will have an opportunity to speak to the physician once the launch reaches the dock, where I am told everything is in waiting," Sayers finished.

She could see that the interview was at an end, and rose.

He stood painfully, reaching his hand out to her. "Madame, my lady, permit me to take this opportunity to thank you, on his behalf, and on behalf of the ship's people, for all your exertions. I have only to add that in this very minute the launch for transporting him is in preparation, while the water is relatively quiet, the tide flowing in."

They shook hands, and she walked out, half in a daze. Once again her life was taking an utterly unexpected turn.

She pocketed the letter and purse and went up to the deck, where she found a party of big, strong pigtailed seamen carrying the captain's cot, step by careful step. Perkins had tucked him mummy-tight down into the cot, a sheet over his face to ward the sun.

Parrette stopped her, and mutely handed her the bonnet that during those long hours of waiting she had made over into something smart. Anna obediently put it on, tied the ribbon under her chin, and then reluctantly pulled on the gloves that Parrette handed her, before being bundled into her traveling cloak, also new-furbished.

When she was done, the men were still involved with their tackles, so Anna ventured down to the sick-berth to take her leave of the midshipmen. Mr. Bradshaw cried almost tearfully, "Oh, that I had known, I would have written a letter home!"

Though she still did not believe she would actually travel to England, she could not prevent herself from saying, "Should all come to pass, I will call upon your family myself, and carry your best wishes, shall I?"

He flushed, his whole countenance changing. "Tell them about the battle, will you, Mrs. Duncannon?" He held out a hand, and she gripped his fever-warm fingers. "And you might also hint that an increase in my mess allowance might not go amiss, as the indent for someone my size is significantly more than it was when I was no bigger than a walnut. Only don't put it so, if you will, but make it polite, like."

She smiled and agreed, but her throat hurt as she took her leave of them all.

Parrette was waiting for her at the railing as she watched over the shifting of their trunks into the launch.

Anna and Parrette were helped down last. Anna sat by the cot carrying the captain. She glanced up to take private leave of his ship. Her time aboard it had been short in measure of days, but she had run through all the range of emotions to such a degree that it felt she had lived there for years, whereas Spain was a faint memory, almost a dream, by comparison.

The journey to the wharf was not long in duration. While the seamen watched the water and boat traffic, Anna slipped the letter from her pocket and, uneasy yet intensely curious, she worked her finger under the seal.

The handwriting was a rounded fist, decorated with flourishes that made it difficult to read.

Northcote Manor

Dearest Henry:

I can quite understand your not writing after John died, given everything that has Transpir'd, though you might have thought of Mother. But however, I promised [the word promised underscored three times] myself I would not take up my pen just to Quarrel with you, after all this time.

Emily would have nothing said, or changed, in any way, save the Notice taken that was due to our Position, until she was brought to bed, as she was so very certain she carried a boy, and she found some London man-midwife who assured her All the Signs were There for a Boy. He charged her a thumping ten guineas, too. But it was all for Naught, and poor little baby Amelia made her appearance this fortnight past. Emily scarcely looks at her, so Nurse and I have made her our very own.

We are all at sixes and sevens here. You can have no notion how Horrid John left everything. I know you would rather be

Anywhere but Here, but it is now your Duty. Even if you wish to pass the Title off, our third-cousin Harry's little boy is only Six Years Old, which would leave us in a very horrid Situation.

I beg you will not render our lives Hideous in the Extreme by such a measure. But however, it is now your Decision and you may do what you Like. But you must visit the Solicitor, or at the Least [another half-dozen underlinings] write, that we may know our Fates.

With better hopes, your still loving sister, and I am very sorry you did not write back about the Handkerchiefs I embroidered for you with mourning edgework, though I know my stitchwork is Not All it ought to be —

Your loving Sister,

Harriet

Anna refolded the letter, more confused than enlightened. The only thing clear was that the captain had a sister, and she felt it was his duty to return home.

She tucked the letter back into her pocket as Captain Duncannon was brought up to the dock as carefully as possible. She watched anxiously. Had he stirred, or was that an effect of the motion that could not be completely avoided?

He was still again, but breathing. She listened to that breathing as they were conveyed in the back of a wagon with two other badly wounded men from other ships. Anna was scarcely aware of her surroundings, hearing only a mix of Spanish and English voices.

Every jolt she felt in her heart, the more because one of the men groaned feverishly. Parrette stayed by her side, a silent presence, as they followed the orderlies into the military hospital, and the captain was carried to a cool, quiet room away from the general wards.

When the captain was lifted from the cot to the waiting bed,

SHERWOOD SMITH

this time she was certain she saw his head move beneath the covering sheet, and one hand flex.

"He wakes," she cried. And then lower, "He moved. I am certain of it."

"I saw, too," Parrette said.

A man in a physician's scratch wig and black coat had appeared, a tired-looking man with enormous side-whiskers that came all the way around his face under his chin, leaving his cheeks and mouth bare.

He glanced into the cot, took the captain's pulse, looked under his eyelids, then shook his head solemnly. "It is only the movement of the cot. He is in a coma. The danger is extreme," he added, low-voiced. "There must be no voices, no excitement at all." He turned to Anna. "You are Captain Lord Northcote's lady, I apprehend?"

There was that title again! She touched her pocket containing the letter before saying, "I am."

"I wish to assure you that he will get the best of care, but what he needs most of all is quiet. Generally in these cases, if the patient survives the initial crisis, there is a strong possibility that he will waken. But I must warn you that the vitreous humors are suffused."

"What does that mean?"

"It means there is a decided chance that he will wake blind. I warn you of possibilities, to emphasize the severity of the case. We cannot speak of certainties."

At her shocked expression he relented enough to add, "I venture to hold out a cautious hope. Even if he does wake blind, there is always a possibility that with time, and perhaps some judicious blood-letting, that the humors will clear, and restore his sight. But he must be made to be quiet, completely quiet, with no excitement, no speech, even, until the crisis is safely past."

"How long will that be?" she asked, aware of Parrette behind her, and at the door, a young midshipman restlessly waiting.

The scratch wig inclined in a bow. "No one can say. It could be an appreciable time. If he does waken in possession of his intellects, he is going to require absolute quiet, and a room devoid of light. You could do the most good by going ahead to prepare his

288

home to receive him."

He bowed and turned away to one of the several men waiting for his attention. Anna, left alone, became aware of whispering, and when she turned her head, it was to discover Parrette in close conversation with a stout middle-aged woman wearing a coarse apron over her linsey-woolsey gown, a plain cap on her head.

Anna nearly stepped away when she recognized the brown stains on that apron as blood. Parrette said, "Mrs. Sperring here says they are over-charged in this place."

"It's severe, your la'ship," this woman said in a broad accent that Anna found difficult to understand. At least the woman was too tired to speak quickly. "Severe, like. We've no proper place for a lady. We're running out of beds as 'tis."

"She tended wounded on one of the other ships," Parrette said.

To this Mrs. Sperring added, with a mirthless laugh, "Afore that I was running powder, skipping like a boy."

The two women looked expectantly at Anna, who recognized moral certainty. Though she was supposed to be the lady of rank here, it was very clear where authority lay. It was her place to bow to greater need, and withdraw.

She said slowly, "Is there perhaps another physician? Another hospital? Somewhere I can take him, where there is no crowding?"

Mrs. Sperring laughed. "Bless you, dearie, this *is* the best. And the admiral's own man, you just spoken to. There ain't any better, not for a month's travel in any direction."

Anna let her breath out. Gibraltar was little more than a rock in the sea, poised between two continents, with war all around. "Lieutenant Sayers spoke of England."

Mrs. Sperring's broad brow cleared. "Yes, your la'ship, the very thing. You can do no better than that. On his waking, he will want to know you are there."

"Very well. Thank you," she said, and finding Perkins hovering beside the door, she went up to him. "Are you being let to stay?"

"It's orders," Perkins said, loud enough for that gallows-faced cove in the scrub wig to hear. "It's orders, I'm to be right here. I'll sleep right here on the floor next or nigh him."

"Oh, thank you," she murmured and slid the letter into his

hand. "When the captain wakes, pray give this to him. Tell him the seal is broken because Lieutenant Sayers said I must open it."

Perkins touched his forehead. "I'll see to it, Missus Capting, your la'ship, that is. The lieutenant told me the news. You can lay your life I'll see to him. Good journey to you."

"Thank you, and to you."

"This way," Parrette said. "They await us."

Two hours later, as the tide turned, she and Parrette stood together on the tiny deck of the *Mermaid*.

They watched until the harbor receded to an unevenly curved line below the towering Rock, and the ships dwindled to dots with gently swaying masts.

The captain of the *Mermaid* waited until the harbor had dropped below the horizon before sending his single middie to his guest. The boy touched his hat respectfully. "Captain Neville's duty, ma'am, and should you like to join him for dinner, the watch is about to change."

Anna knew what that meant: she mustn't keep him waiting. Nothing short of the worst hurricane, or the heat of battle, kept the navy from its regular round of whistles and bells, and a captain's invitation was tantamount to stringent command.

She paced beside the midshipman, a thin, earnest-faced boy, and descended the short distance to what was a fine little cabin, divided into two chambers.

Captain Neville, wearing his formal blue coat, hovered outside the carved doors of his cabin. He was very handsome in the English style, fair-haired, blue-eyed, with a ready smile. "Welcome aboard, Lady Northcote," he said. "Pray accept my wife's best wishes and earnest excuses. She is unwell, and desires me to assure you that only illness prevents her from joining us. But if you wish to wait upon her following the meal, you would be most welcome."

Anna said what was proper as a white-gloved steward quietly served a meal. Charles Neville guided the conversation along unexceptionable topics. In this way they soon arrived at music.

Finding his guest very well informed on a subject he relished, Captain Neville kept them at it until the cover was removed. Remembering the dinner aboard Nelson's flagship, Anna scrupulously withdrew, freeing Neville to return to the deck.

Anna perforce then had to call upon Lady Lydia, lying in the sleeping cabin adjacent. One look at her made it clear that being unwell was no pretext.

Lady Lydia, so lively and pretty aboard the flagship, was almost unrecognizable, her hair tangled, her complexion greenish with nausea. "You are here at last," she said fretfully. "On no account, I told Charles, must the smells of food be permitted inside here. Oh, I am so *very* ill, this motion will be *mortal* before I can ever get home." Her lips worked, her face paled as she clapped her hand to her mouth.

Anna said hastily, "I shall withdraw now, shall I? I will visit you on the morrow. Perhaps you will feel better." She closed the cabin door on the poor young wife.

Parrette was waiting. She took Anna down to the tiny canvas-walled space that belonged to the lieutenant, now made over to the guests. There were two hammocks, one low, and one high, as there was nowhere else for them in the small ship.

Mindful of how sound carried, she repeated the gist of the letter to Parrette, speaking in Neapolitan.

Parrette, watching her with narrowed eyes, waited until she was through and then observed, "You are now Lady Northcote, and you must now go to his home."

"So everyone seems to expect of me. I will do what's right, but he never told me of this home, or these people, and I expect it is the same for them. How am I to thrust myself upon people who *I* expect have no idea I even exist?"

"You will do it because it is your duty." Parrette shrugged. "Speaking of everything that is proper, Lady Lydia's Mrs. Timothy gave me the cast aside magazines, and I shall address your clothing. If they waited upon the birth of a possible heir, then the death is not recent. You will not be required to wear black. *Toutefois!* You will be in proper half-mourning when you step off this ship in London Harbor, or wherever they choose to land us. I am going to need to visit warehouses as soon as may be. You've only the two gowns in correct shades."

Anna thanked her, but with a grave, almost absent air. Parrette's brows snapped together. "You have misgivings?"

"Not about the clothes," Anna said hastily. "Thanks to you. It is this place we go to. About that I have misgivings."

"Where else should we go?" Parrette asked, and seeing Anna's uncertainty, pushed on relentlessly. "It would be madness to return to Spain. Or Naples, with war there, too. Back to France? Do you think, even if Company Dupree were to return to Paris, would you have your place back? Is that what you truly want?"

Anna sat on the lower hammock. "I want him to be well, to talk to me, to decide together if we are truly man and wife. After that, I can look to the future."

"You *are* man and wife," Parrette said. "But a marriage is not the piece of paper you signed. That began it. A marriage, a good one gets made and remade every day." Her voice trembled.

Anna studied Parrette's steady gaze, knowing that Parrette had had the worst of marriages, and yet she had done her best. Anna knew she had nothing to complain of, except fear of the unknown. And that was everyone's fear during wartime.

"Then we are off to this Yorkshire, wherever that may be, to await his recovery," Anna said, and felt guilty when she perceived the tension easing from Parrette's brow.

Twenty-three

THE NEXT MORNING, AS the sloop sailed with slanted deck before a driving wind, Parrette made Anna put on her second-best silk day gown, a soft silver-gray, from which Parrette had unpicked the green and crimson embroidery, and removed most of the lace.

After breakfast she went to the little cabin where she found Lady Lydia sitting propped on pillows in the cabin. Lady Lydia looked less green than she had the previous evening.

Her maid, a silent woman hovering in the background, had managed to dress her hair with a fresh ribbon, and she wore a bed jacket of ribbon-threaded lace.

"Good morning, Lady Northcote." Lady Lydia eyed her visitor with an expression not unlike a discontented pout, before she forced a smile, twining a curl fretfully around a finger. "This illness puts me all out of patience. It is by rights supposed to be worse in the mornings, but *I* am plagued with it all through the night. You ought to be grateful you are not in child while being tossed unmercifully by the billows, is all I can say."

Anna murmured a sympathetic politeness, to which Lady Lydia replied with a sigh. "At all events, I know it is ill-bred to tender congratulations. Charles told me this morning that no one aboard *Aglaea* — no one in the fleet—had actually known that Lord Northcote, the previous baron, had died Christmas last year. And here I'd thought Duncannon had had scruples about using the title until he should find out if the baby was a boy. At any event, I am now to discover that Emily Northcote was *not* delivered of a boy, and I must say—but no, I am not to indulge in *commérage*, Charles says. So I will say nothing about *her*, but I believe I can say that I pity Miss Harriet Duncannon with all my heart, as she was to be presented to society last spring, as I was."

Commérage. The English word was 'gossip,' as if using French mitigated the meaning. Lady Lydia became absorbed in untangling the ribbons tying her bed jacket, and Anna caught the last of a sidelong glance, and shifted the subject. "Pray, if you would be so kind, I must consult your advice on a point of English etiquette."

Lady Lydia's face flushed with pleasure. Few people disliked being asked for advice. "Your accent is so charming! Let us speak in French," she said, switching to that language. "Then we are less likely to have the servants prating all over, whatever we might say." Her French was good, if stilted—probably, Anna thought privately, as stilted as her own English.

"As you wish," Anna replied in French, which was a relief, as she had been puzzled how to get the wording right without lying, yet come at the problem that she faced. "It is this. It is possible that my husband's family knows nothing about my existence. Do I write them to announce my existence? I cannot think of any way that would be considered well-bred. Yet it seems wrong not to apprise them."

"Ah," Lady Lydia exclaimed.

Anna intuited from that exclamation that she had answered a question that no one wanted to ask directly. *So the captain kept our marriage as secret as I did? Moreso,* she thought, remembering her drunken confidence to Hyacinthe, and the result.

"You need not put yourself to the trouble," Lady Lydia stated. "In this very ship, there is with the dispatches a letter writ by the admiral himself, going to the captain's family." She added quickly, "It is to be hoped that he recovers, but in case, well, the admiral felt it his duty to write to all the families of the wounded officers under his command. Charles is to carry these, and official dispatches, straight to the Admiralty. In that letter, there will be formal thanks for the service you rendered. He wrote that way for us all, I had it from one of the middies who helped in copying and sealing the letters."

"That is very good. And yet my question remains: I know I ought to write to them once I am in London, to say when I am coming. What is the etiquette of this letter?"

Lady Lydia's smile vanished. She had a general notion, of course, but even stronger was her immense dislike of one of the members of this family. "I can assure you, they will be looking for you in every post chaise that comes up the road." And at Anna's doubtful expression, "You must realize that you are now the principal woman in the family. It is *they* who ought to be waiting upon *you*. Nothing, I assure you, looks more particular than to trouble them with letters, nothing so odd, so quite out of the way. You perhaps do not perceive your importance, now that Captain Duncannon — Captain Lord Northcote — inherits."

She plucked at the ribbon in her bed jacket. "In truth," she said in a low voice, "since Charles is to inherit nothing of note, I'd as lief be bearing a girl. You can *dress* girls, whereas boys? Nankeen and broadcloth, and then they go off to Eton. They go off to Oxford. You only hear of debts and larks, and then they are off to war, or worse. A girl...a girl is at home, and there is all the world of fashion when she comes of age." She sighed. "That gown you have got on is very elegant. Was you ever in Paris?"

"During the Peace," Anna said, determined to say as little about her life as possible.

"And so was Lady Bessborough, sister to the Duchess of Devonshire! Did you meet?"

"We did not. I did not travel in such circles."

"Of course — you were a mere Mrs. then. Did you ever meet Josephine Bonaparte?"

"No, but I did see her once or twice, at the opera and the theater."

"Oh! Was she as beautiful as they say?"

"Very," Anna said honestly.

"Josephine Bonaparte! Gowns from Paris! You will no doubt find our English fashions hideous to the worst degree..."

When Captain Neville appeared a while later, and found his wife talking animatedly, Anna caught such a grateful look from him that she determined how to be useful on this journey: she must entertain his wife.

As a result, Captain Neville was so pleased with his elegant guest that he insisted upon Lady Northcote accompanying them after they landed at Falmouth. "I will be expected at the Admiralty as soon as may be," he said. "But I promise the White Hart is a fine hostelry—my wife will be able to rest there, until I am granted liberty. And you will find it much easier to find your way from there, rather than the dockside."

A crowd of the curious waiting for news gathered expectantly when the *Mermaid* floated up to the wharf, sails thundering as they spilled air. They were gratified not only by the sight of the young captain shouting, "Dispatches!" as he hurried down the side and away up the wharf, but by his being accompanied by two young and pretty ladies, one being supported by maid-servants, and the other, exceedingly elegant, interestingly clad in a French gown in colors of half-mourning.

No one quite knew how the news got about, but before Lydia and Anna were installed at the White Hart, it was known that the mysterious Parisienne in half-mourning was none other than Lady Northcote, whose husband was one of the Cape Trafalgar captains, now recovering from wounds in Gibraltar.

From thence their party was conveyed to London, and once Anna and Parrette were established at Grillion's Hotel in Albemarle Street, they parted with mutual good will.

As soon as they were alone, Anna said to Parrette, "How long do you think we ought to stay?"

Parrette said firmly, "Until you have a wardrobe fit for a lady. An *English* lady."

When Anna grimaced slightly, for she'd glimpsed some examples of what she assumed to be English fashions on the journey into London, Parrette said, "You will have to become accustomed to covering your head at all times. Frenchwomen of rank did, also, before the Revolution. In England, there are also gloves whenever you go out of doors. But the gowns... I will not entirely throw away what I learned from Le Roy in Paris. I've seen nothing here that drapes as well. But this is a cold climate, it wants more covering, and you are going to require a set of kerseymere spencer jackets to your gowns, and a fur-lined pelisse. And stays," she added firmly. "They will think you indecent if you do not wear them."

Anna sighed at the prospect of stays, remembering her mother lacing herself tightly. But warmth, that sounded very well. Two months ago Anna would have claimed that her exquisite cashmere shawls would be enough, but that was before experiencing the bone-aching cold winds as *Mermaid* sailed around Ushant toward the Channel.

Gratefully Anna conceded, thinking that given extra time she could return to dancing. Sitting in the carriage, she had become aware of her stiff neck and back, her arms and legs all awry. Sometimes it felt as if the ground still heaved beneath her, and she had to catch hold of something to steady herself.

"Thank you, Parrette," she said. "As for my part, though Lady Lydia assured me there is no need to write, I shall put my question to the hotel people. I am certain they can direct me to a respectable bookseller where I might find a book of etiquette for my letter. I will copy it so I make no mistakes. And that means we must settle on a date for them to expect us. I am thinking we have not enough money from the captain to stay long at this expensive hostelry and to buy new clothing."

Parrette agreed. "This is why I must get myself to the warehouses. You will be able to sew the long seams, while I see to the cut, the fit, and the trim."

Anna had no objections to that. Since neither of them had the least notion that Anna was now a wealthy woman in her own right, they calculated carefully how much they could spend on fabric and accouterments, hotel, and carriage hire to the north.

Anna's laboriously written letter — it required a dozen sheets of paper, and a twice-mended pen before she was satisfied — was copied from a book by a Reverend Trusler (a name Anna could not pronounce, which gave her misgivings), with only names and circumstances changed.

After the letter was added to the post collection at the hotel, Anna felt very much like a cannon had been armed, the slow-match lit, and was only waiting for the order to fire.

She was committed. Now she must prepare herself as much as she could. The cries of English voices in the streets were ever-present reminders of how inadequate was her comprehension of the language. She could understand little of anything they said.

So she skimped on meals enough to purchase two novels, with which she hoped to improve her English: *The Modern Griselda*, which the bookseller promised was written by a popular writer, and *The Wonder of the Village*, by another popular writer. Anna hoped by the first to learn something of what she might expect of a modern Englishwoman, and what she might expect from English country life.

They bought every newspaper, both aware of the luxury of not having to hide their interest. There was a great deal more about the glorious defeat of the French off Cadiz, and the sad news of more deaths, but by the time they left, no mention of the captain. Anna hoped that post with promising news might await her in Yorkshire.

By the time of their departure, Anna had made little headway in one book. It seemed to be a story about a poor young man who kept encountering unlikely adventures that proved to show how prodigiously thrifty, moral, and studious he was. Anna laid it by in favor of the next.

Their decision to go by post rather than the stage, or even the Mail (which only traveled at night) sufficed to empty the captain's purse, save a few shillings, but at least they both had the satisfaction of knowing that the trunks strapped on the back contained the smartest clothing Parrette's clever fingers could contrive. She had found out what a superior lady's maid wore, knowing that her own entry into this new household was as important as Anna's.

In Anna's trunk, in addition to all the other necessary garments, lay lace caps suitable for a married woman. Parrette had refused to even think about a widow's cap, that being, she reasoned, nothing but an invitation to ill luck at the most, and perhaps even sin.

The advantage of hiring the post chaise was not having to be crammed in with other passengers, especially those who regularly rode on the rooftop and frequently entertained themselves with noisy drumming on the roof of the equipage, and rocking it worse even than the road ruts. They had experienced enough frights during their long journey from Naples to Paris that neither wanted a repeat of the experience if they could avoid it.

The chaises apparently ended their journeys at inn-yards. At Barford Magna, the coachman assured them, they were sure to be met by someone from the manor to carry them the rest of their journey.

Their chaise stopped at every second posting inn for change of the horses, enabling them to step out and refresh themselves. There were enough shillings left for a small meal for each, and for the douceur the coachman expected. Between these stops, Anna read aloud and Parrette sewed.

Anna sometimes paused to laugh, but the farther she got into the story, the more dire was Parrette's frown. At length she put down her sewing and scowled. "A more contrary example of a wife would be difficult to find. Is this book a good example of a marriage?"

Anna smiled. "I believe the idea is comedy. She is very like Katharina, although the husband is nothing like Petruchio!"

"Petruchio," Parrette repeated, and scowled again. "*Commedia dell'arte* is low. You ought not to be reading such a book! What will they think in Yorkshire?"

Anna laughed. "Katharina and Petruchio are characters from an English play. You remember? Mama had me read it, oh, when I was ten. She translated it into French so that I would understand it." She laid aside the book. "I have promised never to talk about my days in Dupree Company. You were right, too, if Lady Lydia is anything to judge by. Lord This, Lady That. But if I am to hide my tastes and opinions altogether, what kind of a life is that? I am strongly tempted to tell them everything at the outset to get it over."

At Parrette's look of dismay, she relented, and said, "I will not. You know I will try very hard to please them, and to be polite, and, in short, play my role as a titled lady." And when Parrette gazed out at the bleak countryside with a troubled expression, Anna said, "Perhaps I have not thanked you enough. Perhaps I am seen to be taking your goodness for granted, and all your arts—"

Parrette waved her hands. "No, no, I need not hear that. I know you are grateful, and that you appreciate what you call my art. And it *is* art," she amended, in a different voice, permitting herself a small smile. Then she was earnest again. "But to hear you saying that you play a role, it mislikes me much."

"You and I, we were agreed I must play a role," Anna said, surprised. "That was when I was a mere Mrs., and this time with Lady Lydia convinces me that even more is expected from a titled wife."

Parrette said, "I do not like to hear you talk of roles, as if there is a false seeming expected." Her black eyes narrowed.

Anna smiled as she laid aside the book. "False seeming? It seems strange, that I am told the marriage vow is sacred, and yet all around me the reasons for marrying are not sacred at all. My own marriage? Was to gain information. Yes, I remember what you said once about how a marriage is made *after* the wedding."

Parrette looked down at the thick skin on her left thumb, rough from years of needle-pricks, and said slowly, "The Captain is a good man."

"Was he in question?" Anna asked.

Parrette made a quick, impatient movement. "He is everything your dear mother wanted. Everything! I think... perhaps I can put it best by saying, I trust and pray that the time comes, soon, when you are not playing a role. That you will know yourself as the English lady she wanted with all her heart and soul."

It was Parrette's turn to gaze out at the brown, muddy ground and the gray, tumbling rivers reflecting the low steel-covered sky, and presently she shook her head. "When we met, your mother took me at my word. She could have been justified in thinking about me what many did, that I was a mere camp follower, that I was a thief, and no good. And there were things I did to survive while I followed Bonaparte's army to Italy, that I regret. Oh, of the most bitter, my regrets."

She faced Anna. "I played a role, when following the army. It was a dreadful role, but it kept me alive, and in hopes of finding my Michel. I played another role when she hired me. I made myself into what she expected, but then... you see? She believed in the truth of it. Never questioned. I lived that truth. I pray most earnestly every night that your role will become your truth."

Twenty-four

BARFORD MAGNA WAS BY anyone's definition a very small town, but the signs of prosperity were there in the well-kept buildings and the paved street. It lay along a meandering river through excellent land kept in good heart by its landowners and farmers.

Crowning the highest point of High Street was the church, with the vicarage a short walk away, discreetly sheltered by an avenue of yew planted in Queen Anne's time by the vicar's gently-born wife.

The other end of High Street was dominated by an equally prosperous posting inn, named the Boar and Eagle. To the locals, it was The Pig, shortened version of "The Pig in a Wig," an ancient joke having to do with a certain style of full-bottomed wig called the Eagle, and an unpopular judge during the Restoration. The inn had been handed down through several generations, the owners wisely catering not just to the traveler with enough money to want the comfort of well-aired beds and good food, but to the local merchants and laborers who provided steady custom.

The common room that opened onto the stable yard was where Northcote Manor's John-Coachman and his apprentice Noll waited, the latter stiff and self conscious in his seldom-worn livery.

They knew the regular routes and habits of hired post chaises. While not as regular as the Mail, these usually arrived during winter between two and four, so as to avoid darkness closing in.

It was safe to say that everyone in Barford Magna awaited a glimpse of the mysterious wife of the new Lord Northcote.

Several miles away, Henry Duncannon's younger sister, Harriet, paced between the rooms in the new wing of the Manor, delighting in the expanse of shining floors, every bit of brass, silver, or gilding bravely shining in the watery afternoon light, the wood polished to a gleam. Signs of neglect had been judiciously hidden away. She herself had tended to the remains of the garden, as poor Pratt, the only gardener left, had not had the time, the rest of his men having been turned off.

She paused to look out the windows toward the sweeping drive, which was still well graveled, though beginning to show what would probably be deep ruts come spring. Would the new Lady Northcote's sharp eyes detect them?

Harriet clasped her hands. Everything, *everything* depended upon this mysterious woman Henry seemed to have married, did she know that?

Harriet moved away in an unsuccessful attempt to escape that sick inward sense of having made a terrible error. She hated not knowing if this lady had seen her letter to Henry — her letter that she knew her family would consider forward and impertinent to the worst degree — and if she had, would she betray her?

A mellow gong resounded from the clock in the hall. One. Even if they arrived at the Boar and Eagle at two, there would be time wasted as John-Coachman got their traps (their dunnage, as Henry always said) into the gig. After that an ever-so-slow-drive, and then maybe arriving right before dinner.

There might not be opportunity for private conversation even then. That would not do.

Henry had told Harriet on his last visit that the great Nelson had always said never to dither, but to board 'em smoke and oakum, or smoke 'em and oak, which made a bit more sense; the only part she was certain of was that sea captains mustn't dawdle.

And whatever was good advice for the great and glorious Nelson's own captains by reason ought to be good advice for anyone else, surely?

She paused at the foot of the staircase. She knew her mother had retired to her room with her hymn book, and Emily was in the morning room, prosing away to Mary about what she thought she had detected in that stiff, formal letter the mysterious Lady Northcote had sent, written as if she had been alive in the First George's time.

Harriet must meet the lady first. If she got away without being seen, the others wouldn't know until it was too late. After that, she trusted, she would have the protection of company manners.

She flitted up to don her habit, her sturdiest hat, and a muffler, and then she let herself down the back way, through the old part of the house to the stable. She had her mare saddled in a trice. Then, avoiding the drive altogether, she rode through the paddock and the cow pasture, leaped the fence, and galloped cross country. Though there was a thin rain falling, it felt cool on her face, and she laughed aloud.

As Harriet cantered down country lanes toward town, from the other direction, Anna and Parrette bowled along the last distance toward the town.

Anna had been expecting to see the beautiful green England of her mother's stories. Instead, the ground was iron hard where it wasn't mud, the fields mere stubble, the trees barren. Even the rivers seemed to run brown under a low sky the color of steel. The sun, when it appeared, was so pale and low in the southern sky that it seemed a different sun altogether from the one she had always known.

The chaise carried them through a last small village, the streets muddy, the austere buildings closed up tightly. Except for the glow of candlelight in a window here and there they would have looked empty of life.

By then the sun had already begun its downward descent again, and it was too dark inside the chaise for Parrette to see her thread. She folded away her work and they sat in silence until they entered Barford Magna at last, and rolled into a paved square before a rambling inn.

The windows at the ground floor glowed as the chaise came to its halt in the stable yard, the horses blowing and steaming. Stable hands ran to them, and others to hitch up the manor horses to the family carriage, which had been waiting these two hours.

At that moment Harriet rode into the middle of the noise and movement. She reined her horse moments before John-Coachman handed a lady out of the chaise.

Of course she would be beautiful. They had all expected *that*. If Henry were to marry so oddly out-of-hand it would not be to a plain pudding of a girl. This was a slender, graceful young lady who did not look all that much older than Harriet herself, but she was worlds beyond Harriet in the article of style. Her traveling clothes of sober dove gray looked like something in one of those illustrated magazines from Paris. Even her maid looked smart.

Harriet gained an impression of curling dark hair and dark eyes inside the bonnet, and then she impulsively dismounted and splashed across the courtyard before John-Coachman could hand them up into the family carriage, waiting at the other end of the drive.

"You must be Lady Northcote," she said. "Please say you are! I am Harriet Duncannon," she added belatedly, her face flooding with color. *Oh, thank Heaven no one at home was present to hear that!*

A neat hand in pearl gray took hers in a light grip. "I am 'appy to meet you, Miss Duncannon." She spoke with a French accent.

Anna and Harriet looked at one another, liking what they saw. Anna descried a fleeting resemblance to the captain in this girl's strong chin and proud nose, and the color of her tousled hair under her hat. Harriet's smile was broad, reflected in the quirk of her wide-spaced eyes: there, the resemblance was pronounced, and Anna's heart constricted.

"I could not wait," Harriet exclaimed, and as Noll loudly thunked one of their trunks onto the top of the carriage, she stepped near and whispered, "Did Henry receive a letter from me?"

Her voice was low, her face anxious. Anna hesitated, sensing she was missing something, but what? "He was in a coma when I left," she replied evasively. "The physician insisted I come ahead."

There was no mistaking the short sigh of relief. Anna mentally set aside all the questions that had formed around that letter as her words registered on Harriet.

"*Coma?*" Harriet exclaimed in horror. "The papers said injured, they did not say what. Oh, pray, has he wakened?"

"I do not know. The physician held out hope," Anna said, and when Harriet dropped her gaze, clearly unconvinced, Anna murmured, "I was told that it was not to be expected, that I imagined it, but I believe I saw his head move. I felt his hand move under mine." Now she could put forward her own question. "By chance, have any letters arrived for me?"

"No post for you, I am sorry to say." Harriet shook her head, her eyes filled with tears. But then she dashed them impatiently away and took a deep breath. "I had better ride back. They do not know I'm here, but I couldn't wait. *Thank* you."

Without saying why she thanked her, Harriet turned to the ostler who waited at her horse's head. He threw her expertly into the saddle. She guided the horse away with a practiced flick of her wrist and a smile over her shoulder, then she was gone.

Anna found the liveried man waiting to hand her into a fine carriage; when she had climbed down, she was too weary and anxious to pay attention to details, but now she was startled to find herself gazing straight up into a pair of handsome blue eyes in a face like a marble carving. John-Coachman gazed back, used to these reactions, though he took no particular pride in it. God had made him what he was. What he chose to do with himself was what was important.

He liked the way the pretty French lady dropped her gaze at once, gave a nod of thanks, and climbed straight into the carriage. He was secretly amused by the distrustful scowl sent his way by the tiny, beak-nosed woman who climbed in after her mistress, and reached for the door as if to shut it before he could. He closed the door, tipped his hat, and mounted the box.

"Here is a rug to put over your lap," Parrette said.

"I am fine as I am," Anna said.

"You do not look fine," Parrette replied, eyeing her.

Anna leaned her head back, careful not to crush her bonnet. She decided against explaining the increasing sense of fraud that she could not avoid feeling. As if she were not just encroaching, but stealing the captain's home, and would she not be resented by his family? It seemed impossible that she should not be.

"Nerves," she said finally. "So much depends upon first appearances."

Parrette could see Anna's uneasiness in her countenance. She said nothing — there was nothing new to say.

The carriage was so smoothly sprung that the jouncing was scarcely noticeable as they rolled up High Street. Anna looked for the bookseller's shop owned by Midshipman Bradshaw's family. She spotted it, and had enough time to perceive leaded glass windowpanes glowing upstairs, then they were past.

They turned alongside a small, beautifully built stone church in the English style, its steeple rising above surrounding bare trees. She did not recognize many of the types of trees she saw here, except that they were all drearily barren.

Past the churchyard the road took another turn, and soon they were in the countryside again, gray and brown as ever. How could her mother have ever thought this land green? The darkness slowly closing in seemed to settle in her heart. She tried to bolster her nerves by reflecting upon Miss Harriet Duncannon's friendliness.

She was not left long to brood. Over a bridge, down and up, then Parrette said, "Look this way."

Anna slid over to the opposite window, and beheld the place where she must live. The Manor lay on rising ground, a gentle, forested hill to the north sheltering it from the worst winds. The house was not symmetrical; it had two wings, built in different styles, but from the same stone so the effect was not unpleasing. She was relieved to see that it was not all built in that odd style she had seen in London, a style she later would learn was called Palladian, admired by high society. Accustomed to the arches, awnings, and flowerboxes of the south, and Paris's charming variety (under the revolutionary damage), she had found London in November, preparing for winter, unrelievedly grim.

Archways she saw, though no flowerboxes. The new wing, constructed in the New Gothic style, pleased her eye, and even more pleasing was the promise of golden light in the windows.

Harriet arrived home, at a flying gallop. She had just enough time to throw off her habit and huddle back into her day gown, shivering as no one's fire was freshened until it was time to change for dinner. She slipped out of her room then slowed when she saw her mother halfway down the steps to the entryway. So the carriage had been sighted on the hill already!

"Oh, I hope and pray there is no bad news," her mother said

softly as Harriet joined her, then she sighed. "Harriet, child, how have you contrived to get your hair so untidy?"

"Only you could get into a scrape just coming downstairs," her elder sister Mary said fondly, reaching to twitch an errant lock and tuck it up.

"Oh, bother," Harriet muttered, and then added daringly, "No one will notice *me*." With relief, she turned to watch Diggory open the front door as the carriage bowled along the last of the drive and drew up. Beyond the steps the servants had already gathered outside in a straight line.

It was exactly right, but for Anna it was the worst possible introduction. She was intimidated to discover the line of servants on the gravel, ignoring the thin, chill rain, and at the great doors several ladies looking exactly alike at first glance. She did not want to get out of the carriage.

However, here was a powdered footman in fine livery coming to the coach door, and letting down the steps. She could not sit inside forever. She must face the audience. She straightened her shoulders, chin high, ribs tight, and out she stepped.

Rustle, rustle. The entire row of servants bowed and curtseyed.

What was she supposed to do? At Naples, suspended between servants and royalty, she had known every degree of deference. In Paris, there had been no bowing. Shipboard life had had its own etiquette. She remembered what it was like to be ignored by those who considered themselves greater, and she nodded to each pair of eyes she met as she approached the wide, shallow front steps.

Her heartbeat thundered in her ears. When she reached the top step, four women, two in black bombazine, gave slight curtseys. Harriet, now wearing an ugly gray gown, lurked behind a tall young woman in gray who looked somewhat like her.

Anna responded with her own curtsey, and then the eldest and shortest of the women came forward, her curled hair beautifully powdered under a large, lacy widow's cap in the style of a previous generation, her voice high and faint, "My dear Lady Northcote. Welcome to the Manor, to your home, that is. And how did you leave my son?"

This had to be the captain's mother. "I left him with his steward watching over him, as well as the physician appointed by the admiral," Anna said. "Lady Northcote, I apprehend?"

The elderly woman had a beaky nose, and pale blue eyes that squinted. The nose, at least, Anna recognized.

"Oh, oh," the dowager fluted tremulously. "I ought to have waited for a formal introduction, I know. Do forgive me, dear Lady Northcote, forgive a mother's anxiousness for news." She turned to the other woman in black, whose fair beauty was startlingly enhanced by those black clothes.

"May I present Lady Emily Northcote?" the dowager said with even more of a tremor, and the beautiful one dipped her knee again as she held out her hand.

Anna took that hand, meeting a searching gaze from thick-lashed blue eyes, even more striking in hue than those possessed by the coachman. This had to be the wife of the former baron. *Emily?*

"My daughters," the dowager Lady Northcote went on, first indicating the tall one in gray with the thin beaky nose, "Mrs. Elstead, and my younger daughter."

"Mrs. Elstead," Anna murmured, and smiling as Harriet curtseyed as if they had never met, "Miss Duncannon."

Harriet strictly suppressed her own smile, but she was thrilled to the heart. The new wife had not betrayed her! That had to be a promising sign. Unless she was a designing minx, the way...no. She wouldn't let herself even think it, because everybody said her thoughts were forever writ on her face.

"...the drawing room," the dowager was saying, "while your trunks are bringing in. You might wish for something hot to drink before we change for dinner. We keep country hours," she explained, leading the way past the old-fashioned furnishings by Ince and Mayhew, ornate, yet formidably spiky to Anna's eyes, to a large drawing room that overlooked a garden in the back, which framed a lake.

This was the formal drawing room. Furnishings were grouped around a broad marble fireplace in which a good fire snapped and crackled. Covering most of the parquet floor was an exquisite Aubusson carpet of Renaissance floral designs in shades of blue and gold.

The dowager led Anna to what she would come to recognize

as the best seat, neither too close to the fire nor too far away, and as soon as the ladies had settled around her, the butler appeared again, a tall, stout middle-aged man who supervised the row of housemaids carrying in an elaborate tea service and a tray of tiny cakes.

While a young maidservant handed around the tea and cakes (Anna, though ravenously hungry, did not know what to do with these, and so she declined, confining herself to the tea) the dowager put forth a series of polite questions about the post chaise, the roads, the weather, and the journey.

Anna replied with polite nothings that she had already rehearsed to herself. She was unsettled by the manner in which her auditors paid much more heed to her inane words than they were worth. Was her English at fault? She began to reply with increasing brevity.

On the floor below, Parrette was conducted to the house-keeper's sitting room, where she sat down to tea and fresh scones.

Mrs. Diggory, the elderly housekeeper, enumerated the staff, beginning with her nephew Mr. Diggory, the butler. After she had named them all, she added that Parrette would meet them all at the servants' meal, and then straight-away launched into the questions that the ladies upstairs wanted very badly to ask.

This was the interrogation for which Parrette had prepared herself.

She launched into her prepared speech. The Ludovisi duke got his due mention, and Parrette stressed the likelihood of Eugenia's father having been on his Grand Tour before he chose to stay on the continent to take up his abode in Florence. She said nothing untrue, but she suppressed Eugenia's mother's origin, the dueling school, and the fact that Eugenia had had to go out as a governess to visiting English families.

As she went on to Signor Ludovisi and the royal palace in Naples, she covertly watched these words impact her audience. These were *English* English, the people Eugenia had desired most for her daughter. She must not speak amiss.

The housekeeper poured out more tea. Mrs. Diggory was a bony woman, with large gray eyes half-covered by thin eyelids in which the veins were prominent. Parrette found it impossible to descry her expression.

"It came as quite a surprise, as you might expect, to them upstairs, to discover his lordship's marriage in the newspapers," Mrs. Diggory said as she passed the cup and saucer to Parrette. "A recent event, I take it?"

"Not at all," Parrette said, pretending she did not hear the insinuation. It was no more than she had expected.

She took a sip of the vile concoction, longed futilely for coffee, then said, "It happened nearly six years ago. It was arranged by the English legation, but then the fleet was sent away. Her ladyship," Parrette said these words with subdued enjoyment, "did not see him again until we were in Cadiz, and Admiral Gravina himself arranged for her to rejoin his lordship."

The housekeeper's mouth pursed, and those veined eyelids rose a fraction. Parrette set down her cup, wondering if the news would get through the house faster than she would.

Then it was time for the personal questions. She stated only that she had worked at Naples' royal palace for the Ludovisi family. That was twice the royal palace had been mentioned. Anna would have hated such showing away, Parrette knew, or at the least would have been embarrassed, but Michel had told his mother that a foreign accent could be fatal with English servants. "But if you've got the least connection to a duke or two, even better, a prince, fling 'em into the ring," he had advised.

She had done just that, and she measured her success by the politeness of Mrs. Diggory's tone as she offered to show 'Mrs. Doofloo' to her room.

In the drawing room upstairs, the stilted conversation labored on until a single chime from an ormolu clock on the mantel prompted Lady Emily Northcote to venture on her own carefully rehearsed question. "Should you care for more tea, or something else to eat, Lady Northcote?"

"No, thank you."

"There is just time for a swift tour of the house, or should you prefer to retire before dinner? That is," she corrected herself with a little smile that looked as rehearsed as it was, "forgive me, *you* may order dinner put forward, if you wish. I am not to be giving orders anymore. This is now your house."

There was that false note. Not musically. Her voice was well-modulated; Anna's practiced ear detected the result of careful lessons. But her *tone* was a note off, reminding Anna of Therese Rose. A quick glance at Harriet's expressive face reinforced this impression: Harriet gazed at her sister-in-law with lips compressed.

Your house. "I shall be happy to sit down to dinner at the hour of custom," Anna said with polite deflection. "I am conditioned by the bells aboard ship. They are ab-so-lute!" Anna tried to mimic their English speech, but her accent *would* come out, she could hear it in her own words.

She was disgusted, but the dowager found it fascinating, recalling her to her young days when the glittering French court was the epitome of *ton*; Mrs. Elstead wondered where Henry had found her; Lady Emily Northcote suppressed a flash of irritation that her rational mind knew was unjustified; and Harriet was enchanted.

She bounced up. "Mama, *pray* permit me to take Lady Northcote over the house. I promise we shall be quick. There will be plenty of time to dress." She turned to Anna. "Would you care to see the house now?"

"I would be grateful for a chance to walk about a little. I have been sitting in that carriage, oh! Too long."

More curtseys, and Harriet led her out of the drawing room, pausing in the hallway to say impulsively, "I love your accent. Of course Henry was *amazingly* ravished, though Mama hates when I use that word. Oh, it's been a *thousand ages* since anything interesting has happened in this house. Come, should you care to see the old wing first? Then we can come back to where it is warm. We cannot heat the house as we once did, alas. I quite dread winter..."

Harriet spoke so quickly that Anna did not retain the half of what she was told. Names and dates flew by as they walked downstairs again, past a beautiful double staircase and through carved doors into a hall with marble floor and vaulted ceilings. Harriet waved a hand this way and that, then paused, one hand tucked into her armpit. "Do you know English history?"

"I was put to memorize all the Kings of England as a child, but I cannot tell you much more than their dates," Anna said. "And that puts me in mind of a question, may I ask?"

Harriet smiled, fingers interlaced—liking very much to be consulted, for she was usually suppressed. "Please do!"

"Lady Emily, she is the daughter of a duke or a marquis?" Anna remembered Lady Lydia.

"No, she is never Lady Emily, for that *would* be a duke's daughter. She is *Lady Emily Northcote*, being the second widow in the family, when there is a new baron and his wife. Three Lady Northcotes!" Harriet grinned, and said confidingly, "Mama had to go and look it out in some old book about titles and orders, when we first found out about you. And I must say it put Emily in quite a—" She caught herself up, blushed, and turned to the pictures on the wall.

"Our family is quite old. At one time," Harriet went on, "we had cousins on either side of the water due to peace treaties that ended with marriages, during the time of the Edwards. Things are not nearly so wild now. But this house was built before the Puritans ruined everything, and so it was fairly stripped by them. With the Restoration, the family returned and had all new furnishings. The old great hall was turned into a ballroom. Fancy how horrid, the anterooms all opening into each other. That includes the bed-chambers!"

"It is that way in the older palaces," Anna said.

"Palaces!" Harriet cast her a wide-eyed look. "You are not what anyone expected at all, and I must say..." She clipped her lips into a line, used both hands to fling open a carved and gilt door, and waved a hand. "The ballroom. It can actually be very fine when it's decorated, and warm. But it really is dreadfully old-fashioned. When it's like this you half expect a ghost to come out of the shadows, wearing a Louis XIV wig."

Up a carved stone stairway, to the state rooms, where she said, "This is the Baron's Bedchamber, though no baron has slept in it for at least a hundred years. That fence before the bed! That horrid high canopy over the bed, which incidentally is as hard as a plank. So high a canopy cannot possibly have been able to keep any warmth in. But Charles II slept here on a visit, and it is said that at least one of the Pretenders also stayed here, though we are *not* Catholics. My ancestors were friends with the Aubignys, who *are*, and connected to the Stuarts. Anyway no one has changed a thing. They just repair everything and put it right back as it was."

She let them out a side door into a long gallery with fireplaces at either end.

"Those high-backed benches are beautiful," Anna said, pointing.

Harriet lifted her chin as she gazed at the lovingly polished wood gleaming in the weak light, the unforgiving flat benches with the backs carved with Biblical scenes. "Oh, they are beautiful, and I guess some ancestor paid a lot. But have you actually ever sat in one? Those carvings knock the back of your head unmercifully, and as for sitting…"

She half-shut her eyes. "I had a governess, Miss Porter, before she was sent off two years ago, I do not know why. She told me that women wore a great deal more clothes back then, and heavy things with their hair piled in for hats. So maybe they carried their cushions around with them, so to speak. But can you imagine sitting in here, the room full of smoke, for the chimneys all smoked back then, trying to dance? I wonder what girls my age danced to, especially if you were wearing a dress with sleeves dragging on the floor."

She hopped and twirled lightly in bouncing bourrées past windows lining one wall, and stopped at the first of a succession of great, mostly gloomy ancient paintings of ancestors on the opposite.

Harriet began naming each and adding a comment, most of them saucy, which caused Anna to laugh. "…and there, Lady Fortuna—isn't that a dreadful name, Fortuna? It is no wonder she was quite horrid. Infamous over the countryside, I assure you. My grandmother Dangeau once confided to me that her brother said there was a general wish that she might be sent abroad, to teach Frederick of Prussia and his dragoons a lesson in manners."

And then on to a lady whose towering headdress seemed as large as her body in its beautifully painted satin and silk court gown. "Great-great Aunt Sarah, married three times. Her uncle was an earl, and her sister married another earl, which made her top the nob something dreadful. No one could sit in her presence unless she said they could, and she wouldn't let them, so the stories go, if she was the least degree unhappy with someone, and so Caroline, her son's wife, whom she loathed, fainted dead away once. She was seven months in child. It's said that Great-great Aunt Sarah snubbed her three husbands into their graves. She was very beautiful, though."

Harriet sighed, her head tipped to one side. Then smiled as she bounced farther down the gallery and lifted a hand toward a charming portrait of a lady painted as a shepherdess, as if shepherdesses ever wore silk, Anna thought to herself.

"That is great-grandmamma! She was wonderful. I was so very, very sorry when she died, though she lived to be well over ninety. She told me she had very fine ankles, which is why she loved the fashion for shepherdesses in paintings. Very bold, but you can see a painting of the first water. Mama leaves it up here, because my grandmother, who could be quite horrid, had it put here lest looking upon it would make her daughters turn out fast. Can you believe the absurdity? But Papa and John would not shift it, even after Penelope and Caroline moved to Whitstead."

Who are Penelope and Caroline? Anna thought, but did not speak.

Harriet kicked out her slippered foot in its thick, warm stocking. "I think my ankles are just as fine, but I do not, at all, perceive how having 'em painted would make anyone *fast*. Though I must say, I am not quite certain what fast *is*, except bad manners in girls, for nobody ever says it of boys, no matter how abominably they act. But that," she said blithely, "is neither here nor there, and it is quite cold. Let us go."

"The rest of the family is not here, then?" Anna asked, wanting to see a portrait of the captain.

"Oh, no, they are all in the downstairs gallery. Beginning with my elder sisters Penelope and Caroline, by Papa's first marriage," Harriet explained as they ran downstairs to the first floor in the new wing. Anna had begun to feel the chill deep in her bones, and was glad even of a slight lessening of the astonishing cold that Harriet seemed not to feel.

On the opposite side of the ballroom they had first seen was the library, and more formal rooms; along the wall was another gallery, much shorter than that in the old wing, for the layout here was in the newer cross. These rooms opened off a central space, or a hall, rather than into one another.

"Penelope," Harriet said, pointing up at the head and shoulders painting of a stern-faced young woman in an old-fashioned hat and square-necked gown. "I think she was born an old maid. She is every day of forty-five, and pretends to extreme poverty ever since Papa sent her and Caro away to Whitstead, which is a very pretty house, I assure you, though small. Penelope makes a *virtue* of penury, though she is very well to live. Better than we, ha ha!"

She caught Anna's wide look, and flushed, knowing she was gossiping. But the beautiful Lady Northcote had said nothing crushing, so she went on, "Penelope is well content with single blessedness, though she professes to regrets, but the *true* regret is that she, and Papa both, would not permit Caro to marry unless the elder sister did, and so Caro, who loves children, teaches at the village school, and on Sundays, when they come here after first divine service, she creeps upstairs to visit little Amelia, and play with Eleanor and Justina."

Next to Penelope's portrait was one of a young woman with a round, charming smile. She, too, wore an enormous hat and the edge of her gown was square-necked. "You will meet the little girls on the morrow, perhaps. Emily only permits Nurse to bring them downstairs for an hour now and then."

She whirled about, extending her hands to a gilt-framed family portrait. "Here is the family." At either side of the nearly life-sized gathering were full length portraits of two gentlemen, the resemblance pronounced in the strong chins.

"On the one side is Papa, and the other is my late brother John."

The elder wore the satin skirts and red heels and fashionable toupee of an earlier time. The younger was dressed in the modern mode, but in both portraits could be seen a similar erect posture, the haughty shoulders and elevated chin of one who knows what he is worth.

Anna looked past them to the other members of the family. The dowager was there, in a flowing gown of polonaised satin. A young girl leaned against her chair, and a taller girl stood behind her—the present Mrs. Elstead.

On the other side of the chair stood a thin boy who had to be Henry Duncannon, perhaps the age of his midshipmen. In spite of the smooth, rounded cheeks of youth, his chin and eyes were recognizable as Captain Duncannon's. He smiled off in one direction, and Anna fancied he gazed off toward the sea, though the landscape behind the marble terrace on which the family was gathered overlooked the lake behind the manor.

She returned her gaze to the elder son. The former baron, a good-looking young man in a haughty pose, was dressed in the height of fashion some five years past.

"It was so very hot the day the painter sketched me," Harriet said, staring up at her younger self leaning against the fine carved chair that in reality no one would ever leave on a terrace to be ruined by wind and weather. "And insects *would* buzz about my face while I was supposed to stand still. I thought it positively *spooney* at the time, but now I find I am glad it was painted," she finished soberly. "Henry left not soon after, and I was so disappointed. We were always good friends—when I was four or five he promised he would not permit anyone to call me *Harry*, which he loathed because of the way John..."

She shrugged sharply, and turned away from the picture. "That is all we have of Henry, I am obliged to confess. Papa never liked the expense of having us sit to artists, so he confined himself to what he thought was due to the honor of the house. And that meant only John, the heir, to be painted on his coming of age. Henry, of course, was away, and, well, he stopped writing."

She felt she had said too much, and mounted the stairs. They rapidly passed by a series of tall doors all alike behind which Harriet reeled off bedchambers and sitting rooms, and then at last Harriet opened a double door and looked back with a curious expression.

"This is the baron's suite," she said in a lower voice. She beckoned Anna in, shut the door, and glanced about the quiet sitting room, blessedly warm from a roaring fire. "I'm afraid you have all Papa's old furnishings, as Emily insisted on taking all the new ones with her."

To Anna she looked as if she were about to say more, then she turned away, stretching her hands to the fire, and then added, "However little Henry will want those, we can comfort ourselves with the reflection that he, at least, can do what he thinks best. I am certain, that is, it cannot come as a surprise, surely, that he and Papa did not agree."

Anna had spoken little beyond what was polite. Each time Harriet caught herself up, Anna suspected she was curbing the impulse to blurt out what she ought not to say.

Thoroughly sympathetic, Anna pretended not to notice the pauses, the quick sideways glances beneath puckered brows. But now it was her turn for impulse.

"No," she began, and halted.

Harriet turned around so quickly her skirt rustled over her slippers. "No? But they did not agree." She wrung her fingers. "I am not telling tales. Everyone knew it."

Anna said gently, "No, he did not tell me," and at Harriet's hurt expression, she could not stop herself. "He told me nothing at all about his family."

At that moment the air stirred as the far door opened, and in came Parrette with a tall, thin woman in a housekeeper's cap, neat gray hair beneath it.

Harriet said quickly, "Lady Northcote, this is Mrs. Diggory, the housekeeper. We thought you might prefer to meet the staff properly later, after you've had a chance to rest, but as she is here."

Mrs. Diggory curtseyed. "Lady Northcote. If there is anything I can do, pray send directly."

"Thank you, Mrs. Diggory," Anna said. "At this moment perhaps I ought to set about readying for dinner, is it not so?"

Parrette stood against the far wall, her new cap on her head. She dropped a little curtsey.

Harriet was positively burgeoning with questions. She cast a wild glance at Anna, then said, "I ought to leave you to it, and get ready myself." A quick bob and she let herself out the carved door at the same time Mrs. Diggory quietly vanished through the plain door at the back of the room.

"I've got water for washing through here," Parrette said. "Everything is *sens dessus dessous*—what would you say in

English?"

"At sevens and sixes," Anna said, proud of remembering this expression from her reading.

Parrette showed her into her new dressing room, which had been papered in patterns of pale blue irises on an ivory background. It was new paper, reminding her again that she had so recently displaced this Lady Emily Northcote.

The dressing room opened into a bedroom containing a heavy maplewood bed with silk swags that called Lady Hamilton's rooms to mind.

Parrette, at her shoulder, said, "I'm told this was the bride gift of the old baron, for The Captain's mother. It was put back here this past week."

"I hope at least the bed is well aired," Anna said, "even if it looks as if it's been sitting there since my mother was a girl."

Parrette uttered a laugh. "Trust me to see to that."

"Where have they put you? I do not see a room. Is it adequate?"

Parrette clipped her lips closed. No, that attic was not adequate for anything but perhaps rats. The rooms were tiny, and of course not heated. But there was nothing Anna could do about that now. She must concentrate on putting her best foot forward, and Parrette thought to herself, *I have endured much worse.* "It will do. Now, come and wash your face and hands, put on the gown I've laid out, and I will dress your hair."

While Anna divided her attention between the unfamiliar room and getting ready to face them all at dinner, Harriet had flitted to her bedchamber, where waited Polly, the upstairs maid who hoped to be promoted to lady's maid once Harriet would be granted her own servant.

Polly was exactly Harriet's age, granddaughter to Mrs. Diggory. The girls had known one another all their lives. "Oh, miss," she said as she straightened up from stirring the fire. "Her lady's maid is French, and did for royalty somewhere far foreign. And, she told grandmother, straight out, that the new la'ship is related to a *duke.*"

Harriet would no more snub Polly for presumption than she would fly, though she knew who would scold her for permitting unbecoming familiarity. "A duke? Ha, that's capital," Harriet said as she wrestled impatiently out of her ugly schoolgirl mourning gown and into her equally ugly schoolgirl dinner gown.

For the first time she was actually glad she had been stuck wearing her old mourning gowns for Papa, with the seams let out. Perhaps Henry's lady would take her to London for her come-out clothes, once mourning was got over. A thousand times preferable to making them herself, as Emily had insisted she must do—not that getting anything made up by old Miss Reed, the local dressmaker, looked any better.

As she sat, controlling her impatience while Polly brushed out her hair, she reflected that fun as it might have been if the new Lady Northcote had been some low wretch, talking vulgar and flashing diamonds all over, as Emily and Mrs. Squire Elstead and Penelope had expected, this lady was infinitely preferable. Everything about her was beautiful.

So Henry had not only neglected to write home, he had not told his bride about his family. "And I know who is to blame for that," Harriet muttered under her breath as she scowled into the mirror.

Polly nearly dropped a pin. "Did I prick you, miss?"

"No, no, I only had a disagreeable thought," Harriet said. "About a disagreeable person."

Polly understood at once, and maintained a prudent silence.

Twenty-five

ONE OF THE SERVANTS showed Anna where the family gathered before dinner. There she found an attractive man dressed in the height of fashion, his hair the color of wheat in the candle light. His smile was easy, his manner friendly as he bowed over her hand when presented to her as "Mr. Elstead."

This must be Mrs. Elstead's husband. When the butler announced dinner, he offered Anna his arm. She remembered her lessons in rank. "Should not Lady Northcote lead the way?" she asked, turning to the elderly dowager.

The dowager pinked. "A bride always leads the way."

Anna hesitated. She was not a bride in the sense that she understood it, a woman newly married. But she would not keep dinner back.

They proceeded into a dining room done in the Egyptian style popular a few years before. Anna took in the gleaming, glittering table setting. She would learn that Mrs. Diggory had put out the finest Meissen Blue Onion, and the crystal Waterford.

"If it is not too disagreeable," the dowager said as soon as they had been served, "may I ask how you left my son?"

Anna gave them an exact description of his wounds, and what the physician had said, and finished with, "Lt. Sayers promised to write to me if there was any change."

"Lt. Sayers? Did you go aboard Henry's ship?" Harriet asked.

"I was there from Cadiz to when we landed at Gibraltar," Anna said.

Mr. Elstead's silver clattered to his plate. "Was you at the battle?"

"Yes." Anna gave a little Gallic shrug. "But I saw nothing."

Mr. Elstead then took over as principal talker, to Harriet's private disgust. She liked her brother-in-law very much, but she had read every word written in the newspapers about the battle, which he now insisted on retailing to the family, and she had heard his droll stories about stitchers at fences, and other hunting mishaps, time and again.

She wanted to hear more about Henry's lady's mysterious past, but the lady herself spoke no more than fifty words from the white soup through two complete sides and four removes to the towering dessert of savory jelly *a la Bellevue*.

Anna watched carefully for the clues to the mysterious custom of English ladies retiring. As the servants carried away the dessert trays, Anna saw Lady Emily Northcote make a motion as if to rise, then sit back, her brow constricting and her mouth pressed in a line. A heartbeat later her face smoothed.

Anna smiled at the dowager. "What is your custom on retiring?"

The dowager blinked rapidly, flattered to be asked, which her daughter-in-law never had done. "It is your place to choose when we go."

So Anna rose. The other ladies rose with her, and because she had no idea where they were to go, Anna offered her arm to the dowager, who led the way through two doors to the drawing room.

This room was pleasantly warm, with branches of candles set at every wall. Anna took in the paintings, the fine paper above the wainscoting, but her eye lingered on the fortepiano in the corner, with a harp set up next to it. She remembered the captain's love of music. For the first time she began to look forward to her stay: surely she was come into a musical family?

Mr. Elstead sauntered in from the dining room, laughing as he said, "I am a very sad fellow. I cannot abide sitting alone."

On his last word the tea things were brought through the

unobtrusive servants' door and set upon a fine Pembroke table. A servant poured. Once again the talk was general.

After the tea things were taken away, Mr. Elstead genially said, "How about a round of whist?"

Anna was about to admit that she did not know these games when Emily said in her sweet, soft voice, "Must I remind you, brother, that we are a house of mourning?"

That statement had the effect of breaking up the family party, the dowager saying that her head ached and she must retire.

Before she left, she turned to Anna, peering in her near-sighted way, and said kindly, "You must be very tired from your travels. Pray rest tomorrow, if you wish."

Anna then remembered that today was Saturday, and she would be expected to attend church on the morrow. Yet another requirement for manners she barely remembered.

She did not have to pretend to exhaustion. She was grateful to retire to that room with the blue flowers, and yes, the bed was not only aired, but a warming pan had been inserted between the sheets.

She fell asleep trying to remember if her mother had ever mentioned how very, very cold England was. All Anna remembered hearing about was the beauty and the green.

Sunday was a long, slow, cold day during which the sun never seemed to rise at all.

Anna woke late to discover the family gone. She heard women's voices in the mid-afternoon after they had returned from church, but the clearest one was high and sharp, so unpleasant on the ears that Anna retreated to her bed, coming out when she could not bear her own company any longer. Outside, rain fell steadily.

In the dining room, cold food was set out, unappetizing to Anna, who craved warmth. At least the family had dispersed to various parts of the house. But no sooner had she thought that than Lady Emily Northcote appeared, and set about filling a plate. The dowager appeared a moment later, sending Anna a tremulous smile as Anna rose yet again to curtsey.

The talk was polite yet desultory. Anna ventured no questions, or even observations. Her head ached; now that she was downstairs, she longed for her room, which at least did not require her to listen to quick speech, and formulate properly spoken answers.

She clutched her tea cup to her hands as the door opened once again, and a primly dressed woman brought in two little girls and a baby. The girls were told to curtsey to "Lady Northcote."

The girls stared fixedly at Anna, neither speaking, and Anna stared back, wondering what to say.

But she discovered she was not expected to say anything. Lady Emily Northcote said only, in return for their polite little curtseys, "I trust you are being good girls for Nurse." She did not look at the baby at all.

The girls were led to the dowager, to whom they performed their curtseys for the third time, and then they made their escape; before they vanished, Anna saw the youngest one's little fingers steal into the hands of the nurse.

The door shut upon them. Lady Emily Northcote turned to Anna. "It is time to ring for the carriage, but if you do not feel well enough to attend evening service, pray do not feel obliged."

Anna said, "Thank you."

She retired to bed, oppressed by the cold, the heavy silence, the unappetizing cold food.

She shivered under the covers, and daydreamed wild plans. She must get away, perhaps leave for London, and try the theaters. But even her imagination weighed her down with disagreeable realities. She had not worked with her voice for weeks. She did not know the season's new operas, or what the English might be partial to.

She fell asleep at last, and dreamed of arguing pointlessly with some faceless man at Covent Garden, which looked vaguely like the Feydeau.

Anna woke the next day relaxed and warm under the bedclothes, but when she sat up the cold air rushing beneath the covers caused her to lie flat again. It had to be too early. She was going to turn over and attempt to return to sleep when she became aware of small noises through the open door to the wardrobe.

She lifted her head. "Parrette?"

"Ah! I was about to send Polly in to make up your fire," Parrette said. "A very good girl."

"Who is Polly?"

"You will meet the staff after breakfast," Parrette said. "The family is sitting down to it now."

"So early?"

"It is half-past nine," Parrette stated.

Anna gasped, glancing at the dim blue light in the windows. "I thought it was sunrise!"

"And so it was, a little while ago. The sun rises late here. Very late. But I am told that all the hours stolen from you now will be given back in long twilights come summer. I have a bath waiting. The water will chill fast," she warned.

Anna had no trouble believing that and whirled out of bed.

A short time later she arrived at breakfast, reflecting that she thought she understood why the English cumbered themselves with gloves and hats as well as extra layers of clothing. In spite of the many chimneys and well-tended fires, the house was full of cold drafts along the floors and stairways.

The dowager, Harriet, and Emily stared when Anna appeared wrapped in the second of her cashmere shawls, the one made of blues, greens, and gold.

She said, "I hope you will forgive me. I chose the least colorful of the two. It is just that I am so very cold." As Harriet reached a cautious finger to touch the silken fringe, and the dowager blinked rapidly, Emily looked blank. "If it is offensive, I will have breakfast in my chamber," Anna offered.

"No, no," the dowager said faintly, hands fluttering. "We quite understand, don't we?" She cast a look of appeal at her daughter and daughter-in-law.

"We are only among ourselves," Emily said smoothly. "And in point of fact, the required period for mourning could be said to be ending soon."

"Six days," Harriet stated.

"Harriet, dear," the dowager began.

Harriet said, "Mama, begging your pardon, but I have been in black clothes this ten ages. John wore a black hatband for six months after Papa was gone. I think if anyone would understand giving over the black after the expected year and a day, he would. Except that I have nothing fit to be seen in."

No one responded to that sally, and the dowager turned to Anna, peering near-sightedly at her shawl. "Did Henry give you that, Lady Northcote?" the dowager asked. "It is very, very beautiful."

"Thank you! No, I bought it in Spain," Anna said as she helped herself to eggs and toasted bread. "It is said the fashion for these shawls began with the new empress of the French."

"Yes," Harriet spoke up. "I read about them in a magazine at Jane's. It is said that Josephine has hundreds and *hundreds* of them."

Emily sent Harriet a glance, and Harriet sat back with a sigh.

Anna turned her gaze away, not liking to see the only talking person suppressed so coldly. She had spied little silver trays beside the plates: this had to be the post. Lady Emily Northcote's bore a slim pile, and the dowager one or two. Anna's tray at the foot of the table was bare.

She suppressed a sharp sense of disappointment, the captain, and his ship and crew foremost in mind. She cleared her throat, and made an effort to speak into that cold, formal air, but it felt as if her words fell dead. "I hope I may come to you for advice on how to go into the town. Where is a path that I may walk? I must needs make a call."

"You are spared the necessity of social calls until the hatchment is taken from the door," said Emily.

"You will meet the neighborhood at church Sunday next," the dowager put in with an air of offering a compromise.

Anna thanked them both, but then: "This is a call of necessity. I promised a certain midshipman that I would visit his family, and I mean to do that straight away. I feel certain no family would care to wait a day longer than necessary for news of their son."

"A middie?" Harriet asked. "From the neighborhood? Who is he?"

"His name is Bradshaw. He told me he lives in High Street. I believe I glimpsed the shop when we arrived. What is the proper time for this call? What is correct in England?"

"I should think customs are very different from what one is used to, living in a royal palace," the dowager said.

Royal palace? Parrette had obviously been talking! Anna strictly suppressed the urge to laugh.

"Royal palace?" Emily repeated, and Anna wondered at the avenues of communication in the household, especially as Harriet did not express any surprise, but looked down at her plate with a half-hidden smile.

The dowager blinked at Anna. "I did hear correctly, you lived in a royal palace?"

"That is correct, Lady Northcote. In Naples," Anna said, and to them all, "And so? If I walk out along this road in front of the house, will that take me into the town?"

Harriet began to say, "It's faster to go through the meadow —"

A glance from her sister-in-law caused her to subside.

Emily's expression shuttered, her beautiful face smooth as marble. Then she said in her sweet, precise voice, "Speaking strictly upon point of etiquette, you need not call at all. There is of course the matter of our mourning, but there are also our differing spheres of life. I have no notion, of course, of what is deemed proper in royal palaces of foreign places, but here, it might appear... That is to say, sending a letter would meet the case as well, do you not think, Lady Northcote?" she turned to the dowager.

"I am sure I do not know." The dowager was very much flustered. She turned her weak eyes to Anna. "Did dearest Henry request this of you?"

Anna was almost tempted to lie, which caused a pulse of irritation. She felt a moral right to make this call, though she did not particularly expect any pleasure from it, which ought to supersede the niceties of social expectations. But did it in these people's eyes? She had no intention of hiding what was right behind the captain's name, but what *would* he expect?

She remembered him staggering out of the orlop wounded, because his duty was most important, even more than his life. "He did not, but I believe he would want me to carry out my promise," she said, seeing a slight stir in Emily. No more than the tightening of a shoulder, the turn of her head, but she sensed currents here impossible for her to penetrate.

"At all events," Anna said. "While my husband was unconscious, and unable to be consulted, I did promise this boy, wounded in service of his kingdom, that I would call upon his parents directly to convey his words. I said nothing of writing a note."

Emily said, "Then of course you must keep your promise. But, if you will permit me to observe, there is no necessity for walking into town through the dirt in the lane. We have riding hacks. Do you ride, Lady Northcote?"

Anna was obliged to admit that she did not.

"You may take the little gig," the dowager said. "Noll is a very safe driver, if you do not drive. He takes me about quite comfortably."

"Thank you," Anna said. "And the time?"

"No doubt they sit down to dinner very early," Emily said. "You will not wish to put them out, so you might make a morning call."

"Then I had better put myself right," Anna said, but then she looked as bewildered as she felt. How to go about getting the gig?

Harriet bounced up. "I will go tell Noll to hitch up the gig. Would you care for company? I would be happy to point things out."

"Thank you," Anna said gratefully.

Diggory bowed Anna out the front door, where Noll was waiting, at the same time that another carriage drove up. Diggory recognized the squire's carriage, and with a flick of his eyes sent the footman running outside to the carriage door. For the squire's wife, he would not go himself.

He withdrew to await her arrival so that he could announce her, while outside Mrs. Elstead—known with her full approval in the neighborhood as Mrs. Squire Elstead, now that her son was married to Mary Duncannon as was—stepped out of her carriage. Rendered curious by her son and daughter-in-law's accounts of the bride, she'd decided on the pretext of calling on the bereaved widows to see this person for herself.

Spying an unfamiliar bonnet and a very elegant French jacket cut from subdued black cloth on the lady just climbing into the gig with Harriet, she bustled with more haste than she might have. Anna thus met the gaze of a handsome woman in her forties whose vivid blue eyes glanced pointedly at her waist before raking up to her face.

Harriet said hastily, "Lady Northcote, may I present Mrs. Squire Elstead?"

Two wary curtseys, and Anna's soft, accented voice was heard, "I trust you will forgive us, but we were this moment departing."

"Pray, do not stand upon ceremony with me, Lady Northcote!" Mrs. Squire Elstead's high voice was curiously grating on Anna's ear. "I am one might say almost in the family, with a daughter widowed in this house, and my son having married Miss Harriet's elder sister Mary."

She appeared to be contemplating more speech, but Anna curtseyed again. "Thank you. Fare well."

She climbed into the carriage. That insinuating glance she could interpret very well. She struggled to understand and to forgive. It was probably a natural assumption, given that no one here had ever heard of her, that she had married the captain out of hand. But she could not bring herself to forgive that avid look at her waist.

The gig began to roll. Anna saw Harriet studying her, and to get past an uncomfortable subject she said, "I noticed the instrument in the drawing room. The harp as well. I hope that I am got into a musical family?"

"My sister Mary played the harp. She and Henry used to play duets until he was gone, and sometimes she played when Emily sang. Only my mother and Henry were keen. The fortepiano is my mother's. She left off when it became too difficult for her to see. My governess did her best by me, but however it didn't take. At all events," she added with a rush of polite afflatus, "I should very much like to listen if you play."

Anna had been considering admitting to singing. She knew that much was considered 'genteel' as long as one did not do it for money. She decided it was better to wait, and smiled at Harriet's mendacious enthusiasm. "You are safe. I am an indifferent player, suitable only for accompaniment as well. Tell me instead about the library. What sort of books shall I find?"

"Oh, a great many bores," Harriet said. "Things they say you ought to read, but no one ever does. That is, aside from a parcel of novels, as my mother was used to be a great reader."

"But no longer?"

"She would, but she cannot now see the pages. Sometimes I read to her. Especially this year, when we cannot go out, and it seemed to rain forever. I got through all three volumes of Sir Charles Grandison, which she is partial to."

"Do you recommend it?"

"I have nothing to say to it, except once they get into the cedar-parlor, you know a thousand pages of prosing is sure to follow. Frederick, you met him last night, my sister's husband, you know, he said once after I'd been reading a chapter to the family during a rainstorm, that if he ever met a fellow like that, he would kick him down the stairs for a ranting coxcomb."

Without waiting for an answer, she pointed. "Ah! When the weather is nice, the short walk through the meadows comes out at this turning. Then you follow this road along the river. It is a very pretty walk, and when I was small we were used to walking to church when the weather was fair. Then up the hill there. You can see the steeple beyond the yew avenue, and High Street is below on the other side..."

While Harriet chattered to Anna, Mrs. Squire Elstead—safe in the knowledge that the new Lady Northcote, as she supposed she must call her, was away, the dowager elsewhere in the house, and that irritating hoyden Harriet gone as well—closed the door so that she and her daughter would be left alone, and indulged herself with a long, disparaging description.

"...and when my own son declared she was positively the most elegant woman he had ever seen! Frederick must have been in liquor. That can be the only explanation."

"But she *is* elegant," Emily said, each word hurting the more because it was true. "She is at least as elegant as anyone in the Devonshire House set, and a great deal prettier."

"A great deal *younger*, that I will grant. That brown skin? Brown eyes of the most commonplace? My cook has brown eyes. A nose that wants distinction—but I have said all that. At least there is no evidence of a sixth months child, but what Henry was about to marry in this scrambling way, I cannot conceive. I suppose it is too sanguine to assume something can be done about it."

"Apparently," Emily said slowly, "it is *not* recent, however it came about."

"Impossible," Mrs. Squire Elstead declared, her cheeks quite red. "Surely someone would have known. Dearest John would have known."

"How?" Emily declared, the anger she had strictly controlled flaring to heat. "You know very well there had been no communication between them since *my betrothal*."

The anger broke on those last two words, and the squire's wife, who had longed for a title her entire life, eyed her daughter with as high a degree of anger. "I worked hard to bring it about. A berothal that you agreed to with every evidence of delight, Emily."

"I was eighteen."

"What has that to say to anything? You were delighted with John, who was eligible in every possible degree. You agreed with your father and me that throwing yourself away on a titleless and penniless second son, especially one who might end up crippled, or worse, who would be away for ages, would be the madness."

"Henry and I were in love," Emily muttered.

"You were boy and girl," her mother retorted. "And you had been quarreling, as I recollect right well. You did not want him throwing himself away in the navy any more than anyone else, and as for that stupid horn of his! So ill-bred, the manner in which blowing it distorts the face. Very well for a certain class of person, as you yourself quite rightly told him."

"To no effect," Emily observed.

Mrs. Elstead snapped her fan irritably. "Those sentiments are mighty pretty upon the stage, but people of breeding do not prate of maudlin sentiment as if it replaced duty and responsibility. Furthermore, it is abundantly clear that he forgot *you*, if what you say is true. When did he marry this female? And what is her place? Who are her people?"

"The newspapers, when they mentioned she was aboard Henry's ship with him, said only something Italian."

"Which could be anybody," Mrs. Elstead stated. "Or nobody."

"Without knowing more, there is no use in looking in Debrett," Emily said. "My mother-in-law has not seen fit to question her, and it is not my place. If her maid is to be believed, this Lady Northcote is connected with some Italian duke, and was born at the royal palace in Naples, or some such thing."

"*Italians*," the squire's wife said, raising her palms dismissively. "There has to be something ill-done about this entire affair. If they were people of birth, then Henry's family ought to have known. It is a simple matter of breeding and good taste."

But there was no force to her words. Dukes, royal palaces — those were very difficult to disparage, and then there was all that endless talk of war, so she took herself off, her mood very much the worse. After all her care, her hopes settled in her daughter who alone of her offspring had the proper ambition, here was John wilfully getting himself killed before he could bear a son, as he had been willful in all else. There was nothing to be done about *that*.

Emily saw her mother off, then retreated to the morning room to sit alone, staring out at the bleak gray lake and barren trees. She did not know what she dreaded more: hearing that Henry was dead, or seeing him return.

She lifted her chin. Her mother was right in one respect. She wasn't a girl anymore. If Henry did return, he must find her unchanged, with a heart as ready for him as it ever had been. There might be a deal of trouble to be got over, as he had managed to entangle himself, but these days, more marriages ended than began. London was full of such tales, and the *beau monde* shrugged.

Six days. She could not wear colors at once, but he had always loved to see her in white. As for this Neapolitan foreigner and her prating of promises, there was no doubt that vulgar, pushing Bradshaw woman would use any opportunity to force herself upon them, bringing her entire set with her. If Henry returned to find the house full of tradesmen's wives coming to call, what could be better?

Twenty-six

THE INSIDE OF THE bookseller's shop smelled delightfully of books. Until she stepped in, Anna had not been aware how booksellers' shops smelled alike in Paris, Seville, and in this kingdom.

A tall, stooped man, obviously the proprietor, was busy talking to a couple of men. On a high stool at the back, a ledger angled toward the window, perched an equally tall, thin young man of perhaps twenty. He resembled the older man in every respect except for the side-whiskers he was attempting to grow.

Harriet started toward the proprietor, confident that her rank entitled her to interrupt him, but Anna put out her hand to stay her. "I would rather wait until the shop is empty," she murmured.

Harriet shrugged, and both turned to the table displaying the latest books. They were much the same as those Anna had seen in London, save she found a play by Duval, *Le Menuisier de Livonie.* On the shelf below, a title caught Anna's eye: *Right and Wrong, or the Kinsmen of Naples.* Anna took it down.

Harriet glanced at it. "Oh, we have some by that author. *Moss Cliff Abbey*—I had to read it to Mama. Such stuff! Are there really haunted abbeys all over Europe?"

"None that I ever saw," Anna admitted. "But then I have not been all over Europe. Just in the south, mostly, except for a tour of France—"

She remembered that she must not speak about her days as a singer, and fell silent.

Harriet did not notice. "That is more than I have ever seen! I have yet to see *London*. I ought to have been presented last spring, but, well, I know it is ill-bred to complain about *that*. And yet it is very hard, especially when a cousin of mine made her come-out, and a vast number of her friends. It would have been a great deal of fun," she finished wistfully.

At that moment the two gentlemen touched their hats to Mr. Bradshaw and departed. The proprietor advanced on the ladies with the books. When the bonneted heads faced him, he recognized Miss Duncannon from the Manor, then checked himself when he apprehended an unknown lady with her, one dressed in the height of fashion, though in the colors of half-mourning.

Harriet said, "Mr. Bradshaw, this is Lady Northcote, the *new* lady Northcote, just come among us yesterday."

As Mr. Bradshaw bowed, Anna said, "I am come with news from your son aboard the *Aglaea*, sir."

Mr. Bradshaw's entire countenance changed. "My son! Would you honor me by entering our parlor upstairs? Endymion, put down your pen. You must tend the shop in my absence. Please, ladies?"

He moved faster than Anna would have expected from such a tall, gaunt man, leading the way through the store to a narrow stairway at the very back.

Upstairs, his wife, scolding the poor maid-of-all-work, broke off, listening to the voices on the stairs. Under her husband's familiar rumble were the accents of a lady.

She dismissed the maid to the kitchen, hissing, "Get out the fine tea things, and be ready if I ring!" then whisked herself into her parlor.

Mr. Bradshaw was talking as he led the way. "I beg pardon for the darkness. I know this stair so well, have lived here man and boy forty-one years, and..." He was still talking as they emerged in a small hallway.

He opened another door, surprising a lady pouring over a copy of *Corriere delle dame*. She ostentatiously laid aside the magazine that she could not read, but she loved the pictures, and even more loved being seen with the famous fashion magazine all the way from Italy.

Putting on her most polite smile, she gave a quick twitch to her best lace cap, which she had crammed on so fast she suspected it was not quite straight, and advanced on the beautiful new guest.

"Mrs. Bradshaw," her helpmeet said, "permit me to present Lady Northcote, who does us the honor of a call with news from Beverley."

"Lady Northcote!" Mrs. Bradshaw exclaimed, curtseying prettily.

Anna surveyed her hostess, a small, round woman with reddish ringlets escaping from under her cap, and blue eyes that Anna remembered mirrored in her son's face, if he resembled her in little else.

"I... I, *pray* enter," Mrs. Bradshaw said. "Forgive this dreadful little room, it is merely where I sit of a morning. If Mr. Bradshaw had thought a moment, he might have brought you to our drawing room in proper form. I never go downstairs, you see, it was a condition of marriage, as tending a shop is nothing I have been used to..." She chattered on in this manner as she led the way through two more narrow doors into an airless room stuffed with too much furniture in a grand design of the end of the previous century.

"Pray take a seat, and I will ring for some refreshments."

Anna said, "Please do not trouble yourself. I do not mean to disturb you. We shall only trespass on your time long enough for me to discharge my promise."

"Oh! I am so grateful, you may be certain. A mother's tender care for her child... Perhaps you are not yet a parent, and here I am, mother of five boys, though you might not think it to look at me. Five boys! And each a cause for anxious care." She blinked dry eyes, and indicated one of the satin-covered chairs, as if she would press her visitors into them.

Anna sat on the edge of one, Harriet on another, and Anna launched straight-away into as much of the history of the battle as she knew, dwelling only on that which affected young Beverley Bradshaw.

As she spoke, she sensed inattention in Mrs. Bradshaw, whose gaze darted about as if looking for something, perhaps a way to keep them there? She was a contrast to the father, whose eyes gleamed with unshed tears. He leaned forward slightly, as if to draw the words out of her the faster.

Twice she had to go through what little she knew of the battle, dwelling on every detail of Mr. Bradshaw's wound, and every word he spoke. From there Mr. Bradshaw asked after the captain, and on hearing of his wound, said everything that was proper.

Mrs. Bradshaw then spoke up, having a great deal to say about the glorious Nelson, who the newspapers predicted was to have a grand memorial after the new year. She repeated every trite expression that had been written in the newspapers these weeks, after which Anna and Harriet at last were permitted to rise and take their leave.

Mr. Bradshaw accompanied them downstairs, during which time Anna had thought about how best to present his son's earnest request for an increase in his mess allowance. Mr. Bradshaw understood at once, and promised it should be seen to, and he thanked her for having a care to his boy.

They were thus in perfect agreement when they reached the front of the shop. Before Anna gained the front door he took up the two volumes she had been looking at, and pressed them into her hands.

"Please take them, Lady Northcote," he said earnestly. "Gratis. It is the least I can do for such a kindness. Beverley has not been the most diligent correspondent. We make every allowance for boys that age, and I know he is kept busy enough. But…wounded in the service of his kingdom, and under such glorious circumstances…" He wiped his eyes, and when she accepted the books with thanks, he scarcely would allow even that as he bowed her out of the shop.

As soon as they climbed into the gig, Harriet exclaimed, "I did not know you were *in* the battle!"

"As I explained, I saw very little."

Harriet turned to gaze at her. "I thought you were in a ship somewhere nearby, safe."

"We helped the surgeon."

Harriet's eyes rounded. "I did not think ladies would be permitted."

"There were women on the battleships, of every degree, on both sides," Anna said, and as the gig rolled up the street toward the high point, she told Harriet about the French woman who had nearly drowned.

"So they rescued her, but did not throw her back into the water when they knew she was French?" Harriet asked.

"The boat was filled with French rescued from the waters. Our hold was full of Spanish prisoners. We carried them to Gibraltar."

Harriet frowned at the low gray sky, and the liquid mud in the lane. "It seems so odd that they begin by banging away at one another with cannon, and then next thing you know, they set about rescuing those who survive it."

Anna said, low, "I don't understand it myself, but I am glad that they did pull those drowning wretches from the sea. There was much death enough."

Silence fell between them, except for the creak of the gig, the crunch of wheels and clop of hooves. Far in the distance winter birds chattered and cried. Harriet wanted to ask more. The newspapers said nothing about 'death' in such a way as to cause that closed downward look, the gloved hands gripping so tightly. The newspapers had contained long columns about the glory of the victory Admiral Lord Nelson had gained before his heroic demise, and a lot of confusing details about the movement of ships of the line, unhelpful if one had never so much as glimpsed any kind of ship.

They reached the manor and parted to change. Harriet was surprised to find Emily waiting for her, to ask after the success of the new Lady Northcote's first call.

"We only stayed fifteen minutes," Harriet said. "She talked about the battle, and their little boy, and then we left, except that the bookseller pressed two books upon her."

Emily sighed. "I expect Mrs. Bradshaw will use those as an excuse to encroach, but that is a matter to be addressed later. Is that all you talked about, then?"

Harriet was surprised at questions from this quarter. Emily was far more used to suppressing what she called bumptiousness or pertness, as if Harriet were eight and not eighteen. Feeling important, she said, "Yes. Except when we set out, she'd noticed the fortepiano and asked straight off if we were a musical family. She expected it because of Henry. I know you did not like it, but he was a capital player."

"You mistake," Emile said smoothly. "I am exceedingly partial to music. No one is more. It was just that I thought his instrument poorly chosen. One does not really appear *comme il faut* blowing upon horns of any kind, but that is neither here nor there. If he is to come home, I think it appropriate that we consider music again. So much less tiresome than card-playing, and as you said, a few days from now even the highest stickler could not be expected to fault us for indulging a wish for music." She smiled brightly as Harriet tried to hide her dismay. "Perhaps if Lady Northcote plays, she will play to me. I must look out my favorite songs."

Anna thought no more about the morning after she laid aside the books she had been given. She longed to resume her dance and her singing, but she knew nothing of the customs of this house. She walked along the walls of her new chambers, feeling liked the caged bird of the fairy tale.

But that was mere self-pity. She must simply stir herself, and find a way.

The door opened, and Parrette entered. "Mrs. Diggory was expecting to take you over the house, and the elder Lady Northcote has decided to accompany you both. You are free?"

Anna exclaimed, "I would not for the world have her to think me remiss in any attentions. Will you take me to her?"

The introduction was made, the dowager peering near-sightedly at Anna. They toured the house from candles to linens as the lady related anecdotes from her own life, and those she had learned from her mother-in-law. Anna was more interested in the elderly woman than she was in the little stories about persons unknown who had sat in this chair, or had that window put in.

When they reached the library, the dowager indicated one row of shelves containing books that looked less decrepit than the remainder as she said wistfully, "When I was a bride, I spent many a happy hour here."

"Why do you not now, if I may be permitted to ask?" Anna said.

The dowager blinked rapidly. "It is merely my stupid eyes. They refuse to see unless I can get very close."

"Have you considered spectacles?" Anna asked.

The dowager's eyes widened, then she looked away, and murmured something about "the baron" and "bluestockings" and "vulgar appearance...not for the world."

Anna said, "I confess I do not understand English custom, and I hope you will put me in the way of what is right. But on the continent, it is well known that many *queens* wore spectacles, so they could not be considered vulgar, no?"

"Queens?" the dowager repeated.

"Marie Antoinette did, I know. The present emperor is said to wear them, as well as one of his brothers. Before the Revolution, the Duc de Richelieu, and for that matter, Louis XIV, and also Catherine the Great. I learned this because the royal oculist at Naples's palace once showed a design that the Empress of all the Russias had made popular, and another ordered by the Queen of Naples, sister to Queen Marie Antoinette."

The dowager blinked again. "Well!"

At the end of the tour, Anna noted that the tone of the dowager's voice had shifted from minor to major. She smiled and excused herself as Mrs. Diggory said, "And so, my lady, if you wish to order any changes..."

Anna had been thinking. She said, "I believe that it would be best to carry on as you are accustomed, until such time as my husband returns."

Mrs. Diggory curtseyed, but Anna saw the dowager's subtle reaction, a quick anxiousness, when she spoke the word 'husband.'

When Anna came downstairs for dinner, she discovered the younger Elsteads had joined them. Everyone behaved as if this were a regular occurrence, so she accepted it as such.

It was somewhat of a relief, as she liked Mr. Elstead. He was handsome to look at, but more important, he was agreeable, with a fund of mild talk that successfully banished that cold dead silence prevailing over the rest of the family meals. Dinner thus passed pleasantly, and this time Anna knew what to do and when.

As soon as the ladies had withdrawn, Emily walked to the fire, turned to face the rest of them, and said with a bright smile that was pretty to look at, but managed not to convey any of the warmth of her brother's, "I believe that Harriet has the right of it. John would be the first to hail a return to normalcy, and so I propose that we recommence certain quiet pursuits, such as evening music."

Harriet sat upright. "But we have not had music since before Papa died."

Emily said calmly, "*We* did, however, at *my* house. Your elder brother often asked me to perform when we were courting. You know your brother Henry was musical, and while one might deplore the instrument he favored, there is no denying his passion for the art." She turned to Anna with that smile. "Is it true that you play? If you would honor me by providing accompaniment, I will pass the time with a couple of John's favorite airs."

The dowager said, "I would love to hear music again." She then added in a curious tone, "I would play again if I could see the page."

Emily did not pursue that. She gave her mother-in-law a gracious nod, and said, "When Frederick rejoins us—"

At that moment the door opened, and there was Mr. Elstead.

Anna rose and crossed the room while Emily informed her brother of the plan for evening entertainment. Anna was uncertain whether she ought to offer to sing. There was always the danger of the truth to oppress her, but oh, to sing again!

On a fine table she found a stack of music, most of it yellowed with age. Very little was familiar, mostly British, with a few old-fashioned French or German airs. The accompaniment was simple enough: she knew she had only to get the chords right, and to follow the tempo of the singer.

She sat down to the instrument, and softly touched the keys. The sound was good. Someone had seen to it that the fortepiano was kept in repair.

"This is most kind of you, Lady Northcote." A rustle of bombazine, and Emily was there. "I trust this will serve as a fond reminder." And without pausing to wait for an answer, "Can you play this?"

She pulled from the pile a hand-written musical sheet with "Robin Adair" written at the top.

"Oh, my mother taught me this when I was small," Anna exclaimed with pleasure.

"That is capital," Emily said, her tone the warmest it had been yet. She took up a stance beside the fortepiano.

Anna played the opening bars, and Emily began to sing. Anna soon determined that indeed, someone had instructed Emily in tempo and phrasing, but not how to open her throat. She stayed true to her note in the middle range, either shrill or breathy on the high notes, especially in "Katharine Ogle." She then sang "The Last Time I Came O'er," which she prevailed upon her brother to sing with her.

The voices blended pleasingly enough. Anna glanced at the listeners, who smiled and nodded. Anna could have put them right in several places—phrasing, breathing, everything, but she kept her own counsel. At least she was hearing music again.

Then Harriet surprised them by saying, "Mama, come. Play to us, do. How about Souter's Rondo? Remember how I used to dance to that?"

The dowager pinked. "I do not think my fingers remember it. But perhaps..." She halted there, then turned to her elder daughter. "Come, Mary, take a turn."

Mary Elstead rubbed her hands together. "I wish someone might have told me you wished to have music again. It has been these four years at least since I have played my harp, at least since I was married. I would have to practice before I could be heard."

"I confess," Mr. Elstead said easily. "I do enjoy a game of cards, and Mary plays a capital hand of whist. But I've no objection to music, as long as it is no dirge."

"Whist?" Mary said. "We can have a hand now. Lady Northcote, do you play?"

"I do not. But I do not mind watching, that I learn."

Harriet brightened at once. She would have hated to be the one left out, and they would have expected her to offer, being the youngest. She partnered with Emily against the married couple.

Anna watched for what she hoped was a polite amount of time, finding the game tedious and incomprehensible. When she was certain the others were too involved in their play, she withdrew to sit by the dowager.

That lady had been bending over stitchery by the fire. She paused in her work, blinked Anna's way, then said, "Already things are better now you are come among us. I never thought to hear a note in this house again."

"Is this room never used in the mornings, then?" Anna asked.

"No. It is very cold, in winter, this side of the house. We sit here in summer." The dowager stirred a little. "I am thinking about what you said. If Henry comes home, and..." Once again she paused, and Anna wondered if the lady was so in the habit of being interrupted she rarely finished a sentence.

"Should you care to be read to?" Anna offered. "I must practice my English, and there are many delightful books in the library."

The dowager brightened. "If you will pull the bell, my dear, I will send for Madame de Genlis. I have not heard French spoken properly since my visit to Paris. This was well before the troubles. Would you greatly mind?"

"I would be happy to."

And so Anna's third evening passed more pleasantly than she had hoped.

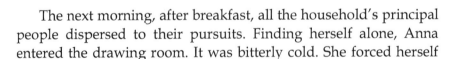

The next morning, after breakfast, all the household's principal people dispersed to their pursuits. Finding herself alone, Anna entered the drawing room. It was bitterly cold. She forced herself to move, and in moving, discovered all the old pleasure.

She danced through all her old patterns twice, thinking about Hortense and Lise, Catherine and Helene, even Ninon. Where were they all now? She hoped they were happy.

When she had finished, she was warm, except for her fingertips. She sat down to the fortepiano and softly keyed a chord. Then, equally softly, she began her drills.

Each note thrilled her with pleasure. All the joy was back. Up the range and down again, and then she began an aria, pitching her voice to the limits of the room. For an hour she sang, and then, feeling refreshed in body and spirit, she was able to go about her day playing the role of Lady Northcote.

Several days passed in a similar manner.

There were two days left before mourning would officially be over when Anna came down to breakfast and, for the first time, found a letter on the silver salver beside her plate. Her heart drummed as she worked her finger under the seal.

Aglaea, off Gibraltar

Lady Northcote, I write certain of your forgiveness for the necessary delay, because you, as a wife of an officer in the service, will understand the Demands that permit one in my position little free time.

But however, I have gained a Respite, and my first task is to do myself the Honor of writing this Letter. I am delighted to report that Captain Lord Northcote is awakened, and in full possession of his Intellects.

I was not permitted a long interview. The medical Men insist that quiet is Necessary, and he said his head Ached fit to break. Plus they have his eyes firmly bandaged, which he has been ordered to endure for at least Twelve Weeks, possibly Three Months, if the head-ache persists.

His first Question was to ask after you, and following that the ship's people. I take Great pleasure in reporting that we lost no more than we had. Our Butcher's Bill was severe, but many ships suffered a worse. Once we discharged our prisoners, we set about repairs, though the Weather continued ill for some days.

But however that, too, has passed, and I will close with a piece of good news: this Letter will go with the next packet, and with it, or soon after, you will find Captain Lord Northcote arriving in Yorkshire for his Recovery.

Your obedient serv't to command, Theophilus Sayers

Anna laid the letter down carefully, as if it might vanish. Then she looked up to discover a row of waiting faces.

"He is well, and is to return," she said breathlessly.

The dowager put her napkin over her face and burst into tears.

Twenty-seven

THE FRIDAY ANNIVERSARY OF the baron's death, Anna expected the house to be colder and gloomier than heretofore.

The dowager was certainly subdued through the day, but Anna could not see a material change in others of the house-hold.

On Saturday, mourning officially ended, and the hatchment was taken down from the door. Other signs of deep mourning vanished, from black hatbands to bombazine gowns.

All week long, Parrette grimly endured her freezing room, at first retiring with a pot of hot water in order to warm her hands so she could sew. Only the water cooled so rapidly. She discovered that servants were permitted one candle end at a time. She used hers to warm her hands as she considered this new household.

Saturday morning, as the servants bustled about removing the signs of mourning, Parrette considered them carefully before settling on Polly, among the youngest but not too young and silly. Taking care to catch her alone, though she knew nothing would prevent Polly from gossiping as she would, Parrette said, "In this country is it still against the law if I look for a Catholic church?"

Polly gaped at Parrette, then said, "I don't know, ma'am. But you ought to put your question to John-Coachman, Mr. Cassidy as was before he took over as stable master. He being from Ireland, is Popish."

Parrette had never ventured into the stable area. She found it scrupulously tidy, the animals munching in their airy loose boxes, or running about in the fenced area beyond.

As she minced across the mushy ground in a pair of pattens left for general use, her skirts held high, the stable master saw from the horses' ears and tails that a stranger approached. Parrette reached the door and glanced up at a handsome blue-eyed face. John-Coachman had been cleaning a hoof-picking tool, which he set aside. "Ma'am?" he said on an inquiring note.

Emboldened by Polly's words, she said firmly, "I am told you follow the true church. If that is so, where I can attend Mass?"

John-Coachman's expression of reserve altered to politeness. "You can ride along with me and my daughter Peg, if you wish, then, ma'am. There is a chapel at the Aubignys', where a priest comes to us Sundays and most Holy Days. We leave prompt at six o'clock, for I must be back in time to take the family to St. Andrews Church."

Parrette found his slow voice, with its slight lilt, soothing after the sharp, high English voices that were sometimes very difficult to follow. "Thank you," she said. "I will be here before six."

And the following morning she was, having laid out everything for Anna, who was to attend church for the first time with the family.

Anna was scarcely less apprehensive than the town was interested.

At last Barford Magna was to be vouchsafed a glimpse of the mysterious new Lady Northcote. Mrs. Bradshaw had lost no opportunity in describing to a few friends the occasion of her surprise caller, swearing them to strictest confidence in respect to the family's mourning, in comfortable expectation of the word spreading all the faster.

Between her and Polly's brother Ned, the first footman, who often spent his free evening among his cronies at the Pig, Anna's fame had spread, gaining glory with every repetition.

Though Dr. Blythe was much esteemed by his parishioners, it is safe to say that scarcely anyone heeded his sermon that Sunday. People were too busy gazing into what could be seen of the Northcote family pew, and afterward watching for a glimpse of the duke's daughter who had crossed from Paris to Spain in a coach-and-six to marry their new baron, Boney's frogs having waited in the offing out of respect, until the honeymoon was over.

Lady Emily Northcote looked like a golden angel, wearing pure white with no ornamentation. She had been overheard to say on her way into church that "Lord Northcote always loved to see me in white." In this way, she signaled that there would be no extended half-mourning, though the new Lady Northcote was correctly dressed in dove gray, a gown (so said those who considered themselves experts, Mrs. Bradshaw in the lead) come straight from Empress Josephine's own dressmaker.

Anna was unaware of this simmering interest. Her apprehension was due to the fact that she had not attended church since her mother was alive. St. Andrews was small—Anna's memory was of the beautiful Duomo ni Napoli, and the chapel at the Palazzo Calabritto, where the English legation had stayed.

This church was built of mellow stone, its arched windows in triune pattern glorious with color. But what Anna detected with her trained ear was how beautifully sound carried within those walls. Someone had understood sound, and music, in building it.

The rhythms of the liturgy, the rise and fall of English voices in the poetic cadences, reached back into her childhood memories. Even the hymns evoked memories, her earliest love of music. She still did not understand how she stood in relation to God, after her father's alteration at the end of his life from negligence to a desire for the comfort of absolution, and the casual atheism of some revolutionaries followed by the evident relief of many Parisians at Napoleon's permission for the churches to reopen, and following that the deeply ingrained religious traditions of Spain. What she heard at the end of the benediction was the beloved voice of her mother whispering, "God loves you."

So, though few of Dr. Blythe's parishioners heard his words, Anna did. The sermon drew from Bible verses Anna had only the vaguest memory of from childhood, but she felt comforted by Dr. Blythe's homily, and his prayer that Napoleon Bonaparte would find peace in his heart, that all the nations might return to peace.

Then there were more liturgical responses. Anna remained silent, not trusting her memory enough to follow what everyone else seemed to know so well. So she rose when they did, sat, knelt, and bowed her head, her spirit bathed in the comforting sound.

When they came out, there was Dr. Blythe. "Welcome among us, Lady Northcote," he said. He was a tallish, balding man with the light eyes so common in this part of the world. Anna liked his smile.

Anna dipped a curtsey and thanked him, wondering if it would be polite to comment on the service. But what was proper to say? She was evidently not expected to say anything, for there was a sense of pressure behind her. The line must move forward.

She stepped onto the flagstones before the church to discover people gathered in little groups talking. She understood from the way people came up to them, greeting them all, that the family was no longer prevented from social intercourse.

Anna had a few moments to observe this before being confronted by Mrs. Bradshaw, who made a bustle and business with her curtsey, then said in a high, carrying voice, "Lady Northcote, I beg you will forgive me for this presumption, but I simply *must* thank you again for bringing us news of our dearest Beverley. I live in hopes of receiving a missive—"

An arm slipped through hers. There was Emily, who gave Mrs. Bradshaw the briefest of nods. "Come, your elder sisters-by-marriage are waiting to be properly presented," Emile said to Anna and gently but inexorably led her away.

Anna glanced back apologetically at Mrs. Bradshaw, who performed a small, jerky curtsey, her face flushed. "I trust my husband will bring news," Anna called over her shoulder.

Mrs. Bradshaw curtseyed again, then was lost from view as Emily brought Anna to women wearing spinsters' caps under their bonnets, their faces familiar. As Emily performed the introduction, Anna remembered them from their portraits, made when they were considerably younger: the Misses Penelope and Caroline Duncannon.

Penelope appeared to have aged the most. There was a prim set to her mouth, and lines furrowed her brow as she said, "I trust you will forgive us for neglecting to call during the week, Lady Northcote." Her voice was deep, and Anna could hear the possibility of melody under those flat tones. "But the family understands our case. Caroline and I are not to be profligate; the carriage we usually hire was either in hire or it rained, and there was our duty to our brother's mourning, which may, in the strictest sense, now be regarded as permitting a quiet family gathering."

A draft of cold wind blew a few withered leaves across the mossy flagstones. Anna shivered, glad of her sturdy gloves, and Penelope pulled her black knit shawl closer about her as she began to inform them how dreadful the weather had been this past week, and predicted a worsening, as Caro's bonnet turned.

Anna could not help glancing in that direction, but all she saw was Dr. Blythe, who talked to an elderly couple, the woman all but hidden in a worn calash, the man wearing a dun-colored coat shiny with age.

Dr. Blythe glanced their way—at Caro?

"Come, Caroline," Penelope said sharply, interrupting herself. How could Anna have thought that voice musical? "You will catch your death standing about in this wind. It is time to depart."

The social circle around the family broke up, parishioners bowing and curtseying as the family moved to the carriage.

Harriet caught up with Anna, smothering a laugh behind her gloved hand. "Penelope *would* think that Caro still is attached to Dr. Blythe." She chuckled. "Fancy that! He must be fifty if he's a day, and she's nearing it. "

Anna thought of her father, who had been a year shy of fifty when he met her mother. As a girl she remembered their shared smiles, and his hands when he would pass behind Mama's chair, how he would caress the back of her neck, or touch her shoulder.

But she kept her thoughts to herself as Harriet rattled on, "They probably want to talk about the school. Caro teaches the great girls in household arts. Oh, Jupiter! Now that mourning is over Penelope is *still* going home with us. I ought to have known. Guess who must sit back, which I don't mind, but not with her sharp elbow in my side, just so she gets out of ordering a Sunday dinner."

Large as the coach was, they were a tight fit, Penelope directing Caro and Harriet in the calmest manner to sit with their backs to the horses. Then, with an air of sacrifice, she placed herself in the center of them, leaving the opposite bench to the dowager, Emily, and Anna.

When they reached The Manor, it had clouded up again. Anna was glad to get to the drawing room, where tea things were in waiting. They got their cups and sat down.

Penelope said, "Lady Northcote, if you will forgive my asking, how does it come about that the family was not informed of your marriage?"

Instant silence, into which the dowager uttered a faint protest.

Anna had been expecting this attack all along. Her only surprise was that they had waited thus far. "You must put that question to Lord Northcote," she said.

"But he is not here," Penelope rejoined, with the assurance of she who stands firmly astride the pinnacle of moral authority. "And you are come among us alone, so suddenly."

"I did not know anything about communications he might have made," Anna said. "He was sent out with the fleet very soon after we were married."

"You did not exchange letters?"

Harriet laughed at the idea of her brother writing *billets doux*. Penelope sent her a reproachful glare, and she sobered.

"Once. But then I was obliged to leave Naples, as they were daily expecting attack from the French."

"Oh, how dreadful," the dowager exclaimed.

"Europe," Harriet said, "is in a dreadful state. I am surprised anyone can get a letter, or send one, with Boney romping about."

"Harriet," Penelope stated, "if you cannot speak with the delicacy expected of your age and position, you would do well to keep silent."

The dowager roused a little at this attack on her daughter. "However it was expressed, Harriet is quite right." She turned her head, and blinked in Anna's general direction. "How did you come together again, my dear? You were in Cadiz, before the glorious victory, were you not?"

"Yes," Anna said. "Admiral Gravina told me himself that he once was an ally of England. In honor of that, I believe, he somehow made occasion to send me to the British fleet, to be reunited with Captain Dun—with Lord Northcote."

The mention of the Spanish admiral appeared to intimidate even Miss Penelope Duncannon. She accepted that with a minute nod, saying after a moment of reflection, "How did you come to be in Cadiz?"

"I was there," Anna smiled, "for the opera. The Company Dupree performed."

She knew she treaded dangerous ground, but she resented Miss Penelope Duncannon's minatory tone.

"Opera," the dowager repeated on a sigh. "Oh, it has been a very long time since I have seen a performance. There was that beautiful one by Gluck, *Orphée et Eurydice*—"

"Opera," Penelope stated, "ill bears close examination. So much of it is preposterous, when not outright immoral."

"I did not care for the recitations, but oh, *beautiful* music," the dowager said. "When Orfeo, sung by a woman, you know, finds Eurydice dead—I often wished that arranged for the fortepiano, before my eyes made it impossible to see the music sheets."

"A woman dressed up in man's attire?" Penelope gasped.

At that moment Diggory arrived to announce that the meal had been laid out in the dining room.

Penelope made it plain that the subject of opera was as well left behind as she followed behind Anna and Emily, the latter having once again taken Anna's arm. Emily said in her perfectly modulated voice, "You and I must unite to bring music back to this house. Henry will find that a fine welcome, do you not agree?"

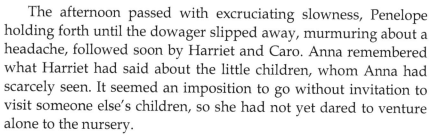

The afternoon passed with excruciating slowness, Penelope holding forth until the dowager slipped away, murmuring about a headache, followed soon by Harriet and Caro. Anna remembered what Harriet had said about the little children, whom Anna had scarcely seen. It seemed an imposition to go without invitation to visit someone else's children, so she had not yet dared to venture alone to the nursery.

A bit later on, once again the little girls were brought down to make their curtseys, which brought Harriet and Caro also. Then the girls were banished and everyone else retired to the dining room for the cold meal, after which they pulled on coats, hats, gloves, and shawls to venture out to the coach again. After evening service, the dowager made the offer to the elder Duncannon sisters to carry them back to Whitstead, as they had known she would, and so the evening ended.

Monday was free of visitors. Anna offered to read to the dowager, who accepted with pleasure. They sat side by side in the morning room, one reading and the other doing tedious hemming in tiny stitches—almost entirely by feel, as she could not see well enough for fancywork—as outside the sleet hissed and roared.

In the afternoon, the weather cleared. The dowager vanished somewhere with her daughter, and Anna took her book upstairs to her room, where she could sit next to the fire with a shawl about her until it was time to dress for dinner.

When Parrette came in, she was blowing on a knuckle and wringing her hand. Anna, in the midst of unfastening her gown, stopped. "What happened to your fingers?"

Parrette scowled at her blotched hands. "I cannot stitch with gloves on, so I use my candle to warm my fingers. And I got impatient day before yesterday. Burned myself stupidly; it is all but healed, except that I splashed hot water on my finger just now, and it hurts again." She wrung her hand.

"Candle? Why would you do that?" Anna shivered as she loosened her gown, and the obvious answer struck her. "The servants' chambers are not well warmed?"

"They are not warmed at all," Parrette said grimly. "It is worse in that attic than on board the ship for space, and no fireplace."

"I wonder if my husband knows," Anna said.

Parrette wrung her hand a last time, and then threw Anna's dinner gown over her head, and twitched it into place as Anna shrugged into it. "*You* could fix it, but I daresay it is better to wait. They have such peculiar customs, here."

"I? Fix it? How?"

Parrette uttered a breathless laugh. "Everyone seems to know it but us. You are a very wealthy woman."

"I thought the household was in bad straits."

"The household is, but it seems that your husband inherited his own fortune from a relation on his mother's side, and has never touched it."

Anna felt as if someone had struck her on the side of the head.

She turned to gaze at Parrette. "Have you been gossiping with the servants?"

"Yes," Parrette said. "Do you want to hear it, or not?"

Anna's struggle was brief. "Only if it is true. Gossip so often isn't."

"I cannot prove what is true or what isn't, but they all believe that it was discovering that his second son had inherited a vast amount from some relation that caused the elder Lord Northcote to go off in an apoplexy."

"So he had not this wealth when we married?"

"He had nothing. He was not even given an allowance. Whatever he did he must contrive himself."

They contemplated this, having learned something of the complicated affairs concerning meals on board a ship. If the officers had not a private allowance of some kind, they might have to eat the same food as the ship's crew. And repair their uniforms as they could, or indent for what they could not repair, as their earnings were scant. Captain Duncannon had possessed beautiful silver serving dishes and fine porcelain plates. So all that was relatively recent acquisition? Again, much was explained.

Anna nodded. "And so his leaving me to the Hamiltons was necessity. But that was then. Now, how are we to address your situation? Shall I order those rooms to be repaired?"

Parrette tipped her head to one side. "I think you would upset the household entirely, especially if you put that ahead of the many other things that need doing."

"But your hands! This is intolerable."

"The servants find ways to warmth," Parrette said. "Yesterday Peg Cassidy invited me to join them over the stable, when you are at dinner. It is very congenial, and warm enough *there*."

Anna said slowly, "The housekeeper did not show me your rooms. And I never thought to ask. *Bon!* This is a question I will be putting to the captain, when he gets here." Yet another thing to add to her sense of anticipation, mixed with...not dread. There was too much hope, and good memory for that. Brief as it was.

So much depended upon his reappearance! Anna had supposed it was only she who thought about him, imagined conversations, questions. Expectations. But in their own ways, the entire household seemed to be in a mode of rehearsal, no, of waiting, until the main actor stepped upon the stage.

Parrette stepped back, gave a short nod, and said, "You'll do. Better get yourself downstairs."

Anna plucked up her shawl and left. Parrette straightened the room, picked up the basket of work waiting outside Anna's door, and sped along the servants' hall to the back stairs. Here she met Polly and Peg Cassidy, who were waiting for her.

Parrette, who had long ago schooled herself to brace for the future, and to never' anticipate, as that brought nothing but disappointment, had found herself thinking about the prospective second visit all through the day.

Tuesdays, Anna discovered when the fire was lit in the formal parlor, were understood by the countryside to be their At Home day for morning calls. These calls would be duly returned toward the end of the week.

However, before breakfast was over a heavy, sleeting rain set in. The storm lasted three days, keeping everyone indoors, and on Thursday, when the weather cleared, Anna discovered the dowager gone somewhere with Harriet as driver; not, ordinarily, an event to cause notice except for Emily's surprise, indeed, her quick expression of disapprobation before her expression smoothed.

Anna was not certain what to make of Emily, even without the memory of her husband's whispering of that name. More often than not Emily's tone, some of her words, reminded Anna of Therese Rose, which caused an instinctive distrust. Not that Emily was as friendly, or as good company. It was that sense of falsity, of words and tone not quite matching, though outwardly she had been scrupulously civil.

Further, her musical evenings so far compassed her own performance, with polite-nothing sayings offering the others an opportunity before Anna was requested to accompany Emily's singing, which occasioned an exclamation from Frederick Elstead that they made a beautiful pair, that someone ought to paint them. Emily simpered, but at no time did she appear to think it necessary to ask Anna if she had another sort of performance in mind besides accompaniment.

Anna was not certain what she ought to say if she did. She sensed that Emily had been regarded as mistress of the household, that she had once led the way in everything. Anna was aware that her own singing far surpassed Emily's modest talents and training; she sensed that Emily would be put out of countenance. She resolved to let the matter lie until Emily might think of asking her to sing. But she wanted to sing again.

She must simply content herself by singing alone.

The resumption of social life meant that when the drawing room was heated, Anna became wary of taking up the room for her own purposes. Anyone might come in.

Then she remembered that long gallery in the other wing. It was equally cold, if not colder, but she had learned in Paris that movement made one warm, and oh, the space!

She made her way quietly to the deserted gallery, low slants of wintry light splashing the paintings with dull color. As her husband's ancestors gazed out into infinity over her head, she danced up and down the marble floor. Once her body was warmed, she hummed a note, and cautiously tested the sound. There was an interesting echo, but that would swiftly blur into unbearable murk.

She therefore took to walking outside in the bitter wind. The ordered garden gave way to a profusion of trees and hedges that surrounded the lake. Once she was out of sight of the house, she ran her scales and sang.

As her voice echoed among the trees, she was learning to appreciate unexpected moments of grace: the subtle sun rays in the mist, the silvery branches against the sky, the smooth hills accented by hedgerows. England might not be as beautiful as her mother had promised, but it was not after all as dismal as it had appeared on her arrival.

When she returned from her first walk, she paused to look at the house sheltered beside its hill. It was so peaceful. The wounds of battle were blessedly distant. She could understand what motivated the men of the *Aglaea* to protect their homeland against the devastation Napoleon Bonaparte caused elsewhere.

But she could not comprehend the motivations of Bonaparte,

seen now and then at the theater in Paris, sitting next to his exquisite wife. *Why* would he invade England? What use would the properties of an island be when he held already the whole of Europe in his grip?

That Saturday, after her dance practice in the gallery and her morning walk for singing, she returned to find everyone gathered as customary for tea and Cook's poppy seed cakes. Harriet presided, a proud look on her face as she wore a new gown.

Anna recognized the stylish lines instantly. Though the garment itself was a plain round gown, suitable for a girl not yet presented, and the color was a subdued pale lavender with little ornamentation, there was no mistaking the fine fit, the pretty line of the yoke in back, the little puff sleeves at the shoulders, framed by a sedate ribbon before lengthening into the long sleeves common in England, especially at this time of year.

Even more surprising was the expression on Emily's face, almost affront.

"You look very well in that new gown," Anna said to Harriet.

The girl preened. "Is it not fine? *Infinitely* better than anything that can be got from Miss Reed. Your Duflot is teaching Polly."

Emily turned to Anna. "Am I to understand that your woman makes your gowns, Lady Northcote?"

"She makes most of them, yes," Anna replied tranquilly.

Emily bit back an exclamation, remembering that the conjectures about Le Roy and Paris had all come from others. At no time had this foreigner made any such claim herself. She had said nothing about her clothes at all.

When Anna went upstairs later to dress for dinner, she said to Parrette, "That was a fine gown you made for Harriet. Poor thing, they seem to have neglected her altogether."

Parrette made certain the doors were shut, then said in Neapolitan, "When we sit above the stable while you are at dinner, I have been teaching Polly what I know." She smiled at the thought of those cozy evenings, with the smell of freshly parched coffee beans smothering the odor of horse as John-Coachman made the coffee himself.

Anna, seeing that smile, was surprised. She had so rarely seen Parrette smile, especially in that way. But then Parrette's brows twitched into a frown. "Miss Harriet is not the only one neglected. There is but the one man in the garden, until spring, and then the kitchen maids will be expected to do most of the weeding. Miss Harriet thinks she is to go to London in spring, but…"

She let that lapse, and Anna laughed. "I know. *When Lord Northcote returns.*" The household's expectation might be almost as intense as her own, though perhaps for different reasons.

Parrette twitched curls about Anna's face, stepped back and cocked her head. "Polly wishes to be promoted to lady's dresser. She's a quick learner. And a good turn requires another good turn, for Polly put me in the way of meeting the Cassidys, so that I might hear Mass in the Aubignys' private chapel."

Anna exclaimed. "Is there no church? Is hearing Mass against the law in England?"

"It was, I learned," Parrette said. "But they changed the law not long after our revolution broke out. Though it is thought best to bide quiet, as John-Coachman says, as there is still ill feeling." Parrette frowned, and added, "Some of it is on account of war in Ireland, five or six years back, the Irish, mostly Catholics, wanting independence in the way of the American colony."

War everywhere, Anna thought as she disposed her shawl about her elbows. Why was it necessary to forbid worship if it was not one's own tradition?

She recollected that the legation in Naples had had to build their own chapel, as the king had forbidden an English church to be built. Her mother had told her that Lutherans and Catholics and Church of England and the Jews as well all worshipped the same God, and read out of the same Bible, or half the Bible, with the Jews. But when kings and governments meddled with religion, there was another excuse for war.

That evening brought another change: the dowager appeared at dinner wearing spectacles. She said nothing about them, but commented in a brisk tone, "I wonder when we may safely begin looking for Henry?"

Anna smiled across the table at her. "I thought to count up the days from my own travel, but I know not how much time he spends when he lands. Oh! I wake every day in hopes of post, saying when he is to come."

"We're all looking for Henry's return," Frederick Elstead said genially.

Frederick and Mary Elstead were dining with them, as they often did. Mary ignored the commentary about her brother. She was regarding her mother's spectacles with faint surprise. But she said nothing, and Emily, who had not been consulted, decided not to take any notice, in hopes that the silly old fool would take the hint and recollect what was due to the family, if not to herself.

After dinner, as the women passed into the drawing room, Harriet came to Anna and said low-voiced, "I would have told you but she desired me to keep her secret." She pointed at the piano. "Now she can play again." Harriet made a face. "If Penelope doesn't attack her first, and scare her into putting them away."

"Why should she do such a thing?" Anna asked.

"Because Papa set his face against anyone making such a *spectacle* of themselves, and Penelope will fuss about what others might say." Harriet smothered a laugh. "Do not be suspecting him of a pun. Papa would never have so lowered himself." Her expressive brows contracted. "My brother John was *far* worse. How would it look—we would be made a laughingstock—people would ask us when we were to set up shop-keeping. He was quite, quite—"

Whatever she was going to say was cut off when Emily interrupted in a smooth, brisk tone. "Tea, Lady Northcote?"

It occurred to Anna that there was one more person in that house who had set her mind against spectacles as well, though Emily *said* nothing. But Anna sensed it in the way Emily looked everywhere else, as if the sight of those little framed lenses offended her.

Sunday dawned with tiny flakes of snow falling. The wheels of the coach crunched along the road to church, where, as before, people gathered before and after the morning service. And as before Penelope Duncannon decided when the family was to leave, marching through and rounding them up like a scolding nanny.

Anna was peripherally aware of Caroline speaking with Dr. Blythe, something she would have paid scant attention to had she not noticed the way Dr. Blythe looked after Caroline when her sister pulled her firmly away.

Surely there could not be anything wrong in talking to the minister after church, Anna thought.

She was distracted when Penelope addressed the dowager the moment the footman had safely shut the coach's door. "Lady Northcote," she stated. "I had no wish to draw the stares of ill-bred persons, but I would be failing in my duty if I did not point out that Papa would never have countenanced the wearing of spectacles at any time, but most especially in church."

"Why not in church?" Harriet exclaimed. "Such rules are *spooney!*"

"Harriet!" Penelope gasped in shock.

Emily said in a low, cold voice, "Harriet. You will permit me to point out that vulgar expressions are never tolerable in persons of birth and breeding, but are particularly unacceptable on Sunday."

Caro turned to Penelope, and said, bravely, "Oh, but Penelope, what can possibly be wrong if Lady Northcote is enabled to see her hymn book—"

"Caroline, you interrupt me," Penelope snapped.

Caro looked down like a chastened schoolgirl instead of a woman of forty years.

"Nor," Penelope went on, "would have my late brother, little as we agreed. We should have agreed on *this*."

"I think—" Caro began.

"Caroline, please. Must you continually put yourself forward? You know better, at your age. Good manners requires the eldest finish speaking." And to Emily, "I very much loathe to point it out, but those have so vulgar an appearance."

"I agree," Emily stated calmly. "But my authority in this household has been superseded."

Anna was about to speak—to say she hardly knew what—but Harriet leaned forward. "You may think what you wish, Penelope, but I take leave to tell you that you are wrong about vulgarity."

"Harriet Duncannon!"

"Would an empress ever be called vulgar? How about the queen of the French?"

"What nonsense is this?" Penelope demanded.

Anna tried a peace-making deflection. "Those spectacles are modeled on the fashion put forward by the Empress Catherine the Great. She took the fashion from Queen Marie Antoinette. I learned this in the royal court at Naples."

"Yes," Harriet exclaimed. "*And* the oculist showed us in a book. Other great ladies wear them, a *vast* number. So they *cannot* be vulgar."

The dowager said in her timid voice, "I did so appreciate seeing my hymnal. And I can now play the instrument again."

Penelope stared at her, and, her face very much reddened, turned Anna's way. "You, Lady Northcote, may be looked upon in some wise as representing my step-brother, until such time as he returns to his home to take up his responsibilities. Do you mean to say that you approve of this start?"

Anna very much disliked being pulled into this dispute, but she recognized that she had perhaps been a cause. Deference she would try, but she would not attempt to placate so direct an attack. "I understood that I am come into a musical family," she said. "If spectacles will serve to enable the Dowager Lady Northcote to see her music, I can only applaud. I saw many such in royal houses," she added.

Penelope sat back, pushing her hands into her muff. She muttered under her breath; when they drew up before the house, her tone became scolding as she vented her emotions in her patient sister's direction. Anna heard the words "French manners," and "royal houses," but chose to pretend to deafness.

The rest of that day dragged on wearily, Penelope having managed to destroy what was supposed to be a day of peace. She carried her disapprobation all the way to church again, only unbending long enough to accept her expected ride home.

The next week saw many changes.

On Tuesday, it seemed that the entire countryside crowded in a continual line of carriages to pay their calls. Everyone sat stiffly in the traditional circle on the fine chairs in the formal drawing room. Their conversation was as rigidly defined: the coldness of the weather, the prevalence of colds, fear of sore throats, which took up the requisite quarter hour.

Anna remembered her mother telling her that one must never be caught rudely looking at the clock, though calls must be strictly limited. As she listened to the flow of talk, it occurred to her that people who had been making and receiving these calls all their lives must have trained themselves to know how much to say, and to listen to, before the time was over, the same way a musician trained to find the true note, or to beat the correct tempo.

She heard herself presented over and over, which intensified the sense that she was merely playing a role. She did not catch all the names in the series of pale faces that paraded in and out, their accents identical, and their conversation nearly so.

The only person she recognized was the rector, Dr. Blythe, who kept up a gentle dialogue about gardens until it was time to go. On leaving, he issued a general invitation to call at the parsonage.

He said to Anna, "The ladies know that though I am a bachelor, my housekeeper, Mrs. Eccles, is famed for her pies, and likes nothing better than to serve my parishioners. She is happiest seeing her good things eaten. I will admit to an ulterior motive, in hoping to elicit your interest on behalf of our school. But that may wait until you have had time to look about you."

He was the last. When the household stirred again, Anna took the opportunity to address Harriet. "What am I to understand by his invitation?"

Harriet smiled, glad to put the elegant lady right, glad to be asked. "Why, he is a bachelor, you know. In the ordinary way, we would not call upon him. But his being our rector changes things. Everyone calls upon him. And it's true about the pies," she added with the earnestness of youth.

Anna was able to get away soon after. Now that the dowager could read for herself, Anna had no obligations, and she was learning to take her walk when she could. She could dance in the gallery at any time. No one went there. But her singing depended upon the weather. The least clearing of the sky found her out on what was becoming a familiar ramble, along pathways lined by stones now mossy with age.

She had found a grotto where sound cupped pleasingly, and her only audience was birds and the occasional little creature. When she had emptied her heart of song, she ran back, refreshed even though she shivered.

After dinner that night, the dowager introduced two changes. First, she had invited her eldest granddaughter, whose first uncertain attempts at music under Nurse's guidance had revealed, she said, a great deal of taste.

And then she sat down to the fortepiano herself, playing the sonata that Haydn had written for the once-famed Miss Jansen, whom the dowager had heard play at a private subscription concert at a ducal manse before she was married.

The dowager attacked the piece with a vigor that surprised Anna from so gentle and timid a woman. Here was clearly a joy in music akin to her own, and proof that the lady, however aged, was still very much a part of the world.

The dowager also made it clear that she preferred to make her own music rather than serve as accompanist for Emily's singing, and so Anna continued to fill that post. She had no need to practice that.

While she played, her gaze wandered about the room, from fire to framed pictures, then was caught by the earnest little figure sitting on the edge of her chair, watching her mother. Eleanor Duncannon clasped her thin hands tightly, and her lips parted.

When her mother sang one of her favorites, "Robin Adair," the child began to sing very softly. Anna easily differentiated the child's voice from her mother's louder one, and liked what she heard. She was thrown back to Maestro Paisiello's music chamber, always warm and bright from the brilliant Neapolitan sunlight, as she began singing at about the same age.

When Emily had finished, and was putting away her sheet

music, Anna got up from the instrument and approached the child. "Are you partial to singing?" she asked Eleanor.

"Oh, yes," the girl said. "Nurse tries to teach me. Until I can have a governess, which was to happen and then my papa died—"

"Eleanor, little girls do not put themselves forward." Emily appeared, her voice smooth as always, but Eleanor flushed and dropped her gaze. "Forgive me, Lady Northcote," Emily said to Anna, "but I do not wish my daughter to develop pert manners. Nothing can be more fatal."

She stretched out her hand to ring the bell. Nurse, who must have been waiting in the hall, instantly appeared.

In the general motion as the child made her curtseys and the tea things were in passing, Harriet came up to Anna and muttered, "As if she didn't racket all over the countryside with Henry when she was not much older. *I* remember, though I was Justina's age. They think I don't, but I *do*."

Anna said, "Do you think it would be inappropriate to offer Eleanor a lesson? I would go to the nursery, that no one would be disturbed, and the child could not be thought to be putting herself forward."

Harriet did not care one way or another about music, but she loved the idea of circumventing Emily, who she felt ignored those girls shamefully. "I think you ought to."

With this assurance, the next day, Anna found her way to the nursery wing. She could not help looking about with interest. Here the captain must have spent a good deal of his childhood; there were battered toys, demonstrably old, a shelf packed with books, and a low table with scissors, paper, chalk, and all the accouterments of childhood. The smell of chalk dealt Anna an unexpected blow, bringing back her time with her mother, so precious; she had resented the hours her mother had to spend among the royal children, until she was old enough to be included among them for lessons, where she could be relied upon to know her place.

Nurse looked up in surprise at this unexpected invasion of her domain. She was a plump woman somewhere between fifty and sixty whose light hair was going gray. Her voice was mild as she said, "Make your curtseys like young ladies."

Justina resembled her sister in her spindly limbs, but her hair was a light brown. The baby lay in a bassinet, sleeping, as the little girls copied out their letters.

"I came to ask if Eleanor wishes to learn to sing," Anna said, and her reward was the flashing up of Eleanor's eyelids, so that the firelight reflected in her wide eyes.

Nurse said apologetically, "I have started them on their letters, but music, well, I can find out some notes, but I never put myself forward for governess duties."

Anna said, "As it happens, I had many singing lessons when I was small, but I have never taught, so this would be an experiment for us both. If Miss Eleanor has the interest."

"Oh, *yes*, Lady Northcote," the child said, bridling. Before Anna could speak she launched into "Robin Adair" in a high, quick voice, mimicking her mother's studied gestures as she sang.

Anna waited a verse through, and then walked over to the battered spinet in the far corner. She pressed a couple of chords, shuddered and lifted her hand. No wonder the child sang flat. The spinet was hopelessly out of tune.

She said, "Try this." Softly, so softly, she dropped her jaw, rounded her lips and sang a C.

Eleanor sang it back. It was close enough that Anna smiled and said, "Good! Now try it here." She touched her ribs. "Not here." A touch to the throat.

Eleanor sang it exactly the same, though she stuck out her middle.

Anna said, "Listen to the difference." She touched her own throat, squeezed up and sang a shrill note. Then she opened her throat, her hands at her middle to show how deep she breathed, and sang it again, low and pure.

Eleanor's eyes widened. "Oh, that's *pretty*. I want to do that."

Anna smiled back, patiently instructed the girl a little longer, until she had the main idea, and then promised to return again if Eleanor practiced.

That evening, Eleanor did not appear after dinner, on the orders of her mother.

Twenty-eight

I MUST NOW BEG the reader's indulgence, well aware that however few of us enjoy the polite duty of formal calls, still fewer want to hear about someone else's.

Still, following Anna on her first round of Barford Magna's principal families—or those whom Lady Emily Northcote considered to be first—will demonstrate, in contrasts, the characters of the three ladies who pulled on hats, gloves, and pelisses that frosty morning.

Anna's only emotion was curiosity to see how English people lived.

Harriet had learned to cordially loathe formal calls before the year's respite required by mourning. That is, she had hated her status as schoolgirl, which Emily, whose sense of delicacy dictated a submissive and above all silent demeanor for girls yet to be introduced to society, had encouraged.

Unfortunately, in recent years, only the two had performed this strictly regulated duty that Emily, as principal woman in the parish, felt she owed the neighbors. As the dowager's eyesight had dimmed, so had her willingness to careen blindly over the countryside. She preferred to visit her friends singly, for as long as conversation lasted, and those friends accepted this gentle idiosyncrasy.

Now that she was no longer principal lady of the parish, Emily had to find sufficient motivation in showing her replacement the way. For there was certainly no pleasure in the tedium of visiting on dull country people. Emily longed to be in London again, among clever people of fashion and rank; there, the strict fifteen minutes was a necessity due to the numbers. One must not accidentally neglect anyone, or the next brilliant ball, or talked-about soiree, might pass with one only hearing about it after the fact.

Buried in Barford Magna as she was, she was aware of every dull ticking of the clock.

At least, Harriet thought privately as they climbed into the impressive carriage with the Northcote arms painted on the side, the worst would be got over first. That, and she had a spanking new gown to show off, for the first time in her life, and Polly had learnt that French way of doing up her hair.

The Elstead family lived at the Groves, closest to the Manor. Squire Elstead was a stout man with large side-whiskers, his bulging waistcoat well-dusted with snuff. He seldom spoke. When he did, he invariably prefaced each remark with a self-deprecating, rattling chuckle, to which his wife listened apparently unmoved. Anna could not help wondering what it might be like to spend one's life hearing that noise.

"And when shall we see Henry return among us?" the squire's wife asked.

"I hope very soon," Anna replied, trying not to hear insinuation in the lady's tone. Nature might have given her an irritating voice. Anna would assume nothing more.

"I am certain it cannot seem too soon for some, naming no names," Mrs. Squire Elstead said archly. "And I, for one, look forward to his account of the last glorious day of our dear Nelson..."

Mrs. Squire Elstead was very much the queen of her over-heated drawing room. Her youngest daughter Cicely, a fair-haired girl a little younger than Harriet, and newly returned from a select school in York, sat mumchance by her mother with some fine sewing on her lap.

Harriet chose a chair on the other side of Cicely. The two girls exchanged a brief whispered greeting until a quelling glance by her mother silenced Cicely. Mrs. Squire Elstead talked steadily, touching on the coming memorial for the Glorious Admiral Lord Nelson, and repeating in lengthy superlatives what the newspapers had said.

Anna's attention showed a lamentable tendency to wander. The room was filled with a great deal of fine furniture. One end of the room was dominated by a full length portrait of Emily, which had to have been done when she was about the age of Harriet. She wore a gown with a long train in the Grecian style, with the heraldic appurtenances of a barony as part of the background. It was clear that Emily, or at least her marriage, was the pride of the house.

The other end of the room was dominated by an extremely handsome long case clock with a white dial. When the clock bonged the quarter hour, Anna rose with alacrity. No wonder Frederick and Mary Elstead came so often to dine at the manor!

They proceeded next to a fine house south of town, where dwelt Mr. and Mrs. Rackham.

Mr. Rackham, a genial gentleman with snuff dusting his sleeve, greeted them on his way to his book room, asking mildly, "I trust we shall see Henry back among us soon?"

Here we find the greatest contrasts. Anna was struck by the differing tones between Mrs. Squire Elstead and this gentleman, though the question was essentially the same: this man listened with an air of pleasure unlike the squire's wife's smile of suppressed bitterness.

Outwardly, that is, perceivable only to us, there existed a contrast between the two Lady Northcotes: there was Emily's contempt for fat Mrs. Rackham, gorgeously dressed in the silk and lace of ten years previous, when she could very well afford to keep the fashion; against that existed Anna's sense of comfort as her hostess presided easily over an old-fashioned parlor with its striped paper, and delicate furnishings covered in pale blue satin, rather worn but kept painstakingly clean.

On the other side of the room sat their son Thomas, a tall, thin young man just turned twenty, whose shirt points required him to stare straight ahead. His short-sighted sister Jane peered at the visitors, smiling when Harriet sat down by her.

Thomas murmured, "Did you hear that Robert Colby is back?"

"No!" Harriet exclaimed, and she put her head together with her old friends, talking in low voices as their mother carried over them with tranquil habit, commenting on the weather, the coming holidays, and Admiral Lord Nelson's expected memorial.

It was Emily who summarily cut short this pleasant conversation.

Harriet smothered a sigh, reflecting that they were certain to drive to the Colbys next. She had not seen her old playmate for nearly four years. She was all the more curious now that he was come down from Oxford, after having spent a protracted time in London, and then with grand friends during the shooting season.

Anna looked out at a sizable house of mellow Tudor brick at the end of a winding avenue of poplars, where lived the widowed baronet Sir Robert Colby. He appeared, made his bows in form—asked about Henry, "who I suppose I ought rightly to call Lord Northcote, though I knew him as a boy in short coats, ever talking of the sea"—then vanished, leaving them to his sister, a faded spinster who only became animated when the conversation touched on her many nephews and her young niece Georgiana.

Emily suppressed yawns, Anna struggled to hear Miss Colby's faint voice, and Harriet sat scowling, feeling a sense of personal insult that Robert had gone out riding instead of waiting to greet them.

Well! She knew how to address *that*.

After the requisite fifteen minutes, every second of which all three callers felt they had counted three times over, they proceeded to the north of town, where lay an enormous house built in the Tudor fashion, half of which appeared to be shut up.

Here dwelt the Aubigny family, the only progeny still living at home consisting of two very lively boys in short coats, who were brought in by their nurse to make their bows, then straightaway taken out again. Anna could hear them hallooing and laughing as they escaped, reminding her of the midshipmen aboard the *Aglaea*. So strange—she had spent comparatively little time aboard the ship, compared to her life in Spain. And yet so many memories would intrude, costing her heart-pangs.

But the visit took a turn for the better when Mrs. Aubigny,

correctly interpreting the strain in her caller's eyes, switched to the French she had learnt as a girl sent to a convent-school in Paris, before the destruction of the Revolution. She also asked after Henry, and reminisced about what a fine young man he was, and how proudly she had read of his doings in the great world.

Now Harriet was bored, as the other three conversed about the new empire of France. The fifteen minutes ticked by, then Harriet jumped to her feet. In the general leave-taking, Harriet muttered to Anna that this would be an end, most probably; Anna would meet the others at some other time. Her glance over her shoulder, and roll of the eyes, adding meaning that Anna could not guess at.

The carriage took them last to the parsonage, a rambling house built in an L, for a much larger family. Inside was cheer, the smell of baked apples, and warmth. After many hours of cold jolting over the roads, and sitting stiffly on chairs, it was a relief. The housekeeper, Mrs. Eccles, stayed to chat in a way that made it clear she knew everyone in the parish.

As the carriage returned them to the Manor, Anna tried to capture and hold the idea that these might be the people she was expected to spend the rest of her life among.

If...if.

They all anticipated the return of Lord Northcote, though none as strongly as his wife.

'Lady Northcote!' It still seemed to denote someone else. *Had been* someone else. There were three Lady Northcotes living under that roof, one whose family had grown, the other who retained the title in courtesy but not the authority, though she betrayed by little signs that she would recover it if she could.

Anna noted during the calls that people had been careful to say 'Lady *Emily* Northcote' with a slight emphasis, which Emily accepted with that marble expression and politely modulated voice.

On Saturday, when Mary and Frederick Elstead once again joined them, Mary surprised them by offering to play at the harp. She had resumed practice, and offered them three Scottish airs.

Anna was still debating permitting herself the pleasure of

singing and the danger of discovery; on seeing Emily's impatience with this new addition, and Harriet's and Frederic's honest indifference, she elected to remain in the background, reflecting that at least she was surrounded by music, even if her contributory role was limited.

Sunday they woke to freezing sleet of such an intensity that there would be no church that morning. The dowager did not retire to her rooms with her hymn book as had been her wont. She played hymns on the instrument, with a power that sounded almost defiant to Anna's sensitive ear. She sensed that the spectacles were still a topic of conflict. Harriet repaired to the schoolroom to play with the little girls, and Anna stole to the gallery to dance herself into warmth.

Then Monday morning arrived after a sleety, windy night, and brought with it an express from Mr. Perkins, stating that the Right Hon'ble Lord Northcote would be traveling by gentle stages, and they might expect him by Wednesday latest.

Everyone felt a sense of anticipation. The only outward sign was Mrs. Diggory, and the entire staff, throwing the house into a frenzy of cleaning suitable (Harriet remarked caustically, when she had been politely chased from three rooms) for the arrival of His Majesty, King George, and the entire royal family.

Tuesday brought the first snow of the season. No one would be expected that day, either from London or more close by. Anna was aware that in other circumstances she would have been enchanted to see snow for the first time, but she was aware of a disappointment so sharp that she yanked the curtains closed.

The dowager sighed, and as she had for years that only she had numbered, suppressed her impatience to lay eyes on her son.

Harriet shrugged. Henry would arrive when he arrived. She was off to visit Jane.

Emily looked out, judged that it was not heavy enough yet to keep her inside, and sent orders for her park phaeton to be put to, with the back up. She went out, looked at John-Coachman's silent face, and sensed his unspoken disapproval. He was invariably courteous, but she suspected he thought more highly of the horses than he did of their owners.

"I have changed my mind," she said. "I will ride to the Groves. Pray saddle my hack."

She left him to unhitch the team from the park phaeton and walked around, slapping her whip idly against her half-boot, until she happened to glance up at the paned windows of the gallery in the old wing. Was there movement behind that glass? It had to be a reflection. Or perhaps Mrs. Diggory had extended her efforts into the wing that no one entered.

"Your ladyship's hack is ready."

Distracted, she took the reins, was tossed into the saddle, and set out at a spanking pace. At the Groves, she handed off the heated horse at the stable, and walked in to discover her family sitting over a late breakfast, as often happened in winter. She did not apologize for interrupting, but said, "Henry should arrive tomorrow."

"Capital," Frederick exclaimed, then frowned. "Is he still wounded, do you think? I hope he has not altogether given up riding—"

Their mother interrupted him. "If any of John's hacks are left at the Manor, I would be surprised. Has that French woman sold them all off?"

Emily knew her mother was very well aware that the only selling had been done by she herself, in her effort to stave off the most immediate creditors, after the disappointment of Amelia's birth. This was her mother's half-apology for their acrimonious last parting.

"Nothing," she said, "has been changed."

Frederick shot a glance from their mother to his wife, and as always, the two were in mutual agreement on retreat, Cicely following right behind Mary.

Mrs. Squire Elstead frowned after them. He was so handsome, and Cicely even prettier than her sister, and for what? Neither of them had the least ambition. They might as well have been born ugly, and the money spent on that expensive school in York saved.

Emily glanced at the head of the table. Her father had already gone, of course. "As for Ludovisi, I found out just yesterday that there is indeed a noble family by that name, but there is an infinity of cousins and children. All she'd get out of *that* connection would likely be a worn pair of shoes."

"Mother, that is vulgar."

The Squire's wife jerked up her shoulder. "It is no more than the truth, and it is surprising to hear missish words from a married woman. A once-married woman. At all events, no one but shop girls dress that smartly. I notice," she said, tapping her finger on her coffee cup, "that she does not wear a wedding band. I find that very significant, though your father insists that that is probably some outlandish French custom, their having got up to all manner of disagreeable capers during their revolt. I am going to find out who the mother's people were."

Emily shrugged. The lack of a ring was immaterial. It was as likely someone pretending to be married could buy a band and put it on.

"And further, I saw quite clearly that she waited for you to move at the end of your call. Does she give orders?"

"No." Emily wished that Lady Northcote would be found out to be a jumped-up shop girl, or something like, but she knew better. Shop girls from Paris would never speak so well, or move so elegantly.

"It is different in France," Emily said impatiently. She had heard enough about the freedom married Frenchwomen had, even before all civilized behavior was thrown out the window by the Revolution. Men and women mixed freely in their salons, where it was reputed that wit and style were as important as good birth. "Mother, I want you to give the Christmas ball. It is too soon for us, even if there were no Lady Northcote in question."

"Your father will quibble over the bother and expense," Mrs. Elstead said.

Emily ignored that out of long habit. When her mother misliked a notion, she always attributed the negation to her father.

Sure enough, her mother followed up her remark with a sharper question. "Why should we be put to that trouble? What is to be gained?"

Henry will see me presiding, Emily thought. Out loud, she said, "It will be a fine way to establish us on the old footing, of course.

And you know Papa will want to settle things relative to his desire to serve as Justice of the Peace."

She could see that this was a hit. Her mother had been hinting broadly ever since John's death. While the appointment brought nothing remunerative, it was a position of tremendous prestige, and her mother longed to print visiting cards with 'J.P.' after Father's name, which was as close to a title as she would ever get.

Mrs. Squire Elstead considered, then frowned. "At a ball?"

"Mother, the ball will begin things. Then we will give our customary New Year's party. If Lady Northcote knows nothing of such things, after years in France under that terrible government, I will put her in the way of it."

"And Henry will see you doing it," Mrs. Elstead said.

Emily flushed, but did not deny it. Her mother smiled. "Is she really so incapable?"

Emily had been considering that very question. "She has given no orders, and yet…the household has changed vastly since her arrival. Not that I can blame her for putting it into my mother-in-law's head that women of quality, even noble and royal women, wear spectacles. It might only have been conversation, after which it is as likely that Harriet talked her mother into it. Harriet has become increasingly pert, and though I cannot blame the woman for that, she does nothing to correct her. In addition to all else, Eleanor is suddenly prating of music lessons, as if she were another Mrs. Billington, which she is not, and that occurred after Lady Northcote went up the nursery and taught her a few notes. I cannot imagine why she would do that. Perhaps she only meant well."

"She might have been put in the way of it by Louisa Northcote," Mrs. Squire Elstead stated. "She was *always* tiresome about that instrument. Of course it was the only accomplishment she had, so naturally the Dangeau family must puff it off."

Emily had long suspected that her mother had wished to marry the baron, old as he was, after the death of his first wife. But he had looked higher for a bride, and the Dangeaus had not only wealth and coronets aplenty but also ecclesiastical rank in their family tree.

Her mother went on embroidering a favorite theme. "You

watch out, Emily, or that fool Louisa Northcote will turn Eleanor into a bluestocking, and then you will be stuck with her on your hands the way they are with those spinsters out at Whitstead. A perfectly good house, which *you* might have had, instead thrown away on..."

Emily shut out her mother, whose complaints about Penelope and Caroline were nothing new. Of more immediate necessity was regaining her own position in society. Even if Whitstead had been free, she had no intention of burying herself in a country village that made Barford Magna look the size of London.

Her mother, noticing in Emily's distant gaze that her daughter was not listening, halted mid-sentence. "Do as you will," she said. "I will put Cicely to writing out the invitations. At least the child came back from York with superior handwriting."

Emily took her leave, and rode back to the Manor. She had gained her point. The Elsteads would give the Christmas ball, and her cheese-paring mother would see to it that it was very fine, as she had the newly-returned Henry to impress for her own purposes.

But Emily could not talk to her mother about her own misgivings.

She sensed that there was some mystery; Lady Northcote vanished alone for hours. It was too much to hope that there was some sordid reason for those rambles.

Emily knew the grounds well enough from when she and Henry had been young. There was little likelihood of mysterious French spies (what would they have to spy on?) or sinister Italian banditti (no one had reported so much as a missing hen in a parish where everyone's business became known as soon as Mother laid ear to it), or even a German count who might appear to carry off the object of his desire, married surely on some whim by Henry. She might only be a very good walker.

Emily had been calculating, and surely this Anna Ludovisi—impossible name!—could have been no more than sixteen when Henry had married her. She might not, feature by feature, compare with Emily herself (and Emily studied her mirror carefully for the least signs of age), but she conveyed an aura of beauty, and without any apparent effort. The way she crossed a room drew the eye; Emily could only be glad that apparently she had never thought to ride a horse, nor did she drive. There, she knew she would be superior. Further, if Henry was still tiresome about music, Emily had made certain that she was leading the musical evenings.

The next day, she dressed in a fine gown that had just arrived from London before she was forced to put on black clothes, so she had never before had a chance to wear it. She might have turned twenty-seven this summer past, but nobody would know it to look at her.

Henry had loved her once. All this past year, as she waited for the birth of her child, she had thought about Henry, and how even if she were disappointed of a son, nothing would stand in the way of her marriage with Henry, who surely could get dispensation from his uncle the bishop for marrying his brother's wife. Either way, she would retain her position.

Then there had come that shocking newsprint article, stating that he possessed a wife.

She gave no sign of these thoughts as she joined the others. She had learnt by bitter experience that the flattery and deference of courtship ended with the wedding breakfast. Since then she had schooled herself to suggest, to hint, to encourage a hot-tempered, selfish husband in order to gain her point, and to reveal nothing that he might use against her later.

The day was got through each in their various pursuits until the likely time the express was to be expected. Emily had already chosen the place where she would stand directly under the chandelier, whose light would make a glorious gold of her hair.

When at last the word passed that the carriage was seen turning at the road, and the servants made haste to assemble outside to greet the new baron, Emily made certain to take up her station before anyone else could claim that place. She spared a brief moment of pity for the bride, who was, in spite of her elegance, content to stand between the dowager and Harriet in a dull corner, and then the noise of arrival caused Diggory to open the door to announce his master.

Emily put on her most serene smile, her hand lifted in a graceful appeal—but then she stopped, thoroughly nonplussed: the man who stepped inside his house was Henry indeed, but with a bandage wrapped around his eyes.

She stared, her wits flown.

Anna had also dressed with care because she always dressed with care. She had seen the terrible aftermath of battle, and her expectation was of a man weakened and in need of nursing. She and Parrette had gone round the baronial rooms, discussing what might be best for him: which room was the warmest? The quietest? Anna's own private thought was, *Where shall I sleep?* But she could not bring herself to voice it.

She had spent time living in his family, his house, and his country. Now, at last, she was to be reunited with the man himself, and here he was, being led by Perkins, who was almost unrecognizable in the correct garb of a valet, save for that wooden leg.

Her heart beat fast as Henry entered on Perkins's arm. He was thinner than she remembered the bones of his face above and below the eye-bandage strongly pronounced. Most surprising, even unsettling, was that instead of the uniform she had always seen him wear, he was dressed in the correct garb of a gentleman, though his blue cutaway coat was similar in shade to his captain's coat.

The tide of warmth glowed through her. "Good afternoon, Lord Northcote," she said, her voice betraying a tremor.

Everyone there saw his face lift, and pale, and then flush. "You are here," he said, reaching with one hand, his smile wide and boyish.

Anna stepped forward to close her fingers around his hand. "I am here."

Twenty-nine

HENRY DUNCANNON HAD WOKEN from his coma to discover that he had lost his command, and gained a title.

The latter need not necessarily have precluded the former. There were titled officers aplenty in the navy; of late, in fact, there had been an effort made to promote from the upper ranks of society, the reasoning being that like served better with like, and that the seamen all loved a lord.

Henry Duncannon did not pretend to agree. A good officer might spring through the hawse hole, as the saying went — promotion of a topmast jack whose intellects made him quick to learn and ambitious brought excellent officers into being.

But this title appeared to no longer matter. One of his earliest visitors had been Lord Collingwood, whose voice had betrayed exhaustion as he informed Henry that the *Aglaea* was wanted for other duties. There were not nearly enough whole ships for everything that must be done, so he had promoted the deserving Lt. Sayers and dispatched him to watch the French again.

He finished, "And so my last order to you, by rights, is entirely informal, but no less important. Your duties lie at home at present. You are to recover your health, and put your affairs in order." He had added gruffly, after a short pause, "You will not be surprised to hear that rumor has it your brother saw fit to leave things in lamentable state."

Sayers visited briefly before departing.

"My wife?" Henry asked at the end of their conversation about service matters.

"As you desired, she was sent to England."

"To England," Henry repeated, the sudden splash of happiness taking him by surprise.

"Was that not right? You said to send her home," Sayers responded. "I recollect it distinctly."

Henry's mouth quirked sardonically, and there was the old captain again. "You have done very well," was all he said, but internally, he reflected — not for the first time — on the many stupid years during which he resentfully considered 'home' to be where his sea chest resided. "Thank you," he added. "I know you have been hard pressed, and I will not keep you the longer."

The creak of wood, a shift of a boot, and Henry knew he was hearing Sayers rise and pick up his hat.

What more was there to say? Sayers wished to be gone, exactly as he himself had done on his first appointment. The new captain wanted to be doing, perhaps to win a prize, now that, at last, his own marriage looked to be in the offing.

So they shook hands, and the last he heard of Sayers was his quick step in departure.

After that he must possess his impatience. Sayers might have sent Anna to England, but after his own scrub-like treatment of her, Henry would not have blamed her a jot for taking his fortune and haring off to Italy, or Sweden, or anywhere else in the world but Yorkshire.

But here he was, back at the house he had sworn once never to set foot in again.

Everything had changed. It was now *his* house, his estate. Its affairs were his responsibility. His family was here, only grown older (Harriet sounded quite grown up, something he would have thought an impossibility), his mother wept...and then came that low, beautiful voice, the French accent pronounced, *Good afternoon, Lord Northcote.*

For a moment the vertigo was back, worse than those first few days. *Lord Northcote* was his father, his brother...and *she* was here.

He sustained a sharp desire to hear her lips shape the words

'Captain Duncannon' again, and he almost laughed. He was not aware of reaching until her fingers closed around his hand, and he heard the soft rustle of feminine fabrics, and smelled the faint, elusive perfume he remembered so well.

Before he could find the wit to speak, another remembered voice shocked him, "Welcome home, Henry."

He stilled, the joy vanishing like smoke. "Emily," he said.

Emily, Anna heard again, and recollected that morning in the captain's cabin before the storm struck. Her heart beat painfully.

The dowager had been watching. She heard the flatness of her son's voice on that word—*Emily*—and stepped between Emily and her son, then reached to touch his free hand. "Henry, dear, we have the tea things waiting. Are you hungry at all?"

His stomach was unsettled, and his head ached abominably. Rocking in a coach from which nothing could be seen had rendered him far more ill than ever the sea had in all its moods. But, like sea sickness, he was certain that taking something would subdue the sensations. Besides, if his mother had gone to this trouble, he must acknowledge it; he knew that he had amends to make, and might as well begin now. "Thank you. I am sharp set."

"Good. Cook has put a vast deal of effort into dishes that should please you, though in course we do not know what you prefer anymore. What kinds of foods did you eat on your ship? You must tell us all about it…"

With Anna on one side and his mother on the other, Henry walked, distracted from his mother's gentle words by familiar sounds, and above all, familiar smells. How that furniture polish brought it all back!

Emily closed in behind, scolding herself out of the shock, and the disappointment, of those bandaged eyes. It was not as if she had not known. Though he disclosed little else, the foreigner had made it plain that he had suffered a head wound that affected his vision. But in Emily's mind wounds passed off in a day or two, the way a rose thorn prick faded under a bit of plaster.

She followed the three who walked arm in arm, Henry appearing taller than she had remembered, his features from what she could see more planed, with a terrible scar down one cheek. The dowager was understandably delighted to receive her son once again, but there had been an unexpected alacrity in her advance. What had she meant by that?

Harriet, watching from where she had sat on the bottom stair, chin on her fingers, elbows on knees, eyed Emily, remembering bits of conversations, angry looks, and the terrible day Henry departed, vowing never to return. She had been a child, with little understanding. She had always thought he had left because of John's temper, though she had known about the broken understanding. Had it been *more* than an understanding? Whom could she ask? No one here would talk to her...

"Nurse," she breathed, and pelted upstairs.

Confound this bandage!

Henry had endured it as a necessity, but the moment he stepped into the familiar sounds and scents of his home, he was nearly overmastered by the desire to rip the thing free.

But he must wait. The physician in London had said not before March, or he could not answer for the result.

He needed to see their faces: his mother, whose voice trembled, Harriet, who sounded so grown, Emily, who sounded unchanged. But above all he must see his wife. His wife! Those brief days aboard his ship seemed a dream.

He possessed what patience he could muster as the familiar voices made conversation on topics such as the weather, the state of the roads, and the doings in London in preparation for the holidays.

"When your health permits," Emily said, "my brother and father will extend an invitation to dine. They talk of nothing else besides the glorious victory, and wish to hear every detail from one who was there. And if," she added, "I may be permitted to add, they are not the only ones."

"You did not ask my wife?" Henry said.

There was a slight pause, and Henry was possessed again of a strong wish he could see the circle of faces.

Then Anna spoke in her distinctive accent, her voice reminding Henry of the rush of a river, of the rustle of leaves, though that was not quite right, either. It was a pure voice, soothing to the ear. "I could not give them witness. You will remember I saw nothing from where I was placed."

Emily smiled her way. "Of course a lady would be kept safely well away from the exigencies of battle. We did not think anything else."

Henry said, "She was away from battle, but not from the exigencies, as she was a mere deck below the waterline, sewing the ship's people back together again, she and her maid. When I was brought below, they were both there, well covered in gore."

His mother gave a tiny gasp, and Henry said quickly, "I will forbear anymore description than that. But you must realize that the glorious battle you read about from your comfortable distance is a sanguinary affair, and any *detailed* account is going to make reference to the butcher's bill, that is, the cost in lives. Nelson, long may he be remembered, was not the only casualty."

They responded as he thought they would, demurring, except for Harriet's sigh, "*I* want to hear it."

His mother said, "For my part, I would be glad if you would speak of our beloved Lord Admiral Nelson, before the terrible event. Was he musical?"

"He had a passion for hearing music," Henry said. "I do not know that he played. I can tell you little beyond what was said at captains' conferences, as I served directly under Fremantle. Our frigates were given a different duty, until the very end."

The dowager said, "Thank you, Henry. Perhaps we may continue over dinner? You might remember," her voice trembled again, "that we keep country hours, though you may wish to change that."

Henry said, "Sea captains dine even earlier. Do not change the dinner hour on my account."

The dowager rose, something she had never done before. With dignity strengthened by the return of her son, she said, "Lady Northcote, I am certain that Henry's things have by now been shifted. Shall you take him upstairs so that he has plenty of time to ready himself to dine?" If Emily had hoped to gain a moment alone with Henry, her hopes were dashed when the dowager added, "Henry, the rest of us will remain here by the fire, to stay out of the way if you wish to reacquaint yourself with your home."

Henry rose, hand groping unconsciously. Anna stepped forward quickly to take his arm, and they exited the drawing room.

Neither spoke until he had negotiated the stairway. Once or twice she felt the muscles of his arm tense, and his face lifted as he checked his pace, but before she could speak he walked again.

When they reached the baronial suite, he heard from the rustles and quiet footsteps that there were people in the room. "Perkins?"

"My lord. Your dressing room is this way."

"That can wait." To Anna, "You remember Perkins, do you not? It transpires he was a first footman before he was impressed. I inherited him from the previous captain of *Aglaea*. He has been released from service, so that I could bring him with me. I'd as lief have him to valet than some mincing caper-merchant who will try to stuff me into stays, and cravats two yards wide."

"How do you do, Mr. Perkins?" Anna said.

"Tolerable well, thank you, my lady, tolerable well," he replied.

"Perkins, we will dress for dinner in, say, a quarter of an hour?"

"Aye, sir—that is, aye, my lord."

Perkins had practiced the new address, but habit would obtrude. Annoyed with himself, he motioned to the little housemaid who had brought up the hot water and was busy tending the fire, and they retreated.

Henry waited until he heard the door shut, then he said, with an attempt at humor, "Will you give me leave to call you Anna when we are alone? 'Lady Northcote' is still my mother. Needless to say, I never thought to be brought to this pass."

Anna said, "In truth, I would prefer it, oh, most prodigiously."

He heard a lilt of humor in her soft voice, and smiled. "Thank you. Will you take me around this room, that I may learn where things are? The rest can wait. I am better if I learn a room at a time."

She sprang to comply. At the first chair, he ran his hands over the old-fashioned shape, sniffed, then said with a curious grimace, "This is my father's chair. I am to gather we were given all his old furnishings. Well, well."

They proceeded from there, Henry counting steps under his breath. He interrupted himself from time to time by asking questions. First: "Who gives the orders? I hope that you have begun as I would have you carry on. Though I trust you would consult my mother when possible."

Anna said, "I have been content to leave things as they are while I make a study to learn the custom here, and until I know your wishes."

He paused, his hands feeling over a little table. "There will be a lot of changes. We will begin in here, but I want you to make *your* wishes known. I want you to be comfortable."

"Thank you. Everyone has been most kind."

"Everyone?" He paused, the light on the angle of his cheekbone sharp, his mouth compressed.

Anna could not guess at his mood, but she said, "Your sister, Miss Harriet, has been generous with her time. She has put me in the way of things. Your mother has been most welcoming."

"I am very glad to hear that," he said, noting the absence of Emily's name. He refused to introduce it between them. Things were already devilish awkward, when he could not see anyone's face. "And now, I will try on my own. If you see me about to trip, sing out, but otherwise, I must make my way."

He moved about with a careful, sweeping step that argued a good deal of practice, as he counted to himself. Twice she nearly spoke, but his reaching fingers encountered the obstacles, and he let out a soft, "Hah." And then, "Perkins changes my bandages at night, with only a twist, and I keep my eyes shut as instructed. But there are times when my eyes will open, and I believe I catch a gleam of light beside my nose." He touched one side. "Or it may be only my imagination. There are sometimes quick flashes of light when I would swear my eyes are closed —"

A knock at the door, and here was Perkins again, with Parrette behind him. He expelled his breath, knowing he had not said a single one of the things he had thought up over the endless days lying blind at Gib, and then during the endless journey. It would all have to wait yet again.

They separated into their dressing rooms. Anna lingered in

their salon in case he wished her arm. When he came out, tall and fine in his evening clothes, he carried a wrapped packet in his free hand, which he surrendered to Perkins with a subdued murmur. Then, "Anna?"

"I am here."

They started down the stairs together, Henry counting under his breath.

In the antechamber before the dining room, Henry recognized his brother-in-law's laughing voice. "Frederick," he exclaimed, then felt a warm clasp of his hand.

"Good to see you returned at last, by Jupiter!"

"Mary, are you here as well?"

"Here am I, Henry. And very glad to find you home again."

Harriet spoke close by. "Henry, please let me take you in."

He smiled. "Harriet? If you wish, though I thought that Mother and I might lead the way. Sit near me, that I may hear what you have been about."

Harriet laughed. "That will take all of two moments to relate: nothing, and nothing."

"We shall see about that," he promised, and Diggory, seeing him ready, announced dinner, then opened the door.

Henry felt his mother's thin fingers close around his hand. He listened to the rustle and shuffle as everyone fell in behind; Harriet chattering to Anna about what to expect for dinner, and Frederick wondering aloud to Mary and Emily what they ate aboard ships.

Under cover of their voices, Henry murmured, "I hope that we may talk together later, Mother, but I wanted straight away to apologize to you for my long silence."

Her voice trembled as she whispered, "Oh, my dearest, I quite understand. It was a terrible disappointment..."

His knuckles collided with the back of his chair. He could not see the others and had no intention of having his conversation overheard. He patted his mother's hand. "We will talk again later."

On the beautiful damask tablecloth the Meissen and the Water-ford had once again made their appearance, though Henry could not see them.

Anna, delighting in the beauty, reflected on the fact that she could give the order for these to be seen everyday. The thought gave her pleasure, but she decided that it, like so many matters could wait until she and Henry understood one another better.

Dinner was a long affair. Henry successfully interpreted the servants' welcome by the number and quality of the many dishes served. He tried to eat something of every one, inured by years of service dinners, and he found the lingering headache from the chaise diminishing to bearable proportions.

Frederick introduced the topic of food on shipboard, and they discussed similar matters until, over dessert, Frederick exclaimed, "Hey day, Henry, it's a capital thing, your being back. I hope you mean to stop on?"

Frederick, though closer to Henry's elder brother in age, had been his friend. John had preferred his Eton and London acquaintance, in particular those with money and rank. Though the Elsteads' wealth was by no means trifling, Henry well remembered that Frederick had been kept on short commons (as was he), his mother hoping that he would seek a bride with a larger dowry and more exalted relations than Mary.

But Mary and Frederick had had an understanding from childhood, exactly the same way Henry and Emily had. Or Henry had thought they had. Distinctly recollecting Frederick's honest dismay after Henry discovered that his brother had secretly cut him out, with Emily's willing connivance, *At least I was not altogether the last to find out what everyone else had seen.*

Henry did not reply as he might have. Frederick was not to blame for anything that had happened, but neither had he helped. Frederick, when trouble loomed, was apt at playing least-in-sight.

So Henry said only, "I cannot make any decisions until this bandage comes off. I cannot even attend Nelson's funeral."

Frederick's polite mumble of commiseration—he could not imagine anyone wishing to attend a funeral—was muted by his sister's composed speech. "I believe I speak for us all in admiring your wish to honor the fallen hero, but we may unite in expressing consternation at the idea of your taking such a risk. The crowds no doubt will be vast, and unregulated, made up of mariners and other rude persons. And though many of your peers will be there, indeed, the very number suggests a rational attitude: one more or less will not be missed. You are better safe among us again."

The dowager, whose primary emotion was relief at having her son home again, agreed fervently, echoed by her elder daughter. Anna observed Henry's bent head, the tight line to his shoulders down to his hands, and sensed something amiss. She kept silent.

Frederick said encouragingly into the pause, "And there is plenty to do here. And you know, m'father begged me to say that he will be along to offer any help he might be called upon."

"Such as?"

"Well, he might take on the duties of the J.P. That has rather fallen behind. We were forced to hire a stipendiary magistrate for a year, but all that can wait until Father calls upon you."

Henry was struggling to get a rein on his emotions. From Nelson's funeral to justice of the peace! He had not thought past striving to get to that memorial if he could. But he knew he would not be able to endure the coach ride again, much less the jostling. So it was time to force his attention to the duty before him.

John had taken the place of their father as justice of the peace? Another thing to look into. But he became aware that the clink of eating utensils against porcelain had ceased. He put down his own utensils, and sat back.

The rustle of cloth and the moving of chairs indicated the ladies were rising, and next came the sound of the footmen removing the covers. Henry was left with Frederick, who chattered amiably about the shooting season and similar inconsequentials. Yes, Frederick still seemed to prefer the safety of least-in-sight, and Henry decided not to interrogate him. He would do his own investigations, beginning with John-Coachman, whose opinion he had trusted as a boy.

"Shall we join the ladies?" Henry asked.

Henry did not have to see the company to know that he would be expected to be principal speaker. Diggory brought the packet to him, as instructed. "Permit me to begin by saying that events being what they were, I have not had an opportunity to bring gifts, save this music for the fortepiano. Mother, the top sheets are an arrangement by a German fellow named Beethoven. The sonata is his eighteenth, in case you decide you like him. There are seventeen before it. This one is called The Hunt. If your tastes have not greatly changed, I believe you may like it. The rest are some airs I found in Italy and other ports."

"Henry! You could not have found anything I wanted more! Bless you, dearest."

"Oh, Mother, it is as well you have those spectacles now," Harriet called out.

Henry waited until the exclamations died down. His head panged anew at the sharp voices, the clatter of tea cups and spoons, and he fought to master the annoyance that had followed Emily's complacent words about Nelson's funeral. *One more or less might not be missed.*

She was not to be blamed. Her attitude would be regarded as rational, just as she had said. But there was something he *could* speak about, as soon as he sensed that the servants were out of the room. *Get it over*, he told himself, once convinced the room had cleared. "While I was in London waiting upon tailors, I took the opportunity to consult our man of business."

He waited as his mother exclaimed softly, Harriet sighed with satisfaction, and the infernal clink and clatter halted. He said, "It will come as no surprise that the family's affairs are left in wretched order."

He curbed his patience as everyone had to exclaim or protest yet again. On board ship, no one spoke unless asked a question by their superior officer, and he found himself longing for those days.

His head ached anew, and his temper got the best of him. "I am certain of your expectation that I will execute my duty, as my own inheritance from my great-uncle, the admiral, has lain largely untouched in the funds. I have also been lucky enough to do well in prize money. But I do not intend to throw good money after bad."

The complete silence following these words caused him to wish he could see their faces. Silences, he had discovered, possessed a surprising degree of qualities. He could not quite parse this one now. "Beginning with the sale of that expensive house in Hallam Street," he stated, and inwardly was pleased when he detected a short inward breath that had to come from Emily.

Then Harriet wailed, "Then I am not to go to London again?"

"Harriet, dear," the dowager began nervously.

Henry hated to hear that worry in his mother's voice. "Not at all," he said in Harriet's direction. "Your making your bow to London society was at the forefront of my mind, which occasioned my decision. Handsome as that house might be—I could not see it, but I am assured of that—it was quite unsuitable in every other way."

His voice sharpened. Anna's neck prickled at the undertone of anger that she sensed more than heard, and then gazed in surprise as Emily reddened.

"It appeared that my brother and his wife preferred a house in town that admitted no more than two comfortably, but the place is altogether unsuitable as a *family* house."

Anna gained sudden clarity then: the former baron and baroness had spent time in London, leaving the rest of the family in Yorkshire. With Harriet underage, and their daughters mere babes, it made sense. The question was, had Emily expected to return to London alone this coming spring, if the place was unsuitable for presenting Harriet?

"It should bring an excellent price, and as for your visit to London, Harriet, your Grandmother Dangeau wishes nothing better than to launch you from Cavendish Square."

Emily listened with growing horror, so surprised she forgot to mask her emotions, and Anna thought, *She did. She had expected to return to London on her own.*

In this, she was incorrect: Emily had expected to return with Henry.

He, it seemed, was not done. "That puts me in mind of another thing. Why is it that the stable is crowded with a landau and a park phaeton, besides the family coach and my mother's gig? Where was this newly ordered barouche-landau, which was the first item I was dunned for on my arrival in London, to be fitted?"

Emily said with a calm she did not feel, "It was to be kept in London. I need scarcely point out that they are the fashion nowadays." As Henry's frown only deepened, "And as for selling them off, I did cause to be sold all my husband's carriages and the main of his horses. As for what remains, my thought was only of your wife. A lady must not be perceived to be dowdy. It is positively fatal."

"Am I to understand that my mother is dowdy when she goes about in her gig?" No answer was made to that, and Henry turned in the direction he believed Anna to be sitting. "Do you drive, Lady Northcote?"

"I do not," she said, but her heart smote her at the undisguised shock in Emily's face, and she added, "I would like to learn."

"That can be arranged," Henry said, his voice cool again, his smile strained, curving tightly on one side. "But even after you do, I feel certain you will not be driving three carriages."

Henry stopped himself. Though he had been appalled at just how badly his brother had run the estate into the ground, he knew his response was splenetic, that John was responsible for most of the bad decisions and waste. John had clearly thought only of his own convenience, and perhaps he enjoyed the éclat gained from the spectacle of his beautiful wife driving about in the handsomest equipage, but Henry was certain that Emily was behind the order of that devilishly expensive barouche-landau.

He forced himself to pause, to finish the tea he had not wanted, and then to say, "Perhaps it is best to leave this question for another time. I apologize for my disagreeable mood, caused by tiredness from the long journey."

Everyone rose. He heard Anna's step, smelled her elusive perfume, and then came her quiet voice. "Shall I accompany you upstairs?"

"Please," he said, holding out his arm.

Neither spoke until they reached their sitting room. Her heart had quickened its beat; and she sensed by the angle of his bent head that he was deep in thought.

As for Henry, by then he had had time to thoroughly regret his ill-temper. When he heard the door close, and knew they were alone, he kept her hand in his as he said, "Anna. I beg your pardon. I promise my manners will improve on the morrow."

The morrow. Between that and now was a night.

All his rational, sensible questions went out the window, leaving him standing there blind, painfully aware that he had no experience of courtship whatsoever. And yet he had come to England fully intending to court his wife if he was lucky enough to find her there. She deserved that much.

But he sensed her waiting, and though the back of his neck prickled with embarrassment, he forced himself to get the words out. "We have begun our married life, so to speak? That was not entirely a dream."

'Married life'. As if one night in a swinging cot meant anymore than…one night in a swinging cot. But these were the polite words to be used, she expected, and she guessed in the flat line of his mouth, and the redness of his face below the bandage that he was uncomfortable.

She suppressed the memory of that breathed word *Emily*, and said, "We did."

His voice dropped low. "I—I am so confounded…" He gestured, his fingers tense, his palm up in supplication. "With your permission, I would so rather wait until we can see one another. To begin with one another the right way. I know I was…"

Her fingers closed on his. "You were a ship captain in war. We may wait as long as you wish."

He let out his breath. "Thank you. We have had the damndest beginning, and it's entirely my fault we know too little of one another. But this I apprehend so far, you are a woman of sense, and kindness. Good night." He brought her hand up to his lips and kissed it. Then he lifted his voice. "Perkins?"

The dressing room door opened. "My lord?"

Henry and Anna parted, Perkins leaving the room last and blowing out the candles.

Out in the hall, Emily, who had followed them upstairs after a suitable period, stood where she could observe the glow of light under the separate bedroom doors, and smiled to herself before she passed quietly to her own room.

Thirty

THE NEXT MORNING, ANNA sensed a different atmosphere in the house. She had begun a habit of rising after her room warmed, but that morning she got up before the fire had been lit. She dressed in haste, her breath frosting between her lips as she wrest-led into her clothes. Even those sturdy kerseymere spencer jackets were not warm enough, and she wore her thickest cashmere shawl over all, still shivering, when she went down to breakfast.

Early as she was, she saw by the empty eggshells on a plate being carried out by Ned, the first footman, that Henry had risen long before, and was already gone. She sat down and thanked young Thomas Akers, the second footman who was carefully pouring tea. Of course she ought to have expected that. Early rising being another shipboard habit.

Emily appeared before Anna had drunk her first sip of tea. She was dressed exquisitely—and disappointment tightened her face when she saw only Anna at the table.

But she murmured a pleasant greeting to Anna, and to Harriet, who burst in a minute later, dressed for riding.

Emily stayed only long enough to drink a single cup of tea, then she left. Harriet, alone with Anna, was in tearing spirits. She too rushed through breakfast, then hurried off, pausing only to kiss her mother, and to mutter, "Cicely and I are riding to meet Jane and Thomas Rackham, to ride over to the Colbys'." Where she intended to get a glimpse of Robert Colby.

The dowager smiled cheerfully. Even her spectacles seemed to gleam, in spite of the dull gray light outside. "Pray tender my respects to Mrs. Squire Elstead and Mrs. Rackham, dearest. Where is Henry?"

"I saw him with John-Coachman," Harriet said before she closed the door.

The dowager nodded, and she turned to Anna to ask what she thought Henry might want for dinner.

After breakfast, Anna went upstairs to the schoolroom, where Eleanor was waiting for her. She surprised Harriet there, her hat swinging on her arm by its ribbons, as she spun the baby Amelia about the room, dancing the Boulanger as Justina mimicked her steps. The infant laughed, waving her hands.

Eleanor sat at the side with a put-upon air, but when she perceived Anna, she advanced, all smiles, and they began their lesson.

When they finished, Harriet had gone, and Justina danced around alone, waving her arms. Nurse had Amelia on her lap. Until now, the infant had been either asleep or looked at Anna and cried, which Nurse had said was common with babies presented with a new face.

Perhaps Amelia had seen Anna often enough by now to regard her as familiar, for this time the baby gave Anna a pink-gummed grin, and waved her fists. Anna approached cautiously, uncertain what to do. She held out a hand, and the baby grabbed her finger and tried to convey it to her mouth.

Anna gently freed her finger, looking uncertainly at Nurse, who laughed silently. "That's what they all do, straight to the mouth. You did, too. We all did." She patted the low bench on which she sat. "Come. Take her upon your lap."

Anna obeyed, listening to Nurse's easy voice instructing her. It occurred to her that, just as she gave lessons to Eleanor, she was receiving lessons about infants. Amelia stayed quietly on her lap for a short time, then leaned toward Nurse, arms out, making fretful noises.

While all this was going on, behind the stable, Henry stood next to John-Coachman, whose slow Irish lilt reached back into childhood. John-Coachman had always seemed this enormous, wise older man, but Henry reflected now, there was no sign of age in his voice. When he had been hired at the Manor, and shortly after had thrown Henry onto his first pony, he could not have been much older than Harriet was now.

He had just finished giving Henry a succinct report on the state of the stables. No personal observations, only demonstrable facts.

Most of it Henry knew already from the bills at the solicitor's. There were no surprises, but it was good to have it all corroborated.

He had always trusted John-Coachman's opinions. And so, at the end, he said, "What did happen to my brother?"

A brief silence was followed by the crunch of gravel, as if the coachman shifted position, and then came the slow murmur. "It was given out as an accidental fall while riding. Which was true enough, it was, but you should probably know that he crammed the fence."

Henry winced. "Sounds like my brother never changed. Was the horse damaged?"

"Knees. Chest. I was afraid we might have to shoot him, and sorry I would have been, for Champion is a great-heart, and I had the training of him. Her ladyship would have had him shot, but I could see the welts on his flanks. When I pointed them out, she told me that if he healed, she would sell him off. I did, and she did."

"Did he go to a good stable, at least?"

"Oh, yes. Sir Robert Colby wanted him for his eldest boy, who is a good rider, though at present thinks himself a blood. But he is well up to Champion, have no fear."

"Robert? He was a schoolboy when I left. I cannot picture him in a gaudy waistcoat and pantaloons like some Bond Street beau. *Anno domini*, eh?"

"Will you be riding again, then, my lord?"

"Depends what I find when these damned bandages come off. Thanks, John-Coachman—though I suppose if I am 'my lord' now, it ought to be Mr. Cassidy."

John-Coachman uttered a breath of a laugh. "John-Coachman will do fine. It's an honest living, and I wear the title with pride."

"That's more than I can say for mine, right now." Henry smiled, and gestured to Perkins, who he knew was waiting out of earshot to conduct him back to the house.

Anna and Henry did not see one another until late afternoon (it was already dark, something Anna still was unused to) when they met in their sitting room before readying for dinner.

"Anna," he said, head tilted slightly as he listened.

"I am here, Lord Northcote."

He smiled, then attempted to mimic her accent. "*Nort-cout.* When you say it like that, almost I am resigned to a mantle I never wanted to put on. Will you say my given name?"

She complied, careful with her pronunciation as always, but the result made him smile the wider. "*Onn-ree.* 'Henri' is a fine fellow, who has a flattering word for everyone, and does not miss his hammock. Does not even know what a hammock is!"

Anna could not help laughing. "You would find many Frenchmen disagreeing."

Henry's smile flattened, but he said quickly, "No, I can hear you taking breath to apologize for reminding me. Do not. I cannot see you, but I feel certain I can safely talk to you about what happened at Cape Trafalgar, for you were there. You will know a little of how I feel, how we all feel. The…the elation and the grief, sometimes felt in the same breath."

"Yes," she said, remembering that breathed *Emily*, "I thought it was different for men."

He was sitting back in his chair, looking tired. "Many will insist that it is, but sometimes I wonder how very different our emotions are, underneath the trappings." He flicked his cravat.

Anna was distracted by the single lock of curly dark hair hanging over his bandaged eyes. Her fingers tingled; she wanted to brush it back. But she remembered what he said about waiting until his bandages came off.

And in any case it was not the right moment. He said, "I have heard, as you no doubt did, strong men cry for their mothers while under the surgeon's knife, whereas I have witnessed two women, the wives of a gunner's mate and a bosun respectively, give birth under the worst of circumstances. One during a hurricano, and t'other a difficult breech birth, twins, while we were in the midst of a running battle with a French privateer, and nary a word did either of them say, beyond the necessary." He grimaced slightly. "Perhaps this conversation is better saved until I can see you."

"I will talk to you anytime," she said quickly, coming to his side. "About anything you wish."

"You are not offended at such subjects? I hear all about me that you are a very fine lady."

She gave a little laugh. "After the orlop? As for the fine lady, I do my best to play the role—" She cut herself off, appalled. That was coming far too close to the truth that she had promised not to reveal.

Henry smiled, clearly with no thought of the theater. "You are probably more deedy at your role than I am at mine. But one thing that bolsters my confidence, I might not be able to strut about London like a Bond Street beau in the way my brother did, but already the tangle of family debt is considerably less." He lifted a hand.

"I wanted to talk to you about that," she said.

"Yes?"

"It is the rooms the servants are obliged to live in. Did you know they have no fire, none at all?"

Henry could have retorted, *Any more than we had on shipboard*, but he was ashamed of the thought. "I did not," he said. "I have never been up there. Is it bad, then?"

"Mrs. Diggory did not take me up there. I would not have thought of it either had not Parrette told me. I have been up there since. Their rooms are no bigger than those little corners the lieutenants live in, but these people have to spend their entire lives there. I would like very much to amend that."

"Then we shall do so, come spring." He smiled. "Take your time to plan it any way you wish. Commencing construction before winter begins would convince them my brains were permanently addled."

"Begins?" she repeated, horrified.

Henry laughed ruefully. "I suppose it isn't funny, but you

have no notion of a proper winter, do you? Well, we shall wait a few months, but until then, content yourself with this: I expect that your Parrette, and the others, find ways to warmth or they would not have survived this long. And I can give orders to that effect, to make certain."

The door opened, and Perkins poked his head in. "It wants twenty minutes before the hour, my lord," he said in a faintly accusing tone.

"And Parrette will be awaiting me," Anna murmured, crossing the room to the opposite door.

"We will talk again, after the tea is drunk," Henry said.

"I will look forward to it," she said.

And so it was. Dinner passed pleasantly. Afterward, though the dowager hurriedly suggested music, as if to ward off any unpleasant scenes, there was nothing to hurry for. Henry sat back and listened to his mother play, and Emily sing, with a polite smile. Tea was drunk, and the dowager asked her son if he had any wishes with respect to the holidays.

"I have been gone so long that I am completely out of habit," he said. "Make your plans. Accept what invitations you will on my behalf. You and my wife may arrange it between you. You have only to tell me when to put on my coat and hat, and I shall get myself down to the carriage at your hour."

Emily smiled composedly. Once he had loved her, and his anger over that house on Hallam Street convinced her that he still retained something of that passion.

She had expected him to return to heel when she snapped her fingers, and had been disappointed of that, but on reflection she discovered that Henry was far more interesting now. He had gone out, traveled, fought, and learned to command. He possessed wealth that he had not squandered at the gambling tables, or on his own pleasures.

To crown it all, he made no mention of his dreadful instrument. Nor did he display transports while listening. Another few such evenings, and she was confident that cards might be safely introduced, no, that would not suit, until Henry's bandages came off. She might lead conversation, or find a fashionable book to read aloud, and so a gradual return to a civilized pastime.

The family retired in the best of tempers when they parted for the evening; Henry's head ached, but that ache, it seemed, was his constant companion anymore. At least he was not as weak as he had been those initial, endless days: he had only had to withdraw once to lie quiet for a time.

Henry was proud of all he'd managed to get done in spite of his weakness. When Anna entered their sitting room, he told her about his day: after his tour of the stables he had met with Pratt, the gardener, promising that all his hirelings were to be brought back.

He had also, with Perkins' help, begun to sort through the sheaf of bills flung into the escritoire.

"It is as well I had London to prepare me," he said grimly. "My brother had not paid his tailor in a year, and yet the week before he died he had sent to order another two dozen shirts. When would he have time to wear them all? I cannot say these things before my mother, of course, because John was her son, too, and though *she* never played favorites, bless her, she must feel his loss. Only a blackguard would speak publicly as I speak safely in private now. If I do not say anything, it festers like a bad wound, and as you never knew him, it cannot mean anything. Am I right? What do you say? I wish I could see you."

Anna sat down next to him. "I say that I agree it is better to speak. And you may speak freely to me, which cannot hurt those who knew this brother I never met. How does your head?"

He sighed. "It is better than it was." Hating himself for complaining, he said wryly, "At least until I sit down at that desk again, and Perkins reads me those bills. Stay. I had a thought." Instinctively he turned toward her, though the damn bandage was ever-present. "Will you read 'em to me? I got in the habit of having Perkins read my mail to me, but he is slow and mispronounces anything that might be French. If I hear your accent, perhaps I will not be so irked at yet another creditor clamoring for his due for things that never ought to have been ordered."

"I should be happy to be of use," Anna said sincerely.

And so the rest of the week passed in this manner. Henry and

Anna took up their station in the library, where she could be heard reading out bills and letters to him. He vanished to his room to lie down in the afternoons, when she would get her walk, if the weather permitted. She also continued Eleanor's lessons, and learned to play pat-a-cake and peek-a-boo with baby Amelia, who seemingly never tired of these games.

On Sunday, Henry was first seen at church, his bandage giving him an air of interest and even heroism, so everyone agreed afterward. And Mrs. Bradshaw gained a great deal of pleasure when the new Lord Northcote and his lady spent time talking of their Beverly, and his bravery in battle, to her and her family outside the church, where they could be seen by everyone in the parish.

When it came time to leave, Harriet waited with bated breath to hear what Penelope would do. Indeed, the elder Miss Duncannon set about directing them exactly as before, as if she had come to the conclusion that a bandaged head meant wounded intellects.

But upon hearing her telling Caro and Harriet where to sit, Henry said in a strong voice, "What is this? Seven in this confounded coach? Pen, where is your own carriage?"

A pause, and Penelope said, "Your mother has most generously taken pity on two poor spinsters who cannot afford to be profligate—"

"Nonsense," Henry cut in, demonstrating that interrupting might very well be a family trait. "Not six days ago I sat in the solicitor's office going over the quarterly expenses. You are very well to pass, very well indeed. You could afford a coach and six."

"But...Sunday...there is nothing to be found," Penelope began in a grating, accusatory tone. "How are we to get home?"

Henry made a curious wry grimace. "Then John-Coachman will be put to the trouble of having to go back for you, to carry you to Whitstead. I trust by next week you will have arranged your affairs better." He touched his hat. "Good day to you." He bowed slightly in Penelope's direction and climbed into the carriage, leaving her standing beside it, stiff with fury.

No one said anything until the door was shut. The dowager gazed at her son, a little frightened, but not unpleased: she had been bullied by Penelope since her marriage, and until now, no one had thought to say anything at all to the deceased baron's eldest daughter.

Harriet exclaimed, "Poor Caro! She will have to bear the worst of Penelope's tongue. Especially if they sit down to no dinner."

"Why would they not have a cold dinner, like everyone else? Has that changed while I was at sea?" Henry asked, his lips thinning as the carriage began to roll and sway.

"They were used to come with us," the dowager said. "If John-Coachman carries them back to Whitstead, they will have no way to come to church again, and I am very sure Penelope will not have ordered a cold dinner."

"Penelope and Caro come to the Manor of a Sunday? What start is this?" Henry asked.

"After John's fall," Harriet said. "Penelope *would* come, and Mama did not like to say anything."

Henry considered that, turned his head slightly toward Anna, who he knew by her scent was seated at his right, and murmured in French, "I did not think my brother would have put up with that. The only thing he and Penelope shared besides a father was a cordial hatred for one another." And, "Do *you* wish for her to be invited to the Manor?"

The only person there who did not follow the quick words was Harriet, who had ever been impatient of lessons; why learn French when that nation seemed destined to be at war with everyone forever?

Emily, who did comprehend, also understood that he meant it to be a private conversation.

"I feel for Miss Caro Duncannon," Anna finally said.

Henry turned his head. "Is that why you suffered their presence of a Sunday, Mother?"

"It is Sunday, and Penelope was so certain it was correct, given mourning," the dowager said nervously.

Emily waited—and Henry said, "Emily?"

It was the first time he had spoken to her since the night of his arrival. She said composedly, "At first I tried to remonstrate with her, for she upset your mother so, but she informed me that she had grown up in that house and had more right to it than I did, unless my child was a son." She spoke in her sweetest, most peace-making tone, and waited for his response.

But there was none. The last little distance was traversed in silence. After the ladies climbed out, skirts held well up over the pooling water, Henry said, "John-Coachman!"

"My lord."

"Pray return to the church for the Miss Duncannons, and carry them to Whitstead."

"Yes, my lord."

"Thank you. Anna, your arm?"

He felt the press of her fingers, and pulled her arm against him so they could match pace. He waited until he heard the others' footsteps diminish toward the house. Behind, the noise of the carriage going back up the drive also diminished, and he said in a low voice, "I do feel sorry for my half-sister, but Caro is a grown woman. She made her choice to stay single, it seems."

"To stay single?" she repeated, understanding some things. "Are you certain it was not decided for her?"

Henry frowned in the direction of the house, breathing deeply in the frosty air. "What do you mean by that?"

"Your sister told me a very little, but also there is what I have witnessed. Every Sunday I have observed her talking to Dr. Blythe. I know she does work for charity, but the way he looks after her when Miss Duncannon summons her away..." Anna halted herself. "I think...perhaps I ought not to speak of persons I know so little," she finished contritely.

"Speak anything you like. *I* cannot see. The devil fly away with this bandage! You have no notion how abominable it is, this not seeing. My hands are going numb. I need better gloves. Are you cold? Let us go inside." They began walking again, Anna matching his pace, Henry mindfully taking shorter steps. They fell into rhythm. Presently he murmured, "So that did *not* pass off."

"Pass off?"

Henry twitched as he instinctively began to look about him, then uttered a sharp sigh. "Let us go into the book room," he said as he fought to curb his impatience. "Where we may speak in peace."

Anna nearly laughed, thinking that he could speak in peace anywhere he wished in that enormous house, but she understood. He would conduct this conversation in privacy, and without unduly disturbing the rest of the family.

So she thanked Thomas Akers, the second footman, who closed the door behind them and carefully helped Henry out of his greatcoat. Thomas departed with coat and hat, and Anna and Henry moved to the library, which had not been lit. Anna could not see very well in the dim room, but she pulled her shawl closer around her and sat in one of the vast wingchairs.

Henry leaned back. "Where was I? My sister Caro. I was a boy when all this happened. If you know aught of boys, you can imagine how little interest I took in the matter, save I was fond of Caro, who unlike Pen was kind to us as children. And I always held Blythe in great respect."

"He seems a good man," Anna said.

"He is. He's no sanctimonious piffler. I've met 'em. One of my Dangeau cousins, butter wouldn't melt in his mouth, but he's the worst gambler I've met with, and a skirt-chaser as well. I wonder what his sermons are like? But he wouldn't write 'em. He undoubtedly either buys them or gets them from our mutual great-uncle, the bishop. But I digress. Blythe came to Barford Magna directly he took his degree. I believe his father is a knight. There is nothing amiss with his birth, but coming from an enormous family, he has little private means. No more than fifty pounds a year, if I recollect."

Anna had only begun to understand English money, but she thought that one could live very well on fifty pounds a year, if one were careful.

Almost as if he heard her thought, Henry said, "Leastways, you cannot raise a family on it and maintain your position. More to the point, my father believed that he couldn't, even with the tithe share."

"Tithe share," Anna repeated. "I do not understand."

"Dr. Blythe is a rector, no mere clergyman. The tithe comes directly to the rector. But that was not good enough for my father, and I do recollect his towering rages over the matter, which were matched and raised by Pen's wrath at the disgraceful prospect of a younger daughter being married before the elder. She would never be able to hold up her head again, Caro would be forever put down as fast and on the scramble, the entire family would be positively steeped in scandal. I don't know how true it is, as I never expected to have to—"

He paused, put his head back, then his voice changed. "One thing I can say for certain is that the only thing my father hated worse than poverty was scandal. Blythe's request for her hand was turned down, and that was the end of it. I had assumed that twenty years must have changed things, but if he's been faithful all these years..."

Again his voice had changed. He struck his hands to his knees. "Well, at all events I had planned to call on him in the next week or so." He was aware that his courtship had been abysmally lacking so far, and in a softened tone he asked, "Should you care to go with me?"

"I would, thank you."

"Good. You can drive me, which will free up—no, you said you do not drive, did I hear right? Would you care to learn? You might enjoy tooling about, once you have become more familiar with the place."

"I would, oh, very much."

"I will speak to Noll. He's a bit slow. You have to have patience with him. Something happened when he was small, and he was nearly despaired of, until the Cassidys took him in. This was before John-Coachman's wife died. They raised Noll with their son, who is second mate on an Indiaman, and doing very well for himself. I used to see him now and again when we and the India fleet met in ports. At any rate, Noll's very good with horses, and you may trust him completely."

"Thank you," Anna said, both charmed and apprehensive at the idea of taking the reins herself.

Then he said, "I mean to put in every effort to get affairs settled before this pox-cursed bandage comes off my head, that when I can see again, I may put to sea with the comfort of knowing my duty here was done."

His silhouette shifted as he swung to his feet, a hand outstretched. "It's cold in here, is it not? And probably not lit. You must speak up. No one wishes to sit in the dark. Would you prefer to go somewhere warmer?"

Thirty-one

ANNA'S FIRST REACTION ON hearing his intention had been surprise, followed by a sharp sense of disappointment.

But then she scolded herself.

Of course he would return to the sea. She remembered the sight of him on his quarterdeck, smiling up at the set of the sails. The sea was his first love. Everything else was duty.

She was not certain of her own feelings about these tidings. That warmth was present each time she saw him, but she had learned enough not to trust that sensation, pleasing as it was, nor was she convinced that *he* felt it.

She was pretty certain now that she knew who his "Emily" was. Anna refused to let her mind follow the paths of jealousy. Nothing in life so far had led her to believe that any good at all came out of jealousy promptings. Henry and Emily had certainly known one another when very young. They had probably been attached; whatever he had felt that night after the long battle, his initial wounds, and the burial of his men, must be put down to fever and tiredness. She understood it, and could forgive it.

But she must know for certain that he wanted *Anna* to wife.

And if that happened, she must remember that in the world of the sea, his chosen world, captains regularly left their wives behind for those long cruises.

As the succeeding days sped by, the household began by degrees to reflect the Christmas season. At first Anna was scarcely able to perceive the signs. For her, the cold encroached as steadily as the darkness, every day earlier. There was little sign of Christmas to be found, or at least Christmas as she had remembered as a child in Naples: the bright, warm sun, the music everywhere, and the Strada Toledo turned into a magical fair, with fruit festooned around the king of arbor in the street. All the shops decorated with gilt and ribbons and patterns to delight the eye.

Here, the season was sedate, but she began to observe a brightening in individuals, even if there was little in the way of decoration.

From Pratt, the gardener, to Mrs. Diggory, the servants moved about with an air of purpose; the days of straitened commons and making do had passed. Henry had indeed given orders for a room to be cleared downstairs and a fire lit for the servants until they retired at night.

In her first interview with the new lord, Mrs. Diggory had been given *carte blanche* to hire back those servants who were needed to restore the house to what it had been, and she meant to live up to the trust his lordship placed in her.

"He's no fool, Master Henry as was," she said to her particular friend, Mrs. Pillbury, the housekeeper at Colby Hall, as they sat in the latter's sitting room over their tea and buttered scones. "*He* knows what's o'clock. It's that being a ship captain, Diggory says, and I think he is right. He was used to watching over those seamen, and if there is a worse parcel of rogues than sailors, I hope never to witness them. Eagles an't in it! What's more, if he don't know a thing, he is not afraid to ask, and he listens to a body when she tells him how it's always been done."

The first snow to stick on the ground fell a few days later, developing rapidly to a blizzard that by Christmas Eve left a white world, clear as glass and shockingly cold.

It was the day of the Elsteads' ball. Parrette, put on her mettle, had made certain that Anna would stand out in pale peach silk, with an overskirt draped crosswise from the high waist, and embroidered from the waist down to the hem and all the way around in gold, green, and crimson figures of Egyptian birds.

Crimson glittered at her neck and ears, and in her simple but elegant headdress, woven in among her high-dressed curls. Harriet, too, knew she was looking her best in white muslin beautifully draped and artfully embroidered with flourishes of cherry blossoms and leaves. When she met Anna at the stairs, she exclaimed, "Oh, you look beautiful! Are those rubies?"

Emily, coming in behind as they gathered in the foyer, heard Anna laugh. "No! I own no rubies, or even diamonds. These are mere trinkets, garnets set in filigree. My father bought them for my mother."

"They are a lot prettier than most ruby necklaces I have seen," Harriet began enviously. "Not that I have seen that many. But, I did not know Henry was so tight-fisted. Has he not given you any jewels at all? Not even a wedding band?" she added belatedly, noting Anna's bare hands as she pulled on her gloves.

"My wedding band was lost in the orlop aboard the *Aglaea*," Anna said lightly. "And you must recollect that your brother has spent most of his time at sea, where I am certain there is a dearth of jewels to be had, even if he wished for them."

"Well, at all events, I think those will be thought the prettiest things in the room, even if they are garnets," Harriet said generously, and then broke off as Perkins brought Henry downstairs.

The snow squeaked under the wheels as the family rode toward the Groves for the Elsteads' ball. Of the family only Harriet anticipated the revelries with uncomplicated emotions. Her ambitions therefore reached no higher than dancing every dance, as this was considered a family event, and therefore practice for the girls not yet out.

Anna quieted her own apprehensions about not knowing English dances beyond the minuet by reflecting that Henry of course must sit out, therefore she must. No one would have the least interest in her as a partner.

Emily's anticipation was entirely taken up with her ambitions.

She had engaged Frederick to dance with the new Lady Northcote to make certain (she said) that the lady had a good time at her first ball in Barford Magna. Where Frederick led, Emily knew, many of the young men followed, Providence only knew why; and in the meantime, he was too simple to reflect that if Lady Northcote was kept busy on the ballroom floor, there would be more time for Emily to devote to laying Henry's ruffled plumage.

All went at first as she planned. The house was full, decorated with holly boughs and all the potted plants in the conservatory that her mother had insisted on building as a bride, because she had been impressed with the greenhouses at Chatsworth on her single visit.

Henry was welcomed by all, and conducted by Mrs. Squire Elstead to the best chair in the place. Emily was pleased at how handsome he looked—even the bandage bestowed an interesting air upon him. That scar marring one side of his face could be ignored if one took care to sit upon his other side, but at least he was not rendered hideous by a missing limb. She only hoped that when the bandage came off, whether he saw or not, there would be nothing to disgust in the appearance of his eyes.

Because his father was too stout to dance, Frederick was to lead out the foreigner as principal woman of rank. Emily turned down two offers, claiming her widowhood was too soon for dancing, and watched complacently as her brother approached Lady Northcote.

Then everything fell apart when the lady responded, "I do not know your dances. All I can perform is the minuet."

"But we begin with the minuet," Frederick said, laughing. "My mother would think nothing of a ball that began with anything else."

Harriet took Anna's hand. "Why did you not speak up? Of course there was mourning, but... Well, at all events, as for the country dances, why, there is nothing easier! If you can do the steps, then you just watch everyone around you, and you'll have the figures."

Anna laughed. "So! If you will teach me, I will be happy to learn."

"Then we shall commence following the minuet. Cicely! Come

help me. You shall call, since this is your house."

Emily watched her own sister come readily to Harriet's imperious beckon, exactly as she had since they were small, no matter how hard she had tried to break her sister of the habit. Cicely and Frederick were entirely too biddable, but at least their docility served well now.

She turned away, losing interest, so she missed the moment that Robert Colby, newly returned from his season in London and his extended stay among people of rank, glimpsed Harriet Duncannon for the first time in four years.

Robert had come to lead, and to be admired for his knowledge of the latest idiom, the latest dances and plays, and the excellence of his London tailor. He had not expected to discover his old friend Thomas Rackham taller than he by at least a hand.

But, he saw on entering the Elsteads' ballroom, there was not a decent waistcoat in the place, the cravats were as laughable as those old codgers still powdering their wigs. He fully expected to amaze the girls he had grown up with, and indeed, pretty little Cicely Elstead was staring at him in a gratifying way, but who was that elegant girl with squint-eyed Jane Rackham?

She turned—Harriet Duncannon? Her flapping braids had somehow been knitted up into something very like the way the girls wore their hair at Almack's, and her gown was somehow the nicest in the place, excepting only for the married women. She was laughing in the old style, but it was different. *She* was different, vastly changed in a way he could not have predicted.

Their eyes met, Harriet dipped her head…and then, before Robert could make his leg and claim the first dance, she imperiously beckoned to Thomas.

Perforce Robert turned to Cicely with a smile and an affect of carelessness as the line formed behind Frederick Elstead and the stunning baroness that everyone had been talking about.

Ignoring the dancers completely, Emily advanced on Henry, to discover him in conversation with her own father, Dr. Blythe, and Sir Robert Colby.

She changed direction, sighing with impatience, and glanced at the dancers in order to avoid elbows and knees. Of course Lady Northcote performed beautifully in the minuet. Emily had expected nothing else, and finding Mary Elstead at hand, whiled away the tedium in talking nothings.

When the country dances began, Henry was lost entirely from view by a tight circle of broad blue and green and brown coats, as the men surrounded him to chatter about that tiresome war: she heard "Nelson," "Wellesley," and "India."

In the center of the room, the elegancy of the ordered dance had fast turned into a romp as the younger girls coached the foreign woman in the steps of the country dances.

Anna was relieved to discover that the basic steps were little different than similar dances in France. It was the patterns that had altered. But those, she could follow, and Cicely began to call.

Emily watched derisively as the dance reeled, turned, came together, weaving circles and squares and lines two by two, the foreign woman moving with a grace that caught the eye. Cicely and her friends all danced on their toes, the newest fashion, one Cicely had gained at her school and passed on to her friends. But they were not nearly as assured as Lady Northcote, who seemed to float. Almost the only ones not watching, besides the inveterate whist players, were Henry with his bandaged eyes, Dr. Blythe, and Emily's father, *still* talking away at Henry, while he downed what appeared to be his fifth or sixth glass of wine punch.

Emily turned her gaze back in time to see Anna execute a pretty *rigadaun*, as perfect as any opera dancer.

Emily stilled. Was that it? What if Anna Ludovisi, whose connection to a duke Emily still did not believe, had become an opera dancer? She had no jewels—knew nothing of English dances—but she could discuss all the details of opera.

Bitter fury surged through Emily. She knew it was entirely fancy, that she was putting together clues out of airy nothing, but at the same time she could not but reflect it would be just *like* Henry to marry his mistress out of hand, just to spite Emily, newly widowed and helpless.

Except that the marriage was apparently some years old.

And even if the foreigner *were* an opera dancer, she would not be the first low woman married by a nobleman.

Enough foolish air-dreaming. It was time to rescue Henry from those old bores. Gratitude would be the first step toward regaining his devotion.

But before she took a step, her mother caught her eye, and beckoned insistently. Emily was forced to comply, convinced that her mother's imperious gesture had got half the room watching.

On the floor, the dance ended.

Anna cast a glance toward Henry, who continued to appear well occupied with his old friends. Yet as the third dance formed up, she thought she might have seen that wry smile he sometimes wore.

She was distracted by the appearance of large, smiling Mrs. Rackham, who came up while Anna was standing in the middle of the line opposite the silent Thomas Rackham. "Lady Northcote, I believe I scarcely need say anything, for it is clear that you are a fast learner. But if you should wish to practice, I have the dancing master twice monthly, and all the young people are in the habit of coming to us. We make up a little party of it. I play to them, and they are able to make their mistakes where no one but us can see them, and become accustomed to company manners. I can heartily assure you that you would be most welcome."

"I should be grateful, oh, much," Anna said. "But if this is a regular party, will I not be seen as the intruder?"

Mrs. Rackham, clad in a gorgeous half-dress of yellow over green silk, shook with laughter, her diamond ear drops shimmering in the brilliant light. "Not the least! A married woman will not have her head turned when I say that the very young gentlemen are all agreed in admiring Lady Northcote, my son among 'em."

Anna understood at once that Tom Rackham, he of the high shirt points, danced mumchance not out of boredom, but shyness. She remembered the midshipmen, how boisterous and tender-hearted they were by turns, manfully taking on responsibilities that one would think too old for them, and in the next moment skylarking in the upper rigging. Manhood, she thought, was as difficult to define as womanhood—or wifehood.

Mrs. Rackham, finding the hitherto silent Lady Northcote both agreeable and conversable, stood back as Anna and Tom danced down the line, and when the music ended, carried her to her own friend, Lady Ashburn, whose pale locks Anna had glimpsed in church. Though nothing direct was said, the women conveyed through hints that the senior Lord Northcote had disagreed with Sir William Ashburn over a question of enclosure, a disagreement that his son had inherited along with his land.

That appeared to explain why the Ashburns were not part of the circles of calls. Anna found the lady's slow voice pleasant on the ears, becoming animated only when the question of the school was raised. She wished the children to be taught music. "So useful as well as pleasant, and my father always said it was excellent discipline."

Anna nodded and agreed, distracted by another glimpse at Henry, and the increasingly wry smile thinning his lips as he listened to Squire Elstead talking.

On the other side of the room, Mrs. Squire Elstead had delivered herself of a lengthy scold at Emily for being so obvious about watching Henry. "....and I must tell you that I witnessed every cat in the room looking your way. Even that muttonhead Mrs. Rackham. *Nothing* could be more fatal!"

Emily blushed in vexation, and when her mother finally paused for breath, said in a low, furious voice, "And so you are busy goggling at me while Papa is on his sixth glass of punch. And won't the evening end well if he falls down in the middle of the dishes?"

She walked away, looking for the least objectionable person to talk to as her mother rustled away.

The foreigner was now with fat Mrs. Rackham, talking away to that vulgar Augusta Ashburn, whose wealthy father had been the very tea merchant to find a place for John-Coachman's son on one of his ships. Probably Henry's wife could not even hear Augusta Ashburn's Manchester accent; the woman should not have been invited, but Emily knew her mother was cultivating the Ashburns in case Cicely could do no better than their Bartholomew.

Disgusted with her mother, with the whole dreary set, Emily walked to the corner opposite the musicians, where she engaged Mrs. Aubigny in conversational French, taking care to keep her back to the room. Let anyone dare to say she was hanging on Henry's coat sleeves now!

Though Anna and Henry were still on opposite sides of the

room, their conversational partners were both distracted as the footmen brought in fresh punch.

Anna saw Mrs. Squire Elstead take her husband's arm and walk him away, leaving Henry alone at last.

Anna moved quickly to Henry's side. "Are you quite well? There is punch just bringing in. Shall I fetch you a cup?"

His breath hissed out. The noise had become insupportable; Squire Elstead's voice resembled the buzzing of bees, while every barking laugh stabbed through his nerves as merciless as that first splinter wound. "Anna." He lifted a hand, and she touched his fingers. He clasped her hand. "Who is by?" he murmured.

"There is no one near us," she whispered.

"My head aches abominably," he admitted. "Can you get me out without causing a to-do?"

"Give me a moment." Anna moved away. How did one summon the carriage? It was time for her to learn these things.

She avoided the line forming for punch, and made her way to the side table bearing the plates of little cakes. A silent man in livery stood behind the table. Anna said to him, "Could you summon our coach to the front, without raising notice?"

He bowed, caught the eye of a young footman circling about collecting cups, whispered, and the boy vanished with his tray through a discreet door.

Unnoticed by anyone, Anna and Henry left the ball and soon climbed into the carriage, where he sank back. The flickering light of the lanterns set outside the windows caught the gleam of sweat above the bandage on his high brow.

Henry grimaced as the coach jerked and began rolling. His hand groped for hers, and she took his fingers in her gloved hands. "I'm fairly well scuppered," he admitted in a husky voice.

"Then we shall get you home," she promised.

Home.

The word came out so easily, so naturally. The sensation behind her ribs was too profound for happiness; it almost hurt, and she was aware that she could not be happy while Henry was in distress. Tears stung her eyes, not of grief but a poignant wonder, and she held his hands, and he hers, as they rode in silence.

When they reached the Manor, Henry stirred. "I survived. A month ago I could scarcely sit up without reaching for a basin," he said. "Riding in a coach throws me back to those evil days. Will you walk me upstairs?"

Anna said, "Of course." She nodded her thanks to John-Coachman, who shut the door and climbed up on the box to return to the Squire's house, as Anna and Henry moved slowly inside.

As soon as Perkins's step was heard, Henry said, "I am in dire want of a dose."

"I shall fetch the tincture at once, my lord," Perkins said.

Henry sank into his chair. "Anna, are you still here?"

"I am."

"I shall soon be asleep. I detest laudanum. It always seemed the nostrum for the weak, and it leaves my head foggier than this confounded crease in my skull. But I find I cannot sleep when this devilish ache is on me." He leaned his head back. "I thought I was ready for such an entertainment. Nothing to do but sit! I would enjoy the musicians, at least, but I had counted without the noise. Everyone talks above the music, and every clink and clatter..." He pressed one hand to the side of his head.

So that is what that odd smile is, Anna was thinking, as Perkins came in with a bottle and a tiny glass on a tray. *Pain.*

"I mean to get these thoughts out before the laudanum renders me speechless," Henry said after he swallowed his dose. "I had thought to talk to Caro and Blythe together, but I had forgotten that though my sisters would be invited, Penelope would refuse for them both. Perhaps it is as well. A public gathering is no place for such a conversation."

He thumbed his eyebrow ridge through his bandage, then dropped his hands. "Did you enjoy yourself?"

"Very much."

The laudanum was beginning to dissipate the worst pain, but his tongue felt thick. "As well, because at week's end you will be expected to preside here. The New Year's ball is an old tradition. My mother enjoys it. I might put in my appearance, then retire. D'you object?"

"Not at all," Anna said. "You must do what suits your constitution best. I find I would very much like to learn how to arrange such a diversion, and I know your mother and Harriet will show me how to go on." She spoke without thinking; she thought about saying something complimentary with regard to Emily, but the time had passed for it to sound natural. It would be too awkward, or worse, she might draw attention to an inadvertent lapse that she had not intended.

So as Perkins helped his master to his feet, she wished Henry good night and withdrew, shutting the door noiselessly behind her.

The New Year's Ball was accounted a great success by all who fought their way through snowdrifts to attend. Anna was aware that she *could* be enjoying herself, though she was too aware of a new situation to truly enjoy it. Instead she experienced the success of seeing people well amused.

The dowager exerted herself to entertain the older guests. Emily presided with calm assurance over the ballroom—having privately resolved to permit no one to see her glancing once Henry's way—and Harriet marshaled the younger people in an endless series of games that involved quick wits and a great deal of laughter.

Anna moved about looking serene, safe in the knowledge that Henry had been seen to his rooms not long after welcoming the last guest.

At midnight she stole upstairs, and finding Henry in the sitting room, awake and restless, she offered to read from Graineville's *Le Dernier Homme*, a book Henry had been given as a parting gift by a French lieutenant who had been a patient in the hospital near Henry's chamber. Both had had bandaged eyes; they had struck up an acquaintanceship, mutually agreeing to lay the war aside until the man was deemed well enough for a prisoner exchange.

Some pages in, Henry laid two fingers on her wrist. "The sound of your voice is what I find most pleasing. But this story is devilish strange. Are you at all entertained?"

She said slowly, "I have read about air balloons, but this vision of the last living man in some far-distant day traveling to Brazil to find the only woman, well, my preference is for stories about people in the world I know."

Henry let out a soft breath of laughter, and she studied the glint of gold in the tiny whiskers on his upper lip and along his strong chin, and suppressed the impulse to stroke them with her thumb. "You can lay that infernal book aside," he said, and wished he knew how to court. How to flatter without sounding like a coxcomb, how to please.

Whenever he thought about how much joy he found in her presence, his throat tightened, leaving him without any words at all. *I am an idiot.* "It is a relief that you and I are of the same mind," he said hoarsely. *I am a coward, an idiot, and a fool.*

What could he say, without seeing her face? How would he know it was right? "I thought it a fine gift, but I wonder now if he wanted to be rid of the thing. Have we something better?"

Anna said, "Your mother recently bought *The Lay of the Last Minstrel.*"

"I read that while on blockade. I could hear that again. I like to listen to your voice."

Anna said ruefully, "I try very hard to emulate my mother's pure English, but I am afraid I fail."

"I wish you might never change," he said earnestly.

"You are very polite." She laughed and went to fetch Sir Walter Scott's poem, leaving him to sigh and castigate himself as a lackwit and a poltroon.

On Twelfth Night, it was Anna and Harriet's turn to brave the elements.

The party was hosted by the Rackhams. The oldest gentleman there, Grandfather Rackham, was chosen as king, and the youngest girl, Georgiana Colby, as queen. From their bough and ribbon-bedecked thrones the king and queen commanded the frivolities.

Harriet had completely ignored Robert Colby at the Christmas ball, feeling that he had returned entirely too above himself. At the New Year's ball, he expressed his penitence so adroitly, making her laugh when recollecting how much trouble they'd found themselves in as children, that she found herself relenting.

"*We* found ourselves," she corrected, mock-solemn. "*You* led us there, being an exalted two years older."

"And now I have learnt the wisdom of following *you*." He bowed.

There was no getting around such pretty compliments, and having Robert there, glancing her way from time to time over the younger children's heads, somehow invested with new interest all the old games like Bullet Pudding, which got their clothes covered with flour as they poked their noses into their dishes in order to lip up the bullet, and Snap-Dragon, which involved raisins, parched almonds, and strong spirits.

Mrs. Rackham offered to play her instrument and Robert begged Harriet's hand first as they danced the Sir Roger de Coverley.

But the first cloud on her happiness occurred when they all exchanged partners for the allemande, Harriet with Thomas Rackham.

When they finished and looked about, Harriet caught a derisive glance from Robert's eye, which puzzled Harriet.

She shrugged. And Robert turned his shoulder in a deliberate manner, leaving Harriet looking both puzzled and a little hurt.

Anna had seen the exchange. She caught a few words of a conversation between Cicely and Jane about French dances in England and France, and for the first time, deliberately set out to draw all eyes.

"I can show you what they are dancing in France," she said. "And even a few steps of the *zarzuela*, which they dance in Spain!"

Attention switched to her. In the middle of the carpet, she danced a few measures of the *zarzuela*, which all the girls wanted instantly to try, Harriet leading them, and so the bad moment passed.

During the carriage ride home, she thought back to how enjoyable it had been—almost perfect, except for that moment with Harriet and Robert Colby, and of course because Henry had not been there to enjoy it with them.

Then Harriet said in a sleepy voice, "How fun it was, without Emily looking on and despising us all."

Anna felt like she ought to demur, but she knew that Harriet had the right of it. For so calm and quiet a woman, Emily did have a constraining effect.

She wondered if she ought to say something, but there came a slow breath from Harriet: she was asleep.

Over the next couple of weeks, Anna watched Henry carefully for signs of that peculiar grimace that she now understood as evidence that he was suffering the headache. She learned not to ask how he was feeling, as the others often did. Invariably he would reply shortly, "I am fine."

She knew he did not like admitting to weakness, and he hated being fussed over. He would sit silently, his lips thinned, as well-meaning persons offered him their favorite nostrums, or furnished unasked-for histories of other persons being cured of the headache, wounds, or other illnesses, no matter how unrelated.

She could discern by how high the side of his mouth tightened the degree of pain he felt. When he looked *so*, she would come to his side, touch his arm, and if he groped for her hand, she knew he wished to get away.

At those times he required silence. If he could get away before the pain reached unbearable levels, he liked to be read to out of *The Naval Chronicle*, books of travel, even plays and novels as long as they were humorous.

In this benignant effort she had the full cooperation of the dowager, who watched her son anxiously. She, too, soon saw that he hated what he called "fuss," that is, questions he did not wish to answer, and a stream of suggested cures, however well meant.

"To admit to weakness is a failure," the dowager said to Anna one morning when they found themselves alone at breakfast, while heavy clouds moved in slowly outside, low and threatening. "He was always that way. His father had no truck with his sons claiming illness, as he himself was rarely ill. Illness, my husband declared, was best left to women."

Anna exclaimed, "But women are not weak. That is, we do not possess the physical strength to do battle, or to build monuments, perhaps, but endurance?"

"Endurance indeed," the dowager said, with a rare flash of irony. "When it comes to enduring pain that is infinitely easier than childbirth, men are the veriest babes in arms."

Anna thought of those poor creatures lying so patiently in the orlop, of Sayers and the captain forcing their wounded selves back to duty until they dropped senseless to the deck. Men knew endurance. Perhaps they endured for different reasons, and each sex respected best what it knew.

"If only I may know whether my playing to him is pleasing, or if he sits through it for my sake," the dowager said worriedly, and in that Anna understood the real reason for the conversation.

That, at least, she thought she might venture a question about, but as it happened, Henry had ideas of his own.

He surprised his mother, pleased Anna, and disappointed Emily the next evening following dinner, when once again he asked if he might join them directly rather than sit alone.

He found his way to the couch, and sat by Anna's side. "Mother, will you object to digging out your old Bach? You will not have known this, but I am used to playing arrangements of some that I believe are familiar. I know I heard them growing up. I have been trying to recollect them, and I might venture to play by memory. Whoever is nearest, will you pull the bell? Send for my instrument, please."

Thirty-two

EMILY WOKE AFTER A restless night of angry dreams. Was she truly the only person of delicacy and taste in this house? Harriet racketed about the countryside without the least constraint, the dowager was as vague as her eyesight, and nobody expected true breeding from a foreigner.

But she *had* expected better of Henry.

His years at sea must have coarsened him to an intolerable degree. She could not believe how he had played duets with his mother for over an hour, as Harriet and the foreign woman danced a Sir Roger de Coverley back and forth over the rug.

Emily looked out the window at the white sky. The weather could scarcely be called open, but the predicted snow storm was nowhere in sight. Refusing breakfast, she ordered her maid to put out her riding habit, and was soon venting her emotions in a gallop over the hard ground as the clouds pressed down, an endless gray wool blanket directly overhead.

Much as she quarreled with her mother, she still sustained a driving need to talk to the only person who comprehended, and indeed shared, her ambitions.

Before she reached the crossroad, flurries began to drift down, at first softly. Emily ignored it, rather liking more than not the squeak of snow under the horse's hooves, and the pure and silent white world. But before she had advanced very far she became aware that the white world was closing around her.

Soon, though she would claim to know the road home if blinded, she felt blind indeed, and fear began to pool within her as the tired animal struggled against a rising wind and the merciless whirl of great white clots that stuck to everything.

She had begun to fight against terror when a brief flaw in the wind revealed the familiar chimneys of the Groves. Thankfully, she traveled the last distance, drifts reaching almost to her horse's chest, until she and her mount shivered their way to the stable.

"What sort of a foolish scrape is this?" her mother greeted her. "I warned you that Old Dobbin's corns have been aching this three days at least, and laugh all you will about rationality, you have known from a child he is *never* wrong in the prediction of blizzards."

Emily did not heed a word. She glanced behind her mother, saw the door to the morning room closed, and heard the faint tinkle of her sister's harp from the room beyond. "Mother," she said in a low voice, "Henry's taste is intolerable, his temper worse, and yet I am in love with him as much as I ever was. What am I to do?"

Her mother also glanced back to check the door. She had meant to save her new discovery for some more propitious date, but her pleasure at having her daughter come to her for advice, instead of quarreling, prompted her to smile.

"Well, now, things might not look as black as you supposed. The post has come through, after three days of nothing." She tapped a sheaf of letters with a smug gesture. "I have finally received an answer to my inquiry from the Admiralty. What with one thing and another, the mails from Gibraltar have been slower than ever, but it was worth the wait. I have learned a thing or two about that Anna Ludovisi, or Anna Bernardo, as she called herself..."

By nightfall the winds howled, the snow so thick that nightfall was indistinguishable from day. After Parrette saw Anna dressed for dinner, she was free to make her way to the stable, which had gradually become the best part of her day.

The storm was so relentless that she set aside her usual lantern, knowing that the flame would be snuffed within a couple of paces, and retreated to fetch a storm lantern.

When she emerged from the closet where such things were stored, she spied Lady Emily Northcote's maid, Miss Shaw, sitting alone in the old linen room. This being the room cleared at the baron's request for the use of the servants, as it gained heat from the great kitchen chimney against its back wall. Presently the footmen would appear, playing cards or reading, and perhaps others.

Parrette was going to turn away, but hesitated. The others might come, but she had noticed that they rarely spoke to Miss Shaw, who had been hired that summer, "the third in as many years," Polly had said. Did they ignore her, or did she ignore them?

"Miss Shaw, would you be glad of some company? You can bring your work basket and sit with us over the stable."

Miss Shaw, a colorless woman very much in the English style (that is, complexion, eyes, and hair color looking to Parrette like uncooked dough), turned her way, startled. "I dare not," she said in a faint voice. "My mistress would turn me off for being familiar." She glanced over a thin shoulder as she whispered these words.

Parrette's interest was roused. Was this why Miss Shaw did not consort with the staff? Polly had made a disparaging comment about Shaw being above her company.

"Your mistress is not coming back any time tonight," Parrette said. "And the kitchen fire is going out, as tomorrow is Sunday."

Miss Shaw looked longingly at the French maid, who seemed so interesting, and whose fingers were quite clever. She struggled. Grateful as she was to have found a good place, she was lonely and miserable. If she refused, her choice was sitting there and smelling the vile tobacco of the footmen as they argued over their interminable card games, or retreating obediently to that freezing room. Both choices were so unappealing that temptation defeated her. "I will, then. Thank you."

"Good," Parrette said. "Two lanterns is better than one. I do not want to be lost in this evil weather."

Bundled up, they struggled out into the snow. Parrette knew

exactly where the stable lay, but even so, she nearly led them astray, buffeted as they were by the north wind; they blundered into the wall around the pump. Once she identified where she was, she corrected their steps. From the pump to the wall, and from the wall down the flagged path to the stable, and thence safety of the cozy stable house fire, and the quiet, steady good sense of John Cassidy.

Parrette had another reason for bringing Miss Shaw, besides a care for a fellow creature who was so obviously unhappy. In spite of her own determination to permit no man beside her son into her life, she had begun anticipating every glimpse of that handsome profile.

It had begun so innocently. Parrette had felt mildly vindicated that English speech by the local people left off that impossible 'h' sound, like she did. But the Yorkshire *the* flitted by as a barely articulated 't', with other words blended together in a fashion that had at first made her feel she was learning another language.

In contrast, John-Coachman's slow, lilting Irish was easy to comprehend, and a pleasure to listen to. Gradually she found herself listening to what he said less than how he said it. She distrusted herself for looking ahead to what any man might say, and yet she would never think of denying herself the pleasure of these gatherings.

When she and Miss Shaw arrived, shedding snow in clumps, Peg and Polly were already there with their sewing, the first with linens, the second with Miss Harriet's newest set of handkerchiefs. Noll was also there, sitting by the fire repairing horse tack. Bringing Miss Shaw to add to their party was a way to add another voice, Parrette thought, to put another obstacle between her and John-Coachman.

Not that the conversation ever transgressed into the personal. The closest they ever got was in talking about how they both had a son at sea, and they had compared notes on how little one heard of their dangers: Parrette had written to her son, but had yet to hear back, and the Cassidys had said that they rarely received post more than twice in a year, though the letters, when they came, might arrive in a bunch.

The conversation was so easy and general that Miss Shaw

began to relax. It was as if the threat of her mistress in the next building had been removed, enabling her to participate in the conversation, innocent as it was, as they all went about their work.

When the clock on the mantel tingled ten times, Polly joined Miss Shaw and Parrette in trudging through the drifts of still-falling snow back to the house.

Polly followed Parrette to her room, round-eyed with interest. "How did you get Miss Shaw to speak?"

"I asked," Parrette said wryly.

"We all tried to talk to her last summer," Polly retorted good-naturedly. "She wasn't having any of us."

"She said that her mistress might turn her off for familiarity," Parrette said.

"Familiarity," Polly repeated in affront, eyes flashing wide. "As if Mrs. Diggory wouldn't turn us off, did we dare! But Ned and Thomas never come near the maids, Mr. Diggory sees to it."

Parrette said, "Might there be another meaning to this word?"

Polly shivered in her shawl, putting her mind to the problem. To her, familiarity meant one thing: walking out with a young man, which was strictly forbidden. "Could it? All I know is, Miss Shaw is the third maid in as many years, and that was after Betsy, who grew up in the squire's house, and was promoted to lady's maid. She's now doing for Jane Rackham, a far better place, she says."

Parrette suspected that this conversation was precisely what Lady Emily Northcote would define as 'familiarity,' but she did not like Lady Emily Northcote, and further, knew that Polly could not be turned off by the widow. That was now Anna's prerogative. "Why was Betsy sent away?"

"Because her ladyship caught Lord Northcote following after Betsy up the stairs one morning, when he thought her ladyship was gone calling, and she came back to change her hat. Betsy was in a wax—tried to put him off—but it was she who had to go. The same happened to Miss Porter, the governess, and right after that the next lady's maid, but *she* was pert, and Mrs. Diggory said she was making eyes at him," Polly said. "We all thought, good riddance to bad trouble, for she was on the catch for Ned, too."

"And then?" Parrette asked.

"Her la'ship discovered the next one sitting over tea with Miss Cooper." She named the elderly maid who had been taking care of the dowager for thirty years, who customarily sat with Mrs. Diggory in the housekeeper's sitting room. "It being her night off."

"That would be this familiarity, I suspect," Parrette said.

Polly's eyes widened. "A good gossip over tea is familiarity? The things you learn! All I know is, Mrs. Diggory said we mustn't be anything but polite to anyone new come to do for *her*. And a shame, too, because until *you* came, Miss Shaw had the neatest way with repairing lace, and can turn a seam so you scarcely notice it's there. But we dursn't speak to her, not if it was ever so."

The next morning, when Anna went up to give Eleanor her lesson, she discovered Justina and Harriet dancing about the crowded room. Watching the child's quick steps, an idea occurred to Anna.

At first Justina had sometimes tried to sing because her sister sang, but she was either too young to land on the note, or she hadn't an ear, and Eleanor fretted that Justina was dragging her off key. Now Nurse kept her aside, and Anna had noted that mutinous little face. It wrung her heart, making her feel guilty that she was giving the one sister something and denying the other.

After the singing lesson, she went to Justina, who was listlessly cutting up paper. "Would you like to learn to dance?" she murmured.

Justina's eyes widened. She bridled, and said in a shrill voice, "Harriet teaches me."

That voice sounded unpleasantly like Mrs. Squire Elstead. Wondering if she was deepening her error, Anna said, "That is good. If you do not want lessons with me, it is fine."

Justina held onto her resentment for two heartbeats. As Anna began to turn away, she said quickly, "I want lessons."

"Then come with me." To Nurse, she said, "I will bring her back."

She took Justina's thin little hand in her own, and led her through the upstairs to the old wing, and thence to the gallery. As soon as they entered this long, shadowy room, bisected by occasional slants of light, the little girl shivered. "I'm cold. I hate this place."

Anna was now feeling that sick sense that she had made a grave error. But she draped her cashmere shawl around the little girl, who preened, running her fingers over the soft fabric. Anna said, "Watch me. If you want to learn this, I will teach you. If you do not, then we will return to the schoolroom."

Giving her legs a couple of quick swings to ease tight muscles, Anna moved to the center of the room, and then danced down the middle, combining the leaps and twirls she had performed over and over with Lise and Ninon, and then ended with the Spanish *zarzuela*.

Then, warm and breathless, she returned to Justina, who flung off the shawl as if it were an old rag, and demanded, "Teach me *that!*"

"I could try," Anna said. "But can you do this?" She stood in third position, her feet turned out in a line.

Justina struggled to emulate, her balance wobbly.

"Then this?" Anna lifted her leg straight up.

Justina tried to kick, and nearly fell. Her brow drew down, and her lip quivered.

Anna pointed to her feet. "All dancers begin with the simple steps, and then you learn and build strength." She recollected her early days, the painful struggle, and resolved to stick with the basic five positions. "They do them again and again, until they are perfect. Exactly the way you practice your alphabet, that one day you might write letters beautifully."

Justina was silent, struggling with disappointment that she was not to get taught that beautiful whirling dance. But at least her sister was not getting this much!

So she obediently mimicked each of the five basic steps, and the proper way to get to each.

Anna finished by saying, "You may practice those in the schoolroom. When you get them exactly right, I will teach you how to lift your legs and arms."

They returned to the schoolroom, where Eleanor turned away, looking hurt.

Later that day, Anna brought Eleanor down to the drawing room with its leaping fire, where she could hear the notes played true on the fortepiano. Eleanor was delighted, and Anna, as teacher, found her opportunity to sing, as she could not go on her walk.

She had trusted in the family's habit of each departing to separate parts of the house, but the dowager, drawn by the sound of the fortepiano, entered in time to hear Eleanor singing the last part of "Norah, Dear Norah."

The dowager paused inside the door, holding her breath. At the end, she clasped her hands, her spectacles twinkling in the reflected firelight as she exclaimed, "I did not know we have a genius budding in our midst!"

Eleanor flushed with pride. But she was at heart a truthful girl, and she had forgiven her idolized preceptress for taking Justina away for dance lessons. She exclaimed, "Oh, you must hear Lady Northcote. She sings like an *angel*."

"Then we have a house full of angels," the dowager retorted with good humor, treating the trite expression as childish enthusiasm. "For your mother is also acclaimed for her celestial voice."

"Mama is a beautiful singer," the child said loyally.

"Indeed she is," Anna said, glad to have the subject of her own singing shifted. "Would you like to try 'Toll for the Brave'?"

Eleanor, much shocked, whispered, "Oh, no. Is it not to be a surprise for Mama, and Uncle Northcote? What if *he* chances to come in, before it is ready?"

Anna knew that her husband was in the library with Diggory, wrestling with estate matters, but she would not gainsay the little girl. "You are quite right. We should not like to spoil the surprise." And then, suspecting the real reason the dowager had come in, "Shall we listen to Grandmama play instead?"

The dowager had indeed come in to sit down to the instrument. She warmed up by playing some of Harriet's favorite airs, knowing that her younger daughter was restless being confined to the house. Soon Harriet and Anna were practicing their dance steps, which Eleanor begged to join; when Nurse appeared to check on her charge, Justina took one look and began to grizzle at being left out of the fun.

She was pulled into the circle. They made so much noise that Henry, finished consulting with the butler on household affairs, was drawn hither.

Mindful of what he had told her about noise, Anna said instantly, "We are become too loud. Perhaps a quieter game?"

"No, no," Henry said. "Pray continue. It sounds festive, and I would not interrupt for the world."

They continued for a short time until Justina, unused to being in company, became shrill and over-excited. Nurse took the little girls upstairs. Harriet followed, promising to read to the wailing Justina, and the dowager turned to her more serious music with an air of determination.

Henry groped with his hand, palm open, fingers slightly cupped in what Anna had begun to recognize as his gesture of question. It was a gesture he used only for her, and she came to him at once. "I am here," she said, suppressing the questions he hated.

And he said as soon as they closed the door behind them, "I'm fine. Shall we go into the book room?"

When they reached it, he said, "Truth to tell, I am astonished to discover that I survived Justina's screeching without my skull shattering. That puts me in mind of a question. Mrs. Diggory tells me that the Rackhams have promised their Jane that her governess can go when she turns eighteen this March. Mrs. Diggory recommends her for those girls, who ought to have had a governess these two years. But she says that Mrs. Squire Elstead has taken it upon herself to find out a governess on her daughter's behalf. What do you think?"

"I do not think my opinion is wanted by Lady Emily Northcote," Anna said.

"But *I* want your opinion," Henry said. "I am the one having to pay the salary. Have you met this Miss Timothy?"

"Oh, I have, two or three times, when I have gone to the Rackhams to dance. She is a good woman, liked by everyone. Her French is excellent, I found that out when the others insisted we speak together, and Jane is very well read. Also, she plays well. Mrs. Rackham enjoys playing for these parties, but she is not always free to do so, and Miss Timothy often performed that office."

Anna thought about how Miss Timothy had with a quiet look quelled Harriet and Cicely Elstead's romping when it threatened to become shrill, then said slowly, "She also seems to have a good way with discipline."

"That is what I wanted to hear," Henry said, well pleased. He loathed the idea of anyone chosen by Mrs. Squire Elstead coming into his house; he would tell Mrs. Diggory to cut out Mrs. Squire Elstead before she could land her spy in their midst. "I will put it to Emily on her return, and if she agrees, that will settle the matter. There is a deal else to be done, no thanks to my brother. But death, we are told, forgives a multitude of sins, so the least said the better. If you are at liberty?"

"I am."

"The post was got in finally, and there's a significant pile of letters. Will you read them to me?"

She went to the desk, and began slitting seals as Diggory saw to it they were brought warm sandwiches and tea.

The top letters held little interest for Anna: a long screed from the solicitor listing creditors' bills outstanding; a begging letter from a fellow captain Henry had not seen for a dozen years, seeking a place for a young son should Henry return to sea; another naval friend writing from the North American station, wanting details of Nelson's last battle; a third sea captain who wished for his old friend, a hero of Nelson's Glorious Last Action, to speak to the Admiralty on behalf of his son, a new-made lieutenant, who longed for a place aboard a frigate where there might be hope of prize-money.

The fourth was from Lt. McGowan, who had been sent to London with dispatches.

Sir: I trust you will forgive me, not knowing how you ought to be addressed. That is, I know you are now Lord Northcotte, but is it Captain Lord Northcotte, now you are between commands? At any road, Captain Sayers, on learning that I was to be Sent, bade me write a Letter if I was in time to witness the Admiral's

funeral. We having had a topgallant breeze into the Bay of Bis-
Quay, we not only set t'gans'ls but —

"Anna, you can skip over the details of the wind and matters
of sailing, if you like. I expect it is long and detailed."

Anna ran her eyes down the closely written page. "It is," she
said, and turned over the paper. "Here is where he reaches
Portsmouth...

...everything decked in black, flags a-flying from Grennitch all
the way to St. Paul's. A mate of mine from Orion, 74, saved out
space for me at Temple Barr, and there we were squeezed. It was
altogether a sad Crush, but they were for the most Part sillent,
so you could hear the tattoo of the muffled drums over the clop
of horse hooves in the train of Carriages. In the distance the
boom of cannon salute.

Before the Admiral's body was in approach there was a great
deal of shoving, and trying to see, but when it drew near the
Sillence was profound, and when it was nigh, it was as if some
angel cried "Hats off," because there was no Order spoken, but
we all doffed our Scrapers..."

Anna turned the page, glanced up, and saw Henry with his
hand shading the bandaged eyes. She had seen that tension in the
line of his shoulders, down to his long hands, on the first day.
"Shall I cease?"

"No. Please. Do go on."

"There is very little more."

And after that, the great press kept us from getting anywhere
near the Church, so I cannot report on anything better than the
newspapers. But I promised to write what I did see, and though
we did not accompany him all the way, there was a sense of
shared grief on us all as we moved away.

There is little more to tell: Mr. Leuven has decided to retire, and Jorgensen is now surgeon. He said to thank you again for the Music you sent along of Capt. Sayers, and that they still play Bach. I carry everyone's Respects, and best wishes for you to regain your Health.

Your obedient servant, Lt. James McGowan.

"I wanted to be there," Henry said, lowering his hand. "I would give anything to have been a part of that. I suspect that does not sound rational. The rational being would assure me that one more or less would not be missed." His voice ended on a bitter note.

Anna was certain she had heard those words before, but could not recollect when. She said, "It might be rational to one who has not witnessed how a ship's company, how a fleet, becomes more than a united body of men. They share for that time one spirit."

"That is it exactly." Henry raised his head. "And we mourn together. One spirit. You have said that well. Shall we answer him?"

Anna reached for the ink well and a tray of neatly trimmed pens. She adjusted the branch of candles so that her hand would not form a shadow on her paper. "I am ready."

Henry dictated answers to them all, saving out the description of the battle for last. "Will this be too disagreeable?" he asked. "It seems absurd to mouth out some toplofty proverb about war is no business for ladies. As we were agreed before, we share these memories. But however, you might not wish to revisit them."

"The memories," she said, "are there, whether I write a letter or not. How should it begin?"

Henry paused many times, and she was even put to the trouble of throwing a ruined sheet into the fire and starting anew because he did not like the words he used. But once he reached the last conference with Nelson, the words came more rapidly, if not easier.

Nothing about those memories was easy, except in the fact that they shared them. He could not shock her, because she had seen the results of the violence, and once or twice she could even put him right, especially about the prisoners and the hurricane.

When the letter was done, she laid aside the pen and wrung her aching fingers. She did not speak, but something in her movement caught his ears, because he said suddenly, "I have worked you too long. I am used to a captain's clerk who spends his entire day writing. Forgive me."

"There is nothing to forgive," she said, her heart constricting at the note of real remorse in his voice, the unconscious plea in his open hands. "We have finished them all. It remains only to seal them up and write the direction—"

A knock at the door proved to be Perkins, to announce that it was time to get ready for dinner.

Anna got up and moved to the opposite door, where she saw Parrette waiting.

After another lively evening, at which everyone felt Emily's absence as an advantage, Anna walked Henry upstairs. He was silent, and she feared he had once again succumbed to the headache. When they reached their sitting room, he said in French, "Are we alone?"

"Yes."

"Will you sit by me?" He felt his way to the satin couch.

Anna did, and when he reached for her hand, he slid his fingers through hers. "I had not noticed until this evening, how very well we all are without my sister-in-law."

Though Anna had also noticed, she had thought she was alone in that—that her ambivalence about Emily was her private struggle.

Henry tugged her fingers gently, and she tugged back, a pulse of warmth thrilling through her at the latent strength in his hands. "Did you not notice? I don't think this is mere evidence of my spleen; you were very careful when I brought up the matter of the governess earlier. One would think women would talk about this, but I gather Emily does not talk to you?"

"She is a very quiet person," Anna murmured, choosing her words with care. "And unfailingly polite. And yet there is a differrence. I do not know why. I hesitate to lay blame at anyone's door."

"She is the one who told me that one more or less would not be missed at Nelson's memorial. It might have been kindly meant, and it was certainly rational. But it brought home to me how vast is the gulf between us. And always has been."

He sighed. "You probably have heard that she and I once had an understanding," he said bluntly. "It was a boy and girl affair. Everyone said so at the time. But when you *are* a boy, you know nothing outside your experience. The short version is, she threw me over for my brother. I am certain her family united in wishing her to marry John, who would inherit, whereas at the time I had no prospects beyond what I might gain at sea. The thing I could not forgive was this, I was the last to learn the truth."

"Perhaps that is a mistake made by a girl without experience," Anna began, aware of a confusion of emotions, above all relief and apprehension to hear at last what she had previously only guessed at.

His voice dropped a note, his expressive mouth tight at the corners. "*She* knew what she was doing. She took great care to keep me dangling, and her mother abetted her in it. The entire countryside knew. I did not find out until she showed me John's ring, and he was there in the next room, laughing himself sick at the expression on my face. Ah, to cut it short, I left home, spouting a lot of nonsense best left to Drury Lane. I promised I would never look at another woman, and I was angry enough to keep my promise until the war overtook me, and I had other things to think about." He tugged her fingers again. "Say something?"

"I know not what is right to say, except that I am sorry you were grieved."

"Oh, the grief was gone off within the first year. It was pride and anger that stuck the longest, until they had become habit."

He stirred, and let out a long breath. "I know something about anger, how it motivates, how it convinces one that the subjective is objective. On my coming home, without my seeing anyone, I must rely on voices. And I discovered that I don't above half like her voice."

"Many people have not been trained well to hear pitch," she said. "But she speaks very well. Her voice is soft, and yet clear."

"She does, but under that softness is anger. I couldn't hear it until now, yet I know it is not her voice that has changed. It's always been that way. She is very angry. And it frets at me, the same way discordancy does, or a sharp clatter."

Anna said, "This note that you call anger? It is also what I hear in Mrs. Squire Elstead's voice. Perhaps it is inherited? I think *I* might be angry, if I were to be raised hearing continual scolding and sarcasm. Lady Emily Northcote has had a great deal to bear."

"Perhaps you're right." He uttered a short laugh. "I was so bitter, and thought myself immune to the wiles of women, but oh, there are few bigger coxcombs than boys my age suffering their first disappointment."

"You had a loving heart," she said. "Whatever age, that kind of betrayal is a wound that takes time to heal, just as does a wound of flesh or bone."

He turned her way. His voice deepened. "*Damn* this bandage. I would give my soul to see you now. Anna, has your heart been wounded?"

"I made my own foolish mistakes," she admitted. "But the worst wounds to my heart were the deaths of my parents. My father felt my mother's and little brother's deaths as the worst betrayal. Not by her, but..." She left the sentence unfinished, remembering her father's desperate fury against God, which at the end of his life he had repented, before he, in turn, had left her alone.

Henry was silent, his head bent. Then he said, "I refused to write home, and after a time they stopped writing to me. Even my mother, finally, after my father died. I read about his death in the newspaper when we next touched land, after the brush with the Danes. I was estranged from him. I am not certain which of us despised the other the most, and I had just enough sense to refrain from writing my mother the truth, but I refused to grant her the small mercy of penning the usual things one says. So I sent her a single line." His thumb traced a circle in the hollow of Anna's hand, around and around. "But mothers — most mothers — forgive their children anything. I regret causing her sorrow."

"If she felt it," Anna said, "I can see that it is gone now. She smiles when she sees you, and I never saw her take so much pleasure at anything than when you played Bach duets with her."

"Smiles," he repeated reflectively, and then, "Is Emily still beautiful?"

"Very," Anna said, though it cost her a pang.

The gentle pressure of his thumb on her palm caressed the heel of her hand, then moved leisurely up to rub the underside of her knuckles, one by one. "As beautiful as I recollect you are?" he asked softly.

She uttered a low laugh. "How is one to answer that?" She looked at his profile, bent away, yet she could see the somberness of his expression, the tender curve of his mouth which could be so severe, then smiling, then thoughtful, a thousand subtle varieties of expression in between.

Until now she had suppressed the impulse to brush back the curling lock that fell forward over the bandage, but this time she did not resist. Lifting her free hand, she smoothed back his hair, finding it unexpectedly soft.

His breath hitched; his hand left her palm and slid up her arm. His fingers found her face and cupped it. "I want to court you, Anna. You deserve that, being married willy-nilly to a coxcomb and a fool. But I don't know how."

And so she had her answer, she thought. She might never know why he had uttered Emily's name that night, but she understood that whatever the cause, it no longer mattered.

"This is how," she whispered back as his fingers traveled over her face, reading her features. His touch was tender, tentative, coming at last to her lips.

She kissed his fingers, one by one.

Again his breath hitched, and he uttered a little groan and bent to kiss her. "Stop me," he said raggedly after they broke apart to breathe. "Say the word if..."

But after all he did not need sight, nor she words, to understand the other.

She took his hand, and her bedroom door shut behind them.

Thirty-three

ANNA WOKE TO HAPPINESS, reminding her of the first time she saw dawn's light pouring golden over the crown of Vesuvius.

She wanted to share it with everyone, but when she went to the schoolroom to give the girls their lessons, shrill voices met her ears, the sound punctuated by Nurse trying to calm the wailing baby.

"No, there will be no lesson," Nurse was saying as Anna entered, her cheeks red with vexation. "Go to the night-nursery, Justina, and you to your bedchamber, Eleanor. You may both reflect upon your bad tempers. Look what you have done, upsetting your sister."

Anna said, "Nurse, may I talk to them before they go?"

Nurse dropped a short curtsey, then went into night-nursery with Amelia.

Anna approached the two tear-stained faces. "What is the quarrel about?"

"She is always singing, and never on note, and no one stops her, but she says I cannot go along for her dance lessons," Eleanor stated in a tone of ill-usage.

"I don't want her," Justina wailed. "I want my dance to be my very own!"

Anna's elation dimmed. "To see you two at odds with each other makes me sorry I offered these lessons. I thought your singing, and your dancing, Justina, would give you each joy, and also bring joy to others. But there is no joy now. So perhaps I had better go away again."

Eleanor ran after her. "But what about my lessons?"

"I will come when you and your sister make peace."

The rest of the day was taxing in a different way as she and Henry made further inroads into the tangle of estate affairs.

He tried not to be frustrated with his inability to see, to remember the columns of numbers she had written down, and to understand yet another aspect of farming that made little sense to someone who had spent so many years at sea.

Finally he pressed the heels of his hands to his bandaged eyes in a way she was beginning to recognize, and she said, "Shall I ring for tea and something to eat?"

"Thank you, no. It seems to me that some of these numbers do not add up. Here, let us set this aside for a time. I need to ask some questions of Pratt, before I can puzzle out whether it is I or the steward at fault here. I may as well get some fresh air while I'm at it, but Thomas can walk me out to the gardener's cottage."

They parted, each to separate tasks. When they met again, she looked to see when he was in a room, and so she saw when he lifted his head as he listened for her step. Then he would smile, and she would smile, though she knew he could not see her, and neither could resist a touch, a caress. In that moment, the elation bloomed inside them both, bright as sunrise.

The next day Nurse found her alone at breakfast, as Henry was still being shaved. Nurse apologized for interrupting her, then said with grim satisfaction, "The girls have ended their quarrel. Now they are resolved to give your lessons to each other. It won't last," she added with the freedom of one who has seen almost the entire family in her nursery, under her care. "But it gives them a good start on civility."

"Tell them I will be with them later this morning, after I help their uncle in the book room," Anna said. "Eleanor first, then Justina."

The snow storm lasted the better part of a week, then it took

436

almost that long again for the roads to be cleared.

Emily knew within half a day after her return that something material had changed, something more than the news that the Rackham governess was all but engaged, if she concurred.

Her first reaction was wrath. How dare Henry consult that woman about her own children! But she forced herself to listen to Henry's measured words, clearly rehearsed, as he told her in front of the others, over dinner. Not even a private interview!

"A capital plan," Harriet exclaimed the moment he paused to draw breath. "At last! The girls will like her amazingly."

"So comforting," the dowager said, "to have someone come into the family who is not a stranger."

That *At Last!* was justified, Emily knew, so she forced herself to answer with composure. She knew Miss Timothy as an excellent teacher, and even her mother had found out nothing against her character.

The only thing Emily had against her was that though she was at least forty, she was still a handsome woman. Emily had no desire to admit that she had put off hiring a governess because she did not want any young woman in the house for John to chase after, once she had got rid of that designing Miss Porter who had taught Harriet so abominably. It was undignified to advertise for one sufficiently qualified yet ugly and old.

Now it would be the adventuress's problem if Henry formed a tendre for Miss Timothy's smiling ways. But no doubt the foreigner would have some clever ruse to deal with that, too.

Emily retired to her rooms with a great deal to reflect on. It was not a surprise that the mysterious 'duke's daughter' had turned out to be an adventuress after all, scarcely better than the opera dancer of Emily's fancy the night of the Christmas ball.

It was equally no surprise that she had ensnared Henry, because all men were fools for a pretty face. And men made the laws. A duke might marry a kitchenmaid and everyone accepted it; a duke's daughter who married her footman could be disinherited, even forced into annulment. The only recourse good society had was to refuse to receive low women raised above their station. Emily cared for the opinion of good society only insofar as it served her ambition, and acting precipitously would only lose Henry.

She could confront Henry about his wife, but she suspected he would refuse to believe her, or worse, he would take the woman away, and Emily would be left with nothing. Better to wait until the strength of attachment had dwindled. As it always did.

She hugged her secret, confident it was known only to herself and her mother, but in this she counted without the servants.

Over the next few days, Parrette and Harriet both noticed Polly's occasional absence, her demeanor unwontedly sober.

Harriet twitted her for her glum face, and though there existed a certain amount of friendship between them, Polly had been dinned never to forget her place, and claimed toothache.

But to Parrette she could speak the truth, especially one night after they returned from their usual night at over stable, during which Polly had not spoken a word.

Parrette stopped her in the courtyard, ignoring the snow piled all around, and said tartly, "If you wish to go to London with Miss Harriet, you must do better than this." She pointed at Polly's basket, which held the unfinished work that Polly had been staring at rather than finishing.

Polly flushed, then to Parrette's surprise, she clutched the basket against her, turned around in a full circle to make certain they were alone, and then leaned in and whispered, "It isn't true, is it? That Lady Northcote is a French spy?"

Parrette was so astonished she exclaimed in French, "*Quoi?* Eh, what say you?"

Polly sucked in a shuddering breath. "Rosa, you know, my friend at the Groves. She was waiting outside the morning room when the widow got there, before the big storm."

Parrette had learned that certain of the servants called Lady Emily Northcote 'the widow' among themselves.

"Mrs. Squire has a loud voice, everyone knows that, and Rosa *wasn't* listening a-purpose, but she had to wait there with her tray, and she could hear plain as plain, as Mrs. Squire told her, the widow, I mean, not Rosa, that Lady Northcote was a French spy caught by the Spaniards, in the guise of a company of low musical players," she finished in a breathless voice, having got all that out as quickly as possible. "But she *isn't*. Is she?"

"Naturally not."

Polly sighed a cloud of vapor in relief. "I didn't believe it. Spies creep around looking in windows, do they not? And they carry knives, and perhaps poisons, or they do in the plays put on by the players when we have the fair. But Rosa said that Mrs. Squire got some letter from somebody overseas."

"Whoever it was got it wrong," Parrette stated. "Listen, Polly, I am very happy that you told me. But you must not repeat it to anyone else. Understand? When lies are repeated, they cause nothing but trouble. You must tell Rosa not to share it with anyone else. When was this she told you?"

"T'other day when Widow Emily returned, they sent Rosa after, a-bringing of her dirty laundry. She said she daren't tell anyone at the Groves, it would be as much as her place was worth, so she got it out to me."

"Well, you came to the right person. But it's a lie, and lies are wicked and a sin."

Polly looked if possible even more terrified.

Parrette made an effort to speak less sharply. "We will say no more, but get to our work. I will help you reset this sleeve."

They went inside, and Polly sped upstairs, looking much relieved.

But Parrette was aware of the burden of the widow's spiteful words having shifted from Polly's shoulders to her own. She went slowly upstairs, and went about lighting the candles in Anna's dressing room, and putting hot water on the hearth to heat.

She opened the outer door, and heard the sound of the fortepiano drifting up the stairs, followed by male laughter from Frederick Elstead and Lord Northcote. She had thought The Captain—though admirable in every respect—incapable of laughter, but that had been proved wrong, ever since he and Anna had begun to live truly as man and wife.

And Anna herself?

There was a secret that Parrette suspected, but she had not said anything about that, because time would tell in its own way.

She looked about the room, saw everything laid out and waiting, then stepped to the door again. The music made it clear that their evening was not ending immediately, and so she gave in to temptation, fled down the back stairs, barely pausing to grab her shawl and to shove her feet into the pattens still wet from the earlier journey across the courtyard.

Bareheaded, she hurried back across the court to the stable, where she saw lights still burning upstairs.

She tapped at the door, her heart in a flurry. It was opened by John-Coachman himself, his coat pulled hastily over his shirt. Parrette lowered her eyes, aware that she was blushing like a girl, as she said, "Forgive me, Monsieur Cassidy, but I have me a terrible problem."

"Come in, please," he said. "I trust Polly is not sickening for something? Shall I summon Peg? She has gone to bed, but I doubt that she is asleep yet."

"No, no, do not disturb her, please." Parrette waved her hands. "It is Polly, but not sick..." And quickly, she told him.

As she spoke, she was amazed at herself. Even a month ago she would never have trusted anyone with the truth, much less a man. But as he drew her toward the fire, his gaze concerned, without shock, anger, or fear, she found herself having to stop and explain, and backtrack, until the entire story poured out— everything, right back to the terrible days in Lyons.

He listened, his gaze steady, until she finished the tangle of past and present, saying, "I was going to tell her. But I was afraid. I would not have her overset now, especially. Or to ruin the happiness they both had so long in coming. Yet, I do not know what the widow will do."

John Cassidy rubbed his raspy chin, then grunted. "If she has said nothing so far, I expect she will not. For a time. If she acts in this the way she has in other things, she will sit on the secret, and spring it when it most suits her."

"And then?" Parrette asked, her eyes wide. "And then?"

John looked into her anxious face, and understood the real question. "And then, I truly believe, should anyone accuse his wife of being a French spy, the baron is going to laugh. The navy has a summary way of dealing with spies. If she *had* been one, she would not be here, no, not at all."

Parrette closed her eyes, the tension going out of her shoulders. "I know that much! It is the other, the fact that she earned her wages singing in an opera company. Not low musicians, pah! But she *did* earn a wage. It is not what a fine lady can be forgiven for doing."

John said, "Yes, that is the rule of what is called good society." He gazed into the fire. "I do not claim to know his lordship as well now as I did when he was a boy, but I would venture to suggest he will be less grieved by the tidings that she was a paid singer in a French opera company than by the fact that she could not bring herself to confide in him."

"That is my fault." Parrette clasped her hands tightly. "Ought I to tell her, then?"

John considered a while longer. "I believe your instinct is right to wait, at least a little while. Give them their time of happiness, one might say, their honeymoon."

"Yes," Parrette said. "Yes. Thank you."

She looked up, aware of John standing a little ways away, and she recollected herself. Suddenly self-conscious, she felt another blush burning up from her collarbones, pulled her shawl tighter, and whirled away. "I am sorry to disturb you, Monsieur Cassidy. Thank you."

"It's glad I am you confided in me, Mrs. Duflot," he said mildly. "Good night. God and Mary and Patrick be with you."

Parrette muttered a blessing in French, and fled.

For Henry, everything had changed.

He had promised himself he would never again set foot in Yorkshire. He had sworn never to marry. He certainly would never have wished to grope about the world blinded, and yet here he was, walking about the ancestral home whose smells and sounds brought back so many memories from his boyhood, by the side of the woman whose touch he could not get enough of, whose voice held the power to soothe the pain in his head.

With the flourishing of happiness came an increase in energy, and a sense of purpose. As the days flew by, the affairs of the estate required Henry to learn a way of thinking that was completely unfamiliar. There was a set of new terms to put his mind to, having to do with land and its seasons, but after all, it

SHERWOOD SMITH

proved to be no more difficult than the mastery of the thousands of terms involved with the standing rigging, the running rigging, and the navigation of a ship.

The smiling, obsequious steward who bowed and flattered every time he saw Henry, bowed a little less each time the new baron summoned him to the Manor to answer to the complaints tenants had been making repeatedly, or to explain figures that did not add up.

Anna sat by her husband, calmly reading off lists that had been half-buried, which built a grim picture.

With his words stripped of the flattery and prevarication, it became apparent that this steward had been hired to wring what he could from the land, without putting a penny back. As soon as Henry, who distrusted the man's smooth, oily voice, heard all the reasons why there must be no change—they must continue on as before—he interrupted the steward's excuses.

"As well you are not a naval man. I know how to address humbug when it's offered to me on my own quarterdeck. The matter is simple. If you are not equal to accomplishing what *I* ask, then take yourself off."

The man flushed, bowed jerkily, and left.

As soon as the library door closed, Henry thumbed his eye sockets and said ruefully, "That sounded a magnificent *coup d'oeil*, but that leaves us more awkwardly situated than before. I am now a steward short, yet the problems remain." He sighed. "Well, Rackham offered to function as sea-daddy. Aubigny as well. I had better take my hat in my hand and apply to one or both of them, like a scrub of a middie."

They took the carriage out the next morning, and this first attempt to gain knowledge failed because he brought Anna, dressed in her fashionable pelisse and a smart hat.

Mr. Rackham, as pleasant as his wife, treated the visit as a social call. He could not be brought to discuss the details of land stewardship before a lady. To him it was not *comme il faut*, and the habits of politeness were ingrained. They went away having enjoyed the conversation, at the cost of Henry being as unenlightened as before.

He mulled this problem for a night, and the next morning, as

Polly laid the fire in her bedroom, he said to Anna, whose head lay on his shoulder, "I know what I must do. I'll call on Bradshaw. As I recollect there's a parcel of sons, and if the next one down is as smart as my midshipman, I will hire him as my secretary if he's willing."

Anna smiled; Henry's hand drifted up her side to cup her face. "You're smiling," he said. "I can hear the alteration in your breathing."

"No, no. That is, I think it a prodigious good idea."

"Prodigious! Never change, Anna. But you deflect me. I must know why you smile."

She gave in to a chuckle. "I only wonder what names these other boys have been given."

"Names?" he repeated.

"Your Mr. Bradshaw was named Beverley. And his brother at the shop wears the name Endymion."

"Was he? I know the mids among 'em had a variety of nicknames. If I recollect, he was Stoat, a fact I probably would not share with his doting family. Beverley. Endymion! Poor devils!"

And at the end of a long day, when they were alone again, Henry kissed her, then said, "Hippolyte, Odysseus, and Lancelot."

There was a hesitation—for her day had also been filled with activity—but then she recollected their conversation that morning, and uttered a low, delicious laugh. He joined her.

Then he said, "Odysseus, who writes a fair hand and can drive, begins work tomorrow. He begged me to call him Bradshaw, but if I must differentiate him from his father or brothers, to use William, which was his grandfather's name."

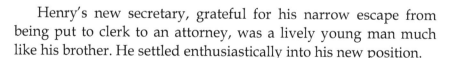

Henry's new secretary, grateful for his narrow escape from being put to clerk to an attorney, was a lively young man much like his brother. He settled enthusiastically into his new position.

Mr. Rackham, presented with an unexceptional secretary accompanying the new baron, began to initiate them both into the intricacies of land management.

Over the month of February, which offered a succession of

storms followed by relatively mild days, Lord Northcote and his secretary were seen all over the parish, visiting tenants and fellow landlords. While Henry was busy with estate affairs, Anna fell into a rhythm of her own: there were regular calls and callers, the informal dance parties at the Rackhams', and social events from dinners to balls. She also learned to drive the gig, a low, sturdy cart hitched to a single horse.

She continued teaching Eleanor to sing, which developed into lessons in Italian, the language of music. Justina showed a surprising aptitude for ballet, and they danced up and down the gallery together. She, too, wished to prepare a special performance with which to dazzle the rest of the family as a surprise.

So the lessons continued, though Anna had all but ceased to sing herself. There was so very much to do, and to think about. In a scarce few weeks the physician would arrive to oversee Henry's bandage removal. What if Henry's sight was restored?

Naturally she must want that for him, because he wanted it so badly. Yet her thoughts continued in a discomforting channel. He would not truly be seeing her, in the sense that there still remained the secret of her professional life. Every time she gave a slight answer to a question that might lead to dangerous ground, or avoided the subject entirely, guilt diminished the pleasure she otherwise felt in her days.

One Sunday morning late in February, snow softly fell on the pony trap wheeling down the white road from the Aubignys' chapel in the early morning light. Peg had stayed behind, nursing a sore throat, so Parrette and John-Coachman attended Mass alone.

They rode in companionable silence for a time, until he said slowly, "We both have a son at sea."

Parrette was surprised at this statement of the obvious. They had been talking about their sons, and sharing their worries about the long silences and the known dangers, for weeks. "Yes," she said.

"And we were each married the once, you and I."

She glanced up at his profile, which she could not help thinking was much finer than any of those statues she had looked upon in Italy.

"But yes," she said.

"And it's glad I am that your husband is no longer on this Earth, or I might have to seek him out to teach him a lesson in manners." The deep voice became more Irish.

"But that was long ago," she pointed out. "And me, I am sorry that your wife is no longer on Earth, because she sounds like an excellent woman."

"And so she was, so she was, God and Mary bless her." He lifted the reins briefly as the horses' ears twitched. But it was nothing but a snow bird bursting from a hedge, sending a white shower along the edge of the road. "I dreamed about her last night. Do ye want to hear my dream?"

Parrette discovered her heart beating fast. "I would."

"I dreamed she looked down upon me from Heaven, and gave me the eye. 'Look for happiness while ye can,' she said. 'Ye'll be here soon enough, now.' Do you feel the same way I do, Parrette Duflot? Any day you come to us over the stable is a day for celebrating. And when you are not there, I'm thinking about you."

When Parrette was fourteen and thought herself giddy with love, it had proved to be no love at all. But she had learned something about love since then. "John Cassidy, you know the reason I cannot say yes as yet. Once Anna finds her way to telling my lord everything and they are understanding one another, then I will know I have kept my promise. And I can look to myself. Can you wait?"

His slow smile turned her way. "I can wait," he said.

Parrette returned to the house, her emotions in such turmoil she felt like a girl again. It was not at all a pleasant sensation. She liked to think ahead, to be prepared for anything. She was mistress of herself, with a good brain and a deft hand. And yet, ever since coming to this house, she had come to see that it was not enough anymore.

Tell Anna, or wait for Anna to trust the baron on her own, before the poisonous widow could do it for her?

I will wait a bit longer, she decided when she crossed the slushy stable yard toward the house.

Her mood was not improved to discover Polly weeping softly in the cold, narrow stairway leading up to the servants' quarters, where Parrette headed to get rid of her coat and hat. "What is wrong?"

In answer Polly held up the new gown they had labored over. It was a delicate muslin with a gauze overdress, figured with tiny flowers. Polly had embroidered tiny gold centers to each flower, and a line of laurel leaves around the neck and the gather at the sleeves. It was one of their triumphs—and here it was, ripped all down the front, the material pulled awry at the high waist. Harriet had obviously been romping in it, and stepped on the hem. Or someone else had stepped on it.

"*Tiens!* It is not ruined, this dress. The gauze along the top? Yes. But look. We can cut here and here, and drape it so, and make it over into a half-dress. High in front, long in back. I saw a picture just like, in one of the magazines. Come. You must get ready for church. You know Noll drives very slowly, and you do not want to be late. I will get started while you are gone."

Parrette scowled as she took the gown from Polly. She had trained Anna to take care of her clothes, and during their Paris days, the dancers had appreciated her work, treating their gowns as rare and precious as money was so scarce.

She liked Harriet, but disapproved of her heedlessness, which seemed to have worsened ever since she found out she was to go to London.

Parrette was right about the heedlessness, but wrong about the reason. Harriet sat in church scowling at the faded blue light in the windows. She was cold, and wanted winter to be over. And how could Anna say that sound was so beautiful in this church? Did that simply mean you could hear Dr. Blythe from the back? The hymns just sounded like people singing, some as croaking as old frogs.

Anyway, she didn't want to hear Bible verses from Corinthians. Those Corinthians were long gone, and they never had a problem like Robert Colby. She was certain she could feel him staring now. Why did he have to come back to Barford Magna at all if he was going to be fun one day, and disagreeable the next?

After church, she dodged around Caro, who was walking slowly with Henry, and she pretended she didn't hear Penelope's sharp, "Harriet, pray slow down. Where are your manners?"

Penelope was standing near the rector like a watchdog, probably judging everyone who came out of church, as if she had taken St. Peter's place at the heavenly gates. Only who'd want into any heaven that Pen approved of?

Harriet looked for Cicely or Jane, so they could talk over the disaster at the Ashburns' soiree the night before. Where were they?

"Harriet."

She spun around, then crossed her arms when she saw Robert. He had always been tall, but now he looked taller than ever, with those high shirt points, and those huge gold buttons on his coat. "I wanted to apologize," he began.

"You ruined my gown," she snapped. "Ruined it!"

"It was an accident," he said miserably, all the words he had carefully planned fleeing from his head. What could he say? You couldn't offer satisfaction to a girl.

"It was stupid," she shot back in a fierce whisper. Both were aware of the rest of the congregation talking a few paces away.

She stepped behind one of the tree trunks to screen herself from Pen, at least, and when he followed, she said, "*You* were stupid. Why do you hate Tom Rackham all of a sudden, when you were in each other's pockets before you went off to university? He's not good enough for your exalted self, now you are come down from Oxford?"

"He acts as if he was the richest dog on the turf," Robert muttered.

"Tom?" Harriet repeated. "Tom hasn't changed. *You* have. You walk around looking as if you have a stomach ailment, and you think you have to claim all a person's dances, and—"

"Stomach ailment?" His surly expression altered to astonishment. Then he flushed. In his mirror, he looked rather like one of those dangerous and brooding fellows in the German novels.

"You have ruined all our fun, with your spooney quarrel,"

Harriet went on. "Everyone is taking sides, or refusing straight out to come when you are invited. Did you really think that everyone was sick, or afraid of slipping on ice, when the company was so thin at the Rackhams' the other evening? Everything was wonderful before you came back, and you turned *all* the boys into spooneys."

He pressed his lips together and bowed jerkily. "I will remove myself from your presence," he said awfully.

Her anger vanished. "Robert," she said, catching him by the arm.

He stopped, looking down at her wide eyes. His heartbeat thundered in his ears.

"Make it up with Tom, please?" Harriet said.

"Why is Tom so all-fired important? Are you attached?"

"No!" She stepped back, irritated. "How did you get that idea into your head?"

"I apologize." He bowed stiffly, and was about to speak again when they both heard his sister Georgiana calling him. "I must go. May I...may I call on you?"

Harriet gazed at him in exasperation. What maggot had got into his head now? He was used to ride over whenever he wanted, usually with Tom, sometimes with Bartholomew Ashburn as well. What did they *do* to him at Oxford? "Of course you may. Don't keep your family waiting."

Harriet turned away before he could respond, and made her way toward the row of carriages. Her mood worsened when she spied Penelope tugging at Caro's ugly old carriage cloak, her breath clouding as she scolded her sister up into the shabby one-horse trap that Penelope had hired from the Pig. Harriet paused to watch Penelope take her place, head high as if she were in a tumbril on the way to the guillotine.

"I feel for Caro," Harriet said, seeing Anna close by. What a contrast she was to her half-sisters' shabbiness, in her bottle-green pelisse with its fur lining, her hat matching with a green feather curving down next to her cheek, and her beautiful smile.

Harriet sighed, wishing she could look that stylish. Even though she was acquiring the right clothes, she could not get the way of moving about so well. Every time she tried before a mirror, she looked like someone had thrust a stick down her neck.

"I hate the way Pen keeps Caro on short commons, just because she's the worst skinflint alive," she muttered as she climbed into the carriage. "She *enjoys* being a skinflint. But I know Caro doesn't. She won't stand up to her, though. Cannot bear loud voices."

Anna had also seen Henry walking about with Dr. Blythe, and once the two had stopped, both glancing Caro's way as she talked to the dowager. She trusted that was a hopeful sign, but said nothing as the carriage door opened and Emily entered, a now-familiar pucker between her fine brows. It would soon become a line, Anna thought, as Emily said, "It is so embarrassing, Penelope hiring that dogcart that a grocer's boy would not deign to drive. Of course she gives no thought to how it must make the family look."

She settled herself, hands crushed in her muff, then added, "If I thought Henry might listen to me, I would ask him to buy them a carriage. Lady Northcote, you might perform this office, as he listens to *you*."

Harriet eyed her, sensing undercurrents she could not define. But she had little interest in what Emily thought.

The dowager arrived with Henry, and they were soon on their way back to the Manor.

Thirty-four

A THAW OVER THE next day meant the formal drawing room fire was lit in expectation of the customary Tuesday callers. Anna resigned herself to duty in spite of a disinclination for sitting downstairs. But when she looked into the room with its inviting fire, she discovered she was alone.

She hummed *pianissimo,* and a pulse of longing seized her. She drew breath to sing, but quashed the impulse. The thought of singing called to mind the confining cage of her promise, moreover the water in the breakfast tea must have been bad. The ill taste was still with her.

She picked up the March issue of *La Belle Assemblée* and had just opened it when she heard voices in the hall: Harriet's high, fierce tones overriding a lower male rumble. By now Anna recognized Robert Colby, the moody fellow whose gaze always followed Harriet about. She was already feeling distinctly queasy; she could not face company now.

"...if you *must* talk to me, you might as well talk in here," Harriet was saying.

Anna nipped up the magazine and whisked herself out the other door just as the hall door opened. Whatever argument the two were having would not welcome a third.

Her impulse was well meant, but Harriet, on finding the room empty, sighed. She thought she'd seen Anna go inside — now what was she to do?

Grown-up manners required that she have a maid present, or *somebody*, even though she was not yet out. Polly was probably sewing upstairs, and she knew she couldn't suddenly tell him they could not talk alone. He would only retort that she and Jane and even Georgiana had been chattering with the boys in and out of rooms since they were all in short coats, and he would be right.

That would start a new argument, and she was afraid that Robert was here to continue the quarrel that he had started after church.

Remorse set in when she recollected her own spiteful words. She was just as bad as Penelope, a lowering idea. She indicated a chair, hoping just to get it over, as he stepped toward her.

She had a moment to notice that he was dressed more gorgeously than ever, his blue coat new and tight above a waistcoat of gold brocade and satin knee breeches that one expected to see at a ball, not on a morning call.

Then everything fled her mind when he knelt down carefully, clasped her hand, and said, "Harriet, will you marry me?"

She pulled her hand away. "Robert, if this is one of those horrid hoaxes you and Tom and Bart was used to play off..."

He flushed beet red. "Hoax?" He sounded genuinely insulted. *"Hoax!"*

She said hastily, "Robert, please sit down, do. Right here, beside me, on this couch. I am not out, as you very well know. There can be nothing thought of in that way, and in fact if I was, you ought to have spoken to my brother, and I would have to run off and fetch Polly, or Lady Northcote, to sit gooseberry with us."

Robert scowled, knowing that all these things were true. But it had sounded so much better in his head on the ride over.

He cleared his throat and tried again. "I asked an honest question, and I know my heart."

"But I...that is..." Harriet flapped her hands.

"Just tell me this, is there anyone else?" he asked.

"No! I don't wish to marry *anybody*. I have no idea of marriage until I have had plenty of time for good fun."

Though once she might have shared her reasons without thinking, somehow the gulf between her and Tom, Bart, and the other fellows had widened: she could not possibly say that her Ponsonby third cousin, and that horridly superior Lady Lydia she had met once at her cousin's estate, were both her age, and already in the family way. From her cousin's letters, they were expected to settle down to matronhood. Harriet did not intend to be mewed up before she turned twenty!

Robert studied her. "So you don't wish to hear poetry, or ought I to tell you how much I admire you? I do, you know. I thought about you often, when I was up at Oxford, and when I returned, you were in every way superior to what I remembered. I thought I would speak before you leave for London, and your head is turned by a parcel of coxcombs and rakes."

She said indignantly, "If you believe I am spooney enough to be swept away by coxcombs and rakes, I wonder why you are here at all."

He scowled. "It's not that, but you having had no experience of the metropolis, which is full of—" He saw that this topic was not gaining him the sympathy he had expected, and abandoned it. "Out of all the girls in this parish, you are the best. Georgiana even agrees with me, and she's merely sixteen. You know she hasn't a hope of ever seeing London, as my father cares only for sport, and my aunt hates the metropolis—"

Harriet gasped, overcome by a sudden idea, and succumbed to laughter. "Robert," she said, wiping her eyes, "if this start of yours is due to your wish to gain a chaperone for your sister next year…"

He looked pained. "I did think it would be capital if you, as my wife, could accompany me to town. And with Georgiana, too, in another year or so. We would have a bang-up time, I am convinced, but that was *not* my motivation."

Harriet got control of her laughter, wiped her eyes with her handkerchief, and smiled. "Marrying me to make me sit gooseberry is the funniest thing I have heard this age, and I cannot stay angry with you. I wish we all could go to London together, including Jane, Tom, Bart, and everyone else."

Robert sighed. "So I don't have a hope, is that it?"

"I don't know. Ask me again in a year, or two years, or maybe *more*. I don't think of marriage with *anybody*. I am as happy to dance with any of you. Except when you look glumpish at Tom."

"Then a year it shall be," he said, rising, and they parted on better terms than they had since his return from Oxford.

As soon as he was gone, the dowager and Emily entered the parlor with questioning faces, the dowager saying, "From the tone of your voices, it sounded like Master Robert wished for a private interview."

Emily sent her a cold look. "Harriet, it is past time for you to be acting the hoyden. You ought to have rung the bell for one of us to join you. You are past the age to require reminding of proper etiquette."

Harriet felt a chill at the notion of Emily overhearing *that* conversation. She said impatiently, "It was just a misunderstanding." And she ran off before either could detain her with a lot of questions.

Anna had retired to the informal drawing room to read the magazine, which she found unexpectedly interesting, as there was an article about Paris. The unknown writer maintained that there were no current great voices in French opera. Vestris was proclaimed the current great male dancer, and Madame Gardel for women.

She paged on, a story catching her eye.

Malice must always have a victim; but I have observed this difference between fashionable malice – I mean the malice of a London drawing room, and the vulgar backbiting of a country neighborhood. The one is content to tease, torment, and play with its unfortunate object; the other is a bloody demon, and demands a complete sacrifice.

Malice, she thought. Was that what she saw in Emily's face? What type was it, or more important, whence the motivation?

Harriet burst in right then, and Anna laid aside the magazine as the words came tumbling out.

Anna almost laughed. Only the increasing stomach distress caused by the spoilt tea kept her from giving in to the impulse. At the end, Harriet said, "Marriage! I don't even want to think about it."

"Then you ought not," Anna said. There were so few years between them, and yet at times she felt ten years older, or more. No, it was not the years, it was marriage that caused the gulf. Or, was it the wish to be married?

She swallowed, wishing she had not drunk that tea. Making an effort to quash the unpleasant sensations, she said, "One thing perhaps we might consider, when the time comes, is your inviting Georgiana to stay in London. Your brother has said he wishes to take me there to attend the theater. Of course you will be with us if you wish."

"A capital plan! Oh, Anna, you are a trump!" Harriet grabbed Anna to hug her, then let go when Anna gave a gasp.

"I am sorry," Anna said quickly. "That tea this morning. Something was amiss. I should send Parrette to Cook ..." She suspended her sentence. "Excuse me." Her voice was muffled by her handkerchief as she left the room precipitately, and hurried upstairs.

She lay on her bed, eyes closed. Presently the door opened softly, and Parrette's quick step approached, her clothes rustling. "Anna, Miss Harriet said you are ill?"

"Please. Tell Cook there was something bad in the tea. It tasted wrong, but I drank it anyway, and it made me sick."

Parrette was silent a moment, then she said in French, "When was your last English visitor?"

Anna sighed. "I don't remember...Christmas week, I think." She opened her eyes, reddening at the new idea that occurred. "Do you think I am in child? But nothing happened before, and I thought it impossible."

Parrette laughed. "Impossible? No. I do know there was nothing amiss with the tea. Everyone drank of it. But," she said as Anna started up, her hand pressed to her middle, "it is perhaps early days yet. Anything can still happen — sometimes the English visitor comes late, or something else goes amiss and it does not take. Oh, that we were in Naples, we could get lemon so easily, or even root of ginger. But I know they have mint laid away in the spice closet. I will get you some."

Anna lay back to consider how she felt. As Parrette said, it was early days. She would say nothing until she was certain.

Over the next few days, the unease persisted. Anna discovered that if she ate plain food in small amounts, and drank hot lemon or barley water, she was able to quiet the symptoms. That, in turn, enabled her to go about her days without anyone asking awkward questions.

She recognized that the greater portion of her unsettled spirits were due to the memory of her mother dying after the birth of her little brother, who had scarcely outlived her.

Everyone had said that her age was the chief fault, that women in their forties often succumbed to childbed fever. Anna was more than ten years younger than her mother had been when she bore her, and she knew herself to be in excellent health. But she would wait, just to be certain, and to understand her own emotions. She did not want Henry sensing her worries.

And she was so very busy. There were teas and dinners to attend, and with Harriet the afternoon dancing. She continued to read to Henry, and occasionally pen letters for him that he did not wish to give to young Mr. Bradshaw.

She also continued the girls' lessons. For the first time she did not leap about with Justina, though Parrette said that dancing was not the least danger. The only women who languished about were rich ones. Everyone else carried on exactly as usual. But Anna found that her stomach did not care for twirling and leaping, at least not now.

On Thursday, the snow had thawed enough that she decided that she needed fresh air, so she would go alone to pay calls. Harriet was already gone, and she did not approach Emily, her excuse to herself that she wished to practice her driving, but she knew she was avoiding the woman as much as Emily avoided her.

She left the park phaeton, which required a team—she thought of it as specifically Emily's—and took out the simple gig.

As soon as she was out in the crisp air, the last melting snows gleaming brightly in the light of the strengthening sun, she knew it was the right decision. Her heart soared: in a few days, Henry's physician would arrive to examine him and perhaps take away the bandages that he had come to hate. The little girls would have their governess in a fortnight, after Miss Timothy was granted an opportunity to visit her family before she fixed herself in her new situation.

And…Anna found she rather enjoyed her secret, until she was absolutely certain.

She got her obligatory call on Mrs. Squire Elstead out of the way first. Fulsome compliments about Lady Northcote's being a true proficient in the world of music, said in a tone that recalled those words about malice, could not disturb her, but she was glad to get away.

Far pleasanter was her call on the Rackhams, where she found Cicely Elstead, Harriet, and Jane with their heads together, planning some sort of party.

She could not help but notice that the beautiful Cicely, who all agreed would be the reigning belle of the parish when she was officially presented to the world, was not as shy and retiring once away from her home. She chattered as much as the rest of the girls, and her soft voice lacked the angry undertone so distinctive in her mother and elder sister.

Anna stayed half an hour, Mrs. Rackham trying hospitably to press her into partaking of jam-filled cakes and custard-tarts, then took her leave. The slight increase in Anna's queasiness prompted her to take the short road to the rectory to break her journey to the Ashburns. Usually she left the rectory until last, but she knew that Dr. Blythe's generous housekeeper would offer simple fresh-baked scones, whose plainness was what her stomach craved now.

So she drove around to the church stable, where the rector's one-armed stable hand took her reins to walk the animal so it wouldn't chill. She thanked him, and had no sooner stepped inside when Mrs. Eccles approached on tiptoe, her aspect excited.

"Lady Northcote," she said in a whisper. "I would never ordinarily take the liberty, but I know with you, there will be no resentment, I trust?"

"No, not at all," Anna said, intrigued.

"It is just that he would come instantly if he knew you had honored him with a call, but right now, he is in the book room with—it is of the first importance." Mrs. Eccles touched her lips with her finger.

"I can call another time," Anna said.

"Oh, that is not necessary. I am sure they are finishing up, and he would be sorry to miss you. I could take you into the kitchen, though I've pies in making, and flour everywhere."

"I will take this opportunity to walk about," Anna said, knowing that the fresh, cold air would be good enough for now. "And you will send for me when he is free?"

"I'll send my Katie to come for you first thing. Thank you, thank you, Lady Northcote. You are all goodness."

Anna stepped outside again, thinking that if goodness were the same as politeness, more of the world would be at peace, surely? She turned her steps to the flagged path alongside the avenue of tall trees. The melting snow was muddy from many feet, making her disinclined to step off the path, until she discovered she had reached the front of the church.

The doors were open. She thought, why not step inside?

She had no plan in mind, but when she walked up the aisle in the empty space, the light through the stained glass windows bright with jewel-toned hues, she took a breath to test the sound, and tried a quick, soft scale. And then another, and yet another.

Oh, that sound! The deeply resonant hush, the brilliant light, the sense of peace, and her own awareness of deeply sustained happiness like a pool beneath the continual flurries of the day's activities, welled up in her. She drew a proper breath, head back, hands out, and began to sing.

She had no idea that Dr. Blythe's book room abutted the little court between the rectory proper and the church. Of the three people in the book room, two — the rector, and Caroline Duncannon, whom Henry had brought on the excuse of visiting the school — were head to head in the most important conversation of their lives.

Henry sat at a little distance, unsure whether he ought to stay or go. He had told young Bradshaw to take the team for a gentle drive, as much to get curious ears away as to keep the horses warm, or he would have called for the boy's help. But he disliked the notion of blundering about a room he did not know, and so he sat silently, possessing himself with what patience he could muster, until gradually a sound was borne in upon him.

Softly at first, so soft he was not certain it was even real, but gradually increasing in volume, rose and fell a beautiful, bell-toned soprano. He lifted his head to listen, his breath catching.

It was so like *the* sweet, pure voice, the one he had dreamed when he was struck down, fighting for his life, which in turn echoed the glorious voice he had first heard years ago, under that dome in Naples that smelled so strongly of fresh paint.

It was, of course, impossible, but grateful for the miraculous gift of unexpected beauty, he intended to enjoy it just the same. Was that "Madre Diletta" from *Ifigenia in Aulide*?

A miracle indeed. He smiled when next came "Air pour les mesmes" from Lully's *Phaeton*, which he had first heard as a midshipman in Rome.

And then, to crown them all, "Ah! Si la Liberté me Doit être Ravie," from Gluck's *Armide* — a heart-wrenching song of the triumph of love over hatred and revenge.

Midway through he was startled by a voice close by, "Who *is* that?"

It was Caroline, whispering in disbelief. Henry became aware that the two had fallen silent.

Dr. Blythe murmured, "I hardly know. At risk of sounding sentimental, it almost sounds as some celestial presence has wandered into my church, does it not?"

Henry stirred. "I would never gainsay the possibilities of miracles, but in this instance I believe there is a living woman singing, as she made a false start on the Lully, and corrected the tempo on the Gluck. With your permission, I would very much like to discover who that is. But can it be done without disturbing the singer?"

Dr. Blythe said, "Perhaps if we go up the back, and look down from the gallery?"

"Lead the way, will you?" Henry said, holding out his arm.

As they made their way, the two whispered together. "I am so afraid that Penelope will be very disappointed in me."

"Caroline," Dr. Blythe murmured tenderly. "If you feel you must wait —"

Henry stopped them. "Before we enter the church, permit me to say one thing. For no good reason Pen has kept you two apart these twenty years. If you flinch now, another day of possible happiness is lost to you. Another week, another year."

"But I do not know what to say to my sister." Caro's voice

trembled.

"I will speak to her, Caro. You need say nothing at all, and if you feel trepidation at the prospect of stopping at Whitstead until your wedding, then you must come to the Manor. You know my mother would like nothing better than to arrange a wedding, and she was balked of mine."

"He is correct, Miss Duncannon," Dr. Blythe said reassuringly.

"Very well, Henry. It shall be as you say. I know it is selfish, but I am too happy to speak against you."

"Good. Then pray let us enter the church; that aria is nearing its end, and I must know who that singer is."

There came an unpleasant interval as Dr. Blythe helped him up the narrow stone staircase. They left Henry seated on a bench and passed beyond him as the remarkable voice continued to shower them with brilliant sound.

Then there was a step nearby, breaking the spell, and the hiss of fabric as someone bent. Caro murmured in a breathless undertone, "Henry, dear, I believe that is your wife."

"*Anna?*" Henry exclaimed, then could have cut out his tongue as the singing stopped.

Below, Anna gave a start, her nerves flaring. "Henry?"

Dr. Blythe took Caro's elbow. "Let us conduct Lord Northcote downstairs, and leave him with his wife."

With the parson's large hand under one elbow and Caro's small one under the other, Henry stumbled his way down as fast as he dared.

Dr. Blythe and Caro left him in the transept. "Anna," Henry said, hands outstretched as he fumbled deeper into the church. The urge to rip the bandage free had never been stronger. "Where are you?"

Anna rushed to take Henry's hand. She, too, trembled, bewildered to find him there. "Henry?" she said again.

"That *was* you," Henry exclaimed, his wits so scattered he could only repeat himself. "That was *you*, Anna? Come, let us sit down. That was you singing? Why did you not tell me?"

Henry held her hands in such a tight grip she gave a little wriggle, and he loosened his grip at once. "I dare not lose you," he said. "It's almost like…no, I cannot explain it. Sayers told me when

I was lying in that infernal hospital at Gib that you had sung for the sickbay, and the midshipmen were all in love with your voice—angels, genius—but I put that down to trite expressions, and homesickness. I see now that I entirely underestimated them. That was you, in Naples, was it not?"

"I—"

"Why not tell me? Why do you not sing, every day, at home? Anna, there are very few things in the world that would give me greater pleasure, give my *entire family* pleasure. Why would you hide this talent, this marvel of a talent?"

It was time for her to grip his hands. "I promised to keep it secret."

"What could possibly be the reason?"

"Because I grew up knowing that the English of good society have very strict rules. One of those is that one must never earn one's living in a trade." The words she had never thought to speak came quickly now. "I was in Cadiz not as a guest, but we were hired to perform before the commanders of the Combined Fleet."

He did not draw back in horror, but bent his head, his profile intent. "Is *that* how you came to Gravina's notice?"

"In a sense. I was a soubrette in the Company Dupree of Paris. We had to travel to Spain when our theater burned down. In Cadiz, someone in our company told the French that I was married to an English sea captain. The reasons are immaterial now, but Admiral Villeneuve himself arrested me as an English spy. I was removed from his governance on the orders of Admiral Gravina. I think he recognized that I was not a spy."

"Married to an English captain sailing under Nelson's combined fleet," Henry said, and uttered a laugh. "Collingwood thought you were a spy, too, for completely different reasons! He ordered me to keep you on board—something I am eternally grateful for now."

He kissed her, his lips missing her face and landing near her ear. They both breathed a laugh, his unsteady, hers breathless.

"I so very much wanted to tell you," she said at length. "But everything I have seen supports what I was taught. There is a divide between what is perceived as genteel society and what is not genteel."

He laughed again, almost giddy. "There are those who will tell you that the word *genteel* is not genteel. Those truly well bred would never let it pass their lips. Never mind that. I see why you did not trust me. My father and brother certainly were in agreement about the niceties and expectations of rank, and my mother probably is as well, as much as so gentle a spirit can be."

He shook his head. "I might have been the same, had I not compounded with men of impeccable lineage who were wafted to the top of command at far too young an age, due entirely to their interests, and not to their abilities. While some officers I trust most are sprung from humble beginnings. Which you are not. I distinctly remember that duke that Jones waved in my face."

"The duke is on one side, but I believe my mother's mother was a housekeeper," she said. "I believe my mother was always ashamed of her own mother. She was so very, very adamant that I must speak well, move well, and never transgress the rules of society, or I would be forever ruined."

"To a great extent it is true," he said. "Except when it isn't. All but the worst snobs appreciate talent, in whatever form it comes. Richard Sheridan, the playwright? You might not know of him, but English society does. He's the son of an Irish actor, but you will find him at the best houses in London. He is one of the Prince of Wales's set, and he's served as a Member of Parliament. Whatever else is testified about him—and there is plenty of scandal, I'm afraid—no one flings either his birth, or the fact that he started life earning his living, in his teeth."

"Is it not different for women?"

"In the main, but there are exceptions for those who lead exemplary lives. As you did."

"I don't know how you could know that," she murmured as he nuzzled her neck.

He laughed, his breath tickling her ear. "The fact that you can say that is testament enough. But Anna, I would be the worst kind of blackguard if I claimed to love music, and yet kept your great talent hidden in my house. I wanted to take you to London to hear a concert. Would you like to give a concert? My grandmother Dangeau would like nothing better than to hire a theater, and invite a select audience. She is always patronizing musicians."

Anna had to take a moment to breathe. Never had she expected this moment! At length she said, "I thank you. Henry, I am good, but I am not great. I sound best in small chambers such as this church. At any vast theater, my voice is lost. Moreover, I have learned that I much prefer to sing when I wish, and not because I must. I care nothing for celebrity; my pleasure is in excellence, whether I sing for myself, or for an audience."

"I hope you will sing for us," he said tentatively. "Though I cannot promise you the audience you deserve, not everyone loving music equally. Colby is a capital man on the hunting field, but he would not know Catalani from a crow. But however, the Aubignys are both people of discerning taste, the Rackhams I know would get immense pleasure, and even Elstead likes music, when he can get it."

Henry paused, recollected where they were, and that his secretary was no doubt tired of driving his pair round and round. "We must go."

"Yes," she said.

He rose, tucked her hand under his, and as they walked out, said, "I have a capital piece of news for you. I brought Caro here myself, and she and Blythe have plighted their troth just now. It is twenty years in coming, but at all events, that is better than forty."

Anna expressed all the delight that he had expected she would, which brought them to their respective equipages. She climbed into the gig, choosing to forgo her call. Dr. Blythe, newly betrothed, would have enough to do, and Anna would not wait a moment longer to tell the faithful Parrette what had happened.

She drove back at a brisk trot, and the moment she got inside, she sent Ned to find Parrette. When Parrette entered Anna's bedroom, she took one look at Anna's smile, her glowing cheeks and bright gaze, and clasped her hands.

Anna told her in three sentences what had happened. Parrette, the determined, steel-willed maid, then took Anna utterly by surprise. She flung her apron over her head, sat down on the nearest footstool, and wept.

"Parrette, Parrette." Anna dropped to her knees by her side. "What have I done? What have I said?"

Down came the apron. "Nothing!" Black eyes snapped above

her ruddy cheeks. "It is my happiness, a thing I never thought to have." In a few words, she revealed her own secret.

"John-Coachman?" Anna exclaimed. "Oh, but that is wonderful! Why did you not say anything before?"

"Because more important to me was keeping my promise to your mother. Which I believe now I can say, truly, I have done."

Parrette's eyes filled with tears again.

Anna patted her work-worn hands tenderly, and said, "What will you do? Do you wish to retire as a maid and become his wife? Oh, and I owe you years and years of wages. You remember I am now wealthy! Henry had agreed that if there is ever peace with Bonaparte I can try to find Helene, and the others, and perhaps do something for them. But you must come first. Do you still desire to set up your shop?"

Parrette wiped her eyes. "You owe me nothing. Everything I did I began for your mother, but then you became the daughter I never had. As for a shop, I have thought about it. If the dressmaker Miss Reed decides to retire, and I think she ought, as she has been behind the mode for a generation at the least, then I might buy her shop with my savings. I could take Susan with me, as she has the cleverest fingers in the house. She is wasted as an upper housemaid. But there is enough to do before that happens." She glanced with meaning at Anna's waist.

Anna laughed, then hiccoughed. "Oh." She pressed her handkerchief to her lips. "Perhaps some barley-water…"

Thirty-five

CARO'S SECRET FEAR WAS due only in part to the expectation of her sister's reaction, but also that she would become, in the phrase, 'The brags of life are but a nine days wonder.' However, her betrothal was scarcely a nine hours wonder.

Penelope Duncannon had made herself as unpopular as the rector was popular. Everyone sincerely wished for the rector's happiness, and if there were a few good but quietly disappointed women who had hitherto been trying their best to catch his kindly blue eye, all were united in agreeing that Miss Caroline Duncannon would make an excellent pastoral wife. In her quiet way, she was very nearly as well-thought-of as her husband-to-be.

The news spread quickly, once Mrs. Squire Elstead got hold of it, and in spite of her funning about Hymenia's saffron robes adorning graybeards and spinsters, the good will of the hearers caused the news to sink into acceptance by the next day.

For those at the Manor, there was a dinner and a ball to go to, and then at last came the evening that Henry had anticipated, without telling his wife all his reasons. Two days before the physician was due to arrive to consult about his bandaged eyes, a sleet storm rose to a gale, keeping the family inside.

After dinner, as usual, the dowager marched with alacrity to the instrument, to play with an air of triumph the Beethoven that she had mastered at last. Henry listened with keen appreciation,

SHERWOOD SMITH

applauded heartily, then said, "Emily? Are you going to sing?"

Emily had not sung for some weeks, ever since the storm that had kept her away; she had given up trying to get them into spending the evening in a more modish manner. She had also noticed that after the dowager played, though sometimes Henry joined her, and the dowager invariably asked Mary Elstead to sit down to her harp, no one had requested her to sing.

Pleased enough by this sign of interest, she rose. "What do you wish to hear?"

"Anything. What is your best air?"

She brought out the sheet music to one of her Scots songs, a pretty one that she prided herself on. The dowager, still at the instrument, firmly resettled her spectacles upon her nose with a slight air of challenge. "I can play that."

Emily gave a faint shrug, and when the introduction was over, performed well, she thought, embellishing the chorus with extra trills.

At the end Henry clapped, but instead of asking her for another, he said, "Anna? How about you? It seems no one has ever asked you to sing, and I think we might repair that error."

Anna had begun to suspect what was in his mind. In truth she felt ambivalent. But she had known that this moment was inevitable, and so it may as well be now.

Harriet exclaimed, "Capital! You've been teaching Eleanor this age. It is about time we heard *you.*"

The dowager added her voice. "That would give us a great deal of pleasure."

"Something from Mozart," Henry said promptly.

"Mozart!" Harriet repeated. "Ask her for something easy. Mozart is vastly difficult."

"Mozart," Henry said firmly.

The dowager began to expostulate that she had no music for Mozart adaptations of arias, but Anna thanked her, reached past her to press a chord, straightened up, and gave them 'Dove Sono' from *Le Nozze de Figaro.*

Henry drew a breath of sheer pleasure as Anna's voice flowed over them like molten gold. No, like the shimmer of light on water. No, angels' celestial choirs? Faugh! All he could think of were

466

threadbare phrases that did nothing to embrace the extraordinary beauty of her voice, much less his pride in her.

At the end, the dowager fanned herself. "Bless me," she said, eyes wide with amazement. "Bless me, who would have thought..."

Harriet bounced up, her brown curls tumbling over one ear. "Anna! That was a *trump!* Why did you not tell us you could sing like *that?*"

Emily sat silently, controlling her fury as she took in Henry's smug smile. He had to have made that suggestion out of malice; she knew very well there was no comparison between her singing and that foreign creature's. Just as well she had kept the foreign creature's secret. He was clearly besotted.

She forced herself to applaud, and then said rather dryly, "From now on you must lead the way, Lady Northcote. As you do in all things."

Anna's sensitive ear caught the mortification that Emily tried to hide. She said seriously, "I take as much pleasure in listening as I do in performing." That much was true, and got her gracefully past having to offer compliments on Emily's singing that she suspected would only prompt the others to make abhorrent comparisons. Though she did not care for Emily, she acknowledged that it was no fault of hers that she had never had Maestro Paisiello in her life.

Her words were intended as a peace-making gesture, but they fell far short of their office. Emily only heard the odious complacency of triumph.

Emily kept herself away from the family for the next day, as she struggled to control her emotions. She was aware that the main of her anger was aimed at Henry. Indeed, sometimes her sensations were more like hate than love.

Even so, she was curious enough to remain at home the day the physician was expected. He had already arrived at the inn in High Street the evening before, everyone in the parish knew by now.

At ten o'clock the hired gig was seen on the drive, brown mud splashing behind the wheels. Diggory opened the door to a stout man in a black physician's coat and a smart physician's bob wig.

"Good day, good day," said Dr. MacAdam, a cheerful man with a red face. "Lord Northcote! I apprehend you have followed my instructions?"

"My man Perkins saw to that," Henry said, Anna at his side. "Lions ain't in it, as they say. Elephants!"

"Excellent. And this is your fine family, eh? Shall we all proceed to your drawing room? I take it we will have good light. I must have light."

The family trailed behind as Henry and Anna walked into the drawing room after the physician. He bade Henry sit on a stool near the window, and before he touched the bandages, he asked a great many questions.

Satisfied that the headaches were all but gone, and most of the attendant symptoms, he said, "Pray keep your eyes closed, my lord. I must watch the action of the pupils, so we will proceed with one eye at a time."

Henry had been feeling the loosening of the cloth around his head every night for months, followed by the rebinding by Perkins's strong hands. At first he had suffered the sensation that the bandages held the shards of his cracked skull together. Gradually that sensation had gone away, to be replaced by an increased impatience at the restriction.

The hated bandage was lifted away at last, and Henry kept his fists tight on his knees, eyelids shut until the physician bade him open his right eye. Light glared, making his eye water. Dr. MacAdam harrumphed and muttered Latin tags interspersed with things like "Good, clear humors...pupil contracts nicely... Now, what do you see?"

Henry squinted, fighting the impulse to open his left eye. He saw a blurry round face under a white wig floating over his head. He blinked, and the blur resolved into jowls framing a broad smile below a pair of observant gray eyes.

He swung his head, and there Anna was, looking back at him anxiously. He smiled, and felicity bloomed in his heart to see her smile back. "I see my wife. The drawing room. A bit blurry, but better than nothing."

"My lord, we will try the left eye now."

"This one open or shut?"

"Oh, shut the right, shut the right. We will try them together in a moment, but first we must watch the…" More Latin.

Henry opened his left eye. There was the glare, in blurred bubbles of light that winked into shadow. He blinked, rubbed his eye, and blinked again. Shadows crawled nauseatingly. He thumbed the top of his eyeball. A brief spray of tiny lights corresponded with an ache.

"Shadows," he said.

"Now try both."

Henry opened both his eyes, and turned his head slowly. Here was Anna again, a little bit clearer on one side, but the other smeared into blur. He could make out her sweet smile, and the tiny dimples in her cheeks. Her smooth brown skin, its color enhancing the warm brown of her eyes—the brown of mead, of amber, of polished wood in clear light. She looked back at him steadily, and when he met her gaze, his heart gave a fierce beat. He leaned to touch her hand. She returned his grip, a private promise: if he had been blind he knew she would have pressed his hand exactly the same. She had married a man, whether he saw everything, or nothing.

He turned his head the other way.

There was his mother, who had aged shockingly under her well-remembered powdered hair, but she wore a widow's cap now. How many years had passed during which he had given her only silence in return for her steadfast love? Guilt pulsed through him as he looked past her to a tall girl with light brown hair done up in curls like Anna's. Could that be Harriet? He remembered her as a spindly twig with tousled braids. Harriet looked like John at that age, save for the bright smile. John had never smiled like that.

Next to her, a golden vision who at first seemed miraculously unchanged. A faint stirring in his heart, echo of the pain he had felt when Emily's image intruded in dreams, pulsed and then subsided. He looked away, at Dr. MacAdam. "My left eye is next thing to blind. Is that it?"

Dr. MacAdam said a great deal about time, and blows to the

head, but what Henry heard was that the medical faculty had little more idea than he did. He had expected no less. Until they could open a living body in order to see its workings and set it to rights the way a clockmaker repaired a faulty pocket watch, there would probably always be at best a combination of guesswork and some experience, and the worst being the outright charlatans preying upon the credulous.

When MacAdam had run out of cautions and assurances, Henry said, "It is better than I expected. I had prepared myself for the worst."

"Wise, very wise," Dr. MacAdam said.

It remained only to invite him to refresh himself, pay him his fee, and send him off.

Henry said to Anna after Diggory had shut the door and vanished into the depths of the house, "Tell me the truth, now. Do I look terrible? Ought I to wear an eyepatch?"

She peered up into his face. "What would be best for you?"

"I hardly know. This side of the world is...soupy. Perhaps an eyepatch would be less distracting to me, but what about others? Did you—no, you have probably never heard of Captain Johnson's book about pirates. I read that as a boy. Made me want to go to sea."

"To be a pirate?" Her eyes widened.

He grinned. "To fight them. But Nelson never wore a patch. Here." He looked around the entry hall. "I am going to reacquaint myself with the house. No, bide here. After being nose-led for months, I am going to take great pleasure in my own powers."

He smiled down into Anna's anxious brown eyes, sensing that she wished to be by his side, but she offered no expostulation.

He set off to explore.

More had changed than he had thought. The house had improved vastly since his departure. He could see John's hand in the new balustrade, the fine Egyptian-patterned papers above the wainscoting, and the furnishings in the formal drawing room, chosen with an eye to pleasing color, and use of space.

Was this John's form of art? John had never liked music, but he had always had a good eye for a painting, and for color and space. Before his arrival, Henry had resolved, if he regained his vision, to rid himself of all signs of his brother, but as he proceeded through his house, he felt the old resentment draining away. John had been bad-tempered, though no worse than their father; he had been profligate and arrogant, but he had paid the price for all those things with his life.

Henry decided, in the time it took to reach the well-remembered schoolroom with its sturdy, cheerfully shabby furniture, that save his own bedchamber, dressing room, and the sitting room, he would not change anything. The best of John could be seen all over the house, and he would preserve that as a better memorial than that stone statue in the family crypt.

In the schoolroom, Nurse, looking very old and faded, had his nieces dressed in their best. The two girls, just emerging into girlhood, dropped curtseys. The baby eyed him, lower lip protruding dangerously.

Henry backed away in haste, and tried to find some conversation for these girls. He had not thought about them until now; no one had brought them downstairs. But he knew that Harriet and Anna spent a great deal of time with them.

"Are you looking forward to Miss Timothy coming to us?" he asked finally.

"Yes, Uncle Northcote," the eldest said, and the smaller one echoed, "Yes, sir."

"Good." He had run out of things to say. With midshipmen, there was an established routine when they first came aboard, but now, he did not know where to begin.

He gave them an awkward nod, swung about, and nearly knocked his left knee into the low table. He must accustom himself to being effectively blinkered on that side. He let himself out, and almost ran into Emily.

"I don't know them at all," he said to her. "You scarcely let them downstairs."

"I kept them from disturbing you," she said. Strange, how much softer her voice sounded when he looked at those large blue eyes, her delicate skin crowned by soft golden hair.

He let his breath out. "And before I came?"

She tried to guess at his mood, and failed. His tone was indifferent, and she strove to reach him. "Nurse did well by them, better than I could. I don't know children," she admitted. "They are loud, sticky, and dirty. I look forward to them reaching an age of reason, and discourse. I will enjoy introducing them in London, if they improve."

"Pray do not let me hinder you," he said, and opened the schoolroom door for her.

She dropped a slight curtsey and passed by.

He continued on downstairs, Emily fading from his mind as he sought Anna. There she was, so different from Emily. Her features, considered singly, might not be accounted as perfect as Emily's very English style, but their *tout ensemble* had become dear in an inexplicable way, and he gazed hungrily into her face, wanting to catch the subtle changes of expression in order to divine her mood. Her happiness had become of paramount importance to him.

They fell into their now-accustomed posture, arms entwined, walking together. But this time he took the lead, and she fell easily into the comfortable rhythm that he had learned to count upon.

Emily, who had gone in search of him in a rare and desperate impulse, found him a short time later in the morning room holding hands with the foreign creature, as if they were girl and boy plighting their troth. They did not notice her; she shut the door softly and went away.

After a bad night full of terrible dreams, she rose late, aware of the throb of a dull headache. She must get out into the open air. A gallop would clear off the headache, if it would not clear her heart or head. She rang for her maid to lay out her habit.

She was crossing the courtyard when once again something flickered at the edge of her vision. She remembered the previous instance, and glanced up at the row of long gallery windows in time to see a small figure flitting past the wavering glass. *Justina?*

She whirled around and ran to the side door, taking the stairs two at a time.

When she reached the gallery, an impossible sight met her eyes: the foreign creature and Justina prancing below the sedate portraits like a pair of performers at Astley's Ampitheater.

The control she had fought so hard to establish vanished like smoke. "*What* are you doing with *my* daughter?"

The two figures at the far end of the gallery stopped and turned, two pairs of wide eyes looking guilty. Emily advanced upon them, her voice rising on every word. "How *dare* you turn *my daughter* into a performing strumpet!"

Anna caught her breath. "Justina wished to learn the ballet," she said.

"Look, Mama," Justina piped up. "I know all five positions, and I can leap like this, and turn a pirouette—"

"Justina, go to the schoolroom."

"Let us all go to where it is warm," Anna suggested, hoping that Emily would calm down if given a few moments. She knew she needed time to collect her wits.

Justina gazed from one to the other, burst into tears, and ran wailing from the gallery. Her voice echoed off the marble as she flitted to the new wing, followed by Anna and perforce Emily.

Unfortunately, Anna's movement served only to heat Emily's temper the more, as it appeared that she had taken control of a situation that Emily felt justified in commanding. *She* was the one wronged.

When they reached the morning room, Anna shut the door. "I am only teaching her the rudiments of ballet. That is all I know myself—"

Emily snapped her riding whip through the air to crack against a table. "No one asked you to do anything to my children. I can tolerate the singing lessons, as that is a necessity for young ladies of good birth, as long as they do not make spectacles of themselves upon the public stage."

Anna gazed in shocked silence.

"Oh, yes, I know who you are. *What* you are. If you think you can—"

The door opened to Henry's hand. "Anna, did I hear your voice? Behold me reading the newspaper! I see here that there is a new comic opera by Guglielmi to be presented in London. And not long after, there is to be a benefit for Grassini. Did you ever hear her?"

He had entered talking, newspaper in hand. But when he got

far enough in and lifted his head so his right eye took in the two women standing stiffly on either side of the fireplace, he stopped.

Emily turned on him, all her determined resolves gone. "Did you know that your wife is a common opera clown, and possibly even a spy for the French?"

Henry squinted from one to the other, then said crisply, "What nonsense you talk, Emily. 'Clown.' You have your mother's terrible habit of making everything and everyone sound worse than it is. My wife was a soloist in a French opera company, driven to earn her living because I neglected my duty to her, and abandoned her to the Hamiltons. I ought to have known better, in retrospect."

The dowager appeared at the open door. "I heard Justina weeping all along the upstairs hallway. Anna, did she fall down during her lesson?"

"You knew what was going on?" Emily turned her way.

"Nurse comes to my powder room every morning to tell me everything," the dowager said, coming in past Henry to face her daughter-in-law. "She always has. We were agreed that Justina was getting quite round-shouldered, and her learning to dance would almost certainly correct her posture."

"I see what it is." Emily's voice trembled. "You have all united against me, and now you wish to turn my children against me as well."

The dowager, much shocked, said, "That is impossible. You are their mother. No one can take your place."

"*She* is trying." Emily pointed her riding crop at Anna.

Hot resentment flared through Anna. She had to breathe out twice to banish it; she struggled not to assume the burden of anger that Emily wished to give her. *Engage and deflect*, whispered her mother's voice in memory. "Your children talk of nothing but how much they wish you to see what they have learnt," she said.

Emily's face twisted. "Am I supposed to be pleased that you would turn them into the sort of woman who makes a spectacle of herself upon a stage for every low bumpkin to ogle and to bandy her name about? I would rather shut them up in a convent."

Henry turned his good eye from one to another. What was he supposed to do here? On board his ship he knew exactly what to do, but he could not court-martial a woman, or stop her grog.

He looked toward Anna, who half-lifted a hand. He understood from her gesture that she deemed this her affair. He forced his voice to mildness. "I will leave you ladies to settle the question."

He backed out and shut the door.

Anna tried once more for compromise, for peace-making. "If you wish, I will cease teaching your daughters at once."

Emily's lip curled. "You ought to have thought of that first."

Anna reddened, guilty and contrite. "This is very true, and I beg your pardon. It all happened by accident, when I saw that Eleanor wished to learn to sing, and I discovered that I like teaching. So when Justina wanted something of her own, well, it just happened, and she was the one who wished to surprise you once she had learnt her little dance."

"Save your breath. I've watched how you insinuated yourself into this household, and though I had thought to spare the family by keeping my knowledge of what you are to myself, I feel it is my duty to our neighbors to let them know what sort of woman has practiced upon their trust—"

"What sort of woman would that be?" Anna asked, calm spreading through her like snow.

Emily paused. Her cheeks glowed with splendid color as she lifted her head. "A common stage actress, to put it no higher."

Anna said, still calmly, "Oh, I do not believe I was common at all! I was, in fact, very good. But not to be compared with La Catalani. But I think the quality of my singing is not truly in question, is it not so? It seems you are attempting to threaten me."

The dowager struck her hand on the back of a chair. "Emily Elstead, if you continue to behave so ill under this roof, I must request you to return to your own home."

Anna heard the tremble in the dowager's voice, and sensed how frightened the older woman was on her behalf. Sorrow crowded her heart, and after that a sense of gratitude for the gentle woman's courage in attempting to defend her.

Though she had sung all the dramatic permutations of 'love' every day during all her years on stage, she had begun to understand the wellspring of the joy she had rediscovered: it was love.

She walked to the dowager and touched her hand. "Thank you. Let me make myself understood."

She turned to Emily. "You seem to believe I can be frightened by your threats. Such fears are, after all, very small, compared to trying to keep from being eaten by rats."

Emily recoiled in shock, and the dowager gasped.

"To keep those rats at bay I danced through the night with the sort of women you would scorn for their humble birth, who had no advantages beyond the skills they struggled to attain. I lived through a battle, sewing up torn flesh as cannon blasted the masts and sails overhead. Your threats hold no fear for me."

"Rats?" the dowager repeated in a whisper.

Humor pulsed in Anna, then was gone as she faced Emily's derisive countenance. "You see your daughter dancing and think only of evil, I find it infinitely sad."

"As for that ..." The dowager cleared her throat. "Emily, if you had at any time acted like a mother to those girls, then perhaps Lady Northcote would have thought of you. Of course she did not, because you have never taken the least interest in those girls."

"That is not true."

"You did not know that Nurse reports to me every day! No, do not remind me that Nurse is my hireling. Here is a question for you: what color are Amelia's eyes?"

Emily glared furiously at her mother-in-law, her throat closing. Tears? Why? When she was the one wronged! And the worst of it was, she did not know the color of the brat's eyes. She could scarcely bear to look at Amelia, whose birth had ruined her life. "Blue," she said, though she knew it was merely a guess.

Indeed, the dowager lifted her chin, acknowledging a hit, but then she said, "I suspect if I told you they were green, you would not gainsay. Yes, they are blue, but I will never believe you knew that. I will state my point, and then I am done. I have been happier since Lady Northcote's arrival than I have been in many years. The girls are happier. Harriet is happier. And Henry is happier. You do not bring happiness to this house because I do not believe you know what happiness is."

Emily whirled and walked out.

The dowager let out her breath, clasped her hands, then said, "Rats? Is that true?"

Anna wiped a strand of hair back with fingers she discovered shook. "Oh, yes." She laughed a little breathlessly. "Hundreds of them. *Hungry* rats. We could hear them squeaking, and if I dared to look, I saw the reflections of their red eyes."

The dowager tipped her head. "I think perhaps Harriet might like that story."

"Then I will tell her it," Anna said, as they left the chamber.

Outside, Emily found Noll still walking her hack; half-blinded by tears of fury, she gained the saddle and rode out.

At first she turned the animal toward the well-traveled path to the Groves, but she knew what her mother would say. She had ruined her chances—she had spoken too soon—she had spoken wrong—everyone was at fault. Everyone was always at fault, except for her.

Return to your home. As if she had not been mistress of the Manor for all the years of her marriage! Now this interloper had replaced her within a few scarce weeks.

Emily wrenched the reins to one side, slapped the whip against the horse's ribs, and galloped hard, but as fast as she went, she could not outride the desolation of defeat.

Anna retreated upstairs, where she discovered Henry waiting. "What happened?" he asked.

Anna sank down in one of the vast old wing chairs, queasiness stirring in her middle. "I feel such regret. She was right. I ought never to have done what I did without asking her."

Henry lifted a shoulder. "I am convinced she would have refused in order to spite you, and for no other reason. Then everyone would be the poorer. And she would go right back to neglecting those girls. If she had exerted herself to find a governess when Eleanor reached five, there never would have been a question."

Anna nodded soberly. "Perhaps. And yet I still feel a sense of failure. She was not merely angry, she was unhappy in a terrible way, I could see it." She paused, and then ventured into what she knew was a delicate subject, but she could no longer settle for silence. "I believe she still loves you."

"She can't. She doesn't know me in the least. When we were young, she was always trying to talk me into being less like me and more like John. You cannot conceive the quarrels we had. What a pair of young fools we were! We would never have made the other happy."

Though Anna was aware how very limited her experience of men was, she did understand how a person could be attracted to someone one had little in common with otherwise, or whom one did not actually know.

"And yet the two of you had an understanding. Feel you nothing whatsoever for her now?"

Henry held out his hand, and she came to him. They walked to the window. She laid her head against his chest, delighted in the low fremitus of his voice resonating through him as he murmured, "Oh, there is still the remains of my admiration. She is still very beautiful. Is that unsettling for you to hear?" He paused to squint anxiously down at her.

"No." She chuckled. "At one time, perhaps, it might have been. But I have learnt that life is seldom like the opera, everyone very, very good, or very, very evil, altogether in love, or altogether in hatred. We are a mixture of everything."

"Just so. So you can listen with perfect equanimity to me when I say that yes, a little of my old admiration is there when I see her, but Anna, even if you had never come into my life, I would not have returned here alone to marry her—even if it were allowed, which I vaguely recollect would not be. She broke my trust, and though I could admire her, I could never love her. I am sorry to have to say it. Perhaps Dr. Blythe would speak a sermon against me if he knew."

She was not yet ready for jokes. "I wish I could find a way to get her to see that I mean her no ill, that we might begin again in peace. We would all be more comfortable."

"We will all be more comfortable if she leaves my house."

"You would not force her to return to the Groves?" Anna raised her head to look at him earnestly.

"No, no, she don't deserve that. Her mother...well, least said, soonest mended. No, while you were in there dealing with her, I was sitting here deep in thought. Perhaps I ought to offer her a season in London as well. I did not yet tell you, but one of my letters this morning was notice from the Admiralty of my prize money for the action at Cape Trafalgar. It is not a spanking fortune, but it will do. My point is, if I gave it to her, she could go to London and return to the smart set. I think she misses London, and if we get great good luck, some likely fellow with sufficient money and title will fall in love with her beautiful face, and take her off to his castle. As far from Yorkshire as possible, I hope."

"Sending her to London is a fine idea," she said. "I think she misses it, from a few things she has said."

"Oh, that much is plain from all those bills I have been paying. If I give her that money she may be as tonnish as she likes, and if the result is she quits this house, we might turn those corner rooms into guest chambers or, who knows? One day they might be needed for another purpose."

Anna had meant to wait, but she turned her face into his cravat, and murmured, "Perhaps sooner than you think."

He straightened up, put his hands on her shoulders, and moved her so he could turn his good eye to her face. "Is that what I think it means?"

"Perhaps so," she said, blushing fiery red.

He laughed, and hugged her, but gently, his mind ranging beyond the startling idea of fatherhood to his house, his estate, and...

"And that is another thing," Henry said. "I am sorry to have to admit this, because the squire was always my friend. For a time I regarded him as the father I never had in my own, but age has brought me to the reluctant conclusion that his heart is as sound as it ever was, but his intellects are not up to snuff. At least, not as a likely justice of the peace."

"Will he not bring his good heart to the task?"

"If only that were so! But I have been having to deal with him extensively on the question of enclosure, and some parish affairs that would be long and tedious to explain, the more because I am only beginning to comprehend them myself. If I believed he could bring a sense of justice with his good intent, I would throw myself behind him, but especially when he is in liquor — which is oftener than anyone knows, not that I blame him — he has a lamentable habit of agreeing with everything the last person said. Most often his wife. Would you wish for Mrs. Squire to preside over questions of justice?"

"No," Anna said on an outward breath of horror.

"Just so."

She turned to him. "You have found a better candidate?"

He colored a little. "My dear, you are looking at the candidate. Rackham insists, Ashburn too, Colby agrees with them, and even Aubigny roused himself sufficiently from his arcane studies to take me aside after a meeting recently between complainants in a question between certain town interests and a farmer, to beg me to apply. They promise to help me to it, and though I still am ignorant, I am discovering in dealing with the estate that it is not so very different from commanding a ship."

She looked into his face wonderingly. "But would that not require you to stop here, and not return to the sea?"

"Can you tolerate an irascible one-eyed man underfoot?" he replied, taking her face into his hands to kiss her.

"I might," she said, "if you give me a barouche-landau, a house in London, a parure of diamonds, and two dozen shirts."

"You may have the shirts," he retorted, and then his answering smile faded. "Along with the letter promising the prize money, the First Lord offered me an excellent sixth-rate recently bought into service, should my eyesight return. If this had happened three months ago, I would have closed with the offer at once. But all this morning, I have endeavored to discover when it was that this house, and all that appertained, became a home that I could not bear to leave. Look out there." He pointed through the window.

Anna gazed out, her eyes widening in astonishment. Sometime in the past few days, the melted snow and the mud had changed. Everywhere she looked grew tender green shoots of grass, and the trees fuzzed softly with green buds. "My mother was right," she whispered softly. "It *is* green. It is a wonderful green."

"Oh, you have seen nothing yet. Just wait until summer. I have fallen in love with this land again, and this house, but that is because *you* are at the center of it. I love you, Anna." He looked down into her face.

"*Je t'aime, Henri.*" And she repeated it in Italian, Neapolitan, and Spanish, kissing him after each.

"Here's an idea," he said, twining his fingers through hers. "We'll get Blythe to let us marry again, this time properly. Even if everyone stares. My mother would love all the doings, and you shall have a ring that you have chosen."

"You think our marriage was a mere rehearsal, then?" She smiled.

"I do. You are now to play the proper role of a bride, and a lady of rank, while I strut about in my new role as bridegroom, one-eyed baron, and justice of the peace. And just as we accustom ourselves to our lofty status, we will be thrown into new roles, as parents, and so we shall dance the new pattern. Did not Shakespeare say that all the world is a stage?"

She laughed, and made unspoken answer.

ABOUT BOOK VIEW CAFÉ

Book View Café Publishing Cooperative is an author-owned cooperative of over fifty professional writers, publishing in a variety of genres such as fantasy, romance, mystery, and science fiction.

BVC authors include *New York Times* and *USA Today* bestsellers; Nebula, Hugo, and Philip K. Dick Award winners; World Fantasy Award, Campbell Award, and RITA Award nominees; and winners and nominees of many other publishing awards.

Since its debut in 2008, BVC has gained a reputation for producing high-quality e-books, and is now bringing that same quality to its print editions.

Printed in Great Britain
by Amazon